Heart of the Storm

by

Debbie Peterson

This is a work of fiction. Names, characters, places, and incidents are either the product of the author's imagination or are used fictitiously, and any resemblance to actual persons living or dead, business establishments, events, or locales, is entirely coincidental.

Heart of the Storm

Cover Art by *Debbie Taylor*

The Wild Rose Press, Inc.
PO Box 708
Adams Basin, NY 14410-0708
Visit us at www.thewildrosepress.com

Publishing History
First Fantasy Rose Edition, 2019
Print ISBN 978-1-5092-2473-9
Digital ISBN 978-1-5092-2474-6

Published in the United States of America

About a half an hour before sunset, the unease she had carried for the past several hours turned into a sudden feeling of dread. Panic overtook all rational thought and settled into her soul. Something terrible had happened. She raced toward her supplies and grabbed her backpack. Her fingers shook as she unzipped the bag and yanked out her phone. She called Greg's number several times over before it dawned on her that he had already boarded a plane headed for Colombia. She wouldn't be able to contact him until the morning.

Despite all attempts to banish it, the dread grew stronger with each passing hour. A growing notion that Wolf and his crew never left the sub took firm hold. The conscientious men of the *Wieven* could very well have remained behind to ensure that all went according to plan. The thought of such an occurrence made her sick to her stomach. What if they could die as she had always feared? What if they died in that sub along with Mercado's men? She couldn't sleep, and she couldn't eat. All throughout the long hours of the night, she restlessly paced along the shore, waiting, hoping, and praying.

By the time the gloomy morning arrived, what little hope she'd carried throughout the long night dissipated. Somewhere in her heart, she finally accepted that her beloved captain wouldn't be coming for her. Not now. Not ever again.

Praise for Debbie Peterson

"This is a real suspenseful page-turning read that had me hooked right away. I would recommend this to anyone who enjoys suspense, mystery and of course romance. I also loved the fresh approach on the Bermuda Triangle!"

~Mother/Gamer/Writer Blog

~*~

"Debbie Peterson has crafted a nice blend of supernatural ghosts, Bermuda Triangle lore, action-packed rescues, and a sweet romance."

~Aubrie Dionne, Author

~*~

"What I like best about Ms. Peterson's stories is how beautifully she handles two people from extremely different backgrounds falling in love. It's that initial flush of romance. There is suspense and intrigue here by the bucketful, but the sweet and tender romance is the star of this novel."

~Mae Clair, Author

Dedication

This one is for my girls,
Jaimie, Shandra, Megan,
Summer, Tammy and Nichole.
Thank you so much for your individual help,
and your unfailing support.
I wouldn't have come this far without you.
And Joshua...what would I have done without you!
Thank you for providing the Spanish!
It added a fun aspect to the book!

Books By Debbie Peterson

Court of the Hawk
Love Letters from Heaven
Bound by Oath and Honor
Spirit of the Revolution
Spirit of the Rebellion
Spirit of the Knight.

Chapter One

Aliyana Montijo slipped out of bed fully dressed in head-to-toe black clothing. She inched toward the bedroom door and crept down the hallway, one cautious footstep at a time.

If they found her outside her room, Emil Mercado wouldn't wait for the final test before he executed her as he so callously planned. Her one advantage? The man had no idea she knew what he had in store for her. The moment she had finished the installation of his new security system, her name topped his list for termination. That didn't mean an amiable exit after the conclusion of her job, either. This Colombian drug lord would accept nothing less than her death.

The sanctity of life meant very little to Mercado. For those who knew his secrets, it meant nothing at all. Of course, if she had encouraged his romantic advances she might've bought herself another month or two. *Yeah, not likely. I'd just as soon take my chances at escaping this place right now, thank you very much.* The very thought of that man touching her made her skin crawl. Besides, she was just about to get everything else she needed to finish up her part in this mission.

Aliyana paused just outside the doorway to his private office, clutching her cloned RFID card a little tighter. As she peeked over her shoulder, she swiped it through the scanner. The low blip granted access. Once again, she gazed down the hallway, searching for the smallest movement or shadow. All remained quiet.

She turned toward the door and touched the numbers on the keypad. Over the course of the past few weeks, she'd collected that four-digit code, one number at a time. Would those numbers still work? In answer to the question, a single click disturbed the silence. She let herself inside. So far, the race against the hands of the clock continued without a hitch.

Under the low security lights, she walked to the desk and turned on the computer. All the while, her heart hammered inside her chest. Each of her fingers took turns pressing against her thumb, as she waited for the boot up process. The simple procedure shouldn't take this long, should it?

Whew! Finally.

Aliyana slipped her small flash drive into the hub and using her own embedded codes, bypassed Emil's ever-changing password. She selected all the files she needed. A few more keyboard strokes and the critical information began the transfer from his machine and into her flash drive. She'd need about five minutes.

Halfway through the download Aliyana took a closer look at the bulletin board Emil must've recently hung. An oversized map of the United States centered the panel. The map contained a series of tiny colorful dots inside the boundaries of Maryland and Virginia. She didn't understand the meaning of those dots, nor could she decipher their significance now. Nothing else on the cluttered board warranted her interest.

Aliyana shivered in apprehension. She rubbed her arms against the chill as she returned to the desk and checked the progress of the transfer. Another twenty-eight seconds and she'd be home free. As her gloved hand hovered above the flash drive, she caught sight of a small stack of papers off to the right. A bright red circle on the top left-hand side of the page grabbed her attention. In bold lettering, the name of the director of the Drug Enforcement Administration headed the page. His home address as well as the identity of his wife and children followed.

Each subsequent color-coded document in that stack contained the same data for other officials of the DEA. The final page recorded a specific time, a single date, and the names of Emil's most trusted lieutenants. Each of those troglodytes had a different colored circle beside his name. Her gaze traveled to the map. She gazed at the papers she held in her hand, and then looked back at the map. The colored dots matched those on the pages.

Emil had spoken of retaliation against the United States so many times in her presence that she'd grown weary of it. He wanted the U.S. government to pay with their blood for shipments lost. Mercado wanted them to fear the power of his cartel so much they would cease interfering in his lucrative business altogether.

Aliyana understood then. She had some elite company on Emil's hit list. Some of the lieutenants' targets were children and that information made her sick. Intense heat filled every vein in her body. Her hands shook as she fumbled inside her backpack and retrieved a high-tech digital camera. She took a series of photographs which detailed the planned attack, despite the lack of time.

She ejected her flash drive and stuffed it inside her

pack. Without making a sound, she turned off the computer and left the room. The hallway remained dark and empty, but not for long. Any moment now, someone would awaken.

With darkness still on her side, she stepped outside and headed toward the fleet of parked cars. Aliyana stopped short. She had arrived too late. Emil's lackeys had already taken her motorcycle. They probably had already stripped it bare and destroyed any evidentiary remains. She couldn't steal something else; there were too many guards. What to do now? The pace of her heart doubled as she clenched her fists. Somehow she needed to get out of here before dawn lit the sky.

The sky!

If she could make it to Emil's Twin Otter before daybreak, she could fly out of here. Then instead of mere minutes ahead of Emil and his men, she'd be hours. She knew the agents in her squad would wonder and worry over her disappearance. Right now, she couldn't help that. She'd get in touch with them as soon as she could.

Aliyana kept her eyes on the guards as she crept to the back of the compound. The bushes provided just enough cover. She slithered over the fence and slipped inside the dense foliage. For a moment she stood perfectly still. Not a footstep or an uttered word diminished the sing-song sounds of nocturnal insects and birds. Though difficult to find her way in the darkness, she turned toward the river and followed its course.

More than once, she suppressed the instinctive need to hurry as she made her way through the hot, humid jungle. Beads of sweat trickled down her face without even the smallest breeze present to help cool her down. At last she arrived at the river dock where Emil kept his floatplane. The first hint of dawn now colored the eastern sky. The faint light revealed the silhouette of a solitary armed guard standing watch over the aircraft. Yet, as a general rule, Emil employed two. With a foot half-cocked, the guard slumped over the butt of his gun. Slack-jawed and with heavy lidded eyes, he had his gaze fixed off somewhere in the distance. The smallest noise would bring him to full alert.

Aliyana circled around until she faced his back. She rushed up behind him and kicked his left knee forward. As he flailed his arms to catch his balance, she yanked him down to her height. She slipped her arm around his neck to cut off his air supply while placing her left hand palm-to-palm with her right. Then she took a single step backward. The guard fell back onto her well-centered body. She pinned him in that position until he lost consciousness. After dropping him to the ground, she grabbed hold of his weapons, and rushed toward the plane.

She tossed her backpack, the knife, and rifle onto the passenger seat and climbed aboard. The fuel gauge showed all tanks full. Aliyana powered up Emil's plane and taxied a short distance down the river.

As she lifted the nose of the craft upward out of the water, a rapid succession of shots rang out and pelted the plane. She glanced down from the cockpit window as she climbed ever higher into the sky. The second guard she expected to see and didn't, stumbled along the bank, holding onto both his rifle and his pants. Any other time, the sight would've made her laugh. The sound of gunfire faded as she turned the craft northeast and toward the ocean.

"All right," she whispered as she activated the autopilot and removed her gloves. "Time to take a deep breath, calm down a bit and plot a course for U.S. soil."

She found the flight charts and whiz wheel. She'd need to refuel at least once along the way. NASJax in Jacksonville, Florida suited her needs best. Aliyana calculated and charted a course. Radio silence was a must for as long as she dared. Emil had ears everywhere. For the same reason, she should avoid Cuban airspace altogether.

As the first tedious hours of the flight passed, her mind wandered in a host of directions. Did the second guard catch sight of her face? Would the glare from the window prevent a positive identification? Mercado had no idea she could pilot a plane or render a guard unconscious. Even if the guard didn't see her, how long would it take him to blame her once he awoke and found her missing? Probably not as long as she might wish. Out of vindictiveness he'd flood her photo and video images from his surveillance cameras all throughout the underworld.

The man wouldn't rest until he received proof 'Victoria Mendoza Torres' was dead. A burst of air turbulence and a massive bolt of lightning jolted the plane. The sudden appearance of thick black clouds swallowed the craft. Aliyana fought the controls. The wrath of the raging storm battered the Twin Otter with relentless fury. She sought higher altitude and the promise of clearer skies. Yet no matter how high she climbed, she remained enveloped inside the unearthly, yellowish gray fog deep inside the black mist. Strange swirling lights surrounded her with no heed to wind direction or velocity. The beams emitted ominous sounds from within each time they bounced off in an impossible direction. Her mind sought for some sort of rationale and found none.

She'd already passed over Puerto Rico. Surely, one of the Bahaman Islands would come into view very soon. If she headed west, she could make an emergency landing at one of the airports—

She dropped her gaze to her instrument panel and found all the gauges spinning wildly, both clock and counterclockwise. At that moment, she had no idea the direction in which she flew. She grabbed the radio, only to find the device no longer functioned. The words 'hopelessly lost' echoed inside her mind.

She dipped the nose of the plane downward and aimed below the tempest. In that same moment she caught a glimpse of churning clouds. The tumultuous winds formed a long billowing portal. That small opening at the end of the tunnel exposed a portion of clear sky on the other side. She charged straight toward it. Before she made it all the way through the portal, the opening slammed shut. Another blinding bolt of lightning struck the plane. Try as she might, she couldn't restart any of the engines.

Aliyana peered through the fog. The raging ocean below loomed ever closer. Large white waves rolled wildly across the surface. Through the haze she stared at the unexpected sight of a stone lighthouse on a small island. She blinked several times just to make sure she saw it. The lighthouse stayed in view. She needed the shelter that lighthouse promised because she couldn't stop the loss of altitude or the rapid descent of her plane.

She set the aircraft down into the water with a resounding thud and a series of harsh bounces. From out of the mist a large ship appeared right in front of her. She avoided colliding with the vessel with a sharp turn to the left. A wave rolled backward and to her horror, unveiled a massive jagged rock straight ahead. The thunderous crash of metal sounded in her ears a split second before blackness overtook her.

****

Captain Wolfaert Dircksen Van Ness cursed under his breath as he strode aft of his vessel and gazed at the twisted wreckage. "Lying ahull, Joris! Fix the helm and drop anchor!"

"Aye, aye, *Kapitein*." Joris roused the crew to the duty.

"Lower and man the boat," Wolf shouted just as he leaped onto the taffrail and dove into the ocean. He thrust his body against the waves and currents until he arrived at the shattered door.

A quick glance told him one life needed saving. *So much the better.*

Water poured into the tail of the tipped wreckage at a rapid pace. Soon the blasted thing would sink. He entered through the crumpled doorway and pulled an unconscious woman into his arms. Blood gushed down her forehead. She had a deep gash somewhere along the top of her scalp. A thick mane of long, sable hair prevented him from seeing the depth of the wound. He had no idea what other injuries she might've sustained during the impact, either.

Joris and Klaus paddled the boat alongside them. After he handed her off to Klaus, he climbed aboard the small vessel.

"To the lighthouse." Once the boat slid up and onto the sandy shore, Wolf stepped out of the boat and scooped the woman up in his arms. He gazed at Joris. "Take a couple of the men back to her craft and salvage as much as you can before the thing sinks into the sea. In the meantime, Klaus will see to her injuries."

"Aye, *Kapitein.*" Joris saluted, shoved the boat back into the water, and climbed aboard.

Klaus followed close behind him as he strode up the walkway and entered the old, deserted lighthouse. The doctor moved ahead of him and raced up the stairs. No doubt he searched for the most comfortable room in which to put his patient. While Klaus's footsteps echoed above him, he took his first good look at the bewitching Spanish beauty in his arms. At least, with her flawless tawny colored skin and raven black hair, he believed her of Hispanic descent. He shook his head over the irony. How many Spanish ships had he sent to the bottom of the sea during his tenure as captain for the Dutch West India Company?

"Bring her up here, Wolf," Klaus called out.

He carried her up the stairs, turned right of the landing, and stepped inside the second bedroom down the hallway. After the doctor smoothed the last wrinkle from the sheet, Wolf laid her on the bed. The room held little else, save a rectangular bedside table where a dusty kerosene lamp sat. A small chest of drawers and a large wooden rocking chair completed the furnishings.

"Would you see if you can find me a cloth or something I can clean the wound with? Oh, and some warm water, if you please," Klaus asked as he focused on his patient.

Wolf headed for the kitchen. He opened several cabinets and found most of them empty. The drawers yielded nothing useful. Bits and pieces of silverware, a few knives, and a can opener lay inside them, but no cloth. He stooped down and peered inside the bottom cabinets. A single medium sized pot gathered dust and cobwebs. He shrugged. The banged up, dilapidated pan would have to do.

He carried it to the sink and turned the handle of the faucet. Rusty looking water coughed and sputtered before it finally ran clear enough to use. In the moment he exited the kitchen, Joris, Pieter, and Johannes burst through the door carrying a vast array of objects from inside the girl's aircraft. They dropped them onto the floor in haphazard fashion.

"See if you can find anything resembling a cloth in that mess," Wolf called out as he hurried up the stairs with his pot of water.

Minutes later, Joris entered the bedroom. He carried a large case with a red cross prominently displayed on the side and a small hand towel.

"This case appears to have all kinds of medical stuff inside it. Perhaps you can find something useful." Joris perched it on top of the table and opened it to the doctor's view. "Pieter found a tattered pillow and some blankets inside a chest down in the living room. He's on his way up."

"Excellent. Thanks, Joris," said Klaus. "Captain, would you fetch me that gauze, right there? Now press it against the wound while I see what I have to work with here."

The doctor made quick use of the hydrogen peroxide, alcohol swabs, and suture kit. With the greatest of care, he stitched the wound in the girl's head. Once he finished the task, he rummaged around inside the case and found a small vial. "How fortunate that someone thought to include antibiotics. Who would've guessed?"

He shrugged away the comment as he grabbed the pillow and blankets Pieter had brought into the room. "One can't stop progress, Klaus. You of all people should know that by now."

"Too bad that progression didn't include some kind of portable x-ray machine, as well," he replied.

"Why? Do you think something is wrong internally?" he asked.

Klaus scratched at the corner of his mouth as he lifted his brows. "I can't say for sure. She has some bruising around her ribcage. But given the impact, I expected no less. In all honesty, I'm more concerned over the damage her brain may have suffered than a few broken ribs. That deep cut means her head sustained a harsh blow. Unfortunately, we won't know anything conclusive until she wakes up and says something. So, my friend, I'm afraid we'll just have to watch and wait."

"How long do you think it'll take before she wakes up?" he asked.

"Your guess is as good as mine. Right now, it's more important to get her out of her wet clothes and warm her up." Klaus drew the blankets over her body and somehow removed her clothing without exposing her body.

Most impressive.

Klaus turned toward him. "Do you mind watching over her while I go through some of the stuff the boys brought in? I might find something else I can use in her recovery."

"I don't mind. Take your time." Wolf slid the rocking chair to the side of the bed and settled into it.

Klaus paused just outside the doorway. "Call me if you see any change. Even a small one."

"Don't worry, I will."

Despite all offers to relieve his watch, Wolf remained at the woman's bedside all throughout the remainder of the day. He watched over her throughout the night, and all during the daylight hours that followed. She hadn't stirred.

Klaus peeked in every now and again as did some of the boys. The doctor checked on her progress, assessed her condition, and took her vitals. Each time it seemed those readings satisfied him well enough. Even so, Klaus remained concerned about the blow to her head. In turn, that concerned him as well.

As dusk approached the tiny island for the second time, a small moan escaped the girl's lips. Wolf leaned forward in anticipation. The tip of her tongue explored the dryness of her bottom lip. He picked up the bottle of water they fetched from the plane and placed a hand underneath her head. At the same time, he drew the bottle to her lips and poured a bit of water into her mouth.

She found swallowing difficult; he could see it. Nonetheless, he could also see she wanted more, and he obliged the need. After several such swallows, her head rolled back. He adjusted her pillow and brushed the long wavy strands of ebony hair away from her face.

"Come now, *lieveling*," he whispered in a gentle tone. "It's time you opened your eyes. You've slept long enough."

In response, she squeezed her eyelids together as she worked her jaw using tiny movements. *Good, she can hear me.*

"That's right, come out of your muddled fog, and open your eyes." As he spoke, he caressed her cheek with the back of his fingers.

She drew in a deep breath and let it out slowly. Her long black lashes fluttered several times before she half-heartedly complied with his request. As she studied the ceiling above her, Wolf was at once mesmerized by her exquisite sea-green eyes. Yet, before he had his fill of the unexpected vision they presented, she closed them once again. At the same time, she lifted a hand and rested it against her forehead.

Her brows knit. "*Dónde estoy?*" she breathed out.

"I'm sorry, *lieveling,* I speak very little Spanish. Very little," Wolf replied. "I don't suppose you know English?"

She turned her head toward the sound of his voice, and with what appeared great effort, opened her eyes. Their gazes locked and held for several quiet moments.

"Who are you?" she asked without a trace of an accent.

He grinned and bowed his head. "Wolfaert Dircksen Van Ness, captain of the *Witte Wieven*, at your service."

"Wolfaert Dircksen Van Ness," she repeated. "Captain of the *Witte Wieven*?"

He nodded as he leaned toward her. "That's right, but Wolf will do just fine. And you are?"

She scrutinized his face for several moments as if she assessed his character. "Aliyana Rosa Montijo and

Aliyana will do just fine. Where am I?"

He chuckled as he folded his arms against his chest and settled back into his chair. "At the moment, we're out in the middle of the Atlantic Ocean, on a small island, inside a deserted lighthouse."

From the frown, his answer puzzled her even further. It seemed she struggled for a memory that would help her make sense of his words. Although he could assist the effort, he'd wait and see how much she remembered herself.

She focused on the thick wooden beams, evenly spaced along the vaulted ceiling. Her befuddlement soon gave way. He could see it in her eyes.

Stunned over whatever details she recalled, she turned her gaze toward him. "Something's not right here. I could've sworn I saw some kind of a…a Black Bart Roberts, '*arr, me hearty*', pirate ship out there on the ocean just before I…just before I—"

A finger went to the bottom of her lip as she stopped mid-sentence and looked him over from head to toe. Her baffled expression returned, and she shook her head.

Of all the stupid things. How could he have forgotten about the look of his clothing? Despite the blunder, he managed a grin. "I take exception to you calling my vessel a pirate ship, Miss Montijo. Personally, I prefer the term brigantine, if it's all the same to you."

Chapter Two

The idea one could dream and take part inside another dream never once occurred to Aliyana. That had never happened before. Yet she couldn't find any other explanation for this bizarre experience. She found herself in a strange bed, gazing at a tall, very handsome, broad-shouldered, man. The man in question had light brown, shoulder-length hair, combed back from his face. His short, well-trimmed beard and mustache seemed darker than his hair or at least it did in this light. He had incredible sky-blue eyes, infectious laughter, and a dimpled smile that would melt the iciest heart.

The only trouble with this picture? The form-fitting black doublet he wore looked like something straight out of *The Three Musketeers*, minus the ridiculous broad-brimmed, large-feathered hat. And it wouldn't surprise her if she found him aboard the ship she encountered just before her plane collided with that massive rock. *If any of that really happened.*

On top of all that, he just told her to call him 'Wolf' using a very charming European accent—probably Dutch. *Okay, Mr. Big Bad Wolf, from which part of my scrambled brain did I conjure a man like you?* She closed her eyes. Perhaps in so doing she could escape this wacky dream altogether and wake up somewhere else. Some place a little more normal.

"Any change?" someone new asked.

The voice sounded quite close. In fact, right now she felt his cool hand as it rested against her forehead. Unless, of course, it belonged to the Wolf. But where did the voice come from? She didn't hear any footsteps, did she?

"Yes," said the Wolf. "But I believe she thinks I'm a hallucination."

Oh, please!

"Did she say anything?" the strange voice asked.

"Quite a bit, considering she just woke up."

"Did she appear coherent?"

"Yes, I think so."

"Did she give you her name?"

"Aliyana Montijo—"

Aliyana let loose an exasperated sigh and once again opened her eyes so she could confront this new delusion. She eyed the owner of the strange voice from his navy-blue peaked hat with its gold insignias to his black polished boots. At the end of her inspection, she wished she had kept them closed. She shook her head and pointed a finger in his direction. "Oh, don't tell me—you're a German Navy Officer from World War Two. Right?"

The new 'hallucination,' in full dress uniform, threw back his head and laughed heartily over her comment. "Doctor Klaus Souter, Miss Montijo. At your service."

Wow—complete with thick German accent even.

"This is just too much." She struggled to sit up, intent on leaving the bed and this crazy dream. However, the mere movement made her cry out in excruciating pain. At once, the doctor eased her back against the pillow. His hands poked and prodded against her sides and stomach. Confusion beset her. How could anyone feel such intense pain in a dream?

"Careful now," the doctor said. "At the very least, you sustained a few broken ribs in the accident and a very nasty head laceration. Keep your movements small, and don't contract your muscles so forcefully for the next little while, hmm?"

Her head did hurt and right now, the room spun around in wild circles. Head laceration did he say? Her fingers crept toward the center of her pain and explored the one-inch gash. She felt a series of tiny stitches on the left side of her head near her hairline as she did so.

"You're lucky," the doctor said, "that the plane had a good medical kit on board. I found it very useful in tending that nasty wound."

Oh, the plane! Her heart dropped into the pit of her stomach and forgetting all else, she turned her gaze toward the Wolf. "My backpack! I have to get to the plane, please! That pack is more important than you realize."

She extended her hand toward the captain. Yet, just before she touched his arm, he bolted upright. He stepped backward in obvious avoidance of any physical contact. She curled her fingers together and self-consciously inched her clutched fist toward her chest. Did he think she had some kind of disease?

This dream keeps getting stranger by degrees.

Wolf smiled at her as he called out for someone named Joris. He'd have her believe he simply rose from his seat so he could gain the man's attention. She knew better.

A third man, dressed in similar fashion as the

17

captain, arrived at the door. He glanced at her before he turned his full attention to the Wolf. "Aye *Kapitein*?"

"Miss Montijo is looking for her backpack. Were you able to salvage it before the plane sank?" he asked as he returned to his seat.

No!

Joris shifted his gaze to her. "Could you describe your backpack for me please?"

She'd go along with this crazy dream, if for nothing more than to calm her racing heart. "The nylon bag is black and about eighteen inches long and about fifteen inches wide or so." She formed the dimensions with her hands.

Joris said nothing but exited the room as quietly as he had entered it. A few minutes later, he returned with a black bag in each hand. He held them up for her inspection. "One of these?"

Relief washed over her as she pointed at the bag in his right hand. "That one there. Could you hand it to me please?"

The man placed the backpack on the bed. She rubbed her hand across the top of the nylon, checking for signs of water damage. Aliyana took hold of the straps and tugged the heavy pack toward her. Yet, just as she did so, intense pain shot through her body. Again. Her eyes squeezed shut. She drew her knees upward and rocked them back and forth as she waited for the agony to pass. At the same time, her hand traveled instinctively to her ribcage.

"Here, let me help you with that," said Wolf.

There was genuine concern in his eyes. For a moment, she wavered in indecision. Whether she dreamed or not, this man didn't pose a danger to her mission. He didn't have the persona of someone who would work for a drug cartel. A circus maybe—but not a drug cartel. Nonetheless, she had to know if her camera and flash drive survived the crash.

She nodded and managed a bit of a smile. "All right, thank you."

"Shall I remove all of the contents for you, or do you want something in particular?"

"Everything, please. I must check all of my electronic devices for damage."

Wolf took her changes of clothing out of the bag. He put her toiletry bag, tool kit, laptop, satellite and cell phones alongside them. All the while he studied the computer and phones as if he had never seen either one before. *How very odd.* Finally, he brought out her camera and flash drive.

"That about does it," he said. "Unless you want me to open the side pouches?"

"No, you don't have to bother with those right now. The left side carries my cords and cables, and the right has just a few snacks inside," she said. "Now, if I haven't exceeded my limit of favors, would you open my laptop, please?"

"Certainly," said Wolf. "Um, which one is the uh—?" His voice trailed off as he gazed down at the clutter on the bed.

"This one," she said. Two things bounded into her mind. One, dreaming had nothing to do with her current situation. Two, the man who worked at prying the lid apart using just the force of his fingers lived his entire life in some remote wilderness—underneath a rock. She didn't have time to think on it. In that instant bile rose to her throat. She needed to puke, and—she desperately

19

needed to use the bathroom facilities as well.

"You just have to slide that little bar, right there, to your right," she said, then took several deep breaths, hoping to drive back the queasiness.

With a sheepish grin that somehow enhanced his looks, he complied. Once he popped the lid open, he turned the computer toward her.

The breathing didn't help. She put a hand to her stomach, the other to her mouth. "I need to get to the bathroom."

Both Wolf and the doctor rushed toward her. Wolf gathered her up his arms as he sidestepped the doctor. In no time at all, he set her down inside the lavatory, down the hallway.

Dizziness befell her and in response, she grabbed hold of the pedestal sink. "Please, could you just—"

"Forget it, Aliyana. I'm not leaving you alone in your current condition," Wolf cut in. "Don't worry. I've seen plenty of vomit over the centuries. I assure you, yours won't offend me in the least."

She hadn't time to argue or assess what he just said. In fact, she just had time to lift the lid of the old-fashioned toilet. While her stomach purged itself, Wolf held her body steady, and kept her hair away from her face. Finally, she took a deep breath and nodded as she flushed the dusty commode. "I think I'm finished. At least for now."

He helped her over to the sink so she could rinse the horrible taste out of her mouth. She wanted to do more than that though. She wanted her teeth brushed, followed up with a hefty dose of mouthwash. But first—

"Look—I really need a moment of privacy, so if

you don't mind?"

He stared at her for several seconds. Surely, he didn't think he could just stand there and watch while she—

"I'll be right outside this door. Holler if you need me," he replied.

"I won't faint, I promise. But while you're waiting, could you bring me the blue bag you took out of my backpack, please? I need my toothbrush and mouthwash."

He merely nodded, turned around, and strode down the hallway.

In her moment of solitude, she gazed down at her unfamiliar attire. She wore a lovely button-up, floor-length nightgown. A ton of eyelet lace adorned the form-fitting bodice of the lightweight, white cotton fabric. The sleeveless, scoop-necked style and cut looked like something out of a nineteenth-century catalog, but the crispness of the material stated otherwise. The clothes she wore when she left Mercado's compound now hung along the rail of the oblong shower rod, which surrounded the white, porcelain, clawfoot tub. They looked freshly laundered.

The moment Aliyana opened the door, she found Wolf waiting with bag in hand. She raised a brow in silent question as she stepped back, took hold of the generous folds of the skirt, and drew the material out to the side. The action exposed part of her legs and bare feet.

"Oh," said Wolf as his gaze wandered over her form from head-to-toe and back again. "The doctor wanted to get you cleaned up a bit last night. We couldn't find anything else inside the lighthouse you could wear as you slept. I hope you don't mind. I give you my word, that all throughout the process, you retained your dignity."

He thrust the case toward her then, clearly wanting to hurry past the topic. She smiled over his obvious discomfort as she took the bag from his hand. "Thank you—for both."

As expected, he stood at her side with his hand against her back while she brushed her teeth and washed her face. Despite the humiliation, she welcomed his presence. The dizziness had returned with a vengeance, and she didn't know if she could get back into the bed without some help. She opened the tiny cupboard, pulled out the towel she hoped she'd find, and dried herself off.

"Are you feeling any better now?" asked Wolf.

"Yes, I am. Thank you." Aliyana gathered her things and turned toward him. "I still feel a little dizzy though, so—"

The comment compelled the man to sweep her off her feet yet again. She huffed out a breath. "This isn't necessary, Wolf. I can walk by myself if you'll just hold me steady."

"Perhaps, you could at that." The charming grin returned. "At the moment, however, you needn't make the effort."

Once they entered the bedroom, she saw that someone had set her belongings off to the far side of the bed and had her blankets turned back. Good, because all of a sudden fatigue overwhelmed her. She could check her camera and flash drive later, right?

Her eyes closed of their own volition just as Wolf laid her on the bed. He drew the covers up around her shoulders and then tucked them around her body. His hand brushed through the tangles of her hair in slow even strokes. She should have taken a moment to run a brush through the disheveled mess. Then again, maybe not. His gentle touch eased her toward sleep. She wanted to thank him for his kindness but couldn't find the energy.

****

While Klaus checked Aliyana's vital signs, Wolf cleared away the clutter from her bed. He placed the slim case she called 'laptop' on top of the table and stacked everything else inside her bag.

"Is she all right?" Wolf asked.

"Yes, quite well, I think," replied Klaus. "You needn't look so concerned, Wolf. Her bout of nausea is just an unfortunate consequence of her head injury. She may go through several more such episodes before it subsides."

"Are you sure nothing else is going on inside her body that needs attention, save the trauma of a few broken ribs?"

The doctor tilted his head to the side and shrugged. "As certain as I can be without some sort of device that allows me a peek inside. But she's coherent; she hasn't run any fevers, and her vital signs are all but normal. Those are all very good indicators."

"We forgot to change the look of our clothing before we let her see us. I'm certain it's a thing she'll recall, despite any corrections we make now," Wolf said. "Not that I have a clue as to what one wears in this particular day and age. At the moment, we have no way of assessing the current year."

"Actually, I can help you with that," Joris said as

he entered the bedroom, clutching a tattered magazine. "January 2017 is the latest month and year I can find among the magazines we took out of the plane. Even if this thing is several years old, the style of clothing should still be acceptable."

"Those magazines are not all we found either," Johannes said from where he stood in the doorway. "Come take a look at some of the stuff yourself. I think you'll want to take some of it back with us."

"Don't be absurd. We're not taking anything that belongs to Aliyana should she remain behind," Wolf said.

"We won't," Joris replied. "We're quite sure nothing we've salvaged belongs to her, save her backpack." He shrugged. "Unless that wicked looking knife and the rifle are hers."

Wolf gazed down at Aliyana. The deep even breathing told him she slept well enough for now.

"I'll stay with her if you wish," said Klaus. "You can fill me in on all of your discoveries when you return."

"No, you can come with us. The hallway isn't that long. We can hear her if she awakens," he replied.

Johannes led the way down the stairs and into the living room. Pieter, Conrad, and Laurens sat on the floor surrounded by several brick sized bundles encased in plastic.

"Drugs?" asked Klaus as he surveyed the pile.

"I think so," said Pieter. "The packaging is different in this decade though."

"You're not suggesting Aliyana's involved in the distribution of drugs, are you?" Wolf couldn't conceive of such a notion. He could see an admirable character

24

within her gaze.

"Not at all. But we can't say the same thing for the man who hired her. You see, he owns the plane she piloted—or at least we believe he owns the plane." Conrad swept a hand toward the documents in the open case. "His name is Emil Mercado. I can't tell you any more than that because my Spanish is limited."

Johannes waved the comment aside. "We can tell you with a fair amount of certainty, that Mercado hired Aliyana to install some kind of equipment about his facilities—probably for surveillance."

"How could you know that?" asked Wolf.

Johannes tossed him a stack of papers from out of the case. "All of those documents show similar drawings of the same facility. They were submitted to Mercado by different businesses, or so I assume. Each set of drawings depict various types of equipment, placed in different positions. We found it obvious by mere presence alone, Mercado used Aliyana's proposal, despite the fact she didn't submit the lowest bid. Oh, and uh—by the way? The name underneath her photograph isn't the one she gave you."

Wolf studied each of the pages with his usual thoroughness. The placement suggested surveillance, but nothing he'd ever seen before resembled the pictures in the file.

Conrad cleared his throat and bounced his eyebrows. "Yes, well that being said, we couldn't help but notice our Spanish lady outshines all her competition, especially since most of the others are male. The only other female? Well—she doesn't even come close."

The boys all laughed, nudged each other, and

winked.

"Whatever her name, there's nothing wrong with Mercado's eyes, that much is certain," said Laurens. "It's obvious that having such a delectable morsel around his facility was worth the extra fifteen thousand dollars he paid for the job."

"Did it ever occur to any of you barbarians that our lady might simply have submitted the superior plan?" asked Andries with a hint of boredom to his tone.

Conrad gazed first at their cook and then looked skyward. He burst out laughing and shook his head. "Nah! Such a thing would be a secondary consideration for any man, I'm sure."

As the boys laughed and exchanged insults, Klaus raised a hand. "Of course, you all realize this leads us to a conundrum."

"That conundrum being—" Pieter prompted.

"Why a woman, hired to set up these things for a virtual stranger, would take off in his plane. For most assuredly, the man didn't give his permission. I'm confident such a man wouldn't part with his personal case, and in all likelihood, his personal weapons, still inside the craft."

Pieter tossed his magazine on top of the table. "Don't dismiss the bullet holes in the plane either. I believe they're evidence she stole the plane, and they protested the theft. Perhaps she ran across something they didn't want her to find, such as these drugs. She then took the only means of escape opened to her at the time."

"Lucky for her then," replied Klaus, "she had the necessary skill to pilot an aircraft."

"These fascinating assumptions aside," Joris said

as he gazed at Wolf, "What do you intend to do with her, once she recovers? Take her with us, or leave her behind?"

"I don't know," Wolf replied. "Since we ended up here in the corridor, we know she has a choice. I believe we should give her the freedom to make it."

"You know it's not an easy task providing someone on the outside with understanding of that choice," Klaus reminded him. "Use me as a case in reference. Taking her with us without full disclosure is quite a risk at this point."

"She'll get full disclosure. I wouldn't have it any other way. Aliyana is intelligent and has both resilience and stamina. If not for the injury to her head, she might already have figured some of this out by now."

"Well, it's your call, *Kapitein*," Joris said. "We, of course, will abide by your decision."

"We don't need to make any decisions right now. Klaus tells me it'll probably take a couple of weeks for full recovery. I won't consider leaving this place until then even if the opportunity arises." Wolf left his seat and gazed toward the stairs. "In the meantime, send all those drugs to the bottom of the sea. We'll talk about the rest of this stuff later. Perhaps Aliyana, or 'Victoria,' can shed some light as to their intended use."

Chapter Three

The incessant hammering inside her head drove Aliyana toward awareness and her fingers to her forehead as she kneaded at the pain. She turned her head to the side and opened her eyes. The Wolf sat in the rocking chair. He had one booted foot resting on top of his knee, his elbows propped on the arms of the chair, and his hands loosely clasped in his lap.

"Good morning," he said. "Are you feeling any better today, Miss Montijo?"

She took inventory. Her ribs let her know of their painful existence each time she took a deep breath. Even so, the discomfort seemed less severe than before. Her nausea had subsided, and she actually wanted something to eat. Good thing she put a few granola bars in her pack. Yet, right now, such fare didn't sound at all appetizing.

Finally, she nodded and inched herself into a more seated position. "If not for the headache, I think I might feel quite a bit better than I did yesterday. I did throw up just *yesterday*, right?"

Wolf had the decency to act bewildered. "I don't recall any such occurrence. However, I do recall taking you to the bathroom, so you could freshen up yesterday, if that's what you're asking."

Aliyana shook her head and smiled. The man definitely had some very charming qualities.

"So, tell me, are you hungry yet?" he asked.

"Ravenous," she said. "I'm just not sure I'm hungry enough for a stale granola bar."

He placed his foot on the floor and with his hands clasped, he leaned toward her. "Andries will be delighted to hear it."

"Andries?" she asked.

"Andries Van Halst is our cook," he said. "And he's circled your room like a voracious buzzard ever since you woke up so he can put his skills to good use."

"There's actual food in this place?" *Didn't he say something about a tiny island and a deserted lighthouse? If someone left food behind, wouldn't it be old and inedible by now?*

"The sea and a lush island have an almost endless supply of food, providing of course, the demand doesn't overtake the supply. One must also know where to find it," he replied.

"Did I hear someone say they were hungry?" A stocky blue-eyed, white-haired gentleman with matching goatee entered the bedroom carrying a plate of sliced, fresh fruit.

"Yes, you did, and thank you," she said, as he placed the small platter on the table next to her bed.

"I'll be right back with a bit of my famous island porridge then." He winked. "The gruel will put a little meat back on those bones, for it looks to me as if you might've lost some."

Aliyana smiled her gratitude. She picked up a piece of papaya and popped it into her mouth as she tracked his retreat through the door. His style of dress caught her attention. The attire appeared far more modern than what the captain and Joris wore—or even the doctor for that matter. She gazed toward Wolf with every intention of making the comment aloud. Yet just as she opened her mouth, she found he now wore a pair of faded blue jeans. He complemented those jeans with a long-sleeved, two-button T-shirt, navy blue in color.

"Is something wrong?" he asked.

She lifted a brow and tilted her head to the side. "Not a thing. Should there be?"

Wolf feigned ignorance, yet the grin betrayed him. "No, nothing I can think of right off the top of my head."

Though she would've challenged his good-natured sham, Andries entered the room with the promised bowl of porridge. "I must say breakfast smells really good."

"The finest compliment you can give me, Miss Montijo, is to return that bowl empty," he replied.

"Anything that'll make the cook happy." Andries gave her a friendly salute before he left the room. She looked at Wolf. "Want to share some of my fruit? It's the sweetest I've ever tasted, and I know I can't eat all of it."

"No, not right now, thank you," he replied. "We've already eaten our fill."

While she ate her porridge, she sorted through the tasks that needed attention. Check her computer, flash drive, and camera for damage. After that, contact her superiors and then find a way off the island. Perhaps the DEA could contact the coast guard or send a helicopter? While she waited for their arrival, she'd get some answers to all her nagging questions.

She shoved her empty bowl to the side of the platter and eased her body toward the laptop. At once

Wolf rose to his feet as he offered unspoken assistance. He placed the computer on the bed, popped the lid, and then grabbed her backpack.

"I suppose you want to try this again?" he asked.

"Yes, thank you. I think I can get through it this time without the drama we all endured last time."

She powered up the laptop. While it booted up, she connected her satellite phone to her computer. Afterward, she retrieved her flash drive and inserted the device into a hub. Her fingers flew across the keyboard as she typed the necessary commands. Wolf watched every move she made. If she didn't know better, she'd think he found the unfolding scene fascinating.

Aliyana held her breath as she accessed her thumb drive. She nodded and sighed in relief. The files for which she had risked her life transferred from her flash drive and into her laptop without incident. Next, she connected her camera to the computer and copied the photos taken inside Mercado's office. Now she'd connect with the DEA servers and download this essential information to them.

Despite the desire and all her acquired skills, she couldn't keep a connection to the internet for more than a minute or two at any given time. Although the satellite phone looked functional, something must've happened to damage it during the accident. She grasped her cell phone and hoped against hope that she'd find a signal. At the very least, she wanted her superiors to know she was alive and well. Certainly they suspected the worst. She could also let them know she accomplished her purpose. If Mercado somehow found a way to listen in, he wouldn't understand anything she said with the code words she'd use. Minutes passed while she labored over the task. Despite every effort, she couldn't find a signal that allowed a link either—but no real surprise there.

"Is something wrong?" asked Wolf.

"Well, some of my equipment must've sustained some damage. I can't keep a satellite signal long enough to make a connection with the outside world. The only thing I get is static." She gave her phone a causal toss. That curious look returned to his eyes and it made her feel a bit unsettled. How could one, so obviously intelligent, remain unaware of technology a couple of decades old? More important, did she want to discover the answer to that question? *Oh, but how ridiculous.*

She took a deep breath and in an exaggerated manner, cleared her throat. "All right, I think I'm ready to hear all of it now."

"Hear all of it?" asked Wolf. "I'm not sure what you mean?"

"Your explanation to all of—this," she said as her hand swept across the whole of her environment.

Wolf shrugged. "I can't see where there is much need for an explanation. You crashed into the sea during the storm. In an effort to avoid my ship, you compounded the problem by slamming into one of the many rocks the lighthouse is meant to divert you from."

Aliyana held his gaze—and her silence—for several long moments. She gave him ample opportunity to continue the tale. When he didn't, she sighed in resignation, and swung her legs off the bed. The action grabbed his attention if nothing else did. He leaped to his feet so he could offer his help. She lifted both of her hands, turned her head to the side, and leaned away from his arms despite a terrible wave of dizziness.

"I can do this by myself, without any assistance from you, thank you very much," she ground out.

"Don't be absurd, Aliyana," Wolf countered. "You can't even hold yourself steady while seated."

"Then perhaps the doctor or a member of your crew can help me instead," she replied through clenched teeth. "Because, right now, I really don't want *you* to touch me. Therefore, would you be so kind as to call one of *them* for me or shall I holler out one of the names myself?"

Wolf shook his head as he gazed heavenward. "Temperamental wench!"

Her mouth dropped as she drew in a deep breath. Before she could make a retort of her own, he scooped her up into his arms. He shifted her weight a little more comfortably and pinned his gaze to hers. "Do you want to use the facilities, or do you need to throw up again?"

She lifted a brow in disdain. "Again?" she asked as her temper rose even higher. So much for the charm she had assigned him earlier. "But you just said I *didn't* throw up!"

"Are you going to answer the question or are you not?" he quipped.

"Ooh! *Tu' eres el hombre más exasperante que he tenido la desgracia de conocer*!" she huffed as she folded her arms and slammed them hard against her chest.

"Sorry?" His eyes danced with sudden merriment. All the while his lips twitched in amusement. "I didn't quite catch all that!"

In response to his mirth, she once again clenched her teeth. Her cheeks flamed as she jerked a pointed a finger toward his chest. "I said, *you* are the *most* exasperating man I've ever had the misfortune—"

The moment she drove her finger forward, her words abruptly ended and so did his mirth. Aliyana touched the tip of her tongue to her lips as she stared. Did her finger really pass through him? She stared into Wolf's eyes, needing an answer. What on earth was happening to her?

****

"Aliyana," Wolf whispered. "Don't be afraid of me. This isn't what you think."

She struggled to make sense of this new quandary. Her bewildered gaze shifted to his arms that still held her fast, traveled their length, and then rose to his face. Those lovely eyes, filled with such delightful indignation a moment ago, now held a trace of fear.

"Who are you?" she murmured. "Better yet, *what* are you?"

"I'm a man, Aliyana, born of this earth, though not of your time," he said.

"You're a ghost then." She stated the words matter-of-factly.

"Yes and no. I guess you could say I'm a ghost part of the time, depending upon the location I'm in," he replied.

"Part of the time? Part of the time! Just what do you mean by that ridiculous statement?"

Wolf looked upward for a moment and then sighed. "I would like to have had this discussion after you were fully recovered. But come on, let's go ahead and get it done now."

"Where are we going?" she asked as he headed for the door.

"Upstairs to the top of the lighthouse," he replied.

"All right. I need to stop at the bathroom first, if you don't mind," she said as a blush stole across her cheeks.

He didn't mind at all. The small delay gave him a moment to form an explanation acceptable to a woman like Aliyana.

Once finished, she opened the door and gazed into his eyes. As he took a step forward, she shook her head.

"Please, I'd like to try and walk up the stairs myself," she said. "Just hang onto me and keep me stable. You can do that, right?"

Wolf nodded and placed a firm hand about her waist. She set the pace as they ascended the metal steps of the spiral staircase. About halfway up, her legs gave way. He caught hold of her body, swept her up, and cradled her in his arms. She didn't make a peep of protest. Once they arrived at the observation deck, he looked down at her face. She had her eyes closed, head tucked inward, and her lips tight together.

"Are you all right?" he asked. "You look a little pale."

"I'm fine really—just a little dizzy and a bit nauseous from all the small turns. Don't worry. I won't throw up on you, I promise."

"Do you want me to take you back to your bed?"

"No, I'm fine, really."

Wolf set her down on the old wooden rocking chair. He grabbed hold of the two-seater bench next to it and turned it around to face her. Once he sat down, he leaned toward her and took hold of her hands. At last, she opened her eyes and gazed into his.

"Take a good look around you, Aliyana. Tell me

exactly what you see." He aimed a thumb at the view behind him.

She took a deep breath and fixed her gaze on the panoramic scene above his head. Her eyes grew wider by degrees. She raised her body a little higher, lifted her chin, and looked in all possible directions.

A hand covered a gasp of delighted surprise. "Oh my—the sky is a brilliant shade of turquoise blue, and I—I see a wide lavender band across the horizon. The beauty of the atmosphere is breathtaking. What makes it look like this? Do the colors have something to do with the anomalous storm we passed through?"

"In a way, yes, but no, not really," Wolf replied. "You see, that particular type of storm merely transported you here. Here in this place, the sky is quite normal."

"What do you mean, here in this place?" she asked as her gaze remained fastened on the view. He could tell she saw more than just the sky, now. The vast colors in the surrounding vegetation also looked far different from anything she'd ever seen before and by expression alone he saw she appreciated the beauty of it. He rubbed his thumbs gently across the top of her hands.

"Please look into my eyes now, Aliyana." With a bit of reluctance, she complied. "I speak nothing but truth in what I'm about to tell you. A lie has no value, nor would it serve any purpose. Would you agree?"

"Oh, you're not trying to tell me I'm dead, are you?" she asked, as a look of horror filled her eyes.

He chuckled. "No, nothing like that."

"Then just come out and say whatever it is you need to say."

"I'll start off by telling you I entered your world in the year 1601 and left it, in a manner of speaking, in the year 1632."

"What do you mean, 'in a manner of speaking'? You keep talking in riddles."

"I didn't die, Aliyana." He held up a hand as she opened her mouth to speak. "I know the questions you have, because once I had them myself. Just let me finish my explanation and then you can ask me anything you want. Fair enough?" he asked.

She nodded as she settled a little deeper into her chair. "Fair enough."

"In my final year as a resident of your current and my former dimension, I served as captain of the *Witte Wieven* for the Dutch West India Company. We sailed the Atlantic between the Bahamas and South America looking for Spanish ships. I'm certain the history books have documented this in great detail. One fine morning in August of 1632, we set sail. We had clear skies and the wind at our back. Several hours into our voyage, we happened upon a Spanish galleon and pursued her. From out of nowhere, and with a suddenness that defies explanation, we encountered the same type of storm you did. Unfortunately, I lost most of my crew during that gale. The seas were so rough we couldn't rescue any of them, though we tried. Strange balls of light surrounded us. Those lights bounded in all directions at once, and the sounds they emitted made our blood run cold."

"Yes, I remember the sounds they made," whispered Aliyana as a slight shiver coursed through her body.

He nodded as he traced gentle patterns on the hand

he still held. "I know you did, and I also know you saw the clouds form a portal, with the promise of clear skies on the other side. You entered it then, correct?"

"Yes," she said. "But the clouds closed the opening before I got all the way through it."

"I know that as well. The gateway closed because two ships, whether sea or airborne, cannot pass each other at the same time while going through it," he said.

She gazed at him for several moments before understanding dawned. "You entered through it from the other side?"

"Yes, I did. This is something we do quite often."

"Why?"

"For the adventure of it—to bring back differing kinds of technology—and occasionally, people that survive without transportation and find themselves lost in those storms." He paused and waited for her reaction.

"Like a navy doctor from World War II?" she asked.

Not quite the direction in which he hoped to lead her, but—"Yes, like Klaus. He served aboard the U84 submarine when we revisited this dimension in the year 1943. An allied aircraft dropped a homing torpedo on top of them, he said. No one survived the explosion, save the doctor. Well, at least none that we saw. We plucked him from the sea and nursed him back to health. I must say it took us quite a while to convince him as to the truth of our tale. For quite some time, he believed we kidnapped and brainwashed him with our outlandish story."

"Why do you think, after almost four hundred years, you're still alive and unchanged physically? Your mortal body no longer houses your spirit, Wolf.

Can't you see that? My hand went right through you."

"Yes, but I can still hold you, can I not? Do you think a dead person from your realm can really do that?"

"I...I don't know. Maybe. I've never encountered a ghost before. I have no way of knowing what a ghost can or cannot do. For all I know you didn't survive the storm and you just think you did because you—"

"I know this is difficult for you to believe. Such would be the case for almost anyone. Nonetheless, what you see right now, what you *can't* feel when you apply enough pressure to my body, is a condition only outside the sphere in which we now live. On the other side of the Bermuda portal, we're still very much alive," he said. "For lack of a better explanation, the change we experience as we go all the way through the portal changes our physical chemistry. This change allows survival in the atmospheric conditions our current dimension has. We are changed insomuch that on this side only—our bodies are more like spirit, with many of the same characteristics that spirits possess. We use those characteristics to our advantage each time we revisit your realm. Characteristics such as moving at speeds you can't possibly detect, enhanced hearing as well as vision. Why, Miss Montijo, I believe we can even walk on water."

"What then—you're telling me you never die?" she asked, her skepticism obvious in tone.

"I didn't say that. We have seen our share of death from those who've crossed the portal. Especially among the ancient ones. The people that existed well before Alexander the Great amassed his empire are now dying off at a rapid rate. But it takes many, many centuries for death to overcome us, save those who die an unnatural death. Of course, the physical age and condition of one's body is a factor in how long one will live, once one passes through the gate," he replied. "Keep in mind none of that applies to those who are native to that dimension. Yet, they too, have extraordinarily long lives."

"What do you mean by the other side of the Bermuda portal? Are you seriously referring to the Bermuda Triangle myths?"

"We've learned the earth has many different parallels, dimensions, spheres, planes, or whatever you choose to call them, just like the universe itself. They all exist simultaneously side by side. And yes, the occurrences inside the triangle are more than just myths. Surely, after your own experience, and by what your eyes see at this moment, you already know this."

"Exactly where are we right now?" she asked, ignoring his comment.

"This is a corridor. It's a harbor of in-between or a *kátholose*, as the ancients call it. These corridors are a place of waiting. Right now, you're not within the dimension you know, nor are you on the other side of the portal," he said. "We find ourselves here because the moment we crossed paths, both gates closed. This is the reason your equipment will not function as expected."

"Are you telling me we're trapped here forever?" Her eyes grew wide in alarm.

"Not at all," he replied. "Just until the next storm arises. In a case such as we now find ourselves, one will come along soon enough. They always do."

"And then what?"

Wolf let go of her hand. With a gentle touch, he traced the contours of her face from cheek to jaw, reassured her with a smile, and shrugged. "Then you choose the direction you wish to go, *lieveling*."

Chapter Four

Caught up in the intensity of Wolf's gaze, it took a moment before she truly understood what he just said. Should she choose to believe him—and for the abundant evidence she found that she did—she could see all the wonders he had already seen. She could come to know all the mysteries he solved centuries earlier. Yet, how many people, given such a choice, left the comfort and safety of their home? So many things passed through her mind. Strangely enough, she discovered part of her yearned to explore that unknown dimension with the handsome captain of the *Witte Wieven.*

"What does one find on the other side of the doorway, Wolf?" she asked as her gaze settled on a distant tree.

"Just everyday life," he said. "There are obvious similarities. Yet, in my opinion we have a far better one than what you have here in the present time. But look, Aliyana, no one is asking you to make a decision about any of this right now. For those who are given this option, careful consideration is required. I know and appreciate that fact."

The comment drew her gaze to his. "If I understood you correctly, you traveled through the portal without knowing beforehand what you would find on the other side or the changes it would make to your body. Also, at that moment, you didn't realize you would leave your life behind. Am I right?" she asked.

"Yes, I suppose you are," he replied.

"So, tell me then, would you have elected to remain behind, if given the opportunity to choose your fate at that time?"

They gazed at each other for several moments. He cocked his head to the side as his eyes took on a faraway gaze. "I honestly don't know. I'd like to believe, just as in all similar circumstances, I'd have wanted to explore the other side of the portal and hang all the consequences."

"Did you leave anything or anyone important behind—like a family, perhaps?" she asked.

"When a man takes to sea, he knows there's always a chance he won't return," he replied. "His family knows this truth and accepts it, as does he."

"How cavalier. Did your wife accept the possibility of your demise so easily?" she asked.

"I've never taken a wife, Aliyana," he replied.

She stared in open amazement. "Never once in almost four hundred years?"

"Not even close."

"Why not?"

He said nothing for what seemed like minutes instead of mere seconds. As she opened her mouth to apologize for prying, he finally spoke.

"I've had relationships, of course. But I've just never found a woman I wanted enough to make my wife."

His answer filled her with a curious sense of contentment, though she didn't know why it should. "Well, I *can't* leave my dimension. Not even if I wanted to. So you see—there's nothing more to discuss or decide."

He sat back in his chair. Disappointment flashed across his eyes. "Why not?"

"Because innocent lives are at stake, and I must try and save them if I can," she said.

"Can you tell me what you mean by that? Maybe I can assist your efforts."

"I don't know what you could possibly do to help the situation I'm in. Besides, you said when the storm arrives you have to leave, didn't you?"

"No, I said one chooses the direction one wants to go," he reminded her. "And you might be surprised at what I can accomplish, if given the opportunity."

Under any other circumstances, she couldn't and wouldn't tell him anything about her work. Nonetheless, she readily accepted Wolf's explanations about her present situation. Nothing else made any sense. The truth was clearly in his eyes and in the environment around her. Obvious as well, the man sitting across from her didn't pose a threat to national security, nor would he have a clue as to how to interfere, even if for some reason he did.

"You can trust me with your secrets, you know," he said after a lengthy silence.

Aliyana considered his statement. "Interestingly enough, I think I could trust you with my life, Wolf. I find I have no qualms about that issue."

"Then will you tell me how you found yourself flying a plane, filled with drugs and riddled with fresh bullet holes?" he asked. "I'd really like to know the circumstances if you'll allow it."

"The plane carried drugs?" she countered.

Wolf nodded. "Yes, it did. However, the entire lot is now at the bottom of the sea. They can no longer endanger anyone should someone else find their way inside this corridor and salvage what they find."

This news didn't concern her overly much. She carried enough evidence against Emil Mercado to seal his fate without producing additional drugs from his private plane. "That's a good place for them." She closed her eyes against a sudden harsh wave of vertigo. The observation deck began a topsy-turvy spin and she found she couldn't focus on a single thing, try as she might.

"Are you all right?" he asked.

"I think I've had enough of sitting upright in this chair, if you don't mind."

He scooped her into his arms, carried her down the tower stairs, and then placed her gently onto her bed. As her head sank back onto the pillow, she dropped a hand against her forehead. She pressed against the pain and dizziness, hoping they'd go away. Once the wild spinning diminished somewhat, she offered a small smile.

"Thank you so much for your continued assistance. I'm sure by now you've grown tired of lugging me about the lighthouse."

"Not at all. I find 'lugging' you about a pleasure," he replied. "Perhaps you ought to get some sleep, now. We can talk later if you choose."

"No." She extended a hand toward him.

In the same instant, his fingers closed around hers. They felt warm and tangible. How did he manage that in his current state? Why didn't his current form go through hers?

"Please sit down. This isn't a clever ploy to escape your questions."

"I didn't think otherwise," he said.

She didn't speak while he settled himself into the rocking chair. All the while she sought a beginning to her story. "I suppose I should tell you I work for the DEA. Until a few days ago, I worked undercover. That means during the past few years, I falsified every possible thing about my life and identity to everyone with whom I interacted, save those in my squad, of course."

"The DE—what?" He lifted a brow.

"The U.S. Drug Enforcement Administration. I'm a field agent."

"How did you get involved in something like that?" he asked.

A quiet breath of laughter followed his question. "The whole thing is my brother's fault really. He became an agent well before I did. He filled my head with enough of his adventures to make me want to take part. In fact, he always made his exploits sound so exciting and important. I badgered him until he helped me get my foot in the door."

"Does he work undercover as well then?"

Aliyana closed her eyes against the sudden pain his comment produced. "No," she whispered as she swallowed past the lump in her throat. "He, uh— became an unfortunate victim of a drug lord in Colombia, by the name of Emil Rios Mercado."

Wolf took hold of her hand and gave it a gentle squeeze. He didn't let go. "I'm so sorry, Aliyana. It seems I keep asking the wrong questions."

"No, it's all part of the same explanation. You see

after his death, my superiors asked me if I wanted to participate in an undercover operation intended to take down Mercado's cartel. I jumped at the chance to give my brother's death some meaning. So, they moved me to Barranquilla, Colombia where we set up a very impressive electronics shop."

Wolf listened to her tale far more intently than she thought he would. He never once interrupted or asked questions. She couldn't help but wonder where his thoughts had taken him. At the end of her narrative he leaned back in his chair as he shook his head.

"It sounds like what you did is dangerous work for a woman."

Heated indignation spilled onto her cheeks over the sexist remark,

He held up a defensive hand. "I don't doubt the quality of your skills or your impressive abilities, Miss Montijo. I simply refer to the risk a beautiful woman takes when in the constant company of so many men. I'm well aware not all of them, regardless of dimension, appreciate and understand the word *no*," he said.

Wolf considered her beautiful? The unexpected compliment banished the scathing retort she nearly made. "Fortunately, other women, many of them in fact, willingly live inside Mercado's compound. And I've learned to handle such risks with amazing temerity when the need arises."

"Meaning you had a great deal of practice," he stated. He scrutinized her face as if searching for any telltale signs of his claim.

"I suppose I've had my fair share." She glanced down at her bedding and smoothed a wrinkle.

"You know, it would bring me a great deal of

comfort, Aliyana, if you told me none of your admirers ever—caused you any harm."

She smiled over his exasperated tone of voice. "Then consider yourself comforted, Captain Dircksen Van Ness. Trust me, I can handle myself."

"So, you went through all of these risks, not to mention time and effort, so you could gain intelligence as to the inner workings of this particular cartel?" asked Wolf.

"Yes, and ferret out the names of his international contacts, bank accounts, shipping methods and lab locations. Things like that."

"I assume you succeeded in this mission."

"For the most part, I did. However, Mercado has a nasty habit of murdering anyone on the outside of his organization whom, even if invited, steps inside and sees things he would rather they not see. Once I finished his security system, I had limited time to escape. So, a couple of days ago, I had my 'going away party.' Later that evening as everyone slept heavily from the over indulgence of drugs and alcohol, I slipped into his office. I downloaded all the information I needed into my flash drive.

"While I waited for the completion of that download, I stumbled across a plan Mercado had concocted. In the very near future, he will assassinate the officials of the DEA, their wives and every member of their family if he can. I gathered that evidence as well. Once I collected all the information I deemed important, I snuck out of the compound. My only means of escape arose in the commandeering of Mercado's floatplane. You know the rest."

She looked down at Wolf's hand, which still held

her own before she gazed into his eyes. "I can't allow Emil Mercado to kill anyone, Wolf, much less innocent children. So, you see—I can't go with you. I must get this information to my superiors in Virginia. My agency must stop this slaughter from taking place. Perhaps, given the rare opportunity of having all his lieutenants in one place, we can take down the entire cartel at the same time."

"I agree you have no other choice in the matter," the captain replied with a sudden look of grim determination. "And I can promise you, we too, will do everything in our collective power to help you in that endeavor."

Just as he finished the comment, Joris, Andries, the doctor, and five other men she hadn't yet met, entered her room. They all carried the same expression of disgust and steely resolve. Apparently, they heard every word she said.

"You have that right, *Kapitein*!" a man with dark brown hair, brown eyes, and long scraggly beard spat. "Men like this Mercado deserve no quarter. I guarantee they'll receive none from me."

"Aliyana, this is Conrad Shaers. To his right is Pieter Van Amburgh; they serve as my gunners," said Wolf. "Standing just behind them is my quartermaster, Cornelius Arians, Laurens Jans, ship's carpenter, and my bos'n, Johannes Tricault."

Each of Wolf's 'pack' greeted her with a single nod of their head. They stared at her then as if awaiting some kind of direction. She had no idea what to say to any of them. "Well, I appreciate the offer, but I'm not sure there's anything you can—"

"Don't you worry about what we can or cannot do

at this point, Miss Montijo," said Pieter, the blonde, hazel-eyed gunner. "Right now our main priority is to get you where you need to go. We'll figure the rest of this out once we arrive at your point of destination."

"What are you talking about?" she asked.

"Come now, Aliyana," said Wolf. "Your plane is at the bottom of the ocean. How did you think you were going to get off this island, if not on board the *Witte Wieven*?"

"Oh, well—I don't know. I guess I hadn't looked that far ahead," she replied.

As if dismissing her concerns altogether, he spared his men a brief glance and then gave her his full attention. "I take it you have all the details of Mercado's plans?"

"No, not all of them. I have the names of each lieutenant and his specific assignment. I know the exact time and date this plot is scheduled to go down as well. As far as the details, such as strategy for entry, methods for termination, and how many men are assigned each squad—"

Her words trailed off as the notion of time in the place he called *kátholose* forced its way into the forefront of her mind. Did time pass differently inside this place of waiting? She drew in a sharp breath as she wondered over the length of her stay.

"What is it?" asked Wolf. "What's wrong?"

"How is time accounted for in this place?" Her heart thumped wildly inside her chest. "I mean, is each day here the same as a day of mine?"

Wolf squeezed her hand in reassurance. "Though I believe the passage of time is accounted for differently in each dimension, in a *kátholose*, time passes according to the dimension of each individual, strange though that might seem. If the sun rises three times during your stay, you'll find it has also risen three times in your world."

"You said another storm would come along soon. But how soon? I don't have an indefinite amount of time to get this information into the hands of the Administration. They have to have time to plan their strategy and get their men in place."

"What kind of time are we looking at?" he asked.

"Just a little over three months," she replied. "I believe Mercado is waiting for summer's end. That way the kids are back in school and vacations are over. For this plot to work as intended, he needs everyone home at the same time."

"Then don't worry," he said. "We have plenty of time to thwart his plans. All you need do right now is concentrate on getting well enough to board my ship and travel over a bumpy sea."

Chapter Five

Wolf stood behind the weathered chair as he brushed through Aliyana's tresses with gentle, even strokes. She propped her elbow on the arm rail and rested her chin on top of her curled fingers. Such had become their routine these past five mornings. She'd wake up and eat a wonderful breakfast prepared by Andries. The captain of the *Witte Wieven* would then whisk her to the top of the lighthouse stairs. He'd settle her into the wooden rocker for a breath of fresh air and some sunshine in this magical place of waiting. Once he deemed her comfortable enough, he'd spend the next half an hour or so brushing the tangles from her hair. Somehow, he made the more intimate act feel just as routine as Klaus taking her temperature.

Now that he had finished his ritual this morning, he sat down opposite her. His large frame all but dwarfed the bench as he propped a booted foot on top of his knee. She smiled. "Thanks, Wolf. As always, that felt really nice."

"Anything to make our patient a little more comfortable and hasten her recovery." Wolf winked. "Doctor's orders."

Aliyana waved a hand in dismissal as she turned her face. "Ugh! That man has way too much time on his hands. If you really want to do something nice for me, you'd give him something else to occupy his time."

Wolf chuckled. "What? And take away his only pleasure? You're the first long-term patient he's had in years. Between you and me, I think part of him enjoys the fact you're still experiencing bouts of nausea and dizziness. Gives him an excuse to fuss, you know."

"So, are you telling me the natives in your dimension prefer a doctor who's a little less fastidious with their health care? Or do people just not get sick in the place you now call home?"

Wolf shrugged. "Oh, a little bit of both I suppose. However, as far as our illnesses are concerned, we can cure most with teas made from herbs or with what nature provides in abundance. That's not to say men of science didn't discover their unique uses and combinations in the first place. And, I should also mention, our time of recovery is quite rapid in all but the most complex cases, which are few and far between."

"What an interesting realm," she murmured. Once again she conjured visions of what one might find there.

"Yes, it is. I think I can speak for every member of my crew when I say we were in no way disappointed once we crossed the portal and took a good look at our new home."

She smiled as she envisioned the scene. "You know, I wished I could've seen the expressions on your faces the moment you realized you were in a different dimension altogether."

"I'll concur with that desire," he whispered. He cocked his head to the side, gazed deep into her eyes, and just tarried there for a time.

She had no idea where his thoughts had taken him. But, that simple look generated a fluid warmth that began deep inside her belly, crawled upward and splashed color onto her cheeks, just as it did each time he gave it. She wondered then, how such a simple look could cause such a physical reaction. Especially since no other man she'd ever known had ever accomplished such a feat. "Well, I suppose I'll have to make do with my imagination."

"Ah, such an image will make for a better tale, anyway. We're a bunch of tough, seasoned sea dogs, after all," he replied. "So, there probably wasn't much to see."

Quiet laughter accompanied a nod. She looked up at the sky and took in the amazing beauty. "How many times have you been here?"

"You mean, here at this lighthouse?" he asked as his gaze strolled about the room.

"Well, yes, of course."

"This is my first visit."

"I don't understand. If you've never been here before then how could you possibly know we are in—in a *kátholose*?"

"You asked if I'd ever been here—to this lighthouse. The answer is no, I haven't. But that doesn't mean I haven't explored many such places before. So far, each one I've encountered is different. I can tell you that oceans surround each of them. They share a common sky, similar vegetation, and dimensional barriers—sizable though some of those barriers might be."

"You've never been to the same place twice?"

He shook his head as his hand scrubbed against his beard. "Nope, not yet."

"Well, that's interesting." She drew her brows

together. "How many different *kátholoses* have you explored?"

"Oh, I don't know, probably a dozen or so—give or take a few."

"And you say they have barriers, as in you can't get through them type of barriers?"

"Yep, each of them has one, and it didn't take us very long before we discovered that fact. The first such place we encountered appeared as nothing more than a mountaintop, rising up out of the ocean in all her majesty. We explored the thing in its entirety in less than six hours. Once we completed our explorations, we took on fresh provisions and set sail. Yet, no matter our navigational direction, within four hours, we arrived at the very same mountaintop. Only the storm, which arrived six days later, allowed our departure."

Aliyana shook her head as she blew out a breath. "Wow, I bet that made for some pretty tense moments."

"Yes, it did. For a while there, we wondered if we might ever remain a prisoner of the mountaintop. However, once we figured it all out, finding ourselves inside a *kátholose* was something we anticipated and looked forward to."

"Do you have a favorite from among those you've visited?"

The way he looked at her took away her breath. A slight grin turned the corners of his mouth as his gaze lingered on hers. Somehow his eyes spoke volumes. Yet he didn't utter a word. She waited for the magical moment to pass. Part of her wanting it to hurry, the other—?

"Besides this one, you mean?"

Unable to string a single coherent sentence

together, she simply nodded.

"Try to imagine, if you will, a cascading layer of silvery water, at least ten miles in radius, water that shimmers like starlight. Yet, at the same time, this tier floats above the powerful ocean waves, at least fifty feet below. The hexagonal shape of the layer splashes downward in an endless waterfall into the sea. Exquisite flora is everywhere abundant. The thick, woody roots of this vegetation create the sturdy pathways that lead to a marbled structure, dark grayish-blue in color, and in the Doric order of the ancient Greek. On the outside, this edifice appears no larger than a modest cathedral. Yet, once one passes through the columns and enters through the magnificent double doors, one cannot determine the structure's breadth, height, or length because there is always one more hallway—one more flight of stairs, connecting to the last."

Her mouth dropped as Wolf painted the delightful scene. "Oh my! How beautiful!"

He nodded as his gaze shifted toward the horizon. "Yes, it is, and it's the one place I hope we'll see again one day."

"How long were you there?"

"About four, maybe five weeks, and that was by choice. We could've caught a storm within three days, but we just weren't ready to leave."

"What did you find inside that building?"

"All kinds of treasures coming from all the different ages and dimensions, I should think. Although you can see these artifacts well enough, you can't touch them because of a shield you can't see with your eyes."

"I take it then that you at least tried to abscond with

this booty?"

Wolf chuckled. "That we did—many times over. We really wanted to take some of that stuff back with us. Especially the navigational and scientific instruments that were unlike anything we had ever seen before. We wanted so much to figure out their specific purpose and discover how they worked."

"Do you ever come across other people in such places? People who actually live there, I mean."

"No, such places are all deserted, save those of us who stumble into them."

"You make all of it sound so exciting." A breath of laughter accompanied the slight shake of her head. "Your stories remind me so much of the yarns my brother spun. They made me want to go and get involved in all of the same things—"

****

She stopped mid-sentence and the dreamy-eyed look disappeared. The haunted expression returned and so did the weight and reality of her mission. Wolf cursed silently as he gazed downward. Though he lost this round, he hadn't lost others. For the past several days, he'd kept her mind off Emil Rios Mercado and his vile drug cartel. The respite had done wonders.

Then again, perhaps she needed to talk to someone about the things that troubled her. After all, how long had she carried the weight of her mission alone without the opportunity to confide in another soul? He leaned forward and tilted her chin upward.

"Do you want to tell me about it, *lieveling*?" He took hold of her hand and caressed the top of it. "Sometimes it helps to talk, and I'm a very good listener."

She briefly lowered her eyes and for several moments, she said nothing. Then she released a slow, ragged breath. "Just a little over two years ago a trusted DEA informant met with my brother and a few members of his squad. They met at an undisclosed location—one that we haven't located as yet. This man provided the details of a secret meeting scheduled to take place between Mercado and a rival drug lord."

"To what purpose do drug lords schedule such a meeting?"

"Territory, drug markets, and trafficking routes among other things. None of the cartels are ever satisfied with what they have. They always want more and they're quite willing to kill each other to get it. One would almost expect their total annihilation after a time, without us even lifting a finger. But there's always someone else waiting to step into their shoes and make it bigger and more lucrative."

"You know, given these circumstances, if I were a drug lord, I'm not sure I would attend this meeting." His comment prompted a quiet laugh.

"And you would be wise not to accept the invitation. Often such gatherings have erupted into violence. Not everyone walks away from them unscathed. Nonetheless, once the body count is high enough, these drug lords are prepared to hear the other out. I suppose they're cocky enough to believe the other is finally ready to give into their demands.

"Anyway, what the informant told them only filled in the holes of intelligence they'd already gathered from other sources. So, our boys planned a strike. The mission, if successful, would've removed two cartel leaders and many of their key personnel. But on the way to the meeting, an ambush occurred. Members of Mercado's cartel hemmed in the two vehicles that carried my brother and his team."

"How can you assign responsibility to just Mercado's cartel, alone, when two drug lords were targeted?" he asked.

"Among the dead, we positively identified several members of his cartel and none from the other. And, Mercado himself bragged about the deed to anyone and everyone who would listen. Although he lost plenty of his own men, he said his soldiers slaughtered the DEA like pigs, right there in the middle of a busy street. He said his only regret was he didn't have time to collect their—"

She couldn't finish the sentence. A hand rested against her throat as tears cascaded down her cheeks.

"Aliyana—"

"I'm so sorry," she sniffed and dabbed at a tear. "I'm supposed to be stronger than this."

"Stronger? No, you mustn't ever think that," Wolf whispered as he traced gentle patterns on top of her hand. "Without a woman's ability for compassion—her tender, sensitive heart, and her tears—this world would be a much harsher place to live, regardless of dimension. Don't you know? Men require these very things to keep ourselves restrained. Without them, the world would find itself in total darkness and chaos."

Aliyana managed a small laugh as she wiped a hand against her cheek. "That's a sweet thing for you to say."

"No, it's just truth," Wolf replied. "So tell me, how did Mercado come to know about the scheduled strike and counter it with his ambush, anyway? Did the information come from this trusted informant?"

"We think there's a good chance that it did. But I'm afraid we'll never prove it now. Within a week of the ambush, the police found him murdered—execution style—inside his apartment. Of course, no one in the entire complex would ever admit to seeing or hearing anything unusual that evening."

"How convenient."

"Isn't it though?" She tsked and shook her head. "But such is the way it is. No one wants the wrath of a drug lord aimed at them. Especially not one like Mercado."

"And so soon thereafter, your superiors recruited you to take up where your brother left off," he said.

"Yes, and you already know the rest of it."

"I know you took the plane out of desperation," he said, "but if Mercado had not confiscated your motorcycle, where would you have gone to elude the cartel?"

"I have a safe house, not too far from the compound," she replied. "I'm the only one who has knowledge of its whereabouts. In Colombia, even the most secure secrets have a way of leaking out. My squad concurred with my decision since we could maintain communication with each other."

"A safe house?" He raised a brow. "What is that?"

"Just what it implies—it's a place wherein a person can take shelter in relative safety from all danger that might unexpectedly present itself."

"I see." He paused for a moment. "How long did you plan to stay there?"

"Well, before I discovered the assassination plot, I thought I'd hide out long enough for Mercado to call off an intensive hunt in the vicinity of his compound. But his plot changed all of that. I didn't make any concrete plans then, of course. But, I still intended to head over to my shelter. I desperately wanted to get the information I collected into the hands of my superiors in Virginia. Once I completed that part of my mission, the Administration would've taken charge," she said.

"Instead, fate stepped in and sent you to me." As her smile grew ever broader over his statement, he shook his head.

"No, don't laugh, I think it's a very good thing we encountered each other. Now you won't have to go this alone. You'll have our help."

She shrugged. "I still don't know what you think you can do."

"Oh, come on, Miss Montijo. I gave you credit for a far better imagination than that." He leaned toward her and raised a brow. "Now picture, if you will, Mercado's men inside a house or a vehicle across the street from their target. They are waiting there, weapon in hand, for the designated moment to strike. These men are laughing and talking amongst themselves about their upcoming assignment. Why, they are going to be heroes to kith and kin, are they not? Men, women, and children will sing their praises in song forevermore. Their names will go down in legend and the stories will survive the centuries, not only in Colombia but throughout the entire world." He glanced heavenward, placed a hand against his heart, and nodded. His dramatic performance made her laugh.

"The final seconds are ticking off the clock now, and just as they raise their weapons, but what should happen? A bunch of terrifyingly hideous, worm-infested, moldy, putrid-looking ghosts storm through the walls of their sanctuaries. Can you hear them screaming at this moment? Those who have managed to hang onto their weapons find them surreptitiously yanked out of their hands. The aforementioned ghosts now turn these weapons upon them." He cleared his throat in a most exaggerated manner.

"Only my concern for your sensitive nature bids me stop the narrative at this point in my story. You needn't conjure the visual image of what these men are most assuredly experiencing at this precise moment in their lives." He drew close to her ear and whispered, "It's kind of embarrassing, really, for them. Suffice it to say, said phantoms then keep this scum corralled until the proper authorities show up, drag out the handcuffs and haul them off to jail."

Aliyana's laughter pleased him. The haunted look had evaporated and mirth took its place. She nibbled at her bottom lip as she shook her head.

"Terrifyingly hideous, worm-infested, moldy, putrid-looking ghosts. Do I have that right?" she asked as her eyes danced with delight.

"Indeed you do," he said as he picked an imaginary piece of lint from his clothing and gave it a nonchalant toss. "Would you like to see the sight? I can call my men up here for a little demonstration, if you wish."

She laughed anew. "I don't think I dare. You forget. I still have to board the *Witte Wieven* and travel with said ghosts."

"Wise decision, Miss Montijo, very wise."

"About that travel." She pointed her finger toward him. "How long do you have to wait for a storm to arise?"

"They're random," he said. "While inside a *kátholose*, we've seen them occur in as little as six hours, as long as thirty days and anywhere in between."

She gasped. "Thirty days? Oh, Wolf, we don't have thirty days to waste—"

Wolf placed a gentle finger against her lips and shook his head. "Don't worry, that only happened one time. On an average, they stir up within a week or two. The key is—we should be ready to board the *Witte Wieven* when the next one arises."

Chapter Six

A full-fledged shower was just what the doctor ordered, at her insistence, of course. Aliyana stayed under the stream of hot water far longer than necessary. A bit selfish perhaps, because a paranoid Wolf waited just outside the door, ready to lunge through it if he sensed the slightest hint of danger. Just as the thought passed through her mind, a gentle knock sounded on the door.

"Aliyana, are you all right in there?" called Wolf from the other side.

She smiled at the anxious tone as she rinsed the last of the conditioner from her hair. Reluctantly, she turned off the faucet, and grabbed a towel. "Yes, I'm fine. I'll be out in a minute, I promise."

"You can take your time," Wolf replied. "I just wanted to make sure you hadn't fainted dead away in the bathtub. You're still recovering you know."

"Oh, come on. Enough of the mollycoddling, already. You're all making me soft," she teased as she slipped into her favorite stonewashed jeans. Once she pulled her white jersey T-shirt with light blue sleeves over her head, she opened the door and returned his charming grin with a smile of her own.

"Are you feeling better?"

"Oh, you wouldn't believe how much better. However, I need just a few more minutes to dry my hair, if you don't mind."

"I don't mind," he said. "Like I said, take as much time as you need. We're in no hurry."

"Careful with those stitches, young lady," hollered the doctor from somewhere downstairs.

"Don't worry, *Doctor*, I will," she called back. She rolled her eyes and wished Klaus had another patient he could smother. Wolf chuckled in response.

Finished with her customary 'pre-Bermuda Triangle' routine, Aliyana gathered her things and placed them inside her bag. All the while, she focused on keeping her feet steady. She didn't want Wolf to postpone this morning's outing simply because of her dizziness. If luck stayed on her side, he wouldn't even notice.

"Are you sure you're up to this?" he asked once he finished his head-to-foot examination of her person.

"I feel fine," she insisted as she stepped into her shoes and tied the laces. "But even if I didn't, I need to move about and regain some of my strength. Ready or not, Wolf, we must leave here at the first sign of a gathering storm. I think you know that as well as I do."

"Yes, I know that. But if you feel as if you're going to fall down or faint, please say something."

"Don't worry, I will."

As they turned toward the stairway, he wrapped a hand around her waist, and didn't let go. He did notice. Should that surprise her? The man's eyes missed nothing.

Once they descended the steps, she took her first good look at the small living room and connecting kitchen. A beige sofa, coffee table and two large chairs supplied the room with furnishings. She spied a wooden table and four matching chairs in the kitchen. Scattered around the empty floor space sat miscellaneous items Wolf's crew salvaged from the plane.

"Where is everyone?" she asked, glancing in every possible direction.

"Ferrying some of Mercado's salvaged equipment to the ship," he said as he opened the door and assisted her down the porch steps.

"That's probably a good thing."

While they traveled the length of the walkway, she gazed out over the ocean to where the *Witte Wieven* was anchored.

"Why do you say that?"

"Because I don't see how this tiny little cottage houses everyone inside at the same time, even minus the junk on the floor. Where does everyone sleep?" She tilted her head to the side as she regarded him. "Or do you?"

"Do what—sleep?" He halted his steps and turned toward her. "We can if we wish. However, on this side of the portal, we find the need doesn't exist. Part of those ghostly characteristics I mentioned earlier."

Aliyana considered that for a minute. "What about eating?"

"We can and do—frequently," he said. "But again, there truly is no need for it outside our realm. We simply eat for the pleasure food gives us."

"That's an interesting phenomenon—meaning the desire, not the need. I haven't come across a man yet that didn't possess a healthy appetite. The location, occasion or time between meals doesn't matter, either," she replied. "My brother and all his friends ate us out of house and home quite regularly."

"I can believe that," he said as they resumed their journey.

They turned toward the back of the lighthouse and made their way into the abundant foliage behind the structure.

"So, how long do you all stay when you go beyond the portal and have the grand adventures you seem so fond of having?"

"That depends on the opening and closing of the gates. We've remained in your dimension for as little as three weeks and as long as six months before we found a gate that would take us home."

"Six months?" That surprised her. "What on earth did you do during that period of time?"

"Oh, the usual touristy stuff," he said. "We sail to different countries. Mingle with the populace to catch up on current events and modern advancements in technology. Of course, Klaus must keep up on all the latest advancements in medicine just in case you've developed something vital to his practice. Then we take a nostalgic look at all of the changes we see and complain about them."

His comments made her laugh. "And along the way, no one ever says a single word about your pirate ship—excuse me—your brigantine either moored off in the distance or sailing the seas?"

Wolf flashed a grin as he shook his head. "Not everyone can see my vessel, you know. For those rare individuals who do, it's just another sighting of a ghost ship they can't overtake no matter how hard they try. More often than not, they believe they've seen the *Flying Dutchman* or some other missing ship of legend."

"I see. Well, how many times have you come back through the portal? Since you went through it the first time, I mean."

"Oh, I don't know. On average, once every couple of decades or so—of your time. Sometimes far more often, sometimes much less," he said.

"Is that because the storms themselves are infrequent, or because you don't take advantage of them every time they arise?"

"Probably a little bit of both. In order to take advantage of the proper type of storm, we must have time on our hands. We must be on board the ship when one opens up, and sail through the portal in our path. And although I must admit we sail often enough, it isn't the only thing we do with our lives," he said.

"I imagine not, but now that you bring up the subject of your antiquated ship, I have another burning question." She swept away the branches of a gorgeous magnolia tree that blocked their path. "Well, actually, you have inspired hundreds as you already know, but we'll start with this one, today."

"Okay, what's your question?"

"Your clothes," she replied.

Wolf dropped his gaze to his attire, and chuckled. "What about them? Are they hideously out of step with the latest fashion for men?"

"No, quite the contrary. But these aren't the clothes you wore when we first met. I just want to know if your Three Musketeers garb is your normal mode of dress within your plane of existence."

"My what?" His smile broadened.

"Cut the innocent act. I can start with your doublet, which fell out of fashion hundreds of years ago, and move on down to your oh-so-stylish britches and knee-high boots if you'd like," she teased.

"No, you needn't go that far. Actually, our clothing is not too far different from your current mode of dress. Curiously and for reasons I've yet to find an explanation for, each time one passes back through the portal, one finds oneself wearing the same clothes they wore the first time they entered through it. We can, however, change the way our clothes appear, to those who can see us."

"You're telling me then, not everyone can see you when you revisit?" she asked.

"Very few actually, unless we will it otherwise." He shrugged. "Again, I suppose, those ghostly traits are the cause. You can see us without any effort on our part because you partially entered the portal and ended up here along with us. Whether or not you could've seen us otherwise is anyone's guess."

"I've always been open-minded," she said. "A time or two I've seen something I couldn't explain. Therefore, I'd like to think I could've seen you as well. After all, a seventeenth-century sea captain would surely have stirred up my life a bit and made things a whole lot more interesting."

Wolf paused for a moment and caressed her with his gaze. "I hope he's doing just that."

In response to the bedlam going on deep inside her stomach, she forgot to breathe. At least, she did until they entered a clearing, with a pool of clear, sparkling water. Water lilies in every hue imaginable floated along the top. A host of dragonflies, sporting wings in a vast array of luminous colors, hovered above the surface.

She gasped. "This is one of the most beautiful sights I've ever seen!"

Wolf eased her onto a large boulder and then sat down next to her. "Yes, it is. You know, we have many such places in my sphere. We have no lack of beauty such as the kind you see on this island. We have countless flowers and trees, the like you've never seen before. They are in colors you cannot even imagine."

"What, no deserts?" she asked.

"A few, but the sands glimmer like diamonds in the sun, and they are never too hot or too cold like they are here," he replied. "They have their own kind of foliage too, and it's far different than what you're used to seeing in such places."

"That's interesting, because I think if someone introduced the subject of parallel worlds before I met you, I would've assumed they were all identical, save the people who inhabit them."

"That would be a rational assumption. However, if someone asked me to describe the difference between our realms, I would simply say our geographical boundaries are far different, and that my world is a little more—intense."

"Intense?"

He nodded as he gazed out over the lake and its surroundings. "The sky, the moon, the stars, and even the look of the sun. So it is with colors, as well. You should see the rainbows and the clouds at sunset, Aliyana. Even the flashes of lightning are unlike anything you've ever seen before."

"You always make everything sound so wonderful, I wish I could see it for myself," she sighed as she leaned forward and rested her chin on top of her clasped hands.

"You still can," he reminded her. "The choice remains open, and I'd like nothing more than to take you with me when I return."

She closed her eyes and dropped her hands into her lap. "I can't think about that right now, Wolf, not yet." He didn't respond but took her hand and held it. As always, a powerful current filled her body the instant he touched her. As their gazes met, Wolf drew in a shallow breath. He held onto it for a moment before he released it. Perhaps he too experienced the same electrifying current she did. Though she should at least try, she couldn't fight the bond growing ever stronger between them. Probably, she could blame her head injury. But she didn't really care. Not right now, anyway.

"Tell me, have you explored the entirety of your realm?" she asked, seeking a distraction.

"A great deal of it," he said. "There's always more to discover though."

"When the gates open, do they ever take you to other dimensions besides the one you reside in now?"

"Not yet." He shrugged. "That might be a good thing. Heaven only knows what would happen to our bodies if we passed through multiple dimensions."

"How do you know there *are* other planes?"

"Because from time to time, other people from other dimensions stumble into ours from the gates in which *they* pass through," he replied. "The world they describe is not the one we hail from."

"That's interesting," she said. "If such is the case, it kind of makes you wonder then, why no one ever 'stumbles' into mine."

"What makes you think they haven't? How do you

know the knowledge of new technological breakthroughs isn't something they chose to give you?"

She combed her fingers through her wind-tousled hair as she nodded. "You do have a point. But tell me, are these other gates from other dimensions found within the Bermuda Triangle as well?"

"No, I don't think so. From what I have gathered thus far, they are located in other oceanic areas. There's one on the Pacific Ocean around the area of Japan, the Indian Ocean, the Baltic Sea, Bering Sea, the southeastern Pacific near Rapa Nui, and interestingly enough—the Great Lakes have a gate, as well. And who knows but there might be a host of other gates awaiting discovery."

"You know, I've read articles concerning the myths in some of those areas. They're quite interesting to say the least. More so now that I've met you…"

****

They sat together in pleasant silence for a time. While the minutes passed, the breeze picked up its pace. Finally, Wolf turned his gaze toward the sky. "I think we're about to get our storm."

"We are?" She placed a hand above her brow and looked heavenward. "How do you know?"

"In answer to your first question, yes, we are. The second? You can just put it down to experience." He stood first and then helped her to her feet. Her eyes filled with sudden apprehension as they gazed at each other. He tipped her chin upward and smiled. "Don't look so worried, *lieveling*, everything will be all right."

"Are you sure? Will we be able to get back to the lighthouse, get our stuff, and get to your ship in time?"

"We have plenty of time for all of that, but only if

we hurry," he teased. "So, come on, let's make haste."

The winds had increased in strength by the time they stepped onto the walkway of the lighthouse. From the corner of his eye, Wolf spied Joris returning aboard the ship's boat. His first mate raised an arm and waved.

"*Kapitein*," he called out. "We're fully loaded and ready to set sail, save the things upstairs."

"All right," Wolf replied. "Just give Aliyana a minute to get her stuff together and we'll be right out."

"Klaus is waiting for her up in her room. If he has time, he wants her stitches removed before we sail," Joris said.

"On our way."

Thick clouds in hues of dark purple and gray formed right above them. With amazing speed, they spread across the horizon. Lightning crackled while the thunder boomed throughout the skies in sudden raging fury.

Aliyana gasped and turned around. "Will we make it in time?"

"We'll make it," he assured her. He opened the door.

Without a shred of caution, Aliyana raced toward the stairs. She swayed as she tried to climb the steps. Wolf scooped her up into his arms just as she lost her balance and fell backward. Once they entered her bedroom, he sat her down on the bed. Klaus hurried toward his patient, with instruments in hand.

"Let Klaus remove your stitches, while I pack your things," he said.

"Put my tools and laptop in first, please. They're the heaviest and can damage my other things if we're not careful," she replied as the doctor tilted her head in a more upright position.

"All right, Aliyana," said Klaus. "The wound looks good, all things considered. More important, I think we should remove the stitches now, rather than attempt the procedure while bouncing over the ocean waves. Just hold still and I'll have them out in no time at all."

"Laptop and tools are now inside the bag," Wolf stated just to keep her mind off the doctor's work. "Now I'm tucking the satellite and cell phones along the bottom, camera, and flash drive along the side. I'm wrapping up the cables and stuffing them inside the pouches—" He paused then as he caught sight of the large serrated knife inside the hidden slot. He pulled it out and held it up. "What's this?"

Aliyana shrugged. "A girl should have a weapon handy, don't you think? You never know what might happen out there, right?"

Wolf shook his head as he sighed. "Have I missed anything?"

"My blue bag is still in the bathroom, as well as all my clothes."

"I'll be right back." Wolf strode down the hall and into the bathroom. He picked up her case and grabbed the clothes off the shower rod. As he turned around, he caught sight of her borrowed nightgown hanging on the hook. He recalled the way she looked, as well as her delightful fit of temper when she wore it and found he couldn't leave without it. He removed it from the hanger, and then headed back into the bedroom.

He handed the clothing to Aliyana. While Klaus fussed over his instruments, she stuffed her things haphazardly inside her backpack.

She held up the gown. "This isn't mine. I only

borrowed it, remember?"

"Keep it. You don't have anything of your own to sleep in, and it certainly isn't doing anyone any good inside this place."

She hesitated a moment before she folded the gown and placed it inside her bag. Once she zipped the backpack shut, Wolf took hold of the straps and tossed it over his shoulder. Klaus closed Mercado's medical kit and grabbed the handle.

"Are we ready then?" Wolf asked.

"Aye, Captain," said Klaus as he swept a hand toward the door.

"Then let's go." Wolf took hold of Aliyana's hand. He led her out of the room and down the stairway. By the time they exited the lighthouse, the storm had intensified. Joris stood inside the boat and frantically urged them onward.

Rain, soft at first, fell ever harder during the short voyage to his ship. By the time they drew alongside his vessel, the small craft pitched precariously from side to side from both wind and rain. Klaus scaled the rope ladder first while Wolf secured the boat to the ship.

For the danger the furious storm presented, Wolf remained a single step behind her. He kept his arms around her during the ascent to keep her from falling into the ocean. Once her head peeked over the railing, Joris grasped her arms and helped her onto the deck. He followed.

"Weigh anchor," Wolf shouted against the roaring winds. "Loose the top sails and heave out!"

"Aye, *Kapitein*," Joris returned.

While the men went about their duties, Wolf escorted Aliyana to his cabin. He tossed her backpack onto his bed. "You'll be safe enough in here while we pass through the gate. I'll return shortly."

"I am *not* staying in here by myself, Wolf!" she huffed. "I'm going topside with you."

He swung his head to the side. "Aliyana—"

"No, you can't make me stay in here." She folded her arms tightly against her chest and glared.

Wolf didn't have time to argue. He simply opened the door and led her out of the cabin, up the steps, and toward the helm. As Joris handed off the wheel, Wolf positioned Aliyana just in front of him. His arms held her fast in a protective embrace as he took firm hold of the spokes on either side of the rim. He glanced skyward and found the dark clouds tempestuously churning in grotesque formations. As each second passed, the fog grew ever broader and thicker. Lightning raged all around and any moment now, the strange dancing lights would surround them. After that, the portal would form and open somewhere in the vicinity.

"Don't be afraid, Aliyana," he whispered into her ear as his ship heaved dangerously to port. "Your body will feel a bit strange as we go through the portal. But the sensation is normal."

"I'm not afraid," she said.

He grinned. No, a woman like Aliyana wouldn't be afraid. In all likelihood, she welcomed and even anticipated the coming experience. Balls of flashing light surrounded them. He searched the seas for the formation of the specific portal they needed.

"To the starboard bow, *Kapitein*," shouted Pieter.

Wolf turned his gaze, as well as his rudder, toward the small vortex of billowing clouds in the distance. As they approached, the gate grew wider and longer by degrees. The moment the bowsprit entered the portal, the ship hummed and vibrated. Glowing streaks of jagged colorful light spewed out like tiny arms that encompassed the vessel. The lights shimmied upward onto the deck, and then crawled on top of it. They slithered upward, covered the masts like entwined serpents, and shot out through the yardarms in brilliant blazing colors. In response, he tightened his hold on Aliyana.

The vibrating currents discharged from the lights gripped their feet and traveled up the whole of their bodies. The intensity of that sensation remained during the journey through the portal. Like a blinking strobe light, the interior of his ship alternated between her seventeenth-century archaic look to her modern form and then back again. Once they entered the clear, warm skies on the other side, the vibrations and the lights subsided and then stopped altogether. She turned toward him. Her eyes danced with both astonishment and delight.

"Are you all right?" he asked.

"Oh, yes, I am," she sang out. She gifted him then with the most enchanting smile he'd ever seen. "And that, Captain, is one of the most amazing experiences I've ever had in my entire life!"

Chapter Seven

In response to her exuberant comment, Wolf and his entire crew laughed. She couldn't help but laugh with them. The captain stepped back and freed her from his protective embrace. Nonetheless, she hadn't the will or desire to stray from his side, so he needn't have bothered.

Cornelius grinned. "I must say, she took to the portal better than most men."

"That shouldn't surprise anyone," said Johannes. "You're talking about a woman who took off in an aircraft under gunfire."

"One who had the audacity to steal the plane in the first place," Laurens added. "We've yet to hear the particulars of that story and it certainly is one I'd like to hear."

"The term 'stealing' is a little harsh, Laurens. I prefer the term requisition, if you please." She turned her gaze toward the captain. "Do you have any idea where we are?"

"On the ocean," he said. "On board my ship."

"Oh, that's really brilliant." A breath of laughter accompanied the exaggerated clearing of her throat. "Do you know, specifically, where we are on that ocean, Captain Wolfaert Dircksen Van Ness?"

"That, I'm not quite sure about." Wolf gazed out over the open sea, then down at the ship's compass.

"However, we are sailing the Atlantic, and heading in a south by south easterly direction. Once night falls, I can pinpoint our location a little more accurately, using the stars as our guide."

"Do you know what? I think I can do better than that," Aliyana said. "After all, my equipment should work now, right? And I have with me a piece of equipment that can pinpoint our precise location."

"Joris, helm," the captain called out.

Once Joris took over the wheel, Wolf followed Aliyana down the short flight of stairs and into his cabin. She unzipped her backpack, yanked out her clothing, and tossed them on top of the feather mattress.

"Here—" Wolf opened a well-worn sea chest at the end of the bed. "You can put your clothes and personal things in here for now. That way you can access your electronic equipment a little easier when the need arises."

She nodded and carried the knotted bundle over to the trunk. Wolf transported her backpack to the table while she put her clothes in recognizable order. Afterwards she tossed her blue bag atop the stack and closed the lid. By the time she arrived at the table, Wolf had already extracted her equipment and powered up the laptop.

While they waited for the machine to boot, she connected her satellite phone to her computer. She then fetched her GPS receiver and turned it on.

"What is that thing?"

"A Global Positioning System or GPS as we call it. This little device locks onto the transmissions of at least four satellites orbiting in space. The receiver will analyze the time differences between them, and then place us on a map of the earth in three dimensions. This instrument can also tell us in which direction we are heading and even how fast we're sailing," she said. "A GPS is especially useful on the ocean, because it finds our absolute position on the globe after it calculates the effects of the wind and currents."

Wolf leaned over her shoulder as the small receiver homed in on their exact location. "No. How can this be right?" she murmured as they studied the screen.

"What's wrong?"

"I don't know. According to this, we're about six hundred fifty kilometers due east of the Turks and Caicos Islands." She nibbled at a nail while she studied the map. "That can't be right though."

"Why not?"

"Because right before I lost my engines, I was approaching the Bahamas. In fact, I expected they'd come in view at any moment. The clouds gathered then and shrouded everything in sight."

"Any other day you might have seen those islands, just as you anticipated," he said. "You must understand that while inside the triangle, a single moment can take you hundreds of miles in any given direction. On top of that, the portal can spit you out almost anywhere within the triangle."

Aliyana mulled that over. "About that portal—"

"What about it?"

"How do you know where it'll take you? Couldn't it have returned us to your parallel instead of mine?"

"Yes, it could. That's why we watch for the direction of the formation," he said. "If the clouds billow outward it's taking us away from where we now belong. If it forms inward, we'll go home."

"That directional formation has to do with just you and your ship? I'm asking because both of us are on board and we live in two different parallels."

"Interesting dilemma, but you're probably right. As the captain and owner of this vessel, I suppose it's up to me to navigate our course."

"All right, I guess I can trust my equipment then," she said. "So, let's chart a course for the eastern seaboard and from the location the GPS has indicated."

"Where specifically, Miss Montijo, do you want to go? The eastern seaboard covers quite a distance as I'm sure you know."

"Well, let's see." She brought up a full-sized map on her computer. "We must choose our route carefully. I don't want the military blowing us out of the ocean for lack of radio contact or proper identification during approach."

"You needn't worry about that," he replied. "Like I said, very few people can see the *Wieven,* much less catch it if they do. We've never once been accosted by any type of aircraft and they've flown directly over us countless times."

"Good. Then let's get as close to Arlington, Virginia as we dare with this ship. Maybe we can sail up the Potomac and drop anchor somewhere near Alexandria," she replied as she pointed out the location.

"I can get just about as close as you desire. While in this dimension, as long as we have a depth of six feet underneath our hull, the *Wieven* call sail in any water in which we can make a full turn. I'll get my charts and plot us a course," said Wolf.

"All right. While you're doing that, I'll access the DEA system and let them know what's going on."

Yet, no matter how hard she tried, or what avenue she took, the DEA system rejected her login. None of her passcodes allowed access, not even her emergency one. "Something isn't right," she murmured as she gazed at the screen.

"What's wrong, *lieveling*?" Wolf asked.

Aliyana shook her head and leaned back against her chair. "I can't access the system to download Mercado's files. None of my passwords work. For some odd reason, they've locked me out of the system."

"Is it because you haven't made contact with them for almost two weeks?" He grabbed another chair and sat down beside her.

"That shouldn't be a factor—at least not yet," she said. "When one is working under cover, the administration anticipates silences. Trust me, they won't get excited over two weeks."

"Then what are the reasons for locking out these passwords?"

"An agent's death, of course. They would certainly lock it if they know one's cover is blown, or if they suspect an agent has gone rogue—" Aliyana paused and then drew in a sharp breath as the notion took hold. At once she entered Mercado's dark web site using his pilfered password. She clicked on the link to his posts and opened the most recent. Together she and Wolf looked down at the picture prominently displayed to the right of the screen.

Her picture.

Underneath the photograph, the bolded words read, 'Victoria Mendoza Torres' AKA 'Aliyana Montijo'. That caption confirmed her worst fear. Aliyana stared at the screen for several minutes and couldn't make sense of it. A way did not exist for Mercado to learn her identity, unless—

Wolf interrupted the thought. "I can read the names well enough, but what exactly does the rest of it say?"

She finished reading the paragraph and then gazed into his eyes. "In a nutshell? Emil Mercado has put a price on my head. That, I expected. However, he now knows I'm a DEA agent and that I infiltrated his compound. That, I didn't expect. I don't think he's discovered my true purpose, though. According to his rant, he thinks the system I installed provided a way for the United States to spy on his cartel. I'm certain by now, he's trashed the system.

"In this paragraph, he says that more than likely I'm already dead. He knows the plane I commandeered never landed anywhere within fuel range. Yet, because he suspects the government has all kinds of secret airports—and he specifically mentions Area 51 in Nevada—he isn't one hundred percent certain of that. Therefore, he's offered a reward of two million dollars to the person who brings him proof positive of my demise. He gives the addresses of all my known residences, should I turn up at any one of those seeking refuge."

Though she didn't speak the language, she recognized a string of curse words bursting out of the captain's mouth. His narrowed gaze, clenched fists and teeth, coupled with the tone of his voice, provided sufficient evidence. *If Mercado were present right now, he wouldn't fare well.* "It's all right, Wolf."

"No!" He shook his head vehemently as he slammed his fist on the table. "No, Aliyana, it isn't all right. I'd like you to explain to me just how this man got your true name and personal information."

"The only plausible explanation is that he received this information from a mole. That's someone who works within the DEA organization itself, for and on behalf of the cartel. I just don't know on which end of the organization he or she works, or just how much intelligence they can get a hold of."

"Then who do you trust with your files and Mercado's murder plot? Whom will you feel secure enough to contact with this information, once we sail up the Potomac?"

Aliyana propped her elbows on the table and dropped her forehead into her hands. Her brother's advice, given long ago, flooded her mind.

"While you're undercover, Aliyana, trust no one. Do not even trust me, for you don't know the circumstances I'm currently facing. I might have a gun at my head or a hidden wire on my person, forcing me to say things I might not otherwise say. Do things I might not otherwise do. Especially if an enemy has a weapon trained on you, and I'm trying to save your life. Do you understand what I'm saying? Until your mission is over and you're officially relieved, don't give away any information until the final debriefing."

What if one of the names slated for execution belonged to the mole? He might believe that adding himself to the list would keep him from suspicion should the plot come to light.

"Aliyana?"

She dropped her hands as she met his gaze. "No one. Right now, I'm afraid there isn't anyone I can trust with the information I have."

"Then what are we going to do?" he asked.

Aliyana said nothing. So many different thoughts flashed through her mind. She found it difficult to put them in any type of order. But she must somehow stop the assassination plot without revealing her knowledge to the DEA, at least not until the last possible moment. That meant she must take care of the problem herself.

"Where have your thoughts taken you, Aliyana?" asked Wolf.

She looked heavenward and sighed. "I don't quite know how I will do it, but my first priority is to stop Mercado from killing innocent people. After that, I'll hand over the information I have. All the while, I'll hope like crazy everything goes well."

"In my opinion, in order to stop Mercado ourselves, we'll need all the missing details of his scheme," he replied. "Do you have any idea how *we* can accomplish such a singular feat from our present location?"

Wolf's determined response made her smile and brought a sense of relief. "No, not yet. But it's a fact we can't gather anything from our present location, nor can we find what we seek in Virginia. Therefore, the first step is to plot a course for Colombia. From there I'll go back to Mercado's compound. I can sneak back into his office. If all goes well, we'll find the missing details."

"You expect me to take you back inside that vile snake pit?" he snapped. "Aliyana, are you out of your mind? Mercado wants you dead. You do understand that, don't you? If you think for one minute I'll let you waltz back in there where you're an easy target, then you—"

Aliyana put a gentle hand to his lips and halted his words. "Do you have a better plan?"

They gazed at each other for several seconds.

"Yes, I do. We'll take you somewhere safe first, and then I'll head for Colombia. Getting inside the compound won't pose a problem for me and my—"

"Where is safe? There's no place on this planet the drug trade doesn't exist. Men of Mercado's ilk are everywhere. My photograph has probably circled the globe at least three times by now. A two-million-dollar reward will attract every unsavory person capable of holding anything from a sophisticated weapon to a rock. So, Captain, where could you possibly find a haven that will guarantee my safety?"

****

Wolf made two decisions. One, he wouldn't let Aliyana out of his sight. And two, whether willing or not, he'd haul her back through the portal with him once they saved the administrators of the DEA. She would likely as not go kicking and screaming, but it didn't matter. She could pout all she wanted after their safe arrival.

"Point taken. But you'll remain on board the ship while my men and I go into Mercado's compound."

"That won't work either, Captain. I know Mercado well. I'm sure he hid the information we need inside an obscure file in his computer. I don't think you can find it, even if I showed you how to get around his password. So, you see? I'm the one who has to go inside. There's no other choice in the matter."

"What if I simply download all his files and bring them back to the ship?" he countered. "You could look for that obscure file at your leisure."

"That would work, if I had a flash drive big enough to hold the contents of his entire computer, which I don't. And *if* you had about four uninterrupted hours inside his private office in order to complete the download," she said. "I can tell you that won't happen, either." She gripped the table as she rose to her feet. "Look, I know the layout of the compound, and I know how to get around the guards. I can slip in and out with no one the wiser. I've done it before."

"We have a long voyage ahead of us, Aliyana. You can teach me everything you know about the man and the inner workings of his compound by the time we enter Colombian waters. I'm confident by then, I can find this file just as well as you can. I'm not letting you go in and that's all there is to it. Nothing you can say will alter my decision."

"You're just the most obstinate man I've ever met!" She shook her head, folded her arms, and slammed them against her chest.

"I think you said something along those lines once before." He grinned over the memory of it.

"No, back then I said you were the most exasperating man I'd ever met and believe me, both terms are accurate!" she spat. "Believe it or not, I can take care of myself. The fact I'm here beside you is a testament of that truth."

"Yes, but now you have me to rely on, as well as my entire crew," he parried. "Don't underestimate us, Aliyana. We're capable of doing things you might think impossible."

"Like what? And don't give me your song and dance about looking terrifyingly hideous."

"How about going through locked doors and walls? I wasn't kidding about that. We can eavesdrop on conversations and no one is even aware we're present.

Don't look so surprised. I told you when in this sphere we're mere shadows of our former selves."

"You don't speak Spanish," she stated flatly. "How then, do you think you could bring back a conversation you witnessed, but don't understand?"

"Are you telling me you don't carry some kind of device that records sound?" he asked. "Ah, I can see by expression alone that you do."

A hand went to her forehead as she closed her eyes. "Wolf, please—"

"Why do you find it so difficult to accept our help inside the compound? Why?"

"Because it would destroy me if something happened to you—or—or your men!" she blurted out. "Even if you have 'ghostlike' qualities, it doesn't mean you can't *die* here, right? I won't let that happen. I *can't* let that happen." She shook her head, as her eyes grew moist with unshed tears. "I don't think you understand that I can't take the pain of losing one more person I—" She clamped her mouth shut and looked away.

Wolf put his arms around her and cuddled her as close to his chest as he dared. "Look, we're far more resilient than you give us credit for. And that pain you speak of? Well, it works both ways you know. So, don't ask me to let you go into that hellhole alone. I'll deny the request. I'm not letting you go in there without us, and preferably I'd rather you not go in at all."

Aliyana took a small step back. "This stubborn determination of yours is a flaw, you know. But I can see you mean what you say. With or without my approval, you're going inside that compound, aren't you?"

"Without a doubt, you can count on it."

"Okay, better then we work together rather than against each other. Maybe even, we'll both survive it."

"So where do we begin, *lieveling*?"

She exhaled a long, ragged breath. "I suppose I'll begin by teaching you the layout of Mercado's compound. The place is quite large and there are several hidden exits and entrances. You and all your men must watch these passageways at all times when inside. Once you've memorized the entire layout, we'll move on to the guards."

The unexpected win gave him a sense of triumph. He scrubbed a hand over his mouth in the hopes it hid his smile. She narrowed her eyes and wagged a finger. "Don't get cocky, Captain. This concession doesn't mean you'll go in there alone. I'm coming with you."

Chapter Eight

Wolf stood at the helm. Though the sky was filled with stars so bright they looked as if one could easily pluck them from the heavens, he didn't pay much attention. In just a little over forty-eight hours, if the winds remained favorable, they would hit the shores of Colombia. They would then sail up the Magdalena. From there they'd take a tributary, close to Aliyana's designated point of anchor.

Once she left the ship's protection, she'd face danger at every turn. The knowledge troubled him. How he wished, during the past two and a half weeks of this voyage, he could've convinced her to remain on board while he and his crew gathered the intelligence needed. *The stubborn woman wouldn't even consider the notion, despite all logical argument.* She only promised she wouldn't take any unnecessary risks.

Her definition of 'unnecessary' didn't match his.

Yet, if honest, he'd admit her courageous, albeit reckless and headstrong, spirit captivated him far more than her physical beauty. He spent his entire life searching for such a woman and could never find her. Now that he found her, losing her to Mercado's hired guns filled him with an unquenchable fear. As each day passed, they grew closer in both heart and mind. Consequently, that fear strengthened each day he stood at her side. He had only one solution to the problem. He could hogtie her and lock her inside his cabin until the mission was over. *Knowing Aliyana, she'd figure a way to free herself and walk her path alone.* That knowledge alarmed him far more than the plan already in motion.

"Penny for your thoughts, Captain?" asked Aliyana.

Wolf's gaze never wandered away from her face as she climbed the steps to the bridge. He shook his head. "No sense in throwing your hard-earned money away. There's nothing in those thoughts worth paying for, I assure you."

She tilted her head sideways. It seemed those lovely eyes of hers penetrated every corner of his mind.

"Please don't worry about me, Wolf. Everything will turn out all right; you'll see. This mission is far too important for either of us to mess it up by dying. After all, I need to get all of the details to Mercado's insidious plot. Once I do, you'll need to get me back to Virginia to stop that course of action from happening."

So much for the glib comment. She saw right through it. "True, but I'd feel better if you promise you won't leave my sight while we're in Colombia."

She dropped her gaze for just a moment. "How can I promise you something over which I have no control? I've already accepted you'll stick to me like glue regardless of what I say, and after careful consideration, I think that's for the best." She raised a brow then and gave him a saucy smile. "This way I know I can keep *you* out of trouble."

"Hmm."

"All right, out with it then," she said. "What else is bothering you?"

"There's something else we must discuss before we

make our destination."

"And what is that?"

"I believe you've taught us well enough the layout of the primary compound, position, and strength of the guards. But you haven't told us what we can expect once we drop anchor. Is it reasonable to assume Mercado will have men watching the rivers, in the event of your return?"

"More than likely," she said, meeting his gaze head on. "But he can't cover all of them, Wolf. He doesn't have the manpower, and it would greatly surprise me if he or his men showed up anywhere near our base of operation."

"Magdalena is a well-traveled river. What if they just happen upon this more remote area anyway?"

"Oh, come on, Captain," she countered, "surely a man who chased down Spanish galleons for a living had to depend on his wits a great many times when things didn't go according to plan."

"Yes, but the other men on board those ships didn't target a specific member of my crew," he replied.

She nodded slowly then, and the slight wilt of her shoulders said she dropped all effort to tease him out of his present mood. "All right, once we make shore, perhaps you and the wolf pack could remain visible to anyone with whom we make contact. I'll simply disguise myself as a member of your rowdy crew until we reach my safe house," she said in a casual tone.

Wolf appraised her form from head to toe and back again. The process brought a delightful blush to her cheeks and just a hint of indignation. "Perhaps you can tell me how any man worth his salt could possibly mistake your gender?"

"A lot of padding, Captain," she retorted.

"I'm not sure even that would accomplish such a feat. What about your face? In case you didn't realize, there's nothing masculine about your features, even if you try hiding them behind some ridiculous facade of facial hair."

"Then you and your men must make sure you keep me surrounded at all times, wouldn't you agree?"

He sighed in exasperation and looked heavenward for whatever help they might grant. "I wish you would just stay on board this ship. It guarantees your safety, Aliyana."

"You know I won't do that. I can't."

Wolf found no point in arguing the matter further. He found Joris standing near the foremast. "Joris? Helm, if you please."

"Aye, *Kapitein*," said Joris as he made his way toward them.

Wolf gazed at Aliyana and held out his hand. "Want to take a walk with me?"

She smiled as she accepted his grasp. "Do you think a walk underneath the stars will change my mind?" she asked, giving him a sideways glance.

"If only."

They strolled along the deck of the ship to the forward bow without words passing between them. Once they arrived at the railing, he turned and faced her. "I take it you couldn't sleep."

"No, I couldn't, and I really tried. For whatever reason, I feel like I've had enough sleep to carry me through a full month of nonstop activity," she replied. "I suppose that's what you must feel like when you visit here."

He nodded. "Yes, it is, and the idea took some getting used to. The first time we returned, we forced ourselves to take a turn at bunk. We thought it a necessity even though we weren't the least bit tired."

"So, how much time passed between the day you first entered the portal to that other dimension and your subsequent return?" she asked.

"My time or this time?"

"They're different?"

"Yes, for whatever the scientific explanation, it seems time moves more slowly in my realm. I have worked at pinpointing that difference, yet the math is never the same between visits. I wondered then if we travel through some kind of time-warp each time we pass through it, if such a notion makes any sense to you," he replied.

She laughed. "Honestly? None of this makes sense to me. I keep thinking any moment now, I'll wake up and find out I've just experienced the most bizarre, most fascinating dream I've ever had. I'll tell people about it in minute detail. In return, they'll just smile, give me a condescending nod, and show me the door. That being said, I must also tell you, you aren't the first person to suggest a time-warp in association with the Bermuda Triangle."

"Is that right?" he asked, suddenly intrigued.

"Yes, the documented story goes that several decades ago, a pilot left Bermuda, heading toward Florida. He encountered a storm, reporting the same type of phenomenon I experienced for myself and which you're very familiar with as well. He went through the cloudy tunnel in the hope he'd reach the blue sky at the end of it. In his case, he did emerge through the other side and discovered the barrier island of Miami Beach directly below him. That meant his plane traveled one hundred sixty kilometers in about three impossible minutes. So, he either topped the astounding speed of three thousand, two hundred kilometers an hour or he experienced some kind of time-warp."

"Interesting tale," Wolf replied.

"I've always thought so." She shrugged as she turned her gaze toward the reflection of stars on the water. "On the other hand, maybe there's some unknown chemical lurking inside those particular storm clouds. Perhaps they produce the same peculiar dream and then lock those of us who pass through it into it for life."

He put a finger under her chin and shook his head ever so slightly. "I certainly hope this isn't a dream we're sharing, *lieveling*. If it is, then I don't want to wake up."

A flush rose to her cheeks as she paused for a moment. Her widened eyes assumed the look of a cornered rabbit. She let go of a nervous breath. He tried very hard to mask his humor over her discomfort.

"Are you serious?" she blurted. "How can you say that when you see the danger I've placed you all in? I'm sure, when you started through that portal, you didn't expect you'd come across or get involved in this dilemma. This is about as far away from *touristy stuff* as you'll get."

"I imagine so, but I'm not complaining." He caressed the length of her jaw as a flood of conflicting emotions passed through her eyes. Wolf detected delight, affection, and a trace of fear. For the moment, he merely smiled and shrugged. "But none of this answers your original question, does it?"

"My original question?"

"Yes, you asked how long it took me and my men to return to this dimension, did you not?"

"You're right, I did."

He looked at the rolling waves as he recalled the memory. "Well, it took us a while, but we finally realized the possibility for a return might exist. We developed a theory. If we were to find a portal that would take us back home, we should sail the ship in the same area the gate opened in the first place."

"When you first conceived of this notion, did you hope you could resume your life, or merely visit?" she asked.

"We never really discussed our options," he said. "We didn't know what we'd find if, indeed, we could return. You must understand the possibility also existed we'd find ourselves in another parallel of this earth altogether."

"Knowing that, you still took the risk?"

Wolf chuckled as he rested an elbow on top of the railing and shrugged. "By far, not the worst risk we're guilty of taking, Aliyana."

"I don't doubt that for a single minute. So tell me, how long did you search for such a portal before you found it?"

"Oh, I don't know, a few months, maybe. All total though, five years passed in our present home before we made our first successful return," he said. "Once we finally made it back, we found over a decade of time had elapsed in this dimension."

"What do you mean by successful return?"

"The cloud formations I told you about earlier? During our first attempts, the formation did naught but take us home again, much like the man in your story. Then one fine day, for the first time, we found the clouds billowing outward. We entered the portal and found ourselves here, in this dimension. We realized then the formation mattered in regard to destination."

"Did you visit your previous homes?"

He shook his head. "Not right away. However, we did plot a course for New York with that intention in mind. We dropped anchor in Bermuda first and that's when and where we discovered the change in our bodies. No one on the island could either see or hear us. Quite frustrating when we simply wanted a tankard of ale just for the pleasure of tasting it again. Conrad eventually helped himself, much to the shock and fear of the bartender."

Aliyana laughed. "Sounds like something Conrad would do."

"Yes, indeed. So, to answer your question, yes, we did visit our homes eventually. But not to visit families who couldn't see us. Rather, we wanted to see how everyone fared during our absence. We found them all well and prosperous. That made leaving them again far more tolerable."

She shook her head as she knit her brows. "But you said if you wished it, you could allow people to see you. So, why wouldn't you just let your families see you and explain what happened? I am sure, after the shock, the visit would've given them joy and some much-needed comfort."

"We didn't have the necessary skill at that time. Showing ourselves took practice, patience, and attaining the knowledge of how one accomplishes such a feat. That information arrived courtesy of an old seaman who had departed his mortal frame decades earlier. We encountered his ghost inside a pub in Florida during our third trip here," he replied.

Aliyana glanced up at the heavens. "You've had some interesting experiences, Captain Wolfaert Dircksen Van Ness. I'll give you that much. And whether I will it or not, you're about to have another one."

"Not to worry," he said. "We look forward to our adventures and always have. They make our lives a little more interesting."

****

In a little less than three days, aided by the light of a full moon, Wolf spied a generous curve along the tributary of the Magdalena River. The heavily laden tree branches surrounding and overhanging the bend would provide a bit of seclusion, if someone passed by and could actually see his ship.

"Take in," he commanded as he steered as close to the bank as he could get her. "Cast anchor and lower the boat."

Aliyana left the cabin a few minutes later, wearing the baggy black tactical pants she wore when first he found her. A bulky, oversized, black sweater covered her form-fitting black shirt. She carried her backpack over her shoulder. Her hair was tucked underneath a cap that sat low over her forehead. A pair of black boots finished off her attire. He didn't laugh or even smile. Instead, he merely offered his hand in silent invitation to act as guard.

Pieter went down the ladder first, carrying his share

of their supplies. He sent Aliyana next, followed by the rest of the crew. Once they were seated on the vessel, Aliyana made quick use of her GPS receiver.

"We still have about a kilometer to go before we leave the boat," she murmured.

"How far is this safe house of yours?" asked Wolf.

"Not far," she whispered. "It's only about two hundred fifty meters away from this tributary."

"Do you expect we'll encounter any people along the way?"

"No, Wolf, I don't think so. The place is far off the beaten path and no one lives anywhere near it. However, since all things are possible, I'll make my steps as quiet as I can make them. Please don't worry."

A thing easier said than done. After they tied off the boat, they gathered their supplies, and trekked uphill in a southwesterly direction. He marveled over just how silently she moved despite the bulk of her clothing. The backpack she wouldn't let him carry didn't hamper her steps.

Twenty minutes later, she halted the journey beside a large hill and swept an armful of thick plant fronds off to the side. Aliyana stooped down, rolled away a cumbersome rock, and entered a small opening. She walked about ten paces, retrieved the light stick from her pack and lit it. He and his men followed her around a narrow corridor and into a massive cavity. She tossed her backpack near her desk, removed her hat, and loosened her hair.

"Wolf, would you hold the light while I start my generator, please?"

While she worked, Wolf took his first good look at the 'safe house' Aliyana created for herself, shortly after her arrival in Colombia. *Now what made me think a woman like Aliyana would actually set up in something resembling a house?*

Still, the cavern had many of the comforts one might find in a residential abode. There was a desk with a lamp on top, a crudely built table with a couple of chairs to match, and something that resembled a bed, with a wooden chest resting at the foot. Next to the desk and her makeshift sleeping quarters sat a couple of large metal trunks. To the right of the north wall there was the shadow from another small opening leading elsewhere.

"Where does that go?" he asked pointing toward the darkened cavity.

"My private shower," she said as she flipped a succession of switches. She gazed at him and smiled. "There's a lovely little inside waterfall around the bend. I'll show it to you later, if you'd like."

The generator sat on top of a natural indentation in the cave wall behind the desk. She had the machine up and running in no time at all. Once a string of dim lights lit up the cave, she set her computer on the table.

"If we're lucky, Mercado will not have found my surveillance cameras."

"And if luck is not with us?" he asked.

She shrugged as she activated the power. "Then we'll make do without them for a while."

One by one, each of his men approached the desk as her fingers raced over the laptop keyboard. The screen divided into sections.

"I have several surveillance cameras in and around Mercado's main compound," she said. "This one here, top left, is his office. The center is his boardroom, where he meets with his lieutenants. These cameras have both audio and video capability, or at least they did."

Wolf pointed at the blank screen far right. "Should we see an image on this one right now, as well as the bottom center section here, or have you not turned them on yet?"

"They're turned on and yes, we should see something. Let me see if I can figure this out." Aliyana worked on the problem for several minutes, to no avail. Finally, she leaned back against the chair, combed her fingers through her hair, and stared at the screen. "Well, the top right camera should show us all activity outside his private office. The bottom center camera keeps surveillance on the main road into the compound. I'm not too worried about that one, though. We can get by without it if needs be. However, the one outside Mercado's office is essential to our task."

"What about these other two?" asked Joris. "Neither looks as if they're functioning properly, either."

"They're not," she murmured. "The bottom left camera should show us the activity taking place inside the courtyard. For some reason though, the image is horribly out of focus. Maybe the birds have disturbed it again."

"Where is this one?" asked Klaus.

"Those static, indistinguishable images are coming from Mercado's bunkhouse. I suspect a malfunction with that camera. We could live without the images if we must, as long as the audio feed still functions. However, we're not going to know if it works until someone shows up and speaks."

"Why did you set one up in the bunkhouse?" asked Laurens.

"Women aren't the only creatures with loose lips, you know," she replied. "Mercado's men always talk about things better left unsaid, especially when they're all together and have a bit of tequila under their belts. I've learned some pretty interesting things that way."

"So, what then, we all just sit here and take turns watching the screen, hoping they reveal the information we seek in the time we need?" asked Conrad.

"For the time being, yes," Aliyana replied. She left her seat and strolled toward the center of the chamber. She gazed at each of them in turn. "I'll show you all how each piece of equipment works so when someone walks into a room you can capture and record both image and audio. In the meantime, I'll devise a way to get inside the compound and either fix or replace those malfunctioning cameras."

Wolf stepped in front of her. He firmed his jaw as he shook his head. "Are you out of your mind, Aliyana? I believe you promised you wouldn't take unnecessary chances and going back inside Mercado's lair simply to change a camera qualifies as an unnecessary risk," he growled.

"That's not true. I must see the keypad outside Mercado's door," Aliyana said. "I'm sure he's changed his code by now. Without that code, I can't get inside his office and retrieve the information we need."

"Not a problem," he shot back. "I'll change the camera for you."

Chapter Nine

"Just how ghostlike are you, Wolf?" asked Aliyana.

"I don't understand what you're asking," he countered.

"You still breathe, do you not?"

"Of course, we still breathe," he said. "Pray tell, where are you going with this line of conversation?"

"I find it obvious someone needs to look after your lives and well-being, since you're so careless with both. You're all prancing about as if you're invincible," she replied. "Ghostlike or not, if you have a heartbeat, you can still die just as easily as I can."

"According to your unproven theory," Wolf countered. "I'm not so sure about that, given our current form within this dimension."

Aliyana held his gaze for several long moments before she whirled and marched over to the farthermost trunk beside the desk. She popped the lid, extracted her Glock, and turned toward him. Aligning her sights, she aimed the pistol just to the right of his chest.

"Should we test that theory right now, Wolf? Don't worry, I promise I won't hit any of your vital organs—as long as you don't move. In the event I might be right, we have a capable doctor right here who can tend your wound. A man in such superb physical condition as you should make short work of recovery, right?"

The men whooped, snorted and laughed. Wolf's eyes danced with amusement as he faced her without flinching. He gave her a lop-sided grin and winked. "Point well taken, *lieveling*. Nonetheless, you cannot dispute the fact we're still better suited for this task than you."

"Perhaps, but let's proceed with a bit of caution. I know only people gifted with such an ability can see you," she said as she lowered her weapon. "But since you're not truly dead, the possibility exists for a motion sensor to pick up your essence and give away your presence. I also wonder if thermal imaging can reveal your presence as well. Mercado has these things inside his compound, so you see they *are* a concern. Well, at least they're a concern to me."

Wolf shrugged. "I have no way of knowing the outcome. In truth, I know nothing about these devices or their capabilities. You must understand, the last time we visited this dimension, we found ourselves in the year 1984."

"Well, that explains a lot, I suppose. However, the fact remains, if a motion sensor can pick up your presence you've no better a chance at accomplishing the tasks than I have." She placed the gun on the desk then faced him.

"That's not altogether true," he replied. "One can't shoot at something one can't see."

"Oh, they could still shoot easily enough," she said, "and they still would, trust me. Those men inside that compound are not only crazy, they're also superstitious. I find it a wonder they haven't killed each other, and for all I know, maybe they have. So, should they get trigger happy, I suppose we could pray a stray bullet doesn't find its mark. On the other hand, they might get lucky and take your life."

Wolf waved away the comment. "You're talking about a risk so miniscule, it doesn't warrant discussion." He held up a hand to halt any heated words. "Look, Aliyana, you face the greater risk as a target they can see. Besides, I believe there are three things in my favor, all which make me the better choice."

"Those three things are?" She tilted her chin upward.

"One—I am sure you know where these devices are located, and we can easily avoid them. Two, you can show me what they look like, so if their positions have changed we can recognize them, and again avoid them. And three, should we set off such a device despite all caution, we can move at lightning speed. We can pass through doors, walls, even rooftops and thereby avoid gunfire. You, on the other hand, are naught but a sitting duck on water with no place to hide, should they discover *you*. If that happens? Mission, over."

Aliyana wondered if he had any idea how it infuriated her when he presented perfectly logical arguments for which she didn't have an answer. Wolf, or a crew member, remained the perfect candidate to fix or replace the cameras she so desperately needed. They could enter the compound any time of the day or night while she couldn't. She'd have to wait for the most opportune time to sneak inside. Several precious days could be lost, maybe even weeks. Still, the knowledge didn't erase her worry over his safety.

The knowing grin tugging at the corners of his

mouth annoyed her even more. "I think I'll conduct some tests before we continue this discussion."

"Tests?"

"Yes. I think I should see for myself what happens when you trip a motion sensor and what you look like under thermal detection. You don't have a problem with that, do you?"

"No, I don't have a problem with any of that," he said.

"Good." With a firm nod, she went to the trunk nearest the desk and retrieved the same type of motion sensors she installed inside Mercado's compound. She connected the fiber optics to the device and set it on top of her table. "All right, walk toward me, Wolf."

He moved forward just three paces before the alarm sounded. Before she could say a word, he held up a hand. "Now, let me see if I can avoid it."

She reset the sensor and watched as he did nothing more than gaze at the thing for several seconds. Then once again, he approached the desk. The sensor didn't go off. He waved his hand in front of the device, still nothing.

"What did you do?" she asked as the crew quietly laughed.

"I robbed it of its energy," he said. "Another ability that your disembodied spirits have and we've attained."

She mulled the notion over and nodded. "I know about that. Ghost hunters report drained batteries and electronic equipment going awry in the presence of spirits. Where does the energy go?"

"We absorb it. After that, we use it for physical manifestation and the manipulation of our environment." He shrugged. "We also use it when we pick things up and move them about—install new surveillance cameras or repair them for instance."

She ignored the blatant comment as well as his mirth. "Do you target a specific item for that energy, like a motion sensor for instance, or do you take all of the energy that surrounds the object as well?"

"Now where are you going with this, pray tell?" he countered.

"If you take all of the energy surrounding an object, you won't know if the camera is properly installed," she said. "You must see if it's working before you leave, since I'll have no way of letting you know."

"We won't find that a problem, either," he replied.

"Look here, Aliyana," Joris interrupted. "We all can and will help with this quest. If you show us where such devices are located, we can deprive them of their intended use while we accomplish our given tasks. Each of us can take a specific camera, thereby working on them all at the same time. We can get in and out again in the proverbial blink of an eye. Trust me."

"Naught but a stroll in the park," added Laurens.

"And Wolf is right, you know," said Cornelius. "You *are* a solid target. Should they discover your presence inside the compound, you have no place in which you can run and hide."

What can I say to that? They have sound arguments. More importantly, should Mercado discover her before she could ransack his computer, they'd never get the details of his assassination plot.

"Put the success of the mission above all else and make each decision with that in mind." She could almost hear her brother give her that same advice for

107

the umpteenth time.

Once again, she approached her trunk. This time she took out her shotgun. "I'm loading this weapon with non-lethal ammunition," she said as she stuffed the rounds into the magazine. "So, if a round finds its mark, you won't die. Unfortunately, if you're anywhere near mortal in this sphere, you will feel some pain. Well, actually, you might feel a lot of pain. That would probably be just as good a test as any to test your mortality."

"You're actually going to shoot us with that?" asked Pieter, his eyes lit with delight.

That annoyed her. "Yes, if I can see your bodies using thermal imaging, I'll shoot you where you stand. Your job is to see that I don't," she replied. "After all, you did say you could evade a bullet, did you not? You said something about moving at lightning speed?"

The entire wolf pack burst into uproarious laughter over the suggested contest.

"All right then, douse the lights," hollered Johannes. "Let's get this done."

"No, not in here. I want you all outside while we conduct this experiment. I won't take the chance of damaging what little equipment I have left by shooting inside the chamber. So, I'll give you a head start. That's fair, isn't it? You can hide anywhere you wish within six, maybe seven meters of the entrance."

"Why the limit?" asked Andries.

"Because that's the average length of each room you'll enter once you get inside the compound. Therefore, those are the boundaries you must deal with."

She stooped down beside her trunk and withdrew

the night vision scope with thermal imaging capability. That took no more than a few seconds. Yet, when she stood and turned around, Wolf and his entire crew had disappeared. Nonetheless, she snapped the scope onto her loaded Benelli M3 and raised it shoulder height. With stealthy steps, she made her way outside.

Darkness pervaded the skies. She panned the scope left and then whirled around to the right. Rather than yellow or red, a solitary figure in cool hues of purple and blue crouched down by a rock. She fired a quick round toward her target. In the same instant, the image disappeared from view. Two other like images popped up dead center. She fired her weapon in rapid succession. Just as before, the images disappeared before she could pull the trigger. She whirled around and shot at the image that popped up from behind and to her right. A pair of muscled arms encircled her body from the left. She used all her skills to free herself yet still retain her weapon. Despite her struggle, the captor yanked the rifle from her grasp. He tossed it off to the side and whirled her around to face him.

Wolf met her gaze with a cocky grin. "I must admit I'm quite impressed with that little maneuver you used to evade my hold. Such a step just might work on someone from your sphere. However, *lieveling*, you missed all of your targets," he whispered with a smug little wink.

She couldn't help but return his triumphant smile, though. "Yes, well—this is one time I'm happy to hear it."

"Aliyana, I promise you, we can take care of ourselves," he said. "Please, let me and my men do this part for you."

Debbie Peterson

"All right, but not until you can install or make the necessary camera repairs blindfolded." Even as she made the comment, a sudden dilemma entered her mind.

"Now what is it?" asked Wolf with a slight shake of his head.

"Exactly how will you shield your presence when you have a solid object in your hand? I can only imagine the looks on everyone's face when they see tools and camera parts floating around."

"If we keep said objects against our skin, it takes on the same physical properties we have now," he replied. "Don't ask. We don't know the reason."

"Our old sailor friend taught us that," Conrad chimed in. "You should've seen the very bizarre spoon collection he had hidden inside the walls of that pub he haunted."

"Interesting you said that. You know, I read something about that once," Aliyana said. "If I remember correctly, a couple found their child's missing toys inside a wall they tore down during a renovation. They didn't have a clue as to how they could possibly get inside the solid sheetrock."

"There! You see?" added Conrad. "No worries."

"Tell me something, Aliyana," said Johannes. "Would you really have shot Wolf had he given you leave?"

Without any hesitation she nodded and said, "Yep."

****

Less than two days later, the entire crew of the *Witte Wieven* met the goal she'd set concerning the cameras. They also proved they could track down every

110

motion sensor she hid and faster than she would've thought possible.

Once she congratulated them on a job well done, Wolf waved off the compliment. "So, when do you want us to go in and get this done?"

"At precisely the right moment," she replied. "In the meantime, would you all take a walk with me? After all, you should know the location of Mercado's compound before you rush out of here with guns blazing, don't you think?"

"You have a point, Miss Montijo," Wolf said. "But is such a journey safe for you right now? You have naught but cloud cover to shield your presence."

"I think I'm safe enough as long as we stick to the forest shadows, and trust me, there are plenty of those."

"Shouldn't at least one of us remain behind to watch over the working cameras?" asked Conrad.

Aliyana opened the trunk nearest the desk, took out a set of binoculars and grabbed her pistol. "The computer can record everything on its own while we're gone. We can watch the videos once we return. However, that'll put us at least one video behind until there's a lapse in activity, so if you'd rather stay behind that's fine too. It only takes one person to know the way in."

In the end, Klaus and Andries stayed behind. Everyone else followed her out of the cave and toward Mercado's compound.

"How far is this place?" asked Wolf.

"About two kilometers to what he considers the territorial border of his kingdom," she said. "The compound itself is another half kilometer inside that and is hidden by the surrounding jungle. However, we can get an eagle's eye view once we climb a specific tree, about a third of a kilometer outside the boundary. Once we're there, I can point out the hidden entrances used exclusively by Mercado and his lieutenants. As far as he's aware, no one else knows of their existence, least of all me."

During the trek, Wolf kept an arm around her waist while the rest of his crew surrounded her. The president of the United States couldn't have had any better guard than what they provided as they traipsed through the thick covering of trees and bushes.

Once they arrived at her tree, she stopped and pointed upward. "I only have one set of binoculars, so perhaps you might all want to take turns?"

Wolf shrugged. She grasped the lowest branch then hoisted herself up into the tree. All the way to the topmost limbs, he stayed right behind her. When they reached a suitable height, she shimmied onto the heaviest bough. She scooted toward the trunk so Wolf could sit beside her. Once he joined her, she peeked through the binoculars, adjusting the power and clarity. The front of the compound and the guards at the gate shot into focus. Right now, she counted four of them. They laughed and talked as if they didn't have a care in the world. That probably meant Mercado wasn't there.

Aliyana handed Wolf the binoculars and pointed. "If you look over there you'll see the main entrance to the compound. In fact, it's the only entrance visitors are allowed to enter."

He positioned the binoculars over his eyes. "I see it. I count four guards at the gates."

"Their relaxed stance tells me Mercado is not in residence at the moment. Straight through those gates is a set of heavy double doors that lead into the courtyard. I slipped one of my cameras inside a small crack above the plaster pillar, opposite the doors. A bird has made a nest inside that crack. The grass from her nest overhangs a bit and conceals the tiny camera."

"Clever," Wolf said. "I see a motion sensor on the right pillar, blending quite nicely with the black iron light on top of it."

"You're right, there's a sensor there. Follow the bars along the fence now, all the way to the right. Once you reach the end of that fence, take a look at the thorny bushes planted down the side."

"I can see them," he said.

"If you follow those bushes, at precisely thirty-three-and-a-half meters, you'll find a trap door, camouflaged with leaves, brush, and a smattering of dirt that looks just as real as what nature produces. If one drops inside and follows the narrow tunnel at the bottom, it'll lead to the boardroom. As I've already mentioned, this is the room in which Mercado holds secret meetings with his lieutenants. You'll find another motion sensor hidden along the fence, directly behind the trapdoor and through the bushes."

"Does anyone stand guard inside the tunnel?" asked Wolf.

"No, Mercado feels the tunnel itself is sufficiently secure since it only leads to the boardroom. There's one door leading out to the corridor. At least one man and usually two, guard that corridor. Unless of course, they're having one of their parties. I'm hoping such an event will take place very soon. Once they all pass out, you can go inside and take care of business."

"Where is Mercado's private office from this point

of view?"

"On the other side, left wing. If you walk down the hall, you'll see a junction. That junction turns both left and right. His office is down the left hall, second door on the right. You can't miss it. It's the only one with an electronic keypad to the right of the door. At this point, he couldn't possibly have replaced the security system he trashed with one similar. However, it wouldn't surprise me if he put some kind of surveillance camera opposite the door to soothe his paranoia."

"I'll make sure to look for one," Wolf replied.

Aliyana painted a vivid description of each room in the building as well as its function and the location of each secret entrance. At the end she sighed. "I hope I didn't leave anything out. Do you have any questions?"

He brushed a hand against his beard as he shook his head. "None I can think of right now."

"I'll create a more detailed map so you study it if you wish," she said. "But in the meantime, if a question comes to mind, don't hesitate to ask it."

"Don't worry," he replied. "We will."

"All right, I suppose we should call someone else up then and repeat the lesson."

Wolf shook his head and thrust his thumb behind him. "There's no need, *lieveling*. If you look around, you'll see you had everyone in attendance all at once. We didn't think it necessary for you to repeat yourself so many times and we can see the compound well enough without the binoculars."

"And by the way, Aliyana," Joris said. "Just in case you wondered, we've already located several solar-powered motion sensors near ground level. We won't have a problem avoiding them on our way in."

"All that's left is to get inside there and do our job," Wolf said.

"Don't worry," she replied. "I know Mercado. You'll go in soon enough, trust me."

Chapter Ten

"What are they saying now? Can you make any of it out?" Wolf watched as the washed-out, shadowy images lumbered about the bunkhouse.

Several animated conversations bounced around the room and all at the same time. Despite the chaos, Aliyana understood the topic well enough. She turned around and faced him. "Well, together—and apart— they just said tonight is a good night for you to go in and fix those cameras. Mercado is throwing a party in celebration of the most lucrative harvest he's had to date. He expects it'll bring in an enormous amount of money and they're hoping for a bonus."

The statement set off a buzz of excited chatter among the crew. Wolf ambled toward his men and joined in the conversation. They went over their strategy yet again for getting in and out of the compound in minutes.

The monotony and boredom of the last several days had made them restless. They dismissed any risk the dangers Mercado and his men presented. They would've marched out sooner if not for her threat of going with them should they attempt anything so foolish. Now, her announcement gave them leave. Yet, it only fueled her worry. With a sigh of resignation, she rose from her chair and slipped out of the cave.

Aliyana turned in the opposite direction of

Mercado's empire. She scooped a broken twig up off the ground. While she followed the twists and turns of the brook's path, she stripped the stick bare. Shredded leaves fell by the wayside as she continued her trek up the mountain. The meandering stream called up childhood memories of simpler days in Alaska, where getting home in time for supper produced her greatest concern. She halted her steps, tossed the twig, and rubbed her arms against the sudden chill. Despite the warmth of the summer sun, a shiver ran down her spine as she considered all that might go wrong. Once Wolf and his men stepped inside Mercado's domain they'd be on their own, and without a shred of experience in such things.

Her shoulder rested against a massive trunk as she stared straight ahead. Yet, Aliyana didn't see a tree, bush, flower, or blade of grass in the valley's terrain below. She had no idea how long she stood there, tormenting herself with all of the 'what ifs' before a hand caressed the length of her back and then rested at her waist. She gasped as she stepped back and twirled around.

"Oh!" The word slipped out of her mouth alongside a ragged breath. Her hand flew to her pounding heart as she shook her head. "Don't do that, Wolf. You scared me half to death!"

He flashed an apologetic grin. "Sorry, I didn't mean to frighten you. I just wanted to provide you with a bit of reassurance. You looked as if you could use some."

She dropped her gaze toward the ground and toyed with a pebble, using the toe of her boot. "That obvious, huh?"

"Perhaps not to everyone." He placed his fingers underneath her chin and tilted her head upward. Their eyes met. "What has you so troubled *lieveling*, or need I ask?"

She attempted a smile. "Allowing you to go in there without me is a little more difficult than what I first imagined."

Wolf shook his head as he encircled her waist and drew her closer. In response, she rested her hands lightly on top of his forearms. How she wished she didn't have to keep his ethereal form in mind every time they touched. Somehow, it just didn't seem fair that he could hold her when she couldn't return the favor as well as she desired.

"You don't always have to rely on your own strength and abilities, Aliyana. You've carried the weight by yourself far too long and such a burden is unnecessary. Right now, and from this moment forward, I want you to rely on *my* strengths and *my* abilities. I have them, you know. Please, please remember, you're not alone in this venture. I can promise you we'll achieve our objectives and get out of there without loss of life or limb. We'll also get it done in a fraction of the time it would've taken you to accomplish the same goal."

"Promises are so easy to make, Wolf," she said as a lump formed in her throat. "They're not always as easy to keep."

****

The haunted look that filled her eyes told him someone had made such a vow and then broke it. Her parents? Her brother? Or did some unknown rival from her past leave her heart shattered? He brushed the notion aside—for now. "Be that as it may, I intend to keep mine."

They stood gazing at each other for several moments, as if under the enchantment of a benevolent witch's spell. Lissa's perhaps? The unbidden thought as well as the possibility made Wolf smile and it warmed his heart. He could see his dear friend in the role of matchmaker. Regardless of origin, right now he wished he could give Aliyana the kiss he longed to give. Yet he wouldn't indulge the desire under the circumstances they found themselves in. He could—and would—wait for a much better time.

Aliyana shattered the enchantment by taking a half-step back as she closed her eyes. She placed a hand against her brow and sighed. "I'll hold you to your promise, Captain," she whispered. "So, don't let me down."

"I won't." Wolf sensed she needed a change in subject. "So, I have a question that I really must have an answer for."

"Do you really? Or are you just saying that so I don't dwell on everything that could go wrong?"

"I really have a question."

"Then by all means, ask away."

He glanced in the direction of the cave. "This 'safe house' of yours. When you first mentioned such a place, all kinds of images popped into my mind, from a grand palatial structure to a dilapidated shack. However, I must confess a dank cave never entered my thoughts. Why would you choose such a place?"

Aliyana laughed and once again leaned against her tree. "Several reasons. I needed a place close to the compound in case I needed a quick escape. I also wanted a structure that would allow uninterrupted surveillance of Mercado's property and the people he deals with. All those times my résumé had me toiling inside governmental buildings? I was actually right here, gathering as much intelligence as I could before I went inside the compound."

"That makes good sense, but how did you know the cave even existed?"

"Well, in looking for a secluded area to pitch my tent, a river turtle crossed my path. Now, don't laugh, but the adorable little thing caught my attention and—you're laughing." She dropped her weight on one foot as she put a hand on her hip.

Wolf clamped down on his mouth. He lifted his hands to the height of his chest and shook his head in protest. "I'm not laughing."

She gazed at him for several seconds and no matter how hard he tried, he couldn't stop the broad smile that appeared on his face.

"You're laughing." Then as a bit of color rose to her cheeks, she shook her head, rolled her eyes, and murmured something in Spanish.

Regardless of what she said, it delighted him no end.

"Anyway," she continued, "I followed the turtle for a time and subsequently, she led me to the cave."

"She?" he asked.

Aliyana nodded as she took on a thoughtful expression. "I think she searched for a place to lay her eggs. However, once I stepped inside her secret domain, the need for my tent and a place to pitch it no longer existed."

"I can't believe you'd even think to pitch a tent out

here in the open. Out here, Mercado or his men could've easily stumbled across you," he said.

"Give me a little more credit than that, Dircksen. I can camouflage a tent better than most. But as I said, the need disappeared the moment I found the cave."

"So setting up your 'safe house' amidst the various creatures didn't concern you?"

She shook her head. "Nope, I evicted all of them first and then kept them at bay with my rock, which fit the opening perfectly, I might add. Well, all but the smallest insects and with my handy can of repellant, they never bother me too much."

"So then you installed your surveillance cameras and on occasion returned to your cave to spy on the inner workings of Mercado's cartel?"

"For a while, yes, I did."

"I'm surprised that whenever you left the compound, he didn't have you followed," he replied.

"Oh, he did." She laughed and leaned in a little closer. "But it didn't take a whole lot of maneuvering to lose the shadows. Mercado's men are far from the sharpest tacks in the tool shed. Of course, my ruse of 'fitting him into my overcrowded schedule' helped ease his mind tremendously. He didn't care if I left the compound on occasion. At least not until the last three weeks of my contract. I only agreed after I demanded more money for my time and he agreed. By then, since I already had everything I needed, I didn't need the shelter of the cave. On the other hand, I had every reason to stay at the compound."

As her brows pinched together, her lips formed a grim, even line. She gazed off into the distance. Wolf shook his head ever so slightly. "So what should I expect with this wild party Mercado is throwing? Do we go in while it's in full swing, or would you rather us wait until everyone is in a drug and alcohol induced stupor?"

The barest hint of a smile grew ever broader. "You know what? With your unique abilities, going in while the party is in full swing just might work to your advantage. Any small noise you make while you fix the cameras will simply blend in."

A small noise did she say? Wolf's gaze swept over the bleary-eyed crowd. The effects of drug and alcohol consumption had already dulled their half-witted minds. If he wanted, he could fire his cannons just outside the gate and these people would never hear the impact. Even if somehow they did, they couldn't respond in the state they were in. He turned toward his men. "All right. I don't anticipate any problems. Nonetheless, Aliyana is watching the screens as we speak. Let's get this done and get out of here before she tires of waiting and joins us."

Each man headed for his assigned task. Wolf strode toward the hallway outside Mercado's office. He didn't have any trouble locating the hidden surveillance camera at the top of the wall and across the corridor opposite the doorway. In this location, Aliyana used a camera that doubled as a working smoke detector. In less than two minutes, he'd have the old one removed, and the new one wired in place.

As he finished up, he stuffed the malfunctioning camera inside his pocket and dropped to ground level. Voices, getting louder by degrees, echoed down the main hallway just as his feet hit the floor. He stood still as the owners of those voices made the turn and approached nearer his position. Emil Mercado stepped ahead of his blond-haired, blue-eyed companion who chattered on about fishing. At least, with the words *delphin* and *barracuda* coming out of his guest's mouth, Wolf assumed he spoke of the sport. His eyes narrowed as he wondered over the second man who had never once shown up under the surveillance cameras.

Mercado approached his keypad, and as he typed in his passcode, Wolf peered over his hunched form. The effort earned him a single number. Nine. Any more than that and Aliyana would throw caution to the wind. Ready or not, she'd descend on the compound. Nonetheless, Mercado and his friend had given him an opportunity he wouldn't waste.

He followed Emil and his companion inside the office, and then moved aside as Mercado shut the door. The blond visitor approached the bulletin board. With a hand on his hip, he waved a hand toward the infamous chart. He said something in Spanish. Mercado shook his head as he opened his drawer and extracted a small steel box. More conversation he couldn't understand followed. Using the key he wore around his neck, Mercado opened the box. The drug lord withdrew a large wad of cash from inside and tossed it toward his companion.

A broad smile appeared on the blond's face as he picked up the bundle and fanned the bills. "*Muchas gracias.*" He gave Mercado a nod as he stuffed the money into his pocket.

Mercado twisted his lips into something that looked like an agitated sneer, with a bit of worry thrown into the mix. "*Has descubierto el paradero de Aliyana Montijo?*"

Wolf whipped his head toward the blond as he narrowed his eyes. The man rubbed a hand across his nose and shrugged, mentioning among other things he couldn't understand, Caribbean, Bahamas, Turks and Caicos. *Did they suspect Aliyana sought refuge somewhere on those islands? If they searched for her there, they surely wouldn't look for her here. At least, not yet.* That was a piece of good news for them.

Emil closed the lid of his box, locked it, and returned it to the drawer. He then cocked his head toward the door as he slipped the chain around his neck. His guest bowed slightly and sauntered toward the exit. All the while, he fondled the cash in his pocket.

Wolf followed them then, breezed past, and joined his men outside.

****

Aliyana watched intently as one image after another filled the void on her computer screen. The various people wandering around in view of those cameras suspected nothing. Wolf completed his task, just as he said he would. She turned toward the companion the captain insisted she have. The ship's cook kept his focus on the computer.

Andries pointed at the top left image that had just popped into view. "There's Mercado. Do you see him?"

"Yep, I sure do and—" Aliyana's eyes grew wide as she sucked in a breath and stared. "What is *he* doing there?"

"Who? Are you talking about the blond man standing next to him? I take it you know who he is."

"Oh yeah, I know who he is. He's the newest member of my team on the U.S. side of things, but I don't have a clue as to why he would be—" She stopped short. A thousand thoughts flooded her mind. Hank didn't know Mercado. Even if the team had him infiltrate the compound in the hope of finding information about her, Emil would never give away the location of his private office. Especially not to someone he recently met.

She watched as Emil opened the door and waved Hank Morris inside. He entered with a familiarity that surprised her. In fact, the whole unfolding scene left her speechless. What she wouldn't give, right at this moment, for the audio feed. But Emil destroyed that portion of her installation after her escape.

"What are you doing there, Hank?" she murmured as he accepted money from Mercado.

"Do you think he's your mole?" asked Andries.

"The possibility exists, of course," she said. "But it just seems so unlikely."

Andries shook his head and shrugged. "Why?"

"Mercado doesn't give his trust to very many people and especially not to Americans. Because of that fact, I don't see how he could've possibly developed a relationship with the man this quickly."

"Well, I can guarantee you he has one." Wolf strode into the cave with the rest of his crew close at his heels.

Aliyana whirled around in her chair and faced him. "What makes you say that?"

"Did you see the exchange in Mercado's office?" He lifted a brow as he flung a hand toward the computer that now displayed an empty room.

"Yes, I did. I don't have any idea what they said to each other though, and I'm sure you don't either."

"Their demeanor alone should tell you they're

familiar with one another. Throw the money and the map into the mix and you've got a sure bet they're working together on something."

"That doesn't always mean what you think it means. Hank might be working undercover. They may have sent him in the hope of finding information about me." She rose from the chair and walked toward him. "For all I know, Mercado found and killed every agent on my team. Should that have happened, then Hank might be the next necessary step. As far as the map is concerned? Hank may simply have asked Mercado about it as anyone might under those same circumstances."

"Hank? You know this man?" Wolf asked as she stopped just inches away from where he stood.

"Yes, in a manner of speaking," she said. "Hank Morris is the agent the Administration assigned to take the place of a recent retiree from our detail."

"Have you met him personally?"

"Met? No, not in the formal sense of the word. However, he attended my last briefing and although we've never spoken to each other, I do know who he is."

"You cannot vouch for his character, then."

"No, I can't."

"How long has he been in Colombia?"

"I can't answer that question either," she said. "The last intelligence I had on the man placed him in the States. You must understand that while I was inside the compound, my team and I had to keep all encrypted messages concise and to a minimum. For someone in my position, that is absolutely necessary."

"Wouldn't you agree then, the possibility also

exists that Mercado and this Hank Morris might have developed a relationship before he ever joined your team?"

Aliyana stared at him for several moments and then shrugged. "All things are possible, you know that."

Wolf huffed out a breath as he turned his focus toward the ceiling. She waited for him to share whatever was on his mind. He didn't.

"What aren't you telling me, Wolf?"

"Mercado asked Morris about you."

She lifted a brow. "Me or Victoria?"

He pointed at her. "You, and in response, Hank used the words, Caribbean, Bahamas, Turks and Caicos. I couldn't understand what they said in between, of course. Nonetheless, I think it's clear they believe you have something do to with that region and therefore, are conducting a thorough search of the islands."

They stood there just gazing at each other while she considered what he said. She did have one explanation for the area of their search—*if* they searched at all. Yet experience cautioned against the obvious answer.

"Go ahead and just say it," Wolf said.

"All right. I do have *one* explanation as to why they might look for me in the Turks and Caicos Islands. Please remember that it might not be the correct explanation."

"I'll keep that in mind."

"As you might recall, those islands were nearest our position when I first tried to make contact with the DEA. Therefore, even though my passwords didn't allow me entrance, the computers traced my incoming signal to the satellite I used at that precise moment. In turn, they could use that information to calculate an approximate location."

"Does this mean you might possibly have other agents from the Administration looking for you as we speak?" he asked.

"Only if they're keeping an eye on the transmissions," she said. "I haven't been gone long enough for a full-on panic just yet. Of course, since I didn't contact my team as expected, there's a chance they might've taken that step for precautionary measures."

"But then they wouldn't have locked out your passwords. They'd have kept them open in the event you needed them, right?"

Aliyana nodded.

"But the mole would keep his eyes open for any hint as to your existence, because he knows about your escape from Mercado, correct? And therefore, in all likelihood is also the man responsible for locking out your passwords."

She sighed. "If he's doing the job Emil hired him to do, then yes, he knows my means of escape. He knows about the use of the satellite phone, and therefore must also have something to do with the passwords."

"The evidence is stacking up against Hank, don't you think?"

"Yes, but as an agent myself, I know things aren't always what they seem. Sometimes we must go brazenly inside the devil's domain and take drastic measures. We must convince him we are on his side in whatever way possible."

"So, you'll just give him the benefit of the doubt and leave it at that then?"

"No, you know I can't do that either." Aliyana gazed at the computer. "Right now I think maybe I ought to—" She paused.

"Ought to what?"

"Check out the web and see if Mercado has shared anything else. Maybe we'll find something new that will shed some light on this quandary."

Wolf followed her to the desk as she resumed her seat. She typed in the URL address and password. Seconds later, her photograph popped into view, along with additional video clips that would help identify her. She didn't click on the links. Instead, she dropped her gaze to the new paragraphs beneath her picture. "What's he saying now?"

"Basically, all indications are that I'm alive and well, but he didn't specify his reasons for making the claim," she replied. "The good news is he also believes I've fled the country. So, at least for right now, they aren't looking for me here."

"Then let's step up the pace, shall we? Let's get the information we need and quit this place while he's none the wiser. We'll start with the number nine."

Chapter Eleven

"Nine?" She raked her fingers through her hair as she drew her brows together. "I don't understand what you mean."

"I know it's not much, but it's the last number in Mercado's current pass code. With the distraction his guest presented, I'm afraid I was too late to catch any of the other numbers. And of course, that leads us right back to good old Agent Hank Morris. So, what will we do about the enigma he presents?"

Aliyana gazed intently at the trunk next to the desk as she brushed a finger back-and-forth against her parted lips. "Well, I think I'll send you back inside the compound for a couple of minutes, if you're willing."

"You know I'm willing. So, what will you have me do this time around?"

She grabbed the handle of her tool kit and headed for the trunk. "You'll install the makeshift bugging device I'm about to make. The task should only take me a few minutes, so hang tight."

Aliyana stooped down beside her trunk and dug around the supplies in her inventory. "Let's see, I must make sure my little device has a remote off and on switch, so when he sweeps his office for bugs he won't find it. And I need to create something he won't pay any attention to should he happen to see the thing."

"You have something like that in there?" Wolf

asked.

"Most certainly, Captain Dircksen." Aliyana met his gaze and smiled. "Didn't you know? A girl can never have too many accessories."

Once she finished, Aliyana placed her fabricated listening device inside a wireless computer mouse that duplicated the one Mercado used. She supposed that the process fascinated Wolf because he stood beside her as she fashioned the bug. All the while, she gave him detailed explanations for everything she did; from the installation of the tiny transmitter inside the board to the receiver they would use to hear the conversations and everything in between. He need only exchange Mercado's mouse with the replica, and then sync the bugging device with the receiver. She couldn't have made his task any easier.

"Finished?" he asked as she completed the final test from across the cave.

"Yes I am. Now, it's your turn." She tossed the mouse toward him.

Wolf snatched it from the air and stuffed the device inside his pocket. "I'll be right back."

"You'll take someone along, won't you?" she asked as she approached him.

"No, I'll just pop in and pop out. There's no need for anyone else to go on such a quick errand."

"I'd feel better if someone went with you, though. Please?"

He took hold of her shoulders and turned her toward the computer screen. "You needn't worry about a thing. As you can see, no one inside the compound is aware of anyone or anything in their vicinity. They wouldn't hear a massive explosion, much less any errant noise I might make. But, if it makes you feel better—Joris?"

****

Once they cleared the cave, Joris clasped his hands behind his back and gave a Wolf a sideways glance. "Tell me something, Wolf, how long do you think it'll take Aliyana to realize we can get her inside Mercado's office without the man's pass code? I mean, if she but thinks it through, she'll know we can walk through the door, disarm the alarm system and open the thing from the inside anytime she desires."

Wolf nodded. "I've already thought about that. I'm praying that with everything she's dealing with, the thought won't cross her mind. Our state of being is a thing foreign to her nature and sorting it all out takes time. If we keep her busy enough, she won't take that time right now. If possible, I want Mercado gone from the compound for at least a day and preferably longer before I take her inside."

"She won't be happy about the deception, I guarantee it."

Wolf chuckled, and as he withdrew the mouse from his pocket, he turned to face his companion. "No, she won't. But I'll suffer her wrath when the time comes if it means keeping her safe. For now, make sure everyone keeps their mouths shut. We don't need anyone bringing the oversight to her attention by a slip of the tongue."

"I'll spread the word. However, I must say, you're a much braver man than I am, Wolf. Much braver—" Joris sucked in a deep breath and exaggerated a shudder.

Wolf laughed as they continued their trek through

the main gate and into the courtyard. They made a full sweep of the area in search of Morris. Not a single blond male stood among the intoxicated revelers, nor could he find any sign of the man as he perused each crowded room and hallway.

"You know, I don't think Mercado invited Hank Morris to the festivities," said Joris as they cleared the final room inside the complex.

"Either that or he didn't stick around once Mercado paid him. More is the pity. I had hoped we could find out a little bit more about the man. There's something about him I don't trust," Wolf replied. "However, we can't worry about that right now. Let's get this swap done. Aliyana is waiting and worse yet, I'm sure she's watching."

Mercado's door stood slightly ajar. As they approached, muffled voices filtered into the corridor. One voice they could hear clearly. The other sounded more like wind through a chimney. That meant Emil probably spoke to someone on his phone. Wolf and Joris breezed through the door.

Mercado stood on the other side of his desk, facing the map. One hand held the phone at his ear, the other rested at his hip. The voice at the other end of the serious discussion had an unnatural quality to it. Why would the speaker keep his true voice hidden from Mercado? Wolf and Joris exchanged glances. Aliyana must hear this dialogue. With a sense of urgency, he withdrew the mouse from his pocket and switched it with the one on top of Mercado's desk. In his haste to sync the mouse with the receiver, he flicked the edge of the pen just as the drug lord turned around. Wolf cursed his luck underneath his breath. Joris gazed up at the

Debbie Peterson

ceiling and grinned.

"*Uno momento.*" Mercado's eyes narrowed as he moved a half-step closer to the desk, leaned toward it, and gazed at the slight wobble of the pen.

The man locked onto the blinking green light, which signified the synchronization process. Once the receiver completed its task, the drug lord backed away. His widened gaze traveled about the room and then shot upward to the ceiling. A moment later, he stood on tiptoes and waved a hand underneath the silent vent. His expression changed from one of puzzlement to horror. His chest heaved. A couple of gulping swallows followed. He then turned a slow circle. Did he seek unseen company lurking in the shadows? Wolf remembered Aliyana had said something about the superstitious beliefs of Mercado and his men.

Did he look for a demon? Better yet, did he fear the spirit of a murdered victim? Joris flashed a devilish grin and bounced his brows as he met his gaze. Wolf held up a hand and shook his head. They would fight off the urge to toy with the man. At least for now. In all likelihood, Aliyana witnessed the unfolding scene and worried over it. More important, he wanted her to hear the remainder of Mercado's conversation *if* the man could gain his wits long enough to speak.

"*Todavía está ahi?*" the altered voice asked, breaking the quiet.

"*S-Sí,*" stammered Mercado.

Once the conversation resumed, Wolf gazed at Joris. "I'm sure we'll have another opportunity. Come on, let's get out of here."

The moment they entered the cave, Aliyana whirled around and met his gaze with something akin to

134

anxious curiosity.

"Did you hear any of that conversation?" he asked.

"Yes, I did," she said. "But what happened? What spooked Mercado?"

Wolf shrugged as he cocked his head to the side. "Fear of ghosts, I think. We'll keep that fear in mind down the road, should the need for such measures arise. Anyway, to answer your question—as I switched the devices, my wayward hand brushed against the pen as I synchronized them. That caused the thing to wobble. As fate would have it, Mercado turned just in the nick of time to see both blinking light and gyrating pen."

"Oh, you should have seen the look on his face at that exact moment. The man turned white as a sheet," Joris chortled. "We could have had such fun with the man, if only—"

The crew of the *Witte Wieven* burst into uproarious laughter and excited chatter. They bandied about all kinds of scenarios that would surely terrorize the members of Mercado's drug cartel. Most especially Emil. Some of their ideas were pretty good. Aliyana joined in the laughter even as she held up a hand in protest.

"Wait—wait just a minute. We're trying to gather some serious intelligence here. That won't happen if we cause everyone inside the compound to flee for their lives," she pointed out.

"Aw, just like a woman! They always take the fun out of things," Laurens lamented.

"Don't they just," agreed Conrad.

"Oh, come on! As I recall, you're all a bunch of tough, seasoned sea dogs, aren't you? So don't pout like a bunch of babies just because you can't have your way. You can all have your fun after we have the information we need—if you still feel so inclined," she added.

"Was there anything in that conversation worth a repeat?" asked Wolf.

"Beside the fact that he won't allow Mercado to hear his true voice?" she asked.

"That too," Wolf replied.

"They discussed the dispersion of Emil's latest crop. Mercado feels that with the productive yield of his harvest, he'll need more than his usual number of buyers. Our mystery spokesman said he would assemble the highest bidders. However, he wants more than his usual cut for this service."

"I take it then, you've never encountered this particular voice before?"

Aliyana shrugged away the question. "Not as he portrayed it today. But otherwise? I don't know. He— or she—used a device we simply call a voice changer. Logic would tell us that if this person wishes anonymity today, then he has always used such a device when speaking with Emil. On the other hand, perhaps he uses it because without it, Mercado would know who he is. And as I've said in the past, once this drug lord no longer requires one's services, that person will die unless he finds a way out of his predicament."

"I find it a wonder anyone works with the man at all," said Andries. "You'd think with such a reputation, he'd have to work his drug empire alone."

"He pays well, so for most, the money is worth the risk," Aliyana replied. "Right now, I'm grateful for that. Without those men and what they know, our mission here would take much longer."

"I have a thought that might speed up the process," Wolf said. "I think it'll get us to Virginia all the sooner."

"I'm all for that," she replied. "What do you have in mind?"

"I think it might prove beneficial if my men and I took turns following some of the key personnel around. We could each take one of your recording devices and record anything we think pertinent to our mission. We can then bring these recordings back to you for translation and intelligence gathering."

"You know, that's a brilliant idea," Aliyana said. "But unfortunately, I only have one such recorder with me. However, I have plenty more back at my shop in Barranquilla, or at least I did. We could take a quick trip there and see if anything still survives. If so, then we can collect them and—"

"I don't want you anywhere near that shop right now. In case you've forgotten, your business address is number one on Mercado's watch list, and whether he believes you're in this country or not, I'm sure someone is keeping an eye on it, just in case."

"Probably," she agreed. "But you could just—"

"Let's just do with the one for now," Wolf said. "We can start by trailing Mercado and if we think another target, such as Hank Morris, is more important at any given time, we'll change our focus."

"Oh, I beg you, let me go first, *Kapitein*," Johannes called out from the back of the cave. "I swear I'll go off the furrow if I don't find something useful to do."

"You're not going without me," said Cornelius. "I think we should go in pairs anyway. Two heads are better than one."

Aliyana laughed as other voices clamored for the coveted assignment. "You're all that bored, are you?"

Pieter shook his head and snorted. "We've resorted to building furniture you don't need, Aliyana, just to keep ourselves busy."

Aliyana bit down on her lip as her gaze wandered about the cave.

During the past several days, Wolf's crew had built several crude chairs, another table much bigger than the original, and a bench. In the process, they had just about used up all her screws, nails, and wood glue.

"*Kapitein*, we could leave right now if you wish," Johannes said.

"I don't think there's any sense in anyone going out right now," Aliyana cut in. "Look at the time. Emil is probably already in bed and if you look at the computer screens, you'll see just about everyone else is out cold too. I really don't think there's anything left for you to find out tonight."

"You never know," argued Pieter as he rushed to Johannes's defense. "Mercado might get a phone call in the middle of what's left of the night. Something that needs our attention and we wouldn't want to miss the importance of it. You must agree that such an act might cut our stay by weeks."

"Keep in mind, Aliyana," Conrad added, "you don't have a camera in the man's bedroom."

"No, I don't, nor would I want one," she said. A shudder coursed through her body as she squeezed her eyes shut. "But in all fairness, I suppose you do have a valid point. Go ahead if you wish. I won't stop you from spying on the inner workings of the man's bedroom—if you have the stomach for it. All I ask is that you please be careful and save all your ghostly shenanigans until we have what we need."

"All right, that's settled then," said Wolf. "We'll go out in eight-hour shifts. I'll let Johannes and Cornelius take the first watch, followed by Pieter and Conrad. Then I'll send Laurens and Andries, followed by Joris and Klaus. If any of you encounter anything Aliyana should hear right away, get back here on the double. Don't wait until it's too late to do something about it, understand?"

"Understood, *Kapitein*." Johannes gave a quick salute and then turned toward Pieter. "Ready?"

"Wait a minute, boys." Aliyana shook her head as she strolled toward the trunk next to the desk. She retrieved a small black instrument and waved it back and forth in the air. "You might want to take this with you."

Johannes grinned sheepishly as he approached her. "Right."

"Once you turn on the power switch, right here, the recorder becomes voice activated," she said. "The minute someone starts talking, it'll record until the cessation of voices automatically shuts it off. The battery will last about twenty hours or so before it needs recharging and I always have the spare charged and ready to go, so—"

While Aliyana rattled off instructions, Joris stepped to his side. He placed a hand on his shoulder and leaned toward his ear.

"If you want to keep Aliyana busy, you might reconsider that trip to Barranquilla," he whispered. "The journey would take her away from here for a time and it would certainly work to our advantage to have a few more of those recorders. I'm sure you could protect her well enough. You could take one or two of us with you if you really think there's a need."

Wolf put a hand to his beard and looked him in the eye as he considered the notion. Joris had a point. "I think you're right—"

At that same moment from across the chamber, Johannes nodded at Aliyana. "That's easy enough. Hopefully, we'll bring back something worthwhile."

"And don't be late getting back," hollered Conrad.

"Not to worry. We'll be back by mid-morning," Cornelius called over his shoulder as they exited the cave.

"Aliyana? Could I talk to you for a minute? Or were you getting ready for bed?" Wolf asked.

"No, I slept half the morning away. So I probably have another hour or so left in me before my mind turns to mush."

He held out a hand in invitation. "How about we go for a little walk then. I have something I'd like to discuss with you."

"A walk sounds wonderful."

Once they made the turn opposite the compound Aliyana shot him a glance. "So, what's up?"

"How long would it take us to get to Barranquilla?"

She stopped dead in her tracks, dropped her mouth, and turned to face him. "Are you serious?"

"Well, I'm seriously considering it," he said. "I need some answers first."

"Why the sudden change of heart?"

"Because having a few more of those recorders could, in fact, save us quite a bit of time and effort. It's quite obvious that not every critical word spoken will be said in front of a camera."

"Yeah, I know that," she said as they resumed their walk. "You don't know how many times I wished I could've placed a permanent bug on the back of Mercado's neck. On all of his lieutenants too, for that matter. Something like that would've given me so much more intelligence, but alas, I think the man actually takes showers—"

Wolf chuckled. "Well, that being said, if what you tell me makes me comfortable enough, we might risk the trip."

"Okay. What do you want to know?"

"Oh, things like how long it'll take us to get there and what kind of terrain we'll cross along the way. Are you aware of a relatively safe place for *you* to hide while *I* go inside your shop and retrieve the recorders? If not, could we find one, and truly Aliyana, I will not argue that issue."

She gazed into his eyes for a time as if she searched for something. The strength of his resolve perhaps? "We could get there in about six hours or so, depending on the river currents. We'll follow the same tributary back to the Magdalena and cross it at the safest point. Once we cross, we can head into the city. My shop is kind of on the outskirts, so we won't travel far—"

"Outskirts denote a more open area, do they not? That would make it easier for Mercado's men or his would-be assassins to spot your arrival and therefore, all the more dangerous to approach," he cut in.

"No, that's where you're wrong. I chose the location because of the abundant terrain the outskirts provide. If we leave just as it gets dark, we can arrive well before sunrise. There's an old abandoned shanty surrounded by some very huge trees and vegetation about two hundred meters from the shop. We can shimmy up one of the trees next to that shack, and from that vantage point, I can point out the precise door you'll enter. You can raid the thing to your heart's content. Afterward, we can take refuge inside the shack until nightfall. Then, under the cover of darkness, we simply retrace our steps and come back here."

Wolf shifted his gaze toward the horizon. "Let me think about it while you sleep."

"What's to think about? You're right about the recorders. The more we have, the better the chances of finding the information we need, and in far less time. Surely you agree that right now, time is a commodity we can't waste."

"That's true, but I won't have you taking unnecessary chances just so we can shave off a few weeks."

"You won't," she said. "Mercado isn't looking for me in Colombia, remember? Even if he assigned a stray man or two to watch my shop, they'll never catch sight of me. I can stay under the radar, Wolf. An agent undergoes extensive training in this area, and I believe I can do it better than most."

Wolf held her gaze as he mulled over their options.

"Just when did you assume control of this mission anyway? I don't recall ever relinquishing my command. As far as I am aware, nobody died and made you the all-powerful supreme leader of this particular quest, either!"

A smile stole across his face in response to her adorable fit of temper. However, in all likelihood, the wink that followed was responsible for setting off the blistering string of Spanish words.

Good thing he couldn't understand a single word she said.

Chapter Twelve

"We could just as easily have taken a motor boat, you know," Aliyana said as under the darkness of night, they drew ever nearer Barranquilla. "There isn't a single soul on this river that would've thought anything of another water craft passing in the distance."

"Do you think that by taking such a boat, we could've traveled the river any faster than what we already have?" asked Wolf.

"Well, no," she admitted. "But you wouldn't have had to exert so much energy along the way."

"I am not exerting any energy and need I remind you, taking my boat keeps you well hidden while we're inside it."

"So you keep saying," she murmured as she watched him work the oars. The ease and skill with which he maneuvered them surely didn't come from his ghostly traits alone. That perception roused her curiosity in a direction she hadn't explored. "You never told me what keeps you busy in your realm."

"Busy?" He raised a brow.

"Well, unless you live in some kind of Utopian society, you must have a job that provides your living."

"Oh. That." He shrugged away her question as he cleared his throat. "I suppose you could say I'm an independent contractor."

"Doing what?" A lengthy silence followed the

simple question. She tilted her head to the side and tsked. "Is something wrong with the question?"

"Wrong? No, not at all, it's just that ah—".

"Are you bound to secrecy then?"

"No."

"Hmm, let me see if I have this right. After I trusted you with—and spilled—the entire history of my life, you can't, or won't, share yours with me?"

"Look, I don't mind sharing—it's just that the answer is rather—complicated, that's all."

"I think I can wade through your explanation if you promise you'll keep all your words small, so a simple girl like me can understand them. As luck would have it, we have lots of time at our disposal—just in case I get lost along the way and you find you must begin your complicated explanation all over again." She smiled.

Wolf laughed outright. "You're a saucy wench. You know that, don't you? All right, here goes. As you might expect, my realm consists of many different cultures with diverse forms of government, just as you have in your own. Similar to your own, a small handful of those kingdoms have enacted laws that forbid their subjects to leave their boundaries without permission. And trust me—in the greater portion of those kingdoms—that permission is difficult to obtain. Even then, they're accompanied by a bunch of ruthless guards to ensure their return."

Her mouth dropped. "They really go that far to keep their subjects secluded from the rest of the world?"

"They really go that far," he replied. "These kingdoms, the majority of them island realms, have built massive, well-guarded walls around their territorial boundaries to enforce this law. These walls keep people in or out, as the case warrants. However, at times, especially during military conflict, economic trade, or sanctioned, scientific exploration, a few citizens will escape their guards and defect to other sovereignties. These denizens have loved ones and friends they want liberated as well. This is where I, along with my crew, come in. We reunite their families within whatever society they adopt as their own."

Aliyana stared as such ruthless dictatorships in her own dimension flooded her mind. "Are you telling me that you just boldly waltz pass these well-armed guards and extract people from beneath their very noses?"

"Well, I don't know how boldly we waltz, but yes, something along those lines."

"How do you get them out of a territory surrounded by massive walls and the heavy guard that patrol them?" she asked.

"Very carefully and by changing up our methods and strategy on a regular basis. If we used the same methods all the time, our success rate would fall dramatically."

Aliyana considered that for a moment. "What's your success rate, if you don't mind my asking?"

A slight grin curved a single corner of his mouth. "We've never failed to reach our goal. However, the danger does exist that one day we might. This reality is something we keep in mind each time we go out. If nothing else, it keeps us on our toes."

"Sounds like a very interesting job, Captain Dircksen. So, how about sharing your latest adventure with me, hmm? Detail by precious detail." She propped an elbow on the side of the boat and rested her cheek against her hand. Though she could see his reluctance, she coaxed him with her most beguiling smile. "Please? I'd really like to hear it."

At once his features softened. He shook his head and sighed. "There's really not that much to tell."

"That's okay, the length of the story doesn't matter," she replied.

"All right—detail by detail. A month or so before we sailed through the portal, a client hired us to retrieve his wife and two young daughters. They were located on one of the tyrannical island kingdoms, known as Adëyrin. They have a unique power source they aren't willing to share or sell to anyone else, at any price. Hence, the reason they keep their citizens locked in. As luck would have it, our client's home was located very near an underground cavern, connected to several tunnels that we had discovered and explored decades earlier."

"Did his family know you were coming to get them out?" she asked.

"No, and that's always the most difficult part about our missions, since—by necessity—we come and collect them in the dead of night. We must take our targets out fast. There isn't time for explanations until after we have them safely on board our ship."

"I can see where that would be a difficult couple of hours for you—and them."

"Yes, well—during this particular mission we used our sub vessel to reach the tunnel that would take us up to the cavern, which rests just above sea level."

Aliyana's mouth dropped again as she drew in a sharp breath. "You have a submarine?"

"Certainly, we couldn't very well succeed without one," he said.

"Well, don't these kingdoms possess the technology to detect a submarine as it approaches their waters?"

"Some vessels, yes. Ours—no," he said.

"Why? What makes your submarine so special?"

"We've devised a unique combination of technology, pilfered from the various *kátholoses* we've visited, and from your realm, and mine. The combination 'keeps us under the radar,' as you would say."

"But your crew is so small. How do you divvy up your men to handle both vessels?" she asked.

"I have a much larger crew in my current dimension, so manpower isn't a problem. To answer your next question, only the men who crossed the portal with me the first time around are willing to venture back and forth. I think that's probably the wisest decision—"

"Most likely."

"Anyway, once we made it inside the cavern, which, by the way, is filled with the most magnificent stalagmites I've ever seen, we stored our underwater gear near the exit. We headed through the limestone tunnels and toward our destination. Some of those passageways were flooded at the time, so we found some air pockets and marked their locations for our return trip."

Aliyana gasped. "What about the children? How did you think you'd get them out in flooded tunnels, for goodness sake?"

"We have breathing apparatuses, unique to our

realm, that accommodate those who need them. You needn't feel such anxiety, Aliyana. We wouldn't let anyone drown. That would defeat our purpose, wouldn't it?"

"Well if you have such devices, why didn't you use them yourself and toss the need for locating air pockets?"

"We travel as light as we can, and we don't need them," he said as if the answer should be obvious. Aliyana shook her head and rolled her eyes in exasperation.

"Once we made our way to the rock wall that would take us to the surface, we simply scaled up the thing and then we—"

"Wait, wait, wait!" Aliyana waved an agitated hand. "How did you intend to get the man's wife and children down this rocky wall?"

"Carry them on our backs, of course. Come now, Aliyana. You're attempting to make a mountain out of the proverbial molehill. We've climbed that rock many times and I can assure you, it isn't that dangerous."

"But the danger increases with additional weight, and you know it," she argued as her mind conjured images of what that rocky wall might look like.

"We managed," he replied with an irritating shrug that said the whole thing was of no nevermind. "Anyway, once we surfaced, we remained in the shadows provided by the surrounding terrain and scaled the woman's housing complex up to the roof. From there, we simply used the fire escapes that led to her rear door. We disabled the alarm, used the key our client gave us to gain entry, collected our targets, and retraced our steps. We loaded our client's family on board my ship and delivered them into the man's waiting arms. So, there you have it. No big deal."

She had her own opinion about the scope of their mission. Nonetheless, compelled by curiosity, Aliyana succeeded in getting Wolf to reveal more of his professional assignments before they arrived at their destination. Each seemed significantly more dangerous than the first, and each revealed his wisdom, cunning, and audacity. Particularly, the mission wherein he impersonated a royal prince to gain entrance beyond the thick, towering walls.

Conrad's cryptic, *"Don't you worry about what we can or cannot do at this point, Miss Montijo,"* and Wolf's *"I want you to rely on my strengths and my abilities. I have them, you know,"* and *"by far, not the worst risk we are guilty of having taken,"* swirled around inside her mind. She'd grossly underestimated the formidable talents of her Wolf and his entire pack. And it made her feel a little foolish.

No wonder the man could so easily assert his authority and command whether she wished it or not. He was a natural-born leader. Very likely, these qualities are what caused her to fall so hard for the cap—*Don't even go there. There's no point. I know it's an impossible situation. At the end of this mission, he'll go home. I'll stay here and continue the fight against the drug cartels. I'll never see him again. Not ever. I must keep my emotions in check.* She closed her eyes against the sudden pain the notion caused.

"Aliyana, are you all right?"

"Y-yes…, of course," she stammered. "Why do you ask?"

"I don't know. For a minute there you looked as if

something deeply troubled you."

His gaze bore into her own and she had the distinct feeling he had guessed her thoughts. She smiled as best she could. "No, everything is fine."

He said nothing in return and for the remaining twenty minutes or so of their journey, they lapsed into companionable silence.

"You can take the boat anywhere in here, Wolf," Aliyana said, pointing toward the west bank of the river. "My shop is just a little way over that hill."

He headed for an area that had an abundance of plumeria, palm and mahogany trees. Large bushes and wild flowers were everywhere present. Once they secured the boat, Aliyana donned her backpack and turned in the direction of her shop. Yet before she could take a single step, Wolf placed a hand on her shoulder.

"Please stay close to me, Aliyana," he begged. "I'll feel much better about having brought you here if you do that."

"Anything to make the captain happy," she replied as he dropped his arm and took hold of her hand. She did want to make him happy. After all, she had one more additional task to undertake while they were here in Barranquilla, and she needed his help.

Once they climbed the hill, Aliyana pointed to the tallest tree, which was surrounded by a variety of colorful bougainvillea vines that crept along fences and tree trunks. "We can see the doors of my shop from that mahogany tree, right there," she whispered.

In no time at all, they had climbed to the topmost branch that could hold her weight. The dim streetlights illuminated the street as well as the row of aging, brick buildings on each side.

"Which one is yours?" asked Wolf.

"Left-hand side, third door from the end of the street," she replied. "Do you see it?"

"Yes. Where do you keep the recorders?"

"In the back room. You'll see the door leading to it behind the counter. Once you're inside, you'll find several rows of shelves on either side of the aisle. I keep the recorders on the right-hand side, third row, and second bin from the top. You'll also need to get spare batteries for each recorder. They're located in the bin directly beneath."

Wolf nodded. "Got it. Is there anything else you need while I'm in there?"

"Yes. If they'll fit in the backpack, I need some more of my parts cases. The small plastic containers with eight dividers. Do you know which ones I'm talking about?"

"The ones that had your nuts, screws and small electronics parts, correct?"

"Yep, that's it. Two will do. They're on the back row, second shelf, left-hand side. I also need more flash drives if the recorders prove a success. Take all that I have left. You'll find those in a bin underneath the counter. That particular bin is just about in the center. You can't miss them."

"Is there anything else?" he asked.

"Let me think." After a slight pause, she nodded. "I have a small nylon tool case, black in color. You'll find it next to the cash register, right hand side."

****

Wolf watched a shadowy male figure that paced back and forth along the darkest recesses of the alleyway, across from her shop. The staggered steps showed he was well into his cups. There was no way of knowing if the man sought Aliyana or another drink to still the trembling hands. He'd find out soon enough though—

"Is that the abandoned shack you spoke of?" He scanned the dilapidated shanty about twenty paces off to the north of their tree.

"Yes," she whispered.

"You'll stay here while I'm inside your shop, will you not?"

"If you want me to, but—"

"I'd like to check out the structure before we go inside. Just to make certain it's still empty."

She nodded. "Good idea."

"Promise me, Aliyana, you won't come down from this tree until I return."

"Don't worry, Wolf. Everything will be all right. I'm in no danger, I assure you."

"Promise me," he repeated.

She raised her right hand to the square and dipped her head. "I promise."

"Don't break it," he said as he gently pressed her hand.

Then he disappeared from her view and headed straight for her shop. Once he gathered everything Aliyana asked for, he turned on a single security light along the east wall. Aliyana couldn't see it from her tree, but the man across the street couldn't miss it. He slowly counted to ten before he shut it off.

The subtle action drew the man's immediate attention. The shadowy figure yanked a pistol from under his shirt and raced across the street. The idiot hammered on the door before he unloaded three rounds through the large, storefront window, shattering the glass. Despite the blaring alarm set off, the would-be assassin hopped through the opening, slicing his hand in the process. Blood dripped from the gaping wound. He stared at it. Wolf shook his head in contempt before he left the man to his utter stupidity and headed for the tree.

As he expected, he met her just as she hit the ground. He stepped in front of her. "You promised you would stay *in* the tree."

"Oh, Wolf, thank goodness!" Her hand quivered as she covered her mouth and squeezed her eyes shut. "I thought—I thought something happened to you and I…"

"Shh, it's okay." He drew her close to his chest and brushed his fingers through her hair. "Everything is fine; I'm all right."

"But the shots, he fired several, and I just thought that—" She gulped.

"All orchestrated on purpose." He cupped her face. "I saw a man inside the alleyway that paced without any kind of clear destination. That made me think he was looking for you and I thought I'd find out one way or the other. Now I know." The faint sound of sirens somewhere off in the distance caught his attention. "I think the local police are headed this way in response to the alarm in your shop. They'll search the area, I'm sure. So, how about we wait in the tree until after they've conducted their investigation? If they're thorough, they'll include the shack in their search as well."

Once they were nestled in the safety of the lush branches, Wolf handed her the backpack. She made quick work of the inventory.

"Looks like you got everything I asked for, despite the incident with the creepy peeping Tom."

"Mark my words, that imbecile won't have enough sense to quit the premises before he's caught."

"What makes you say that?"

"First of all, he won't believe you aren't inside the store and will look for the evidence which can't be found. Second, he'll conduct a search for something to staunch the flow of blood. I don't think you have anything like that inside, do you?"

"No, I don't think so, just some paper towels, but why does he need it?"

"Because he didn't take care when leaping through the window he shot all to blazes. In fact, he mashed his hand down on a broken shard and then stared at the thing as if he didn't quite know how it got there." Wolf shook his head over the idiocy.

"Wolf?"

"Hmm?"

"I didn't see him until he crossed the street." The admission seemed a difficult one for her to make.

"No, but then you couldn't have. He was out of your line of sight."

"Then how did you see him?"

He winked. "Ghostly ability. I could see the distinct movements of his shadow as he paced the alleyway."

"Oh." The word escaped in a ragged breath.

They watched from their treetop perch as the police finally arrived. Within minutes they found and secured the intruder. They also conducted a not-so-very thorough search in the surrounding area. The shack, they ignored altogether. Afterward, they congregated for a brief chat session and then they were gone.

"Wait here until I make sure the shack is empty, okay?"

She managed a small smile and saluted. "Aye, aye, Captain."

"I'll be right back."

Wolf found the two-room shack void of human encroachment. He evicted a couple of mice and one bedraggled bat that anxiously sought an exit anyway. Once he deemed it safe, he went outside and over to the mahogany tree. The first hint of dawn had just appeared over the eastern horizon.

"All right, Aliyana," he called out. "You can come down now."

"Right behind you," she said, her voice low and casual.

He whirled around and faced her.

"I saw you coming and thought I'd avoid the morning light."

"Good thinking." He curved a hand around her waist as he led her toward the cabin.

She stopped at the small, connecting shed, opened the door, and yanked on a rusty ring attached to the wood flooring. "Follow me," she said as she led him through a trap door and down a set of rickety steps. She stooped down beside the nylon bag in the corner and pulled out a flashlight. "You can close the door now."

She turned the beam of light on a second set of steps then headed for them while dragging the heavy bag behind her.

"Here, let me take that for you," he said.

She nodded and let it go.

"What do you have in here?" he asked as she opened the trap door leading into the shack.

Chapter Thirteen

"Clean blankets, comfortable padding, some food, bottled water, a lantern, and a couple of books," she replied. "Unfortunately, I've used this place a couple of times, and trust me—it doesn't come with any amenities or room service." Aliyana dropped her backpack in the corner, turned around, and faced her companion. "Before we get settled in, there's something else I must take care of while we're here. The errand shouldn't take very long and it's kind of important. At least, it's important to me."

"What errand would that be?" He placed the bag and pilfered supplies next to her pack and eyed her with suspicion.

"Check out an apartment building not far from here," she stated, keeping her tone casual. "We can get there in less than fifteen minutes and this time of morning, we shouldn't encounter anyone along our path."

Wolf firmed his jaw and shook his head.

"Two of my team members are in this building. Or rather, they were last time I checked. I believe that whenever possible, all facts should be gathered, not just part of them. The thing is, I must know if the mole outed my entire squad to Mercado. A quick visit to the complex will tell us if they're still here."

"Even if they are, what would that really tell you?"

he asked. "For the time being, you can't tell any of them what you know due to the trust issue. We both know their presence could mean almost anything. Finding your team members there might suggest that at least one of them is in league with the mole. On the other hand, it might suggest the mole won't go so far as having them executed, yet. Killing every single agent on a specific squad would arouse suspicion among the leaders of the administration, would it not?"

"Yes, and that fact alone might help narrow his identity to a handful of individuals," she said. "There's one more thing I should add. If these men are gone, and for many reasons I hope they are, they might've left me a message. If so, it might give us a piece of critical intelligence."

Wolf held her gaze for several moments. "Tell me about this building. Does it face a well-traveled road?"

"Yes, it does, but at this time of morning, there's very little activity on the street. Traffic doesn't pick up much before eight-thirty. That gives us almost three hours to get in and out again. I can also guarantee you that we'll need no more than an hour of that time."

"If all goes well," he pointed out.

"Yes." She sighed. "If all goes well."

"And if it doesn't?" He advanced a single step.

"Then we'll deal with whatever situation arises, as it arises. We both have experience in this area. Besides, if a member of my team left a message, the small risk we face is worth getting my hands on it. Surely you know this."

"Is the specific apartment easily accessible?" he pressed.

"Well, actually there are two apartments inside this

building we should visit. One on the third floor and one on the fourth. We should check them both. And with your unique abilities, they're easily accessible."

"Why don't you just tell me where this building and the individual apartments are located, and I'll check them out for you."

"Because you won't know what to look for if the place is deserted. We've devised several different methods of communication. A scrap of paper with meaningless scrawls might not mean anything to you, but it'll be just what I'm looking for. So, you see, I must go in there and search the place myself. If you return empty-handed, I'll worry that you missed it." She scrunched her shoulders together. "I guess the bottom line is this—I'm going with or without you. But if I had my druthers, I'd rather you come with me. With your help, I can get in and out in no time at all."

Wolf blew out a heavy breath. He lowered his chin and nodded. "Did you bring along some kind of hat?"

"Yes, I did."

"Then get it out and let's get this thing done as quickly as we can."

In less than thirty seconds, she had her hat on her head and her small tool bag shoved deep inside her black tactical pants pocket. "All right, let's go."

Wolf approached her and adjusted the cap. He arranged her hair so that it covered portions of her face and then stepped back. His gaze traveled the length of her body. Twice.

"Come on Wolf, we're wasting time. Let's just go." She could see his reluctance as he took hold of her hand and led her out through the back door. "We'll head south," she murmured.

He wrapped a hand around her waist and turned right. All throughout their silent journey, she remained close at his side. As the apartment building loomed ahead of them, Aliyana lifted a hand and halted their steps.

"Is that the only entrance?" asked Wolf as he gazed on the large glass entry doors.

"No, there are security accesses on each side of the structure and two emergency exits in the back," she said.

"Which entrance do you suggest?"

"The one on the left side is closest to the first apartment we'll check. The inside area is usually empty, and as you can see, this side is still obscured by shadows," she whispered. "They keep the door locked, but that shouldn't be a problem for you, right?"

They crossed the street at the intersection and then slipped into the shadows that darkened the side of the complex. A moment later, Wolf invited her in through the now open doorway. Rather than the elevator, they chose the stairs. They climbed on silent footsteps to the third-floor landing. Despite the vacant hallway, she stepped into the alcove of the darkest corner. "Second door down, left side, apartment three twelve."

"Don't move from this spot unless you find it absolutely necessary," Wolf whispered before he disappeared.

Several minutes passed before he stepped into the hallway and motioned her forward. Aliyana crossed the threshold into the meagerly furnished apartment. The place looked as if it hadn't been lived in for days. Eduardo had removed all his personal items, but left debris scattered here and there across the floors. She could only hope she didn't need to scour through the mess.

"You didn't see any signs of a struggle while you searched each of the rooms, did you?" she asked. "Overturned furniture, bullet holes, blood—"

"No, nothing like that. I'm sure your associate left of his own accord. Now, where do you suggest we begin this search and exactly what are we looking for anyway?" asked Wolf as his gaze swept over the cluttered room.

"Well," she said, withdrawing the tool pouch from her pocket, "I'm looking for a small piece of paper or something that can hide it. I thought I might start with the electrical outlets."

"Excuse me?"

Aliyana laughed at the incredulous look that shot across his face. As she approached the first outlet along the bottom of the north wall, she dropped to her knees. Using a small screwdriver, she attacked the screws that held the plate. "This all stems from the moment I went undercover. Each team member decided on a unique place to stash a message if something should happen that would demand a quick exit. Eduardo, our all mighty squad commander, chose electrical outlets. Knowing this man the way I do, I suspect he used this outlet because it's right of the door. That way should someone burst in while he was hiding his message, he'd have time to stand up and back away with no one the wiser."

"You could've just told me that, Aliyana, and eliminated the need for you to come inside this building altogether," he said.

His tone was filled with reproach, and she paused

at her task. Sighing, she looked at him. "Yes, but if he lacked either the time or opportunity to hide it inside the designated spot, then I'd have to keep searching. While I'm here, I'll even sift through the trash on the floor if necessary. I'm not trying to be a hero, Wolf. Really, I'm not. I'm just trying to stop an assassination plot."

The comment satisfied him well enough, or so it seemed. Once she removed the plate, she spied a small piece of tan tubing that didn't belong inside the wall. She removed it from its nest. A quick peek confirmed a message rolled up inside. She stood up and tucked the tube and the screwdriver inside her pocket. "All right, we're making good time. So, let's head upstairs and see what Shaun might have waiting for us behind door number two, shall we?"

"Give me a minute to check the hall, first."

She didn't wait long. Almost as quickly as he vanished, Wolf opened the door and offered his hand. As they stepped onto the fourth-floor landing and into the shadows, she whispered. "Four sixteen, left-hand side, last door at the end of the hall."

****

Wolf sized up the length of the hallway. He could now hear voices, running water, the rustle of pans, and refrigerator doors opening and closing. In this case, should Shaun's apartment prove empty, he'd need to unlock the door and walk beside Aliyana, rather than have her walk alone. "I'll be right back."

He found the apartment empty with no signs of a struggle. Just like Eduardo's apartment, this too had rubbish scattered about the premises. He unlocked the door from the inside and headed down the hallway.

"Is the place empty?" she asked as he approached.

He took hold of her hand and nodded. "Looks very much like Eduardo's. Come on."

As they arrived, she stood just inside the doorway and scanned the room. "Okay, this time look for a piece of door trim that might've been pried off recently and then reattached," she said as she headed toward the bathroom door.

Wolf focused on the bedroom, checking first the entry door and then the trim around the closet. The side trim next to the wall had a fresh nick on the edge. "In here, Aliyana."

She entered the room with tools in hand. He took the chisel and tapped it underneath the trim. As he lifted the wood away from the wall, a small piece of folded paper fluttered to the ground.

Aliyana picked it up and opened it. Scrawled rows of letters and symbols filled the top half of the page. A series of numbers filled the rest of it. Aliyana smiled.

"This is it," she said as she tucked the note inside her pocket. "We can go now."

Wolf made a thorough sweep of the outside perimeter before he led her down the empty hallway. Just short of the elevator, a bell sounded, and the doors opened. Two workers talked to each other. He and Aliyana couldn't advance without those men getting a good look at her face, nor make it back to the apartment before the passengers entered the corridor. Only one option remained open, and he couldn't say he was at all sorry for that.

He whirled around, stepped in front of her, then made himself visible to the men leaving the elevator with their buckets, mops, and brooms. At once, his lips connected with hers. He cupped her face to shield it from their view. The men responded to the amorous scene with words he couldn't understand. Yet, their appreciative tone and raucous laughter translated them well enough. Aliyana had the presence of mind to keep her hands light against his chest. Then, without breaking the kiss, Wolf turned her around and led her into the elevator.

He tarried even after the door shut because whether she realized it or not, the kiss she returned had nothing to do with acting the part of a lover. Instead, it had everything to do with genuine emotion.

Perhaps one day soon, she'd realize that fact. Finally, he reluctantly broke the kiss and stepped away but held her astonished gaze captive. He winked as he pressed the ground floor button.

The swift journey ended before either of them could utter a single sentence. Wolf stepped to the front, keeping Aliyana hidden behind him. The deserted lobby didn't pose a threat.

He placed his arm around her shoulder. "I think it's best to leave this place the same way we entered it."

With a bemused expression still lingering upon her beautiful face, she nodded as he led her to the door and out into the open.

After arriving at the shanty, Aliyana set up their 'camp.' She tossed her hat, combed her fingers through her hair, and then withdrew her treasures from her pocket. Wolf peeked over her shoulder as she eased Eduardo's message out of the little tube. The slip of paper contained the same type of information, as did the message Shaun left behind the door trim.

"I can see they've used some kind of code, but how

165

does it work?" he asked as she sat down on the layers of padding and made herself comfortable.

"This is called a transposition code." She retrieved a small notebook and pencil from out of her pack. "First, I locate the pre-arranged number, symbol, or letter and then use that to set the alphabet. Then, using the given key, I translate these double-digit numbers below the graph into words. The first number signifies column, while the second signifies row. The words the numbers create are also coded. So, even if someone gets a hold of this message and figures out the key, the words still won't make any real sense."

Wolf sat down beside her as she labored over the scraps of paper. The first two words she scribbled down on the note baffled him. "What is a scavenger hunt?"

Aliyana laughed. "A scavenger hunt is just a game wherein the participants are given a list of bizarre items. The object of the game is to find these items wherever they can. The first person or team to collect all of the objects wins. We always begin with this heading as an additional precaution to keep the message safe. Other than that, the words mean nothing at all."

"If you already know each message begins this way, why bother translating those first few numbers?"

"I do it to make sure I have selected the correct locater." Aliyana drummed her pencil against the notebook as she studied the word she had just completed.

"Is something wrong?" He peered down at the pad.

"No, not really. We've assigned the term whistle to mean train. In turn, train means the members of my squad are no longer in Colombia, but still somewhere in South America. I'm just looking for a logical reason for the move."

"Perhaps they've been reassigned, or it might be that your sudden disappearance without contact prompted the DEA to relocate them for safety's sake."

"All very possible."

"So tell me, what word would your group have used if they were still somewhere here in Colombia?"

"We would've used the word 'daisy'."

Wolf folded his arms against his chest and lifted a brow. "Daisy—," he repeated.

Her lips curved into a smile as she nodded. "Yep, we use the flower to signify a song titled, 'Bicycle Built for Two,' wherein Daisy is a character. However, we toss her to the side in favor of the word bicycle, which indicates shorter distances."

"I see." Wolf watched as she wrote the words for the next set of numbers. "Door prize?"

"Door prize tells me the next word coming up needs further investigation. Now, if he had used grand prize instead, it would mean the following word is crucial to our mission. On the other hand, using the single word 'prize' simply means the subsequent word on the list is something we might want to keep in mind for later consideration."

"So then, what needs further investigation?"

"Just a minute, I'm still working on that one." Her brows knit themselves together as she regarded the letters she copied onto the pad. "Hmm, that's odd."

"What?"

"Just a minute, I want to double check my work." She erased the letters and started again. "The exclamation point in front of this set of numbers tells me to skip each letter three spaces, so—"

"You've written the same word with no deviation," he said.

"Yes, I have," she murmured. "Jomini—"

"You don't have a code for this word?"

"No, but I do know that Jomini was an early nineteenth-century general. During his lifetime, he served in both the French and Russian armies. He also authored critically acclaimed works on military strategy. However, no one in my squad has ever mentioned this name in my presence."

Wolf didn't say a word as she decoded the rest of the numbers. Once she finished her task, she stared off in the distance, lost in her thoughts.

"Cotton ball?" he asked.

"Cotton ball represents clouds, and clouds mean sky. What this is telling me is that during the investigation of Mercado's cartel, they captured the name electronically. The asterisk following the number means star, which in turn means fantasy." She dropped the pad in her lap and for a moment, gazed into his eyes. "Wolf, I think they're referring to the man that uses the voice changer."

"That would make good sense." He pointed at the pad. "Perhaps you'll find confirmation in the numbers that follow."

Aliyana shook her head as she drew a line through the asterisks in front of the remaining numbers. "This indicates everything else is without meaning. They're all pure fantasy meant to throw off anyone else who might get their hands on this note."

"Clever."

"Well, let me see if Shaun has anything to add," she said.

Wolf rose to his feet, ambled over to the window, and studied the landscape for several minutes while she completed her task. Gut instinct said that this Jomini and the unknown voice were one in the same. Did he choose the moniker himself, or did Eduardo choose the name for him? If he chose it himself, did he fancy himself a general of strategy as the name might imply? Arrogant men almost always made mistakes.

"Jomini is our man!" Excitement filled Aliyana's eyes as she waved the notepad above her head.

He turned away from the window and gave her his full attention. "Is that what Shaun told you?"

"I think so. Keep in mind, I'm filling in a whole lot of blank pieces here, but from what I can gather, they followed Mercado into a restaurant. While inside, they recorded Emil speaking to his unidentified companion. Jomini was on the phone and said he had to take the call. Mercado then spoke with a man using a voice changer and before our boys made any headway as to the subject of the conversation, they lost the signal."

"I'm impressed, Miss Montijo." Wolf gave her a playful salute. "I must admit our visit to the apartment complex was worth the risk involved. Especially since we managed to walk away unscathed."

She drew in a short breath and dropped her gaze. A pretty blush spread across her cheeks.

Ah, the kiss they shared. His remark must've called the memory of it to mind. That brought a smile to his face. Perhaps neither of them walked away unscathed after all.

Chapter Fourteen

"So, what books did you include in your survival pack?" Wolf sat down opposite her and settled himself against the wall. He peeked over at the small stack she'd taken from out of the nylon bag.

Aliyana picked up the volume on top, dusted the cover off with her hand, and turned the book toward him. "Not what you might expect. These books are all on ancient history and the world's archeological discoveries during the past couple of decades."

"You have an interest in these things?"

"I would say it's more like a passion. I love poking about old ruins and hearing tales of ancient kingdoms and civilizations. At least from the archeologist or historian's point of view. You like that kind of stuff too?"

"A great passion of mine, as well. Do you ever travel to these ruins and explore them for yourself, or do you just read about them?"

"I visit every chance I get," she said. "Exploring one of these places is the ultimate vacation in my opinion."

"We have many such places in my dimension, you know. Some have survived, in some form or other, for more than twenty millennia. They are truly something to behold. Perhaps once we complete this mission, you'll let me show some of them to you."

Aliyana dropped her head as she sighed.

"I know. You don't want to think about that right now, and I'm certainly not pressing you for an answer. I'm just issuing an invitation to share the wonders of my realm, that's all—"

"Kind as that invitation is, you have a lot more you can share with me right now, if you've a mind to. Do you have any idea how often I've fought off the temptation to grill you, as well as your entire crew, about life in the early seventeenth century? In this dimension, of course. I'm sure the history books have only the smallest portion recorded within their pages. So how much better to learn from someone who actually lived during the time period?"

Wolf shook his head. "Surely you know by now, Aliyana, I don't mind answering your questions. Now is as good a time as any to ask them. Right now, we have a whole lot of time to kill."

"Well, all right then. First question. Were you born in the Netherlands?"

He stretched his legs out in front of him and propped one foot on top the other. "Yes, I was. I was born in the province of Zeeland. My family and I lived on this island until about 1615 when one fine day, we packed up and set sail for Fort Nassau."

"Then you remember your native country as well as your first voyage," she said.

His eyes took on a faraway look as he nodded. "Very well. Zeeland is beautiful, and I have wonderful memories of growing up there. And a sailor always remembers his first voyage. That's when I fell in love with the sea."

"Why Fort Nassau? Did it have anything to do with

the Dutch East India Company?"

"No, my father simply thought it made good business sense to expand his merchant trade into the new world. After moving around from settlement to settlement after our arrival, he finally found the success he sought in New Amsterdam."

"You weren't content with your father's merchant business, then." She leaned back against the wall and draped her arms around her knees.

He chuckled. "No, the business didn't interest me in the least. Having several other sons that could take on the business, my father didn't mind my wanderlust."

"After that first voyage, how much time passed before you sailed again?"

"Less than a year after our arrival. The captain of our ship, a very good friend by the name of Rand Van Locken, noticed my interest during that first voyage. He taught me the inner workings of the vessel as we sailed. One day he sought me out and asked if I'd make a return crossing with him. I jumped at the chance to go. I sailed with him from that day forward. Sailed with him, that is, until his personal life took an unexpected turn. He booted me off his ship and told me it was high time I found a vessel of my own. I heeded his advice."

"You told me that the boys with you now passed through the Bermuda portal alongside you. Had you always sailed together?"

"For the most part, yes we did. We came together under Rand. Not long after I joined the crew, Rand and I found Joris inside a tavern in New Amsterdam. We walked in at the tail end of a brawl. Other than those patrons minding their own business, the only person still standing was Joris. Everyone else was on the floor—bloodied and knocked out cold. We asked about the trouble. His gaze fell on the largest man in the group. He said the scoundrel didn't think he and his cronies should pay his father for their meal or the drinks they'd guzzled. Joris didn't agree. When Rand deviled him a bit about the way he handled their belligerence, he simply said he'd given them ample time to pay. Rand asked him then if he'd sail with us. He said yes, and the rest is history."

Aliyana laughed as she envisioned the scene. "You know somehow that story doesn't surprise me at all."

Wolf laughed. "Nor should it. That was Joris, just being Joris."

"Okay, what about Andries? I mean, he's just so much older than everyone else."

"Rand always told people that he stole Andries from his father. At the time his father sailed for the Dutch Admiralty. Yet, if truth be told, I think his father asked Andries to look after his son, because that's what Andries did, and with unfailing loyalty. One day, after having held every position a ship can offer, he announced his retirement. He said he'd leave the shenanigans to the young and make sure they had decent enough fare to handle the job."

"Dear Andries, he's a good man," she said.

"The very best. I've always felt fortunate that after leaving Rand, he chose to sail with me."

"When did Laurens join the crew?"

"At the very beginning. Laurens actually worked on Rand's ship during its construction. Rand saw him as a man with vast knowledge of ships and one that gave careful attention to even the slightest detail. He offered him the position of ship's carpenter and he accepted."

"And Johannes?"

"Well, Johannes was our gunner, one of the best. I've never once, in all our long years together, ever seen him miss a target. He, along with Pieter and Conrad were aboard a Spanish galleon the day we found them. They'd been imprisoned months earlier by the Spanish and used for slave labor in whatever post they saw fit. Once Rand captured the galleon, he freed all the slaves on board. The minute Johannes boarded our ship, he took over the guns. He blew a hole in the hull of the galleon that touched off the powder magazine. Pieter and Conrad, ever at his side, manned guns of their own. In less time than it takes to tell the story, they had the ship at the bottom of the sea. Rand asked Johannes if he made that shot on purpose. He said he most certainly did. Rand appointed Johannes as master gunner on the spot with Pieter and Conrad serving alongside him as gunner's mates."

"Wow. I think I've just found a new respect for your gunners. I mean, I wouldn't want to get on their bad side."

Wolf chuckled. "Wise decision, *lieveling*. As for Cornelius, the day we presented the West Indies Company with the treasure from that galleon, we crossed paths with him. He served as bos'n aboard the ship known as the *Dolphijn* at the time. The man had earned a formidable reputation. Rand asked him if he'd rather sail with us. In turn he said any sailor worth his salt would jump at the chance to sail with *Kapitein* Van Locken and the *Rood Draeck*."

"The *Rood Draeck*?"

"The *Red Dragon*. The name has a story, but I'll

leave it for another time."

"I must confess a burning curiosity as to the name of your vessel. Does the *Witte Wieven* have any particular meaning to you personally? Or—"

The faraway look returned. "Indeed it does. I chose the name because it pays homage to one of my dearest friends in this life."

"Really? Who?" She blurted out the question before she could stop.

"A very special lady by the name of Lissabeth Capoen, or Lissa as we called her. She's a direct descendent of the legendary *Witte Wieven* and as such has special skills of her own. If not for her, I wouldn't be here talking to you right now. Once, a long time ago, she saved my life. Therefore, after a fashion, I dedicated my ship to her as well as all the *Witte Wieven* who came before and after her."

Her stomach plummeted at the fondness reflected in his tone. She gulped. "You were in love with her?"

"Lissa will ever hold a special place in my heart, Aliyana," Wolf said. "I do love her, as did every member of Rand's crew. However, I was never *in* love with her. That wondrous enchantment fell upon Rand. I'm very pleased to tell you that they were happily wed prior to my leaving your dimension. So you see, it would've been most inappropriate for me to name my ship *The Lissa*."

Relief followed the announcement. "Was that the unexpected turn you spoke of? Their marriage, I mean."

"Yes, it was. Trust me when I tell you he couldn't have made a better choice."

Question after question followed and Wolf answered each of them without hesitation. Everything he said fascinated her. He painted his narratives with such distinction she could see each scene as if she lived them herself. In turn, he asked questions of his own about places she'd visited and the things she'd experienced. He also quizzed her about the newest technological advances they hadn't yet discussed. They talked until the shadows streaming through the windows announced the approach of sunset.

"Not too much longer now." Aliyana peered through the slits of the sun-rotted curtains. "I think I'll go ahead and pack up all this stuff. That way we can leave as soon as the sun sets."

"Sounds good to me," Wolf replied. "I'll go take a look around outside and check the grounds for any would-be assassins hiding in the bushes."

"Well, let's hope you don't find any."

After Wolf disappeared, she rolled up the bedding and stuffed it inside the bag. All the while Aliyana's mind drifted to Wolf's kiss. Until that moment, she had no idea that in his current form, he could give such an exquisite kiss. And that it would stir her feelings as deeply as it had. She found she had the overwhelming desire to accompany him into his realm. She just didn't know if she could—

"Aliyana!" Wolf burst into the room. "Toss me one of your recorders. Do it quick!"

She bounded to her feet. "Why? What's wrong?"

"Hank Morris is approaching your shop, and he's talking to someone on his phone in English. If you hand me the blasted thing, I'll record every foul word coming out of his mouth." Once he had the recorder, he disappeared.

Aliyana hurriedly packed up the rest of her things.

With the backpack over her shoulder and nylon bag in hand, she rushed down the steps. She dropped the bag with the camping supplies in the corner then bolted outside. She turned east and stepped into the evening shadows. From there she climbed the nearest tree and gazed down at her shop. Wolf stood next to Hank with the recorder held about chest-high. In turn, Morris made careful study of the shattered glass. He stooped down and peered inside. Moments later, the man eased his leg over the sill and stepped all the way into the building. Wolf followed close behind.

****

As Wolf breezed through the wall, he recorded every word Hank uttered. The man stopped just in front of him and fumbled along the wall in search of the light switch.

"Hang on a sec," Hank said. Once he found the switch, he flipped it upward and turned a slow circle in the middle of the floor. He then skulked into the storeroom and thoroughly searched that area. Hank shoved his hand in his pocket as he halted. "In answer to your question, I don't see any evidence that even suggests Montijo entered this shop last night. The thing looks as if it's been deserted for quite some time."

"Are you absolutely sure about that?" asked the same altered voice that spoke with Mercado.

Why would this person hide his true voice from Hank Morris as well?

"I'm sure," he replied. "Judging by the scattered animal droppings, I think the gunman probably saw a rat or some other vermin moving around. He took a shot, thinking he found his target and a load of easy money. Instead, he found himself a jail cell."

"You're certain there's no room for doubt?"

Hank rolled his eyes and huffed out an agitated sigh. "Look, don't keep asking me the same question. I'm standing inside her shop right now. I've examined every nook and cranny. Nothing has disturbed the dust here, at least, not anything human. The only footprints I see on the floor belong to someone who wears about a size twelve shoe, and I see, perhaps, a couple of tens. I find nothing here indicating Montijo was here."

"Keep the building under surveillance for a few days, nonetheless," the obscure voice commanded. "At all times, do you understand?"

"Are you out of your mind?" bellowed Morris. "I'm not your witless lackey to command. Lest it slipped your mind, I'm now your equal partner— whether you like it or not—and I won't have you reduce me to mundane chores! Find someone else or better yet, come do it yourself."

"Have you forgotten Montijo could still pose quite a threat? She must be taken care of without delay. If there's even the slightest chance that she's anywhere near the vicinity—"

"We agree on that issue, but find someone else for the grunt job, okay? Besides, do you really think she's dumb enough to come back, here of all places?"

Wolf fought off the overwhelming urge to throttle the man and extract every shred of information he possessed. But that carried the very real possibility of destroying everything they sought to gain about the assassination plot.

"If she has a good enough reason—"

"No. Not even a good enough reason would make her return right now. Not with Mercado hot on her trail.

She'll sit tight someplace safe. If you want my opinion, she's probably in Virginia by now."

"We've seen no sign of her in this location."

Despite the voice alteration, Wolf could hear the controlled anger and resentment in the unknown man's tone.

"Then she's probably still on one of the islands somewhere, looking for a safe exit off the blasted thing," Morris shot back. After a lengthy pause, he took the phone away from his ear and glanced at the screen. "Hello? Are you still there? Hello?"

Hank heaved out an exasperated sigh, swore underneath his breath, and shoved the phone inside his shirt pocket. After one final tour around the shop, he exited the same way he entered. Wolf followed him as far as his car before turning back. He caught sight of Aliyana just as she swung down onto a lower branch of a nearby tree and then dropped to the ground. He expected no less.

"Were you in time?" she asked as she approached him.

Wolf gazed at her as he turned on the recorder. Her eyes grew ever wider as the exchange between the two men abruptly concluded. "Do you have any ideas as to whom Hank would speak to in such a manner?"

She dropped her gaze, shook her head, and shrugged. "Not a clue."

"Would you agree it's the same person who spoke to Mercado and he's in Virginia at this particular moment?"

"Yes, I'll agree with you on that."

"Well, there is that. Come on. We can discuss this after we're safely on the river," he said as he relieved her of her backpack.

They didn't speak again until they had boarded the boat and were well on their way back to the cave. "What're you thinking?" Wolf finally asked.

"What the men said to each other can be taken one of two very opposite ways," she replied.

Wolf chuckled as he shook his head. "You always give Morris the benefit of the doubt. He doesn't deserve it."

"I just won't jump to the wrong conclusion without proof and mess everything up," she said. "I mean, just think about their discussion for a moment. The DEA knows I haven't contacted anyone on my team. That might've motivated a decision to bring Hank out here in the hope he could pinpoint my whereabouts or at least get a lead."

"Why would they send him right now? You said you weren't gone long enough for them to panic," he reminded her.

"That's true, but Mercado's reputation alone might've produced enough concern for them to act. Therefore, it's possible they're trying to locate me before Emil does. They might do this especially if they've discovered the bounty he put on my head."

"No, Aliyana. The man's tone of voice and demeanor clearly states the opposite. I should also think if your scenario were even remotely correct, there wouldn't be a need for Hank's cohort to disguise his voice. Have you forgotten Hank declared himself this man's partner in this scheme? What about the encounter we witnessed between Mercado and Morris? You said yourself they couldn't have built a trusted relationship this soon."

Aliyana nodded as she bit down on her bottom lip. "I'm aware of all that and those things trouble me—far more than you know."

"Well they should. I think we should proceed with a little wisdom here. It's far better to err on the side of caution and think of these men as your enemy. At least, until you find proof that states otherwise."

"I know and you're right."

He gazed upward at the night sky. "I wish now I would've brought someone else along on this journey. We could've handed him a recorder and had him follow Morris."

"Don't worry. We'll get another opportunity. If he's in thick with Mercado, he'll return to the compound and probably sooner rather than later."

"I'm counting on that," he said. "But tell me something, what possible reason could this 'Jomini' have for altering his voice when speaking with Hank?"

Aliyana raised her shoulders in concert with her brows. "Well, the only thing that comes to mind is trust—and this man doesn't trust Hank. Even if Hank knows his identity, Jomini might alter his voice in the event that Hank is sharing the phone call with someone he doesn't want it shared with, such as Mercado. He might even worry that Hank is leading him into some kind of trap for the administrators of the DEA itself. We just might find out that Hank is innocent in all of this and is gathering evidence against our unknown participant and at the same time, is trying to make sure I don't get killed in the process."

"Then why would he give away your position to Mercado? If anything, he would surely point him in the opposite direction."

"No, he wouldn't. He must lay down the facts as they are because Hank knows Jomini would contradict him. That all by itself could be a death sentence for Hank."

The back-and-forth conversation ended the moment they stepped inside the cave where Wolf's crew waited. Joris stepped ahead of the pack. He looked quite excited about something as he handed her the recorder he carried.

"We have a conversation between Mercado and our mysterious voice again," he said.

"How long ago?" asked Wolf.

"About forty-five minutes," he replied. "We hurried back, hoping you had both returned."

"Good job." Wolf dropped the backpack on top of the table and tossed the recorders into the hands of his crew. "All right, pick yourselves a target. Keep your focus on Mercado and his top lieutenants if you can. When your battery gets low, come back and get a fresh one when you see a lull in the action. Most importantly, should Hank Morris return, I want someone to follow him. Find out where he's staying and keep on his tail at all times. He has information we need."

"New developments?" asked Cornelius.

Wolf nodded as he glanced toward Aliyana. "We ran into him at Aliyana's shop." He unfolded the events of their quest and filled them in on Morris's conversation with Jomini.

Aliyana downloaded Joris's recorder and listened to the conversation. She listened a second time for any detail she might've missed during the first go-round.

"What did you discover?" he asked once the boys left the cave.

She tossed the earphones and leaned back in her seat. "Do you want the short version or the long?"

"I want every detail," he said.

"Mercado made the call to Jomini this time. It seems we had two would-be assassins near my shop last night. One of them had wandered into a bar for a drink, out of boredom, he said. He left the place just as the police arrived. Of course, he made a quick u-turn and beat all haste back inside the bar once he spied them. After he got himself good and drunk, he passed out. As he came out of his stupor, he found the guts to call Mercado. He made his report to a very unhappy drug lord. As you might suspect, the man is quaking in his boots."

Wolf nodded.

"Mercado asked our mystery man if he had any evidence that might suggest I had visited my shop as the man claimed. Jomini assured Emil that Hank thoroughly investigated the building and didn't find any evidence of my presence. However, the mere mention of Hank's name set off another heated discussion between them."

"What did they say?"

"Mercado wants Hank Morris dead and he wants him dead right now."

"That doesn't surprise me in the least," said Wolf.

"No, it shouldn't. However, it did surprise me that Jomini wants him dead as well. Just not now. He said the 'timing' wasn't right and that he had to tread carefully."

"Did he give any reason for wanting the delay?"

"Yes, he did. First, Jomini said Hank still had his uses, though he didn't give any specifics concerning those uses. Two, I think our mystery man is afraid of him, although he didn't say it in quite that fashion."

"How so?"

"I'm just filling in the blanks now with my own suppositions, so keep that in mind," she said. "What if Hank has threatened to expose Jomini if he doesn't give in to his demands? The fact that our mystery man doesn't kill Hank now tells me that in all probability, Hank has damning information. Information that just might land him in prison for the rest of his life."

"Did Jomini give any kind of time frame for Morris's ultimate demise?" asked Wolf.

"No. He just said that when he no longer needed him, Mercado could do with him as he pleased."

"Do you think Morris suspects any of this?"

"He'd be a fool if he didn't," she replied. "Still, for Hank to walk brazenly into Mercado's compound, he must think he has the upper hand."

"All the more reason to keep Hank under surveillance," Wolf said. "Anything else?"

"No, that's about it." Aliyana sighed.

"What's wrong?"

"This is all just getting so complicated. We have more questions than we have answers. I'd like to think we've found our mole in the guise of Jomini and that somehow, Hank stumbled onto that fact. But is Hank a greedy thug that simply wants a share of Mercado's very lucrative pie, or is he working undercover to get the mystery man convicted?"

"Are you asking my opinion?" asked Wolf.

"Would I be surprised at your answer if you gave it?" she countered.

He grinned. "Probably not."

"Yes, well, that being said, I also feel I should mention here that neither Hank nor our mystery man has mentioned the assassination plot, together or apart. What if they don't have anything to do with it? What if they're just working the cocaine?"

"No, I don't think so. I believe that at least one of them knows about the assassination," said Wolf. "Mercado couldn't have obtained the personal information of the DEA administrators or you without one of them giving it to him."

"Unless we have an unknown third party."

"That's possible, of course. But I think it's highly unlikely," he replied. "Jomini, by necessity, must keep his inner circle tight. Especially given the magnitude of this plot and sooner or later, it'll unravel."

"Yes, I know, but we're running out of time. What if it unravels too late?"

"Don't worry," Wolf said. "We'll get all of this figured out with time to spare. That, *lieveling*, is a promise you can count on. In the meantime, why don't you try and get some sleep. I know you could use it."

Chapter Fifteen

Aliyana wished she could stay in bed. Perhaps then she'd have that wondrous dream again. A dream that seemed more like a memory than something her mind conjured. She could stay snuggled in her blankets and relive it though. Surely, it couldn't hurt—not this one time.

Wolf walked with her, hand in hand, along the Yukon River. She recalled the cool, gentle breeze as it touched her face. The sun had just set, leaving glorious colors above the distant mountains. Nothing seemed more important at that moment than settling inside her hidden sanctuary before darkness covered the sky.

"You needn't be in such a rush," Wolf said.

"Yes, I do. We must get there before dark."

"Why's that so important, pray tell?"

"So we're in the most perfect place at the most perfect time, of course," she replied.

They followed the path up the gradual slope of the mountain that was covered in pine trees. Halfway to the top, she led him to an enclosure. The niche was made of soft earth, rock, and an overhang of sweeping tree branches. She sat down inside the alcove first, and then patted the ground beside her. Once he joined her, his arm dropped around her shoulder. He cuddled her close to his body and shared his warmth. "I can see why you chose this place as your personal haven," he finally said. "It's amazing."

"Wait, there's more to see."

"Impossible."

"No, really, there is." She positioned herself behind him and covered his eyes with her hands. "No peeking, now."

"Now, how can I peek when you're covering my eyes?"

"And no whining."

"I never whine."

Aliyana held her breath and waited. Once the majestic moment arrived, she dropped her hands and looped her arms around his neck. She rested her chin on top of his shoulder and gazed up at the sky. "The aurora borealis, like you've never seen it before," she whispered.

He smiled as he watched the vivid hues perform their heavenly ballet. "That's quite a sight."

"Despite the passing of years, I never grow tired of seeing the lights dance," she whispered.

He chuckled. "Dance?"

She nodded as her gaze remained fixed on the sight. "Yep. Once, when I was a little girl, a very wise and respected woman told me about the lights. She said they were the dancing spirits of our ancestors and our very dear friends, celebrating the joy of the afterlife. She said if I looked closely, and truly believed, I would see them take shape. Some of them, she said, might even talk to me."

"That's a fascinating legend," Wolf replied.

"I've always thought so."

Wolf brushed his fingers along the side of her face before he swept them through the strands of her hair.

The simple act caused the beat of her heart to skip a time or two and then accelerate. He captured her gaze. The way he looked at her at that moment stole away her breath as a warm flush rose to her cheeks.

"So, I suppose such atmospheric displays within your realm are *far* superior, because *all* things in your dimension are far more intense than mine. Am I right?" She meant to tease, but each breathless word she spoke refused to convey the proper tone.

A slight smile tugged at the corners of his mouth. "That's right. And did I tell you that when we fall in love, the intensity of the emotion is far more powerful than anything you can find in this realm?"

He leaned down to kiss her then, but just before their lips joined, she turned away and covered her mouth with her hand.

Her beloved Wolf shook his head. He took hold of her trembling hand and held it close to his heart. With the other, he lifted her chin. "No, Aliyana I won't let you run away from me this time. Not here, not in this place."

"Wolf." The whispered name coincided with a sharp intake of breath. "I don't think we should—"

"Shh, Aliyana," he said as he grazed his lips back and forth across hers. "Don't think."

The exquisite kiss that followed swept away the last vestiges of her pitiful resolve. Each subsequent kiss—kisses that bespoke the fierceness and totality of his love—chipped away at the fear that one day she would lose him, just as she'd lost everyone else that ever meant anything to her. Then, as if he sensed that very notion, he drew back and gazed at her.

"I see the fear in your eyes, but you needn't be

afraid, *lieveling*," he whispered. "I give you my solemn vow—I'll never walk away. Even should you desire such a horrendous thing, I would fight with every weapon in my personal arsenal to remain at your side. And trust me, with all my charms, I'd win the battle."

A small laugh escaped her lips. She shook her head and closed her eyes. "Please, Wolf, don't make promises you can't possibly keep."

"Who destroyed your trust in such a promise?" he asked.

She dropped her head as she placed a hand at the corner of her brow. "Everyone—a childhood sweetheart that had the audacity to drown on his fourteenth birthday, my parents, all of my grandparents, my brother." She sniffed, shook her head, and wiped away a tear. "Despite all their heartfelt vows, they've all gone to join the dancing spirits in the sky and they've left me here, alone. I think I'm cursed—"

"Look at me, Aliyana." He waited until she complied. "You're not cursed, and I'll never leave your side. Not ever—for any reason. That's something you can count on."

She could see something in his eyes then, some hidden knowledge that somehow made her believe his words. "I love you, Aliyana Rosa Montijo, far more than you know. I've looked for you my whole life and now that I've found you, I can't lose you. You mustn't ask that of me, for that's the one thing that has the power to destroy my heart as well as my soul."

The words all but turned her to a puddle of mush. Nonetheless, she shook her head and bit back a smile. "Well maybe if you asked, instead of commanded—" She let the words hang as he lowered his mouth to hers again. The wondrous kiss quieted her fears and finally wrested the total surrender of her heart. The experience wasn't nearly as dreadful as she had anticipated.

"Come with me," he said after another such kiss. "Please?"

She nodded. Yet, a nod didn't seem good enough for the captain.

"I want your parents, your ancestors, and all the dancing spirits to hear your promise. That way you cannot renege," he said between each powerful kiss. "And I want you to promise because you love me in return."

"I promise I'll go with you," she said as her arms encircled his neck.

"Because?" he drew out the word as he lifted a brow and waited.

"Because I love you."

Her words echoed inside her mind. Somehow she could still feel the warmth and pressure of Wolf's final kiss as she awakened.

She tucked the precious dream inside her box of personal treasures and then locked that box inside her heart. Perhaps every now again, when the pain of their separation became unbearable—for one day he would leave her—she'd allow herself to open that box and relive the wondrous dream.

Reluctantly, she turned over, took in a deep breath and opened her eyes. Wolf sat at the desk all by himself. He focused on the computer screens, and it made her feel a little guilty. Despite the guilt, she took a few extra minutes to gaze at her handsome captain. She wished she could tell him she loved him. Even though she could now freely admit that to herself, it'd be unwise to admit it to him. Most unwise. She tossed her sleeping bag cover off to the side and sat up.

The moment Wolf turned around in his chair, their gazes locked and held. The expression in his eyes seemed reminiscent of the one in her dream. Her heart fluttered in response and despite her resolution, the memory of the dream threatened to escape. She forced it back where it belonged.

"Good morning, *lieveling*. How did you sleep?"

Her eyes widened over the implication of his simple greeting and it gave her the distraction she needed. "Good morning?" she repeated.

He wagged his head from side to side and nodded. "Morning it is."

"Are you telling me I slept a full twenty hours?"

"Give or take a few."

"Oh, Wolf! I'm so sorry," she said as she hurried to her feet and crossed the space that divided them.

He rose from the chair and shook his head as she approached. "No need for an apology. You needed the sleep, and everything has been quiet enough inside the compound. Mercado's hired thugs slept through the night, they woke up this morning, and I haven't seen a whole lot of activity in any of the rooms since."

"Really? I wonder where everyone is," she mused aloud.

"I don't know."

"Have any of the boys returned?"

"Not yet," he replied. "But I'm expecting them to filter in almost any time, so if you want your shower before they arrive, now would be your perfect opportunity."

She combed her fingers through her tangled hair

and nodded. A shower sounded wonderful. "All right, I'll hurry."

****

"No need for that, take your time." Wolf tracked her progress as she gathered her things from the chest near her bed and headed toward the waterfall. Just as she disappeared around the bend, Cornelius entered the cave.

"Did you get something?" he asked.

Cornelius nodded. "I have Liscano speaking to Otiz and during this conversation they mention Hank Morris. Where's Aliyana?"

"Showering," Wolf replied. "Where did Mercado's lieutenants have this conversation? I haven't seen anyone of note inside the compound for a couple of hours now."

"Inside a jeep. They're all serving as armed escorts while Mercado's lackeys transport his harvest to one of his labs for processing, I believe."

Wolf narrowed his eyes as he huffed out a breath. "I think before we leave Colombia, we should make sure everything inside Mercado's empire goes up in flames. I'm talking the fields, the labs, the compound—everything."

Cornelius flashed a grin. "That's a very good idea, *Kapitein*. I don't think it would take us all that long to set something up. After all, Mercado keeps all kinds of explosive and incendiary devices about the place. Johannes would be delighted to draw up a plan."

"That he would. Does Mercado keep these devices near his fields as well as his labs?"

"Labs, yes—fields, no. But we could rearrange his arsenal to fit our specific needs. We could move some of that stuff a little at a time and tuck them away in an obscure place. The jungle is so lush he'd never stumble across the devices once we've hidden them. Then just before we set sail for Virginia, we can clear the compound of its occupants, set off the explosives, and obliterate his entire business."

"Tell me what kinds of munitions you've seen in that arsenal."

While Aliyana showered, Wolf devised an achievable strategy with Cornelius. Each night his men could put various devices in the areas Johannes deemed most effective. A chain reaction of some kind would work best. Destruction of this cartel would bring him a great deal of satisfaction as well as a little bit of justice for Aliyana.

Just as he made the comment aloud, Aliyana walked into the chamber. She halted her steps when she noticed Cornelius's presence. Her eyes narrowed in obvious suspicion. "What's going on? Did something happen?"

"We were just wondering what was taking you so long in there," Wolf said.

"Come on now, you said I could take my time," she countered.

"So I did." He offered her the recorder. "Cornelius captured a conversation between two of Mercado's lieutenants. Since they mentioned Hank Morris, he thought you should hear it right away."

"Hank again, huh?" Aliyana took the device and plugged it into the computer.

Cornelius stood behind her as she downloaded the contents. "If the derisive tone Liscano used is any indication, then I don't think Hank is one of the cartel's favorite people."

"You know, it's the strangest thing but somehow, the man always seems to put people off," Aliyana quipped as she donned her headphones and hit the play button on the computer screen.

Wolf sat on the edge of her desk as she listened to the lengthy exchange between Mercado's most trusted lieutenants. He and Cornelius didn't say a word during the process. Finally, she removed the headset.

"Well, most of what they said to each other is much too embarrassing to repeat. So I won't. However, as far as Hank is concerned, they agree he is making himself a nuisance. Liscano said, and I quote, 'he is putting his big fat American nose where it doesn't belong,' end quote."

"Do they provide an explanation for that comment?" he asked.

"Yes, as a matter of fact they did," she replied. "Hank has demanded a tour of Mercado's empire. He said that he wants to see the way they produce cocaine from start to finish. By so doing, he could point out their faults and help them improve production. According to Ortiz, Hank had the audacity to boast about his knowledge of the latest in drug manufacturing technology, as if they were a bunch of ignorant 'campesinos.' As you can imagine, this rankled them a bit."

"Perhaps they'll use this outing as an excuse to kill him then," Cornelius remarked.

"They actually mentioned that. However, as much as Mercado would like to permanently get rid of the man, he'll show a bit of restraint. He said he'd allow the 'pig' to live—for now."

"Did they mention whether or not Mercado will comply with this requested tour?" asked Cornelius.

"He is, but not in the way Hank intends," she replied. "Mercado plans to take him much farther south, to a factory and lab he no longer uses. He's sending some of his employees ahead to clean the place up and make ready for their visit. Emil wants everything to look as if the lab is in full swing."

"So Mercado is conducting the tour personally then?" asked Wolf.

"Yep, that's what they said. Mercado doesn't trust Hank. Therefore, he wants to observe his every movement, personally."

"How long will it take them to get to this lab?"

"If it's the one I think it is, about three, maybe four hours. Why do you ask?"

Wolf paused for a moment as he contemplated the unexpected opportunity. "How many such places could he possibly take Morris?"

"I only know of two," she said.

"How long would it take to get to other one?"

Aliyana shook her head and shrugged. "Oh, I don't know—perhaps an additional half an hour or so. That's why I think he'll opt for the closest one."

"Did they say when they'll conduct this tour?"

"Day after tomorrow. Hank is supposed to arrive at dawn. If you still want to follow the man, you'll get your chance then."

"So travel time, to and from, is at least six hours, maybe more," Wolf mused aloud. "The tour itself will take some time. What would you think, another hour, maybe two, for him to thoroughly inspect the facilities?"

"Every bit of that and then some," Aliyana said. "Wolf, why are you asking all of these questions?"

"With Mercado out of the way, I think this might be the perfect opportunity for you to go inside the man's office and raid those files on his computer."

"But we don't have all of the numbers to his passcode yet," Aliyana replied. "I can't get inside without them."

He battled a grin and lost. For several long moments, he held her gaze without saying a word. Her confusion dwindled as understanding dawned. She drew in a sharp breath as a burst of anger reddened her cheeks.

"You could've gotten me inside that office anytime you wanted to, isn't that right, Captain Wolfaert Dircksen Van Ness?" she spat. "How could I have been so dense?"

Wolf folded his arms against his chest, flashed a full-fledged grin, and bounced his brows.

"I can't believe you didn't say anything," she seethed as her gaze shot lethal daggers. "You just let me watch that screen for hours on end when such a need didn't exist—"

"Oh, come on, Aliyana," Wolf laughingly protested. "You surely didn't think I'd allow you to go in there until the safest possible moment, did you?"

His humor did nothing to improve her anger. If anything, it only served to fuel it. She shook her head then and let him have it—with both barrels blazing—in Spanish, of course.

And he enjoyed every minute of the delightful display.

Chapter Sixteen

Aliyana didn't take as much time with her morning routine as she usually did. After a quick shower she put on her dark green T-shirt, jungle camouflage pants and matching lightweight, waist-length jacket. She finished braiding the last of her wet hair as she approached the desk. Leaning over Wolf's shoulder, she peered at the screen. "Are they all gone?"

"I'm not certain. The bunkhouse is empty, as you can see," he replied. "But the last man out the door left not five minutes ago. Therefore, I'm not sure they've vacated the property."

"Mercado has a thing for punctuality, so it shouldn't be long now."

Minutes later, Joris burst into the cave and gave them the all clear. "Remember," he said, "the compound is far from empty. The women are still inside. We also have a handful of guards and miscellaneous personnel scattered hither and yon throughout the building."

Aliyana nodded as she collected a couple of flash drives from off the desk. She slipped them inside her pocket. "I know. The compound is never empty."

"Where shall we make your point of entry?" asked Wolf.

"Since all the lieutenants are gone, I thought we'd enter through the tunnel leading to the boardroom."

Aliyana took the tiny flashlight from the top of the desk and tested the light against the cave wall. She then dropped it inside her pocket alongside the flash drives. "The hallway outside is the most direct path to the office other than the one going into his bedroom. But if we use that entrance, we run the risk of running into the woman who shared his bed last night."

"I agree," said Wolf as he abandoned the chair. "So, are you ready to go then?"

She retrieved her pistol from her trunk, checked it over and tucked it inside the slot of her bellyband, made for that specific purpose. "Yes, I am."

"Then, let's get this done." Wolf took hold of her hand as the men led her out of the cave and into the dark shadows of dense jungle vegetation.

Two or three times along the way, the men paused. Aliyana wondered over the delay until she realized they had deactivated the solar-powered motion sensors. Once they spied the main gate in the distance, Wolf halted their advance.

"Mercado's added another guard," Joris said as they studied the four figures standing just outside the iron bars. "When I left, he just had three."

"That's not unusual under the circumstances," Aliyana murmured. "All the better for us to have them outside rather than inside, anyway."

"I won't argue with you there," Joris replied.

"Give us a minute. We'll double check the sensors surrounding the fences and make sure they're all incapacitated before we go in." Wolf gave her hand a gentle squeeze before he let go.

"All right," she said. "Just don't be gone long."

"We won't."

Aliyana crouched down within the darkest shadows. She fixed her gaze on the sentry as Wolf and Joris conducted their search. All the while, the guards paid little heed to their duty. They seemed more interested in the animated conversation passing between them than watching for trespassers. That increased her chances of slipping past them unnoticed.

She had chosen her path by the time Wolf and Joris returned. A single nod to the right indicated her choice of direction. After taking a deep breath, she moved forward, blending with the trees. Wolf stuck right by her side as step by careful step, she inched her way toward the hidden tunnel. Just shy of Mercado's outside border, one of the guards turned away from the others. He ambled to the end of the front fence, close to where she stood. Aliyana made an abrupt stop and stood beneath the tree not more than four meters away from the man's location. She placed a hand close to her gun and stood motionless as he peered into the surrounding foliage. Finding nothing amiss, the guard rejoined his comrades.

Wolf focused his attention on that solitary guard as Joris bounded off in the opposite direction. Once the sentry rejoined his comrades, he stepped in front of her.

"Stay still until the guards move off to the left and away from the fence," he said. "Joris will create a small diversion so you can safely slip past them and ease yourself down the tunnel before the men return to their post."

Aliyana nodded and then shifted her gaze toward Mercado's henchmen. She didn't wait long. Within minutes, the sounds of screams and chaotic flight from a troop of startled howler monkeys filled the forest.

Mercado's men cast furtive glances at each other. They bundled themselves together and strode into the foliage.

She swiftly moved past the perimeters of the fence and made her way down the side railing to the tunnel entrance. Wolf lifted the escape hatch as she eased herself down the rickety ladder and into the narrow corridor. She withdrew the flashlight from her pocket and turned it on, feeling Wolf behind her.

"Where is Joris?" she whispered without turning around.

"Inside the compound," he replied. "He's making a sweep of the boardroom and the hallways to the office. While he's there, he'll deactivate all motion sensors and cameras."

Aliyana nodded as she traveled through the twists and turns of the tunnel.

Joris awaited her at the end of it with the escape hatch open. He offered her his hand and then hoisted her up. "Everyone is busy or is still sleeping. Now is as good a time as any for you to go in, see what you can find, and then get the hell out again. While you and Wolf are inside the office, I'll patrol the hallways."

They exited the boardroom and traversed the hallways without encountering a single heart-stopping moment. Wolf stepped ahead of her as they approached the office in less time than she thought possible. He disappeared through the door and within seconds deactivated the alarm and opened the door. She slipped through the gap and turned on the computer. While she waited for the machine to boot, she checked the map, seeking any noticeable changes to the colored dots. None had occurred.

"Any changes?" asked Wolf.

She shook her head. "No, everything is the same."

He followed her to the desk and perched on the edge as she sat down and inserted a flash drive. She let go of a breath and grabbed the mouse. "Here we go."

Hour after tedious hour passed as she searched through the plethora of files on Mercado's computer. But other than what she had already discovered, and previously downloaded, nothing held any great significance. Disappointment set in. Then, just as she gave the cause up for lost, she took a second look at the file Mercado labeled 'familia.' She had looked through it months ago and found nothing but photographs. Still, she clicked on the folder. Just as before, a multitude of pictures popped onto the screen. But this time she spied a subfolder marked 'family correspondence,' down at the very bottom. Had she overlooked that one?

Aliyana opened the folder. Mercado had saved hundreds of emails, including some from his lieutenants, inside this folder. That piqued her interest. So did the months old email in bold type that said, "Give this information to your mother," inside the reference box. Mercado's mother died several years ago. Intrigued, she clicked the file and read the contents.

Cousin,

Tell your mother she needs to write Uncle Bruce and Aunt Justine, right away. They have moved house so she will need to write them at their new address in Virginia.

Aliyana's mouth dropped at the first names and personal address of a top DEA official and his wife. A couple he slated for execution. The correspondent did not sign his name.

"Did you find something?" he asked.

"Yes, I did, but it'll take some work to decipher the origination of the email and find out who it's from."

Before she could elaborate on the find, Joris popped inside the room. He looked a bit frazzled.

"Time's up, Aliyana," he said, jerking his thumb toward the door. "Mercado and company are just a short distance away from the compound. They have Hank Morris in tow. We've got to get you out of here, right now."

Wolf stood up, rounded the desk, and extended his hand. "Come on Aliyana," he said in a brusque no-nonsense tone. "We're leaving."

"Wait!" She lifted a hand then clicked on the sub folder and dropped it into her flash drive.

"We don't have time for that," Wolf shot back.

"We need to make time," Aliyana countered. "I can't leave without this file."

"I can come back and get it for you tonight, after everyone is asleep," he argued between clenched teeth.

"No, I must have it now and I only need a few more seconds." Aliyana rose from her chair, while keeping her hand cemented to the mouse.

"You're risking your life and this mission unnecessarily, Aliyana!"

Joris shook his head, strode through the wall and into the hallway. Wolf rolled his eyes heavenward and sighed as he clamped down on his jaw. Despite his impatience, his anger, maybe even his concern, she couldn't leave without this file.

"Just fifteen seconds more—almost—there!" She ejected the flash drive, yanked it out of the hub, and shut down the computer. Then, just as they vacated the office and entered the hallway, Joris halted their flight.

"You can't go down that hallway now," Joris said. "It's too late. Mercado is already inside the building and he's heading this way."

Aliyana hesitated for only a moment. "I'll have to go out the window then."

"What window?" asked Wolf. "There isn't a window inside the office."

"No, but there's one inside the room right there," she said, pointing to the door opposite and just down from the office.

"Let me see if anyone is inside," Wolf muttered. A half-second later, the lock clicked, and the door opened. He waved a frantic hand. "Come on, hurry."

By the time Aliyana entered the room, Wolf had already raised the window. Though he motioned her forward, his gaze was fixed on the hallway. Voices grew ever louder. She had indeed run out of time. Mercado now spoke with Hank just outside his office. Aliyana froze. The slightest movement would draw Emil's attention. Her heart raced and climbed up her throat. She looked at Wolf. His gaze darted between her, the men in the hallway, and then landed on Mercado.

Wolf grabbed hold of her hand. "Create a diversion, Joris!"

As the words left his mouth, Mercado headed toward the door which should not, under any circumstances, be open. Her heart sank. The drug lord yelled for his guards as he thrust Hank out of his way and barreled toward the room. In that same moment, Joris made himself visible and then stepped in front of the doorway. As Mercado looked on him with mouth agape, Joris kicked the door shut. He locked it as a multitude of footsteps raced down the hallway toward them. Mercado commanded his men to break down the door and shoot the intruder. In that same moment, Wolf scooped her up into his arms and swung her through the opening.

She tumbled out of the window to the sound of machine gun fire pelting the steel door. "Joris!' she gasped.

"He'll be out in a minute, keep moving!" Wolf commanded.

Aliyana crept through the vast array of tall coffea plants and wild brushwood. A few minutes later, she clambered over the same fence she used the day of her scheduled execution. Joris had yet to join them. "Wolf—"

He shook his head. "Not now, Aliyana, you must keep moving."

Wolf didn't let her stop until they were a good distance away from the compound. Once she caught her breath, she turned and searched the area behind them. Joris had yet to make an appearance. What if he was injured despite all claims to the contrary? She bit down on her lip. "Where is he?"

"He'll be along," Wolf said. "I'm sure he's making sure that no one follows us."

"Do you think they saw me?"

He shrugged. "I don't know. I hope not."

She dropped her gaze as she released a tattered breath. "Wolf, I'm so sorry."

As Wolf opened his mouth to speak, Joris popped into view. He gazed first at Wolf, and then at her. "Don't look so concerned, Aliyana. All is well."

"Are you sure? You don't look so well."

Joris laughed. "Just like a woman to worry over nothing. You needn't have. Those men couldn't hit the broadside of a ship at fifty paces in front of their face."

"Yes," said Wolf, "but the fact remains it might not have ended well for you."

"I know," she breathed out.

"Next time, do as I ask, please?"

"I will."

Wolf turned his attention to Joris. "Did they see her?"

He shook his head. "I don't think so. They never mentioned her name. From what I could tell, they just focused on me. I led them in the opposite direction for a while before I disappeared. I'm sure they're still out there searching."

"Good. Did we have anyone recording that conversation between Mercado and Hank when the events unfolded?"

"Yes, Cornelius and Pieter. They were, and still are, tailing them," he replied.

"All right, tell them to bring us the recorder at the first opportunity that presents itself. We'll know for sure then whether or not they suspect Aliyana may've visited the compound."

"Will do."

"Oh, and also make sure someone follows Hank when he leaves," Wolf added. "Find out where he's staying and who he communicates with in his down time. I'll take Aliyana back to the cave. After all this, she needs some rest."

"Aye, *Kapitein*." Joris disappeared.

Wolf gazed at her then. "Which way do you

propose we go?"

Aliyana swallowed past the dryness in her throat. "Our safest path is the river because of all the trees and bushes growing alongside the banks. They'll keep me hidden well enough. Once we get there, we can follow its course back to the cave. Any sound I make will blend in quite well with that of rushing water and jungle creatures."

Wolf didn't speak again until they were well past the danger of discovery. Not that she minded. She hoped it would give him an opportunity to calm down a bit.

"What were you thinking, Aliyana?" he hissed as they drew near the cave entrance. "You risked your life, not to mention the integrity of the mission, and all for your stubbornness. Do you understand that you were within seconds of discovery and faced the very real possibility of detection and death?"

So much for calming down. Aliyana sighed as she stopped to face his anger. She placed a light hand against his chest. "I'm sorry, Wolf. But you don't understand the importance of my find or that it'll take me quite a while to sift through everything inside that file. I thought it worth the risk if it gives us what we need now."

Wolf said nothing. He simply looked at her, the anger in his eyes still evident.

"I know you're angry and again, I'm sorry. But I knew without doubt, you would never have let Mercado get anywhere near me. If I didn't think that, I wouldn't have finished the download."

****

The comment took the wind right out of his sails.

As they resumed their journey, he shook his head and tsked. "So, tell me about your discovery."

"I stumbled across an email sent to Mercado that gave him the name and personal address of one of the DEA administrators on the hit list."

"You've lost me," he said. "What is an email?"

"Nothing more than an electronic letter. This one pretended to come from a cousin, with no signature at the bottom. I'm hoping that by tracing the header information, I can determine its author."

Wolf considered what she said. "And you're hoping to find other such letters in this file?"

"I think it's reasonable to assume we will," she said.

"Perhaps then, our author will get careless and reveal his identity," he mused.

"I sincerely hope so."

Aliyana tackled the task the moment they entered the cave. Despite all diligence, several hours ticked off the clock and all she had presented him were two letters bearing names and addresses of DEA administrators and their families. She leaned back against her chair, wiped at the moisture gathering at the corners of her weary eyes, and yawned. "I think I need a change in focus. Let's see if we can find out where the letters originated from," she murmured under her breath. She turned her attention away from Mercado's correspondence folder, and onto the three emails that needed deciphering.

"How do you go about doing something like that?" Wolf turned a chair around backwards and sat down beside her.

Aliyana pointed to the information found at the top

of the email. "I start with these numbers right here—they're called IP or internet protocol addresses. I'll trace them in reverse order. These addresses will give me the location of the servers the message passed through during its journey from the sender to Mercado's computer. While I'm at it, I'll hope that our man isn't the least bit computer savvy."

"Why are you hoping that?" asked Wolf.

"Because if he knows what he's doing, he can make it very difficult, if not impossible, to trace the point of origin, other than to say he used a host outside the United States. In all likelihood, we'll find it's one in Russia. If that's the case, then we've hit the end of the trail."

Aliyana spent the next several hours tracing each of the IP addresses. Just as she feared, the trail ended in Europe.

"Now what do we do?" asked Wolf.

"We keep looking," she replied as she swept a hand toward the computer screen. "As you can see, I still have hundreds of emails to sift through."

"Why don't you let me read through some of them while you get some sleep," Wolf said. "The sun will rise before you know it and you'll need some rest before it does."

"Well, if you don't mind, I think I'll take you up on that offer. I really could use some sleep and a fresh pair of eyes might be a good thing. Keep in mind that the emails are all in Spanish. Even so, that shouldn't make any difference in locating the emails we need. Names are still just names and you already know the important ones."

Wolf nodded. "The rest of the message won't make

any difference at this point. I'll mark the ones I think are of value, and you can read them once you awaken."

Aliyana rose from the chair and smiled as she drifted toward her bed. "Thank you, Wolf."

****

Wolf turned to his task and clicked the first unopened email on Aliyana's flash drive. Nothing caught his attention on that piece of correspondence— nor did he find anything of great importance on the five subsequent pages he sifted through, one tedious email at a time. That all changed the moment he read pages six and seven. They contained the rest of the emails that provided the DEA administration's personal information. Several other letters spoke of both Victoria Mendoza Torres and Aliyana. What's more, the emails listed on page seven mentioned the Turks and Caicos Island. In that letter, Jomini finally got careless. At least, with the signature containing the single letter J, he assumed Jomini authored the thing. That single letter might provide conclusive evidence that Jomini helped orchestrate the assassination plot. But what of Hank Morris? He hadn't found his name on any of the emails.

He turned his gaze toward the figure in the bed. Aliyana slept so peacefully he didn't have the heart to wake her with this new information. A few hours more wouldn't make any difference in their investigation. Pieter and Cornelius strode into the cave. Wolf lifted a finger to his lips as he cocked his head toward Aliyana first, and then nodded toward the cave entrance.

Once they stepped outside, Cornelius put a hand on Pieter's shoulder. "We followed Morris from the compound as per your orders. Unfortunately, our quest to find out where he lived took us to an airport. He boarded a flight bound for Nassau."

"Did you capture anything of significance on the recorder?"

"Nothing in English," he replied.

Pieter nodded. "But as far as the conversations with Mercado? Only Aliyana can decide if they're important or not."

"And as far as you are aware, he never once spoke to anyone associated with the DEA organization after leaving the compound?" asked Wolf.

"No, he didn't," said Cornelius. "In fact, the only English conversations we overheard had something to do with his bank account and something called 'wire transfer.' Then he had a couple of nauseating conversations with a woman—either his girlfriend or his wife. In my opinion, Aliyana needn't waste her time on either one of those."

"Do you think it even remotely possible that the conversation he had concerning his bank account might be coded words meaning something else entirely?"

"Not a chance," Cornelius replied. "Both his tone and facial expression verified he argued with someone at this bank. He mentioned something about a transaction fee for the wire transfer. He didn't want to pay it, and he made that abundantly clear to the harried clerk."

Wolf rubbed a hand back and forth against his beard. "That's even more damning."

"What is?" asked Pieter.

"The fact he never made contact with the DEA. If they sent him here to infiltrate Mercado's compound for any reason, then I'm of a mind to believe the man would surely have given them some kind of report once he vacated the premises, even if by code."

"Aliyana will probably beg to differ," Cornelius said.

"She'll say we're not seeing the entire picture," Pieter added. "She'll insist there's another side to his sordid little tale."

"She probably would," Wolf said. "She'll maintain that his full-fledged argument with the banker is nothing more than a clever ruse in case that someone out there is listening to his transmissions."

An exaggerated clearing of the throat caught Wolf's attention. He and his companions turned toward the sound. Aliyana gave him a saucy smile as she pushed away from the rocky wall she had used for support. She dropped her folded arms to her side, stepped out of the shadows and sauntered toward him.

She lifted a single brow as she approached. "Is that what she would say, do you think?"

Chapter Seventeen

"Without a doubt in my mind." Wolf didn't so much as display a shred of contrition. Instead, he met her gaze with directness, a slight bow of his head, and a cocky grin.

Cornelius's smile grew ever broader, as did the one Pieter hid behind the hand now rubbing against his mouth. Both men looked at each other as they fought to quash their humor, and then shrugged when they failed.

"Well—I suppose we'd better get back to the compound and look for another target to follow." Pieter winked at his cohort.

"Yes, you're absolutely right about that. We mustn't miss anything important." Cornelius offered her the recorder. Once she had it, he glanced at the cave entrance. "We'll uh, just dash inside and get us another one before we leave."

"Maybe you ought to just," she teased.

Once the men left, Wolf took hold of her hand and drew her close to his side. As he gazed into her eyes, he cocked his head in the direction away from the compound. "Let's take a walk, shall we?"

She drew in a breath and held it. Why did this single expression, the one that said nothing on this planet—regardless of dimension—mattered more than she did—always render her brain totally useless? And why, oh why, did the recollection of his 'elevator kiss' storm into her mind like an invading army bent on conquest right this minute?

Oh, but what a kiss it was, her heart whispered. In truth, she couldn't find a single particle of her entire body, or spirit, that kiss didn't affect. And it made her wonder how a man, devoid of his tangible form could bestow such a wondrous, magical kiss—

"Aliyana?"

His voice startled her out of her reverie. A guilty flush splashed onto her cheeks as she met his inquisitive gaze. "Hmm?"

A slight smile curved at the corner of his lip as they strolled away from the cave. Had he somehow guessed her thought? *No, surely not. Even ghosts in the true sense of the word couldn't read a person's mind, could they?*

"Did you get enough rest? I didn't think you'd get up quite this soon."

"Obvious by the conversation you just had with the boys," she replied.

"We didn't say a thing we wouldn't have said in your presence and have said in your presence, if you recall," he countered.

"True enough." She dropped her gaze and smiled over the lingering recollection of that kiss. *Get it out of your mind.*

"So did you?"

Once again, heat splashed onto her cheeks. "Did I what?"

Wolf stopped, turned toward her, and shook his head. "The question really isn't that difficult to follow, Aliyana. Did you get enough sleep, or did you not?"

"Oh, that." Aliyana laughed. "Too much,

apparently. I mean, you know you've had way too much sleep when you start dreaming about your work."

"You dreamed about work?"

"Yes, but it was just one of those crazy mixed-up affairs that doesn't make a lick of sense in the light of day," she said.

"We've all had dreams like that," Wolf said.

"Yes, and while we're on the subject of work, did you find any emails worth looking at while I slept?"

"A few, but let's talk about those after our walk, shall we? I think it's important, every now and then, to forget about the concerns of our jobs and refresh ourselves. At least for a while. Such is good for both mind and soul. Don't you think?"

Aliyana breathed out a laugh. "Yes, I do—wholeheartedly."

"All right then. During this walk, we'll pretend you're not a DEA agent. In fact, we'll pretend you haven't even heard of the organization. Deal?"

"Deal."

Somehow Wolf knew she needed this walk. The hour-long respite underneath the shade tree, his stories, his humor, the back-and-forth banter between them was pure delight. She realized that the minute they abandoned their tree and headed for the drudgery of the cave. The drudgery of computer screens and assassination plots—

As they strolled along the path, she closed her eyes. As the delightful scent of plumeria flowers wafted off the breeze, she took a deep breath, and slowly released it. "Thanks, Wolf. I truly enjoyed myself this morning."

"I'd have held you captive a bit longer, had it not been for the gathering storm clouds," he said.

Aliyana gazed toward the sky. The dark clouds, mingled with the rumble of distant thunder, warned of rain. Funny, she didn't notice the approaching storm while she and Wolf sat underneath the tree.

They arrived at the cave just as they were hit with the sudden deluge. While Wolf closed off the entrance, Aliyana leaned over the desk and turned on the computer screen. Wolf had left an email open.

"Cousin,

"All is going well for Grandfather's surprise party later this summer. Your generous donation assures that we'll have everything we need in place, and on time, to make this a most spectacular event.

"Oh, and by the way, I thought you'd like to know that my dear sister, Aliyana, has surfaced from her honeymoon retreat long enough to let us know the Montijos are fully enjoying themselves on the sandy beaches of the Turks and Caicos Islands. Of course, knowing Aliyana the way we do, I think we agree that she'll get it in her head to visit as many islands as she can before she assumes the ordinary life of an old married woman and comes home. I'll keep you updated on the party as well as any new messages from our elusive newlyweds.

Until later, J."

Aliyana read it twice. The date posted was the same day she attempted to contact the DEA. That meant the author pounced on her signal the moment it transpired. In turn, that meant Mercado asked him to watch for any telltale signs that she survived her escape from Colombia. Far more important than that, 'J,' a.k.a. Jomini, a.k.a. the mole, just handed her the evidence she needed to tie him to the assassination plot. She gazed at the rocky wall without really seeing it as unanswered questions flooded her mind.

"What exactly does that email say?" Wolf asked.

She sat down and scooted her chair forward. "Here, let me just read it so I don't leave anything out."

Wolf grabbed a chair for himself. As he settled in beside her, she translated the document into English, sentence by sentence. Once she read the final words of Jomini's correspondence, she met his gaze. "What are your thoughts?"

"First and foremost, would you agree that 'J' is Jomini?" he asked.

"Yes, and it's also evident from this letter alone that he's our mole."

"Can you tell me whom, within your organization, has unlimited access to the personal information concerning its key personnel?"

"I don't really know," she replied. "There are those in the organization who oversee all personnel records for payroll and taxes. How many work in that department? I have no idea. One can also assume the Administrator, the Deputy Administrators, and perhaps even their secretaries might have at least limited access as well. I'm a field agent, Wolf. I really don't know the inner workings of the office."

"We can't identify this man with any kind of certainty then," he mused aloud.

"No, we can't. Our best bet is to catch him in the company of Mercado or one of his lieutenants. I'm not sure that will ever happen, though. If the man is smart, he'll make sure it doesn't happen."

"Tell me, what is your theory about this man and the relationship he has with Mercado?" asked Wolf.

"Do you think that somewhere along the way they may have met face to face?"

"Possible but not probable. I don't think Jomini has ever allowed Mercado to see his face or hear his true voice. If he has any intelligence at all, he wouldn't risk it. Revealing any portion of his true identity would allow Mercado to hold all of the aces," she said. "And as for my theory? Something must have triggered Jomini to discard his allegiance to the Administration and trade away any dedication and loyalty he once had for monetary gain."

Wolf abandoned his chair and began a slow back-and-forth pace. "Desperation, greed, and vengeance are the usual triggers for such action, are they not?"

"I'd say so. Jomini might seek revenge if someone less worthy received a promotion he believed he earned. Perhaps he blames the DEA for a death of someone close to him. Those are just two scenarios that come to mind, but there are others. And desperation? That's a no-brainer. Our friend Jomini gets in over his head financially, either by his own careless actions or circumstances beyond his control. That could lead him to look for a quick and easy way out of his dilemma."

"Greed takes over, and since he didn't get caught the first time around, he finds the payoff worth what he now believes is a diminutive risk." Wolf paused and for a moment held her gaze. "I don't suppose you know anyone that might fit one or more of those categories?"

She shook her head. "No and trust me, I've tried to figure this out since the day I learned of the mole's existence. I've gone over the list of every person I know in the administration many times over. Nothing."

"What of Hank Morris?" he asked.

The question made her smile. "You won't like this, but I think I'll reserve judgment on Hank until I hear the conversation that took place between him and Mercado."

Wolf shook his head as he huffed out a breath.

She lifted a hand. "Wait just a minute before you say it."

"I didn't say anything," Wolf protested.

"You didn't have to. The expression on your face said it all. Anyway, at this point, I don't think Hank is an innocent bystander, although I might be proven wrong. However, I'm not so sure he is privy to the assassination plot."

"I might be inclined to agree with you there."

"You would? Why?"

"Because he spent almost an entire day entrenched in Mercado's drug enterprise, with the expansion of that enterprise uppermost in his mind. I'd think if he had involved himself in Jomini's plot, a discussion of the details would've taken precedence over his crop production."

"Those were my thoughts as well." She glanced at the computer. "Maybe we'll find some of the answers right here. I have recorded conversations that need translation and we still have all those emails to wade through."

"Can we share the computer?" asked Wolf.

"Share?"

"Can you listen to those conversations while I plod through the mail?"

"We certainly can. Come on." She patted the chair at her side. "I'll show you what the Spanish words for party and grandfather look like, so if you come across those again, you can mark them."

Hours passed swiftly enough while she listened to Hank's almost one-sided conversations with Mercado. They grew ever more obnoxious and boastful as the day progressed. She yanked off her headphones, tossed them, and closed her eyes.

"Finished?" asked Wolf.

She nodded. "Yes, thank goodness. I don't know if I could've listened to much more."

"What did you gather from those conversations?"

"One, Hank knows something about Jomini that's keeping him alive. Two, there isn't a shred of proof that tells us he knows anything about the assassination plot. So, there's our quandary."

"Tell me what you're thinking."

"Well, Hank never once mentioned anything to do with the plot. That seems odd to me since the date is looming ever nearer. Hank focused solely on increased production and what he thinks are clever ways to evade detection when entering the U.S. with contraband. Of course, all those ideas are quite expensive to initiate, but that shouldn't be a problem for someone as wealthy as Mercado, right?" she said, mocking Hank.

Wolf chuckled.

"Morris might not realize it, but every time he opened his mouth, he increased his chances of immediate torture and death. The fact that Mercado restrained himself tells me Hank knows something that either Mercado or Jomini, maybe even both, fear."

"If he knows something these men are afraid of, wouldn't his death be advantageous?" asked Wolf.

"Not if Hank has something on the two of them. Something that his death might trigger."

"If Jomini isn't ready to walk away from the DEA just yet, he would tolerate Morris's presence for the time being then," Wolf surmised.

"Very possible. I think Jomini's largest payoff will come at the conclusion of a successful end to this plot against the DEA," she said. "He'll wait until he is paid and gone before he takes care of Morris permanently."

"How will they do that if he has some kind of safety measure in place?" Wolf asked.

"I don't know," she said. "Perhaps Jomini believes he has his bases covered."

"Could be he's manufacturing evidence that'll place the blame on Morris. Hank gets convicted and Jomini walks free," Wolf said.

"You know, you might be right about that, Wolf." She gazed at the emails on the screen. "Maybe we'll find what we're looking for right there. You did say you found a few things that looked promising?"

"At the very least, I think there are a few that need your attention," Wolf said. He took charge of the mouse and clicked. "What is this email saying about you?"

"Well, let's see. It says that someone saw a woman matching my description in a Nassau hotel. Jomini assures Mercado they're making every effort to locate this woman."

"And this one?" asked Wolf.

"The woman in Nassau is the wife of the hotel proprietor. False alarm. They're continuing their search with all diligence."

"All right, this one mentions grandfather again," he said as he opened the file.

"Invitations to the party have been issued," she read. "I wonder what that means."

Wolf shook his head. "I don't know. Unless he's speaking of the men who will participate in the assassination itself."

"You could be right about that," she mused. "Mercado has men working inside the States who are assigned to handle incoming cargo. It makes far more sense to have those men work with the lieutenants, rather than taking men from here."

"Does your organization have the identities and locations of these men?" he asked.

"Not yet. They know they exist, of course, but right now, I'm the only one in possession of their exact identity and location, save Mercado. Obtaining that information was part of my undercover work."

"All right," said Wolf as he scrolled through the messages. "There's one more I think you should read. This one mentions Morris, I believe."

Aliyana gazed at the screen. "HM making himself a nuisance. Using vacation time for a visit to the area. Desires to collect his share of treasure now and in person. See that he receives his fair allotment of the cache without hindrance. All things are as they should be. You needn't worry at this juncture. All you need do is play along."

"Very interesting," murmured Wolf.

"And if you look at the date, you'll see that Jomini sent this email a few days before you witnessed the payoff inside Mercado's office," she said.

"Mercado did as Jomini instructed, but one could see that he loathed every moment spent in Hank's company."

"Given the circumstances, it's easy to see why."

"Well, one thing is certain," continued Wolf.

"Hank knows the true identity of Jomini. Since this is the case, we should concentrate more of our efforts on Hank. Given enough time, Hank just might lead us to Jomini."

"But we're running out of time, Wolf."

"Not too much we can do about that right now. The man boarded a plane for Nassau. We can't do a thing until he returns."

"No." She smiled. "We won't have to wait for his return. There are other ways to track Hank Morris, you know."

"How so?"

"Well, Hank did give us the name of his bank and account number," she said nodding toward a recorder. "I happen to know a hacker who can break into the bank and give us every shred of information inside his file. The file will contain things like his phone numbers, addresses, and at least one email account. Perhaps by using recent posts from his bank account, we can figure out where he is, and where he goes."

"You know this hacker personally?" he asked.

"Well, I've never met him in person," she replied. "But I've worked with him in the past."

"How did you pay him for his services?" he asked.

"Through a DEA slush account that in no way reflects the name of the organization. I simply wire the funds."

"Do you still have access to this slush account?"

"No, no I don't." She turned her gaze toward her trunk. "But I still have enough cash to pay him outright."

"Then you'd have to meet with him in person."

"Well, yes, but that—"

"No, that won't work then," Wolf interrupted. "As you've said, your photograph has circled the globe more than once. I'm certain a two-million-dollar reward exceeds whatever sum you might have tucked inside your trunk."

Wolf did have a point, but she had a solution. "Then you, or one of your men, must pay him for his services in my place. Just don't shake his hand."

He grinned. "That could work. However, we do have a language problem, do we not?"

"No, we don't. My friend speaks several languages. English is one of them and the fact you speak it with a Dutch accent will only gain his trust faster than you might otherwise receive it. Throw in some Dutch phrases, and you'll have him eating out of your hand."

"Now that is some excellent news."

"Isn't it though?" Aliyana laughed as she turned to the keyboard. "Let me make sure he's still around and willing to help us. I haven't contacted him for quite some time now."

Wolf studied the name of her contact. "Sombra?"

"The word means shadow—our hacker's moniker," she murmured. "All right, now all we have to do is await his reply."

Sombra responded within the hour. Aliyana breathed a sigh of relief as she read the message moments after its arrival. "He agrees to the price and selected a meeting place from off the list. There are just a couple of things though," she said as she eyed his clothing from top to bottom.

"What's that?"

"For one, you must wear a red and black poncho,

so that he'll recognize you. He also has a key phrase you must respond appropriately to, once prompted."

"Can you show me a picture of a poncho?" he asked.

"Yes, I can," she said as her fingers raced over the keyboard. Within seconds, she had several examples popping up on the screen.

Wolf stood and backed away from the chair. Aliyana stared in fascination as he instantly cloaked his shirt with an exact replica of the intricately woven poncho on the screen, using the requested colors.

"So what do you think, Miss Montijo," he said as he made a slow turn.

Aliyana's smile grew broader. "I think, Captain Dircksen Van Ness, that will do just fine. Now all we have to do is get to Soledad and back again without incident."

"Soledad?"

"That's where he's agreed to meet us," she said. "Don't worry. The municipality is really not that far from Barranquilla."

Chapter Eighteen

"Remember, Sombra already has the name of the bank, so don't make the mistake of repeating it. Should such a mistake occur, he'll leave before we complete our business," said Aliyana. "The man, like most hackers, is paranoid. As far as he's concerned, he tops everyone's most wanted list."

"Don't worry, I won't forget," he said yet again.

"Well, along with that reminder, I think we should go over the bank account number and the key code I set up for Sombra's use one more time. You can't stumble when you give both. If you do, he'll suspect you aren't who you say you are."

Wolf rolled his eyes and glanced heavenward as they journeyed up the Magdalena River. "Unnecessary, Aliyana. You're looking for something to worry about. I promise all will go exactly as planned."

"Things rarely ever go as planned," she countered. "You know this just as well as I do."

"Then let's just say we'll attain our objective and without a whole lot of interference. I think I've proven myself adaptable to all unexpected situations as I'm confronted with them."

"Yes, you've done that," she said. She lowered her gaze as just a touch of color stole across her cheeks.

"Then I wished you'd reconsider and stay inside the boat while I conduct the transaction. Like you said,

225

the entire exchange should take less than thirty minutes."

"Not a chance," she replied. "You just might find you need my help with a technical term I've overlooked."

He studied her ridiculous disguise. Yes, she'd produced a pair of dark brown contact lenses from somewhere inside that magic trunk of hers. Aliyana had also donned several layers of clothing, topped with a colorful shawl and a ragged scarf. She wound her hair in a tight knot on top of her head and painted gray streaks throughout her tresses. Hideous make-up that she'd painstakingly applied in the hope she looked older, only looked absurd. Anyone who gazed at her face and form for any length of time would see right through it.

"We'll be inside a darkened restaurant," she had argued. "I'll keep this tatty old-woman's scarf atop my head and keep my eyes down at all times. As I've said at least a hundred times now, I'll stay in the darkest corners of the room. No one will give me a second glance. I guarantee it. Besides, no one under the age of forty pays any attention to the elderly and you know it."

Why didn't any of her reassurances give him any comfort whatsoever? The woman simply didn't know how to keep herself out of danger.

"Wolf?" She shot a glance upward and gazed into his eyes.

"Yes?"

"Please don't worry so much," she said. "I'll be fine. I promise."

"I know that." He'd make sure of it—regardless of outcome. Hackers, and assassination plots, didn't matter a whit, if either threatened her life.

He shifted his gaze to the tiny device she held in her hand. How many times had she examined the thing since they boarded his boat? Still, the activity gave her something to do, he supposed. She plugged the thing inside her ear. Again.

She turned around, with her back facing him and hunkered down. "Can you hear me?" she whispered.

"Yes, I can," he replied, through his matching device. "But may I remind you, I can hear you quite well without the blasted thing."

"Yes, but without mine, I can't hear *you*." She straightened her shoulders and sighed. "Well, I think we're as ready as we'll ever be. Once we get in there and give him his fee, we'll leave."

"Yes, but once we give him the money, how do you know he'll keep his end of the bargain?" he asked. "Shouldn't we keep a portion of it until the job is complete?"

"No, that isn't necessary. Hackers build their reputation on satisfied customers. The more successful they are, the more money they can charge. I don't think any one of them would risk their reputation by failing to deliver on their promises. News like that would spread rather quickly. Even more important than that, I've learned hackers live for the thrill of the challenge. Each successful hack gives them that highly desired dose of adrenalin."

They crossed the rest of the river in silence. Wolf suspected that despite all preparation, and all his efforts, she still worried over an insignificant detail she might've missed. Even if such should prove the case, it didn't concern him. In less than an hour, they'd meet with a man who very much wanted the money they offered. Therefore, he'd surely overlook a few missteps, should they occur.

After they climbed out of the boat, he scouted the area. He didn't see a soul, detect any movement, or hear a single breath or heartbeat in the vicinity.

"All's clear." He helped her out of the vessel and then tied it off.

She spared him a quick glance before she moved ahead. "I'll lead the way. Keep a respectable distance behind me. We don't want anyone to suspect we're together, least of all Sombra," she whispered over her shoulder.

"Aliyana—" He paused where he stood and waited until she stopped. She turned around and faced him. "No one can see or hear me right now, but you."

A small smile grew ever broader. "Oh yeah. I forgot."

As he took hold of her hand he gazed into her eyes. "Once I have you safely inside the restaurant, in the darkest possible corner, I'll leave the building. Then, in case Sombra is watching, I'll step out of the most convenient vehicle in the vicinity. I'll go back inside the restaurant, select a table, and wait," he said. "In the meantime, you won't move a muscle or talk to a soul. Don't even speak with me unless it's necessary. Agreed?"

"I've promised that at least a million times already, but here we go again." She crossed her heart with the tip of her index finger to seal their bargain.

Wolf followed each step of the plan to the letter and surprisingly, so did Aliyana. He sat at the table and sipped something called Monserrate Roja. Once he finished the drink, he opened the book with the hacker's fee sprinkled throughout the pages. As he pretended to read, the young woman in the corner across from Aliyana cast furtive glances in his direction. Centuries of experience told him that in the next few minutes, she'd rise from her table and approach him.

If nothing else, the woman found herself attracted to him. Thus, he had passed Sombra's first test without saying a word. He wondered then, why Aliyana seemed so certain their hacker was male. The woman rose from her seat and sauntered toward him—just as he expected. She flashed a coquettish smile, just as he expected.

"*Buenos tardes.*" She slowly turned her body from side to side.

Wolf held up a hand and shook his head. "Sorry, I don't speak a word of Spanish."

"Then it's a good thing I speak, English, no?" she countered.

Wolf kept eye contact with the lady as he closed the book. "Please sit down. I think I have time to buy you a drink before I leave."

"But we haven't been introduced, and I never sit down with strangers. So, shouldn't we take care of first things first?" she asked, giving him the exact phrase in which he must give a proper response.

"Call me anything you like," he said. "Forgive me if I prefer the shadow of anonymity."

Her smile broadened as she sat down in the chair opposite his. "You're not from around here."

"Obvious," he said, meeting her gaze.

"Would you care to tell me what brings a handsome man with a delightful European accent to Colombia?"

"No, not really," he said.

Sombra burst out laughing. "I like you. You're direct."

"Then you'll understand my desire to proceed with the business at hand." He signaled for the waitress who hustled over to his table. "Another one, please," he said pointing toward his glass. "And the lady will have—?"

"The same," she replied.

Sombra placed her elbows on the table and rested her chin on top of her hands. All the while she kept her dark brown gaze glued to his. She didn't move so much as an inch to accommodate their server. Not even when the woman released heavy sighs of exasperation as she attempted to place the ordered beverage in front of the attractive hacker.

From the corner of his eye, Wolf saw Aliyana stop the waitress as the woman approached her table. She uttered something in Spanish and the beleaguered woman nodded. He resisted the need to roll his eyes. Instead, he slid the book toward his guest.

"I've just finished reading it," he said. "In my opinion, it's a very good book. Perhaps you might find it entertaining as well."

She turned it around, flipped through the pages and nodded. "I might, thank you."

Just as she extended a hand toward his arm, Wolf dropped his napkin. He scooted the chair just out of her range, picked up the napkin, and set it on top of the table. A brief look of consternation shot across her features. Nonetheless, he folded his arms against his chest and gave her a friendly smile.

Sombra took her glass and slowly raised it to her lips as she regarded him.

"Perhaps when you finish the book you can let me know what you think," he said, nodding towards the volume.

"I read pretty fast. I think I can have this book finished in just a couple of days. So, if you'll give me your number, I'll certainly share my opinion."

"I have two numbers, actually. Do you have something you can write with?"

"That won't be necessary. I have a very good memory," she replied.

"The most important number is 6394060098 and if you find you need the second, it's 8687940307. Would you like them repeated?"

Sombra lifted a brow and cleared her throat. She then repeated the numbers. "Correct?"

"Correct." Wolf withdrew some cash from his pocket that more than covered the cost of the drinks and tossed the bills onto the table. "I'm sorry, but I must cut our meeting short; I have a plane to catch. So, if you'll excuse me?"

Sombra pushed her glass to the side and leaned as close as she could get without knocking over the table. Aliyana huffed out a breath. Wolf heard the sound without the ear device, even though Sombra couldn't. Nonetheless, he held a tight rein over his amusement.

"Why don't you take a few more minutes and come with me? I could show you my state-of-the-art equipment. I don't live very far from here," she purred. "The tour shouldn't take much of your time. I think you'll be impressed with what you might, um, encounter. I promise you'll still have plenty of time to catch your plane."

Yanking out her earpiece, Aliyana bounded to her

feet. Her cheeks blazed as she shoved the device inside her pocket and marched toward their table despite the pretense of her earlier limp.

His little spitfire was about to explode. Time to leave and the sooner the better.

"I'm sorry," he said, keeping his tone casual. "But I really do have a plane to catch and—my heart is already taken. I'm sure you'll understand." He winked as he rose from the chair.

Before Sombra could respond, Aliyana snatched a plate of someone's leftover fritanga from off a nearby table. As she passed his table, she 'accidentally' dumped the entire contents into Sombra's lap. The woman sputtered and jumped up from the table. She grabbed a napkin and dabbed furiously at her clothes. The hacker whirled toward Aliyana.

"*Aye vieja! Mire de lo que estas haciendo!*" Sombra spat between clenched teeth.

Aliyana dipped her head and tried very hard to look contrite. He tried very hard not to laugh out loud over the exchange. He took that moment and slipped out the door. On his way out of the room, he passed the waitress, as she carried a plate of steaming hot, heavily-sauced tamales toward Aliyana's table. Wolf chuckled, knowing Sombra got off easy.

****

"*Aye, lo siento tanto, por favor permite me ayudarle.*" Though Aliyana apologized, she wasn't the least bit sorry. She grabbed the dirtiest napkin she could find from off a neighboring table and offered it to Sombra.

"*Ya hiciste suficiente, yo no nesacito tu ayuda!*" snarled Sombra. She stamped down hard on her foot and flung the soiled napkin in her direction. Fortunately for her, she missed her target.

Aliyana bit down on her lip to mask a victorious smile. Yes, everything the hacker said during her little hissy fit hit the mark. Though she had 'done enough' it would've given her additional satisfaction to add the food she ordered earlier. But if she didn't leave now, Wolf would worry over her absence. Without anyone the wiser, she palmed one of the larger bills Wolf left on the table and placed it on top of her own. She resumed her limp and hobbled out of the restaurant.

She spied Wolf the moment she cleared the door. He leaned a shoulder against the brick wall just outside and across from the restaurant. The toe of his boot rested against the sidewalk. He met her gaze with a mischievous grin.

"Would you mind explaining what provoked that incident?" he asked as she arrived at his side.

She didn't meet his gaze. Instead, she gave her head a little toss as she sniffed. "We should get home well before dawn, should we not?"

"We should," he replied.

"Well, then we needed to get going." She turned toward the alley and the path that led to the river. "From what I could see, our little hacker didn't seem the least bit amiable toward that goal."

Wolf chuckled as he took her hand, twined his fingers through hers, and drew her close to his side.

"Is something funny?" she asked, giving him a sideways glance.

Wolf shook his head as he struggled to control his amusement. "Nope, not a thing."

Aliyana looked up at the stars as they slipped into

the protection of the dense vegetation. While they walked, she reflected on the events inside the restaurant. Her actions should mortify her, but they didn't. Rather, she felt strangely exhilarated.

Besides, she reasoned, the woman received no more than what she deserved. Sombra had no call to flirt with Wolf during a business meeting. If that wasn't the most tawdry, unprofessional behavior on this planet then she didn't know what was. Wolf didn't encourage her wanton behavior. He didn't respond to her brazen overtures either, even though it might've helped further their cause. So, just what did the woman hope to accomplish?

"Aliyana?"

"Hmm?"

"Why did you think our hacker was a male?"

She elevated her nose a tad as she tightened her grip on her shawl. "Because that's how she portrayed herself on the net. Among other things, her résumé included membership inside an all-male brotherhood of self-proclaimed hackers. I'm sure she used the ruse as an additional way to protect her identity. However, she sure didn't have any trouble revealing her true gender to you this evening, did she now?"

Wolf shrugged as they finally approached the river. "No, but then, given the circumstances, maybe she had no other choice. We told her my stay in Colombia would be brief. Therefore, I don't think she had time to find a decoy she could trust, even if such a thought entered her mind."

"I suppose you could be right." Aliyana stopped by the river bank and removed some of the bulky, cumbersome clothing. Before boarding the boat, she wrapped them inside her shawl, and tossed the bundle aboard.

"Give me just a minute to wash up," she said as she removed the clip from her hair and shook her tresses loose. She scooped up a handful of water and splashed it against her face, then scrubbed off the itchy make-up. After washing out the hair paint, she plucked the contacts and sent them floating down the river.

She felt like a drowned rat and probably looked like one too.

Wolf nodded his approval and grinned. "Much better."

Aliyana laughed as she wiped the dripping water away from her face. "Well, at the very least, I feel better. The makeup made my face feel tight."

Wolf helped her into the boat. As he pushed off the bank, he climbed in beside her. "Speaking of your lovely face, I hope and assume our hacker didn't get a good look at it?" he asked.

She shook her head. "We're safe. As I said, the young pay very little attention to the aged and infirm. And by necessity—Sombra focused her attention—elsewhere."

Amusement crept into his eyes. "Tell me, given the time, would you really have dumped that entire plate of steaming slop onto her lap?"

"Yep, without any hesitation whatsoever," she replied.

"Remind me never to get on your bad side, Miss Montijo."

"Oh, I don't think you have anything to worry about." She tilted her head to the side and met the intensity of his gaze head on. "I think it'd take quite a bit for you to end up on my bad side."

"Good to know," he said.

Their return trip only took half the time, or at least it seemed that way. Why did time spent in Wolf's company always pass so quickly? Hours passed like mere minutes. Maybe it felt that way because they had precious little time left. In just about a month, they'd complete their mission in one way or another. She gazed at the cave entrance with a strange mix of reluctance and resignation.

Joris strode outside. He looked excited about something. "I must say, you two picked a fine time to leave on your little outing," he said. "I want you to know I felt as if I waited bloody forever for your return."

"Why? What's going on?" asked Wolf.

"About eight hours ago, Mercado conducted a meeting with all his lieutenants," he replied. "As luck would have it, I returned for a fresh battery. While I switched them out, I glanced at the computer screen and wouldn't you know? I caught sight of Mercado speaking with his men inside the boardroom. To sum it all up, I think I have most of the meeting recorded on video for you. If not, I know some of the men will surely have the entire conversation stored on their recorder."

Aliyana took in a sharp breath as Joris delivered his news. Her excitement escalated as she made a beeline for the computer and sat down. A half minute later, she isolated the boardroom video, turned up the volume, and clicked the play option. Wolf grabbed a chair and sat down beside her. Several times throughout the meeting, she met Wolf's inquisitive gaze. Yet he didn't speak or interrupt while the video played. Finally, as the lieutenants filtered out of the room, she turned the recording off, and faced her companions.

"Should I assume this meeting concerned the assassination plot?" he asked.

Aliyana nodded. "Yes, it did. But there's more. I'll listen to this a couple of times and take some notes, but—" She paused as her mind raced in a thousand directions all at once. What Mercado said took her by complete surprise.

"But what?" he prodded.

"Mercado plans to kill two birds with one stone, so to speak."

"What do you mean by that?" asked Joris.

"A few weeks prior to the scheduled termination date, his lieutenants will escort millions of dollars' worth of drugs into the United States. They'll disperse them at a specific time and specific place chosen by Jomini. From there the men will make their way to Virginia for the final showdown."

"Did he provide us with any of the details?" asked Wolf.

She shook her head as she shrugged. "No, he didn't."

"Is there any way we can find them out?" he asked.

"Not unless those missing facts come through in an email or a phone conversation. We'd also have to be lucky enough to get a hold of them. The thing is, Mercado might already have this information. If so, he won't speak of it until the last possible moment, if at all."

"We must keep someone with him at all times then," Wolf replied.

"There's one more disturbing thing." She looked back and forth between the men.

"What's that?" asked Joris.

"Mercado usually transports his drugs by way of an aircraft or cigar boat, but—"

"What is a cigar boat?" Wolf interrupted.

She waved a hand in dismissal. "Nothing more than a speed boat, built to outrun the coastguard. Although they're not always successful in that attempt. They've also used handcrafted, semi-submersible submarines. They can be difficult, but not impossible, for the coastguard to detect. But this time—this time they're loading the drugs and transporting them inside a full-fledged personal submarine."

"What do you mean?" Wolf asked.

Aliyana shrugged. "Just that. He told his lieutenants that he purchased a 'luxury' submarine at a fraction of the cost. Translated, this probably means someone captured or stole the thing. He said the vessel has more than enough room to carry the lieutenants, crew, and the contraband."

"Interesting development," said Joris.

"Yes, it is." She rubbed her fingers across her forehead and closed her eyes. "But what are we going to do now?"

Chapter Nineteen

Aliyana leaned back against her chair and studied the cryptic email. The thing didn't make a lick of sense, even decoded. Or did it? She typed the first word that just didn't mesh with anything else, along with the number one hundred fifty into the search engine and hit enter. Despite the thirty-five thousand hits, nothing of importance jumped out at her. Then, on a hunch, or perhaps simple desperation, she added the word 'submarine' alongside the word 'barracuda' that she had previously typed. She hit enter again. This time the search yielded a single hit. She didn't need any more than that.

"Wolf?" she called out without lifting her gaze from the screen.

His hands rested on her shoulders as he leaned over her shoulder. "Did you find something?" he asked.

She pointed at the picture on the website. "I think this is the submarine Mercado purchased from the black market. What's more, I think he purchased the craft somewhere in Asia."

"What makes you think that?" he asked as he settled into the chair next to hers and scooted a bit closer.

"Because that's where I traced the IP addresses off the header, although that might be another false lead," she said. "But look at the internet brochure. It says this sub can dive to a depth of three hundred meters and will hold up to sixteen people. Just look at it. The thing is perfect for his needs."

"Let me take a look at the vessel's specifications before you scroll down," he said.

The one-inch banner emblazoned with the words, "The Barracuda" seemed to steal his attention away from the section he asked for. He turned away from the screen and gazed at the cave wall.

"Is something wrong?" she asked.

He turned toward her. For a moment they simply gazed at each other. Finally, he said, "I think Hank Morris has something to do with the submarine."

"Why do you say that?"

"Because I just remembered something. Do you recall the day we entered the compound and fixed the cameras?"

She nodded. "Of course, I do."

"Hank had a conversation with Mercado out in the hallway just before he went inside the office. At that time, I understood two words. He mentioned the word 'barracuda' alongside a word that sounded like 'dolphin.' At the time I believed he chattered on about fishing and didn't give it any more consideration than that, but now—" He swept a hand toward the screen.

"Mercado has no interest in fishing. I'm not even sure he would recognize the word barracuda as an ocean dwelling creature," she said. "Your scenario would make sense though, since he gave Hank a great deal of money a few minutes later."

"The email did indicate a payoff. Perhaps Hank brokered the deal and then collected a finder's fee for acquiring the sub," Wolf said. "Whatever the case, we now must rethink Hank's involvement. If he knows about the sub, does he also know about the assassination plot?"

"Maybe our little hacker friend will shed some light on this mess," she said. "Or at least provide information that will point us in the right direction."

"We should be hearing from her any time now," he replied. "She did tell me it would only take a couple of days. Have you checked for a reply yet?"

Aliyana grabbed the mouse. "No, I haven't. But don't pin your hopes on what she said. She just might make you wait a day or two longer out of spite."

"I don't see any reason why she should do something like that."

Quiet laughter accompanied a sideways glance. "After almost four hundred years, you still know so little of women. I find that interesting, Captain Wolfaert Dircksen Van Ness—"

"Okay, I'll bite." He cleared his throat in an exaggerated manner. "How would I have earned her spite in such a short amount of time?"

"Well, by not succumbing to her charms or accepting her blatant invitation to 'tour' her lodgings, you dissed her. Therefore, she'll get even in her own little way. Right now, the only way to accomplish that goal is by making you wait."

He seemed totally baffled by her statement. He drew his brows together. "Dissed?"

"Dismissed, humiliated, scorned, take your choice," she said. "Any one of them will do."

"Oh, come on, I didn't do anything like that," he said.

She nodded with tongue in cheek. "Oh, yes—yes

you did."

"I think you're way off the mark, here. After my explanation, I don't think she could possibly have taken offense over my inability to accept her invitation."

"Oh what—your song and dance about needing to catch a plane?" she asked as she shot a glance heavenward and laughed. "Lame, Wolfaert, lame."

"No."

For a moment or two, he didn't speak. He simply caressed her face with just his gaze. In response, a warm flush spread throughout her body.

"I simply told her that my heart was already taken."

The bottom of her stomach gave way. The overwhelming power of his gaze first captivated and then bound her with a mesmerizing spell. She couldn't break it. Somewhere in the back of her mind, she wondered if he meant what he just said, or did he tell Sombra that to keep his cover?

"Wolf!" called Laurens as he strode into the cave. "You've got to come and see this thing for yourself. But you must hurry in the outside chance it's gone before we get back."

The spell shattered, they stood simultaneously and turned toward him. Aliyana had trouble finding her voice.

"See what?" asked Wolf.

"Mercado's submarine has arrived in all her glory." Laurens bounced his eyebrows and grinned. "She's a beauty, too. That vessel rose right up out of the water fairly close to the *Wieven*. I think they chose that spot for its seclusion, just as we did, ourselves."

"Are any of the men from the compound down

there now?" asked Wolf.

"Quite a few of them, actually," Laurens replied. "We could tell something was up the minute Mercado called for his lieutenants and several of his more trusted henchmen. They all boarded a bunch of those cigar boats Aliyana told us about and took off. So, of course, we followed."

Wolf thrust a thumb toward the computer. "Tell me something, does the sub look like that one right there?"

Laurens took a step closer and peered down at the screen. He nodded. "Yep, that's her, all right. The thing kind of resembles a yacht, don't you think?"

Wolf cocked his head toward the entrance. "Give us a minute, will you?"

"Aye, *Kapitein*, I'll be right outside."

Aliyana's mouth dropped. She stared at Wolf as Laurens departed. He wasn't taking her with him. She could see it in his eyes and the firm set of his jaw. At once, she shook her head. "No, Wolf. You can't leave me here."

"Aliyana, the sub is quite a distance from here," he argued. "There's a travel issue for you, which doesn't affect us. You know this."

"I don't care about the travel issue," she huffed. "I can take the boat and row it myself if you're in such an all-fired hurry. After all, while I'm inside, I'm invisible, right? No one will see me."

"Please, Aliyana," he said as he took hold of both her hands and drew them close to his heart. "You heard Laurens. I can't take the chance that one of them will see you in broad daylight."

"I can keep hidden, you know I—"

Before she finished her sentence, he put a gentle

finger against her lips. "I know you can, *lieveling*. I've seen you do it. But no matter how well you stay out of sight, there's still a chance someone will stumble across you. What if one of the men relieves himself exactly where you're standing, or a wild animal catches your scent? Please, for my sake, stay here. I promise you—I absolutely promise you—that once the men have left the area, I'll come back and get you."

She closed her eyes, dipped her head, and released a ragged breath.

"I'm begging you Aliyana," he whispered. "For me. Please?"

What could she say to that? "All right, if you insist. I've plenty here that can keep me busy, I suppose. While I'm at it, I'll look for emails from Sombra."

He let go of her hands and assumed the expression that unfailingly weakened her knees. She managed a smile as she took a half-step back. He winked and then turned toward the cave entrance. Before he took a single step, he unexpectedly paused for a moment and turned back around.

With gentle fingers, he traced the side of her cheek and brushed her hair away from her face. "Just in case the question crossed your mind? I meant what I said to Sombra."

****

Wolf grinned in triumph as he joined Laurens outside. A short while ago, the thought of rendering Aliyana speechless seemed a lofty goal. But, he'd just accomplished it with a simple statement of truth. Perhaps at the end of their mission, he could do it again. He'd whisk her out of this dimension, and into his own. For he could not—and would not—leave this place without her, not when he loved her so deeply, and she loved him in return.

"Do they have a Spanish speaking crew piloting the sub?" Wolf asked, as just minutes later, they approached the sleek vessel near the bank of the river.

"They do, and by the look of things, I believe Mercado has hired that crew to pilot the craft. We're recording all the conversations though. If we're wrong about that assumption, Aliyana can tell us."

Wolf examined every inch of the exterior shell before he dropped down inside. From below deck he analyzed the inner workings of the vessel. He studied the mechanics of the single engine in depth before he joined his first mate inside the cockpit.

"What do you think of her?" asked Joris as his eyes scanned the instrument panel.

"Impressive," Wolf replied. "Have you spotted any weaknesses we can use to our advantage?"

"No. Well, at least not yet. This ship has been put together rather well," he replied. "However, we can empty out her fuel tanks easily enough if that's the route we choose. We could leave the scum at the bottom of the sea well before they carry out their plans. If you'd rather, we can also rob the sub of her power, and hand Mercado's men over to the authorities just before they run out of oxygen."

Wolf paused as he considered the choices. "The latter choice gives the DEA control of their jurisdiction. We could radio the position of the sub before we disable her and let whoever is listening take it from there."

Joris shrugged his indifference. "Whichever you choose. Either way we can stop the assassination plot well before it spills into Virginia. Mission all but accomplished."

They emerged through the hatch just as Mercado and his men vacated the main deck and climbed aboard their cigar boats. Johannes, Cornelius, Pieter, and Conrad jumped aboard as well. Wolf returned their salutes with one of his own as the boats headed toward the compound. The rest of his men gathered around him while the sub crew roamed around the main deck, in full view.

"These men won't sit at the bottom of the river indefinitely," Wolf said. "They don't look as if they have the patience for it."

"No, they don't," Klaus replied.

"I wonder if that means Mercado will load his contraband and take off sooner than we expected," Wolf mused aloud.

"I wondered that as well," Joris said. "According to Mercado's timetable, we're less than a month away from the assassination date. Within that time frame, the man must load this ship, sail to an unknown destination, and unload her contraband. They then must arrive in Virginia in a sufficient amount of time to set up and carry out the planned assault."

"I should think they'd need several days to bring that portion of their plans together," Klaus added.

"At the very least," Joris said.

"Especially when you take into consideration these men have never worked together." Wolf shook his head over the stupidity of that fact. "According to the internet website, this ship has a maximum speed of ten knots. That will be a factor in determining the date of departure as well."

"As will the place they intend to unload Mercado's haul," Joris replied. "Sailing to the Keys would take far less time than, say, heading somewhere in the Gulf of Mexico."

"All right, Joris," Wolf said. "I think I'll leave you here, so you can keep an eye on things. Laurens, I need you at the cave. But first, go back to the compound and let the boys know I'm packing up and bringing Aliyana to the ship. We'll handle our remaining business from here. That way if we must follow the sub at a moment's notice, nothing will hold us back. Andries, I'll need your help in moving Aliyana's equipment out of the cave and onto the *Wieven* as well, if you don't mind."

"Should I attach our line to the sub now or wait until we reach open sea?" asked Joris.

They didn't carry a full three hundred meters by any means, nor could they get any more in the strength required here. But then he didn't really expect the Barracuda would dive that deep, anyway. Wolf gazed at his first mate. "Even though they haven't processed all the drugs yet, I think it's wise to get it done now—just in case. After all, we have no idea when or where they'll load their drugs."

"Consider it done."

"Then let's get to it," he replied.

In less than five minutes, Wolf entered the cave, with Andries a single step behind. Aliyana looked up from her work and took in both their faces.

"Is something wrong?" she asked as she rose from her chair, pencil in hand.

"No, nothing is wrong," he said. "Our strategy needs an adjustment to accommodate this new development in Mercado's plans."

"In what way?" she asked as she tossed her pencil aside.

"By moving our operations to the *Wieven* now, rather than later."

"But Wolf, your ship is too far away from the compound. If I need to get there in a hurry—"

"I can't think of a single reason that would necessitate your return to that place," he cut in. "Can you?"

She shook her head slightly as confusion beset her features. "Well, what if I must go back in and retrieve the latest emails? The ones I have right now might not give us all the information we need."

"If that proves necessary, I can go in and get them for you. Problem solved. There's nothing inside the compound that I, or a member of my crew, can't take care of from this moment on in our mission," he said.

Andries stepped forward then and placed a hand on his shoulder. "Excuse me, *Kapitein*, but what items shall we take with us, and what should we move first?" he asked.

"Aliyana?" asked Wolf.

She gazed about the room, clasped her hands together, and shrugged. "The only things we really need are my trunks, the electronic equipment, and my personal belongings. We can leave the lights and fuel powered generator behind. I will, however, need all of my spare batteries. The order we empty out the chamber doesn't really matter."

Andries set straight to the task. Wolf waited until Aliyana had packed her electronic equipment and personal belongings before he took hold of her hand. "There are a few things I'd like to talk to you about before we leave. Come for a short walk with me?"

"Of course."

They met Laurens coming into the cave, as they were on their way out.

"All set, *Kapitein*," he said. "Everyone is aware of the change and will meet at the ship, henceforth."

"Very good," he said as cocked his head toward the cave. "Give Andries a hand in there, will you? We'll be back shortly."

"Will do." He saluted and entered the cave.

Wolf led her toward the valley. She didn't say a word as they followed the now familiar path. Once they stepped under the shade of their tree, he took in a breath, and turned around to face her. *Where to begin?*

"Despite what you might think, the submarine is the best thing that could've happened," he said. "That's because we can stop the assassination plot at the time and place of our choosing."

"How?" she asked. "How can you possibly track the submarine once it dives under water? You didn't, by chance, bring your own sub along with you, did you?"

He grinned as he gave her hand a gentle press and leaned back against the tree. "No, we didn't."

"Then what are your plans?"

"By now, Joris should've attached a line from our vessel to the submarine. This metal line is unbreakable and just as invisible to their eyes as my ship is. As the sub tows us toward its destination, we can choose when and where we seize control of the vessel. Once we drain her power, we can send a radio message to the proper authorities—"

"The coast guard is our best bet," she said off-handedly. "If you can get close to Puerto Rico, you can use the radio inside the sub to contact them. I know they'll help."

"The coast guard it is then. We'll give them control and let them handle the vessel, its contents, and occupants, however they choose. The important thing is that Mercado's lieutenants and his drugs will never reach their destination. Emil Mercado guaranteed the safety of the DEA administrators and their families the moment he purchased the *Barracuda* and decided to use it to carry out his plot."

He held her gaze as a slight smile appeared at the corners of her mouth. She took in a deep breath and let it go. "That's excellent news. Then we need only concentrate on uncovering the mole's identity. We'll find out Hank's true purpose and capture Mercado. And—we should accomplish that before the sub sets sail. Because if we don't finish this now, Emil Mercado will simply start over and with the mole's help, grow even stronger the second time around."

Wolf chuckled. "Now, how did I know you were going to say that?"

"Because you know I'm right," she said.

"Yes, and I also know this is the most dangerous part of this mission. A cornered animal usually comes out with teeth bared and claws unsheathed."

"I know. We'll just have to be extra careful."

"That means not taking any chances, Aliyana," he said in a stern tone.

"Don't be absurd," she replied. "You know as well as I do that some risks must be taken in order to accomplish this goal."

"Not the risks we can take for you," he countered. "Let us handle those things we're best suited for, agreed?"

She said nothing. Instead, her gaze roamed out across the valley. As she combed her fingers through her hair, she viewed the brilliant colors created by the setting sun. He had no idea where her thoughts had taken her, but he wouldn't let her leave this spot until she made him this promise.

He turned her face toward him. "Agreed?"

"Oh, Wolf, I just don't know how I can make you such a—"

"I do know. You must stay safe, Aliyana. Because once this is all over and we've achieved our goals, you'll leave this dimension. You'll then come home with me. You'll come home with me because I love you, far more than you know." Wolf gathered her into his arms and held her as close as he could. He hadn't intended to do this now, but perhaps a better time just didn't exist—

He cupped the sides of her face. "I've looked for you my whole life and now that I've found you, I can't lose you. You mustn't ask that of me, for that's the one thing that has the power to destroy my heart as well as my soul."

Her eyes widened in surprise. Her hands trembled as they rested lightly against his chest.

"Wolf—" she gasped, just before he claimed her lips in a thorough, unhurried kiss. He followed that kiss with another that proclaimed his love in no uncertain terms. She responded to both with equal passion.

"Come with me," he said again, pressing his advantage. "Please?"

She looked both stunned and amazed. "Well, I don't—I think maybe we should just take one day at a—"

"No, Aliyana. Don't run away from me now. Underneath the dancing lights of the aura borealis, you already promised. But I need to hear you say it again and this time, without the assistance of dreams. I want you to make me this promise because you love me just as much as I love you. Promise me that you'll marry me the moment our mission is finished and come home with me. Promise me."

Tears welled up in her eyes. She wavered for what seemed like forever. Then, by expression alone, he could see she had made her choice. The depth of love she expressed within her gaze alone humbled him.

"I promise," she said as a tiny tear trickled down her cheek.

He wiped it away as his lips hovered above hers. "Because?"

Just as he had once before, deep inside her subconscious thoughts, he drew the word out. She must make the admission vocally, not only for his benefit, but for hers as well.

She closed her eyes and whispered, "Because I love you—so very, very, much."

He claimed another kiss, to seal the vow.

Chapter Twenty

Sometime later, and she didn't know, nor did she care, how much time had passed, they re-entered the cave, Wolf's kisses still warm on her lips. But this time she walked in after having made a life-altering decision. Did that decision frighten her? Perhaps just a little bit. Yet Wolf made a promise in return. He said he'd never leave her, under any circumstances. That even death could not separate them. Those promises helped diminish her fears. Just as she had in the dream he somehow shared with her, she surrendered her heart to the handsome captain of the *Witte Wieven*. She discovered it didn't cause any undue suffering or pain. Only a smidgen of uncertainty and trepidation remained. Wolf vowed he'd overcome those as well.

"Looks like they have just about everything cleared out of here," Wolf said.

She nodded as her gaze wandered over the chamber and then landed on her bulging backpack on top of her now bare, makeshift bed. Her hand flew to her mouth as she turned to face him. "Oh! In all the confusion, I forgot to tell you that Sombra sent the results of her hack. A very successful hack at that, by the way."

A slow wicked grin appeared.

"Did I confuse you, my love?" he asked, using a husky tone.

A breath of laughter accompanied the shake of her head. "I think I'll take the fifth on that."

"The fifth?" he asked.

"Yes. The Fifth Amendment to the Constitution of the United States. It gives me the right to avoid self-incrimination. Didn't you ever read it? If not, you should. It's an amazing document."

Wolf chuckled. Just as he dropped a light kiss on her lips, Laurens and Andries entered the cave. The men didn't make any attempt to hide their broad grins or their approval.

"Now we wouldn't be interrupting anything important in here, would we?" asked Laurens as his eyes sparkled with mirth.

"Would you care if you did?" countered Wolf as he approached the bed.

Laurens stroked his chin, glanced toward the ceiling, and then shook his head. "Naw, I don't think so."

"I thought not." Wolf picked up the backpack and turned toward the entrance. "Let's get the rest of this stuff and get out of here, shall we?"

Under the stars and a waning moon, they traveled toward the boat. From the boat, they crossed the rivers to the ship that bore the name of the legendary *Witte Wieven*. Aliyana thought of the woman who inspired it then and wished she could somehow thank her for saving her captain's life. She couldn't imagine a single day without him at her side.

With the aid of the lighted viewports, Aliyana gazed at the submarine, anchored about thirty meters ahead of and across from Wolf's ship. The shadowy silhouettes of various crewmen moved around inside the vessel.

Laurens climbed out of the boat ahead of everyone else, and then offered her his hand. "I should probably warn you; you have hours of recordings waiting for you inside Wolf's cabin, so good luck with that."

As she placed her hand on top of his, she nodded. "Oh well, it's something that must be done. Maybe we'll get lucky and find something that will help us bring this mission to an end sooner rather than later."

"I'm all for that," he replied as helped her out of the boat and onto the ship's ladder.

"What? Do you mean to say you haven't enjoyed your stay inside the dank, scenic caves of Colombia, Laurens?" she teased. "Or is your stay inside the compound of a drug lord wearing thin?"

He chuckled in response and then stepped to the side, in deference to the captain.

Wolf followed her up the ladder and led her to his cabin. "I didn't ask earlier, but did Sombra give us any usable information?"

"That, I don't know. Her files arrived just as you and Andries returned. Therefore, I didn't get the chance to look at them, as you might recall." She went to the table, gathered the scattered recorders to make room for her laptop, and dropped them inside the table drawer.

"Don't expect me to apologize for stealing you away, *lieveling*," he said as he set her pack on top of the chair. "If I did that, I'd have to apologize all of the time."

Joris called out to Wolf before she could form a witty response. The first mate said something she couldn't quite make out. "What did he just say?" she asked.

"He wants us to evaluate the sub's power since they're using quite a bit of it right now," he said. "Don't worry, we won't be gone long."

"All right. While you're gone, I'll just put some of this stuff into some kind of recognizable order."

Curious over Sombra's emails, she unpacked her computer first and powered it up. Sombra had sent Wolf two large encrypted files. While they processed, she arranged the remainder of her equipment on the desk. After she finished, she put her clothing and personal items inside Wolf's sea chest. Yet, this time, the simple act was far different than what it had been during her first voyage aboard the *Wieven*. This time, it carried the feeling of permanency.

Wolf entered the cabin as she closed the lid.

He glanced at the computer. "So, what did the hacker send us?"

"We're about to find out together," she replied as she sat down and placed her hand on top of the mouse.

"Before we get into that, could you bring up the details of the *Barracuda* again for me?" he asked as he sat down next to her.

"Yes, I can. But why? Is something wrong?"

"No, I just want another look at the vessel's specifications. I didn't study it in depth the first time around and there are a few things I must know about her capabilities."

She nodded as she typed in the web address. "All right—there you go," she said as the brochure appeared on the screen.

He pored over the document for several minutes and then shifted his gaze just above the computer. "Looks like it will, indeed, take all of our combined efforts then," he mused aloud.

"What will take your combined efforts?" she asked.

"Absorbing the ship's power. The vessel's mission capacity is four full days, with an additional four days of emergency life support, should they require it. That's a great deal of power. Therefore, it'll take me and all my men to shut her down."

"Are you sure there are enough of you?" she asked. "What if you can't do it?"

Wolf put an arm about her shoulder and shook his head. "We can do it. Don't look so worried. You'll just be alone for a short time while we carry out this portion of the mission, that's all."

"Oh. That isn't any big deal, Wolf. I think, if I try really, really hard, I can survive on my own without getting into trouble, for at least an hour or two."

"Perhaps you can at that." Wolf grinned as he inclined his head toward the computer screen. "Let's take a look at what Sombra sent us, shall we?"

She slid the mouse forward and clicked on the first file. "Well," she began, "this data returns to a bank in Singapore. Sombra gives us Hank's full name, residential address, phone number, and email account as found on his bank documents."

"Where did he say he lived?"

"Somewhere in Singapore, actually." Her gaze traveled down the list of transactions. "What's more, it appears that he did, in fact, live there for a time. At least two years. This tells me that in all probability, the DEA assigned him to the taskforce in that area of the world, working out of the U.S. Embassy. However, it doesn't appear that he used this account for his paychecks."

"So then, this is his private account," he said. "The one he doesn't want anyone to know about."

"That's what it looks like. He has some rather large incoming wire deposits beginning about three years ago. Here is one and here's another—one here and here—"

"Ill-gotten booty?"

"Let's not jump to any conclusions just yet," she murmured as she scanned through each of the pages. "Though I must admit, you're probably right. I mean, just how many dead relatives can leave him an inheritance? Or how many expensive things does he have that he can sell in such a short amount of time? This could also tie in with the purchase of the sub through his contacts in that area."

"Can you tell by looking at those records when he returned to the United States?" he asked.

Aliyana clicked through page after page of transactions. "Yep, he began using his debit card exclusively in the U.S. about six months before I arrived in Colombia. They didn't assign him to our detail until my last briefing. I have no idea what he did during the interim period, other than he used these funds to maintain a lavish lifestyle, as you can see by the amount of his withdrawals."

"Would they have assigned him to another task force?"

"I don't think so. They didn't mention a point of transfer when he attended that meeting. All they said was that Hank had replaced Cutler, our retiree. Maybe between the two assignments they gave him a generic desk job or something along those lines." She clicked through each page, studying the details of each transaction he made. "After the oath we all take, I can't believe he'd do something like this."

"Is something wrong?" Wolf asked.

As she gazed into his eyes, she shrugged. "You were right about Hank all along. He's working for himself, not the DEA."

"What brought you to that conclusion?"

"Hank is using his personal debit card for all his transactions here in Colombia. He is not using the card issued by the DEA. The first transaction on this ledger right here took place about a week before the meeting you witnessed between him and Mercado. He didn't come here on behalf of the DEA to look for me or to hook up with any member of my squad. He simply traveled here to line his pockets."

"Are these the last of his transactions?" asked Wolf.

"Yes, at least they are as of early yesterday morning, when Sombra hacked into the account."

Wolf leaned forward. "This shows that two days ago he paid for lodgings at the British Colonial Hilton in Nassau. Do I have that right?"

"Yep, that's what it says," she replied.

"I wonder if he's still there or if he simply paid his bill in full and left the island."

"You know what? The purchase of a plane ticket would tell the tale, wouldn't it? Wait, just a minute." She turned to her keyboard and opened another file. "Sombra, sweetheart that she is—and don't you dare say a single word—has also given us the password to Hank's account."

Aliyana read through the rest of Hank's

transactions. The man did enjoy living a lavish lifestyle, and one that an agent's salary couldn't provide. "He didn't buy a plane ticket. However, this one is a transaction from a very expensive restaurant in a very different place. I wonder what he's doing on the Andros Islands, though."

"I don't know. Unless—"

"Unless what?"

"Unless they've chosen the Andros Islands as the place to transfer Mercado's drugs from the submarine to another vessel."

"If so, it'll be a first," she said. "Mercado has never used the Bahamas to distribute his drugs. The coast guard keeps a high presence in the area."

Wolf considered that for a moment. "Then we'll dig a little deeper before we settle on any one conclusion."

"Sombra sent an additional file," Aliyana said as she downloaded the attachment. "I haven't a clue as to what it might contain, but let's open it up and take a look."

"His email correspondence?"

A broad smile stole across her face. "Yes, indeed, and it's the email account listed on his bank records, only here he's using the name Harlan Mooney."

"That's not very original, nor it is very smart if he doesn't wish to get caught." Wolf said. "The man is using his own initials."

"So he is." After she read the brief note from Sombra, she gazed at Wolf and smiled. "Well, it looks like you've made quite an impression on our little hacker, Captain Dircksen."

"Why do you say that?"

"The woman has given you Hank's passwords and email records at no extra charge. Highly unusual."

Wolf shrugged off the praise. "Perhaps we should send a note of gratitude."

"Don't worry. I'll acknowledge the gift in one way or another. After all, we just may need her again."

"Think so, do you?" he challenged.

She faced him. Why did she always find it so difficult to think when he looked at her like that? "Well, you never know. We might—"

"Not if I have my way, we won't," he replied. "My personal goal is to wrap this up before month's end. We'll then find the nearest portal out of here."

"That's less than three weeks, Captain," she reminded him. "You realize that, don't you?"

"Doable, I believe. To that end, why don't we split the chores and see if we can shave a few days off that?"

"Chores?" she asked.

"Yes, I'll take the email since it seems they're all written in English. At least, those I see on the screen are written in English. You can get started on the recordings."

"You've got a deal."

Two hours into the grueling task, Wolf nudged her. Aliyana removed her headphones and set them on top of the table. Once he had her attention, he swept his hand toward the screen.

"I think we might have something here," he said. "Take a look at the header and then read what's just below it."

"Top video of the day," she read aloud. "Study both attachments very carefully, my friend. Study them as if your life depended on it."

They looked at each other for a moment before she clicked on the first attachment. Seconds later, the video screen box appeared on screen. She clicked the play button. The back of a man, average in height and build, dressed in a brown business suit, popped into view. He sat at the table of a busy restaurant, his meal still in front of him. The side angle of his face, though shadowed, appeared deliberately blurred. He held a cell phone to his ear. During a lengthy pause, in which he appeared to be listening, he nibbled at his food. After a drink from his glass, he nodded his head and replied in Spanish to whomever he spoke with.

Despite the chatter surrounding him, Aliyana could hear each word he uttered. Her mouth dropped as she whirled around to face Wolf. She met his steady gaze all throughout the length of the conversation. Once the unknown operative ended the call, the video ended. Her mind raced in several directions at once as she took it all in.

"What did he say?" Wolf asked.

"I am fairly certain the man sitting at the table is Jomini. As you might've guessed, this video is the reason he is scared half to death of Hank," she said.

"Tell me what he said that's so incriminating."

"From what I can gather, Jomini is talking to Mercado. In this conversation, he's giving him the go-ahead to move some decoy trucks to the specified route they must have discussed early on. Everything is in place, he said. The plan is to keep both the ICE and DEA agents focused on the bogus route, rather than on the one bringing in the main haul."

He drew his brows together and looked a bit lost. "ICE?" he asked.

"Oh, sorry. The U.S. Immigration and Customs Enforcement. We work with them quite often in these types of situations."

"I see."

"Anyway, Jomini told Mercado to make sure he employs the men he's willing to sacrifice. He told him to make sure they carry an impressive load of low-quality drugs so as not to arouse any suspicion. Then he ended the conversation."

"So this tells us that Hank walked into this restaurant, either by design or at an incredibly opportune moment. He then took advantage of what he witnessed."

"Yes, and it looks as if he videoed this part of the conversation with his cell phone. From there, all he had to do was copy it to his computer. He distorted Jomini's face so that no one else could identify the man should the video end up in the wrong hands. After that, he sent it to Jomini."

"Do you recognize this man or his voice?" asked Wolf.

She shook her head and shrugged. "I'm sorry, I don't. You must understand that the DEA has over ten thousand employees. I know relatively few of them."

"Well, perhaps we can uncover his identity as we go through these emails."

"Let's see what Hank sent Jomini in this second attachment first," she said as she clicked on the file.

The image of a newspaper article appeared on the screen. The editorial concerned a drug bust that sounded very similar to the conversation between Jomini and his unidentified contact. The newspaper published the article about the time she opened her shop in Barranquilla. However, Hank held onto the information for a full six months before he confronted Jomini with his evidence.

"We need to keep going," said Aliyana. "Somewhere in this stack of emails, Jomini has to reply."

"Don't you worry," said Wolf. "I won't stop looking until we find everything we need."

Less than an hour later, they had completely uncovered Hank's blackmail scheme. Just as Aliyana presumed, Hank had a safety net in place. Each piece of incriminating evidence was ready to be released to the Administrator of the DEA as well as each of the Deputy Administrators, and all media outlets.

Hank had a contact he trusted to release the files upon his instructions, though the person was unaware of the circumstances surrounding the threat.

Wolf rubbed a hand against his beard. "You know what? I don't think Hank knows about the assassination plot."

"What leads you to believe that?" she asked.

"As you pointed out earlier, Hank's interest is in the drug money. He never mentions the plot," he replied. "I think Jomini plans to use the confusion surrounding the assassinations to kill Hank. He won't care, because at that moment, Hank's contact won't have anyone to send his files to."

"In addition, the media coverage surrounding the assassination will take precedence over a scandal. This will give Jomini time to collect his money and escape. Most certainly he'll head for a country that has no extradition treaty with the United States. All of that together makes perfect sense," she said.

"Without a whole lot of effort, we can turn all of this back around on Hank," Wolf mused aloud. "In the process, we can get him to hand Jomini over to the proper authorities."

"What makes you think he'd cooperate in something like that?"

"Desperation will compel it. Especially if he believes that by cooperating with us, it buys him time to figure a way out. He used this evidence to corner Jomini. We can do the same. All we need do is confront him with everything we have right here. With that advantage, we can have him arrange for Mercado and Jomini to be at the same place, at the same time. Of course, we'll make sure he's there as well. We can then have the coast guard or some other federal agency step in. They can take over, and in one fell swoop, your mission successfully concludes."

"That just might work, *if* Hank returns to Colombia before Mercado launches his submarine with drugs and lieutenants in tow," she replied.

"Perhaps we can find something that will lure him here," he said.

Chapter Twenty-One

Wolf rose from his chair as he fought his rising anger. The cold, callous email, in which Hank and Jomini discussed Aliyana, filled him with revulsion. They hunted her with the same merciless persistence a predator stalks its prey. Now, more than ever before, he wanted an end to this mission. He wanted to take her home, and far away from those who sought her death.

The letter confirmed, along with a few others he had read during the night, that neither of the men fully understood Aliyana's true purpose in Colombia. Nonetheless, Mercado wanted her dead and not just because she, as a DEA agent, infiltrated his compound. Jomini insinuated that because she had spurned Emil's advances, his pride and humiliation demanded no less. *What made Emil Mercado think he deserved more than a passing glance from Aliyana, anyway? The beslubbering wagtail didn't even belong in her universe, much less at her side.*

Wolf approached the computer and gazed at the email once more. He didn't see a thing that held any real value to them or the DEA. With the click of the mouse, he deleted the record from their file. Aliyana didn't need the reminder of the price on her head.

A quiet little sigh drew his attention to the bed where she slept. Though she stirred, she had not quite fully awakened. He approached the berth and sat down on the edge of the mattress. A slight grin stole across his face as he gazed at her. How did an ordinary man such as himself win the love of this beautiful, extraordinary woman? Not that he intended to question his luck. No, quite the contrary. He intended to run with it. What's more, he intended to keep it forever safe, at all cost.

Then, as if she sensed his presence—perhaps even his resolve—her eyelids fluttered open. She lifted a hand to his jaw and ran her fingers through his beard. "Good morning, *quierdo*."

He leaned down and gave her a slow, unhurried kiss. That kiss turned into two and then three. Four sorely tempted him, but he quashed the desire, so she could sit up a little more comfortably and take a much-needed breath.

"Good morning, my love," he whispered.

Aliyana regarded him for a moment and then smiled. "I had a dream about you and me." She gave him a sideways glance. "Should I tell you about it or did you create this one for me as well?"

He brushed the tousled hair away from her face and shook his head. "Not this time. So, go ahead and tell me about it."

A faraway look appeared. "It's nothing all that remarkable really. Well, not in the retelling of it anyway. But it seemed we had already gone through the portal. You drew my attention to an ancient temple on a narrow peninsula near the sea. This structure was unlike anything I'd ever seen before. It had four magnificent spires built into each corner and those spires rose straight up out of the ocean. The uniquely colored stones used in the creation of this temple provided it with breathtaking majesty. At that moment, for whatever the reason, an incredible sense of joy filled my heart."

"Did we stand aboard my ship when we viewed this structure?" he asked, suddenly intrigued.

"Only at first, when you showed it to me. Suddenly then, as dreams go, we were on the steps that led to it. Yet, I had the feeling we'd just come out of it, rather than we were about to go inside. We were having a conversation, but I can't remember a single word we said."

"Pity that. Do you recall what the place looked like inside?"

She shook her head. "No, if I ever saw it, I lost the vision when I awoke."

"Anything else?" he asked. In response to the innocent question, a captivating blush rose to her cheeks. At once she lowered her gaze. He wondered over the cause.

She peeked up at him through her lashes. "Right before I awoke, we shared a kiss, and—that's about all I can remember."

"What kind of a kiss?" he pressed.

"Just a kiss." Her tone was evasive.

He slowly nodded and then, unable to resist, he leaned down and gave her a sweet, simple kiss.

"Something like that?" He paused for a moment with his head tilted to the side. "Or, was it more like this—"

This time, the kiss lasted a little longer and he put a bit more feeling into it. Her eyes sparkled. The barest hint of a smile curved her lips the moment he released her.

"Maybe," he whispered as his lips played against hers, "it was more like this." Once he finally let her go, she took in a deep breath, and blessed him with a radiant smile.

"Yep, I'm pretty sure it was more like that one."

"All right, then." He winked as he dipped his head downward. "I'll keep that in mind."

"Well, you could practice a little longer if you'd like—"

A knock on the door ended their playful banter. As he swore under his breath, she merely laughed.

"Yes?" he growled.

"Just wondering if Aliyana is up yet," Andries said from the other side of the door.

"I'm wide awake and raring to go," she said as she tossed her covers toward the wall and swung her legs over the edge of the mattress.

"All right, breakfast is coming right up then," he said.

'Sounds good, thank you, Andries."

Aliyana hid a yawn behind her hand as she approached the computer. She glanced down at the email list he'd left on the screen. "Did you find anything of importance while I slept?" she asked.

"The ones of note are marked," Wolf replied. "But I have a question for you before you read them. You'll see a couple of emails with you as the subject. I think it's obvious from all the possibilities they've discussed in those letters that neither Hank nor Jomini understood your full mission inside the compound. They, however, know you were working undercover. What do you make of that?"

Aliyana shrugged. "I'm not really sure."

"Would those you worked with in Virginia ever have made Hank aware of your mission after they assigned him to your detail?"

"No, I don't think so. Those few individuals who were privy to my assignment would never have discussed it with anyone else. When someone goes undercover, the fewer people that know the details, the better off that person is."

"If such is the case, then Jomini isn't connected to anyone inside your inner circle," he said. "Do I have that right?"

"Right. I can't imagine any connection at all. But to have some of the details as to my presence in Colombia means he would have to work somewhere inside the intelligence or human resource divisions," she replied.

"During this briefing you said Hank attended, did anyone mention Colombia, in any way, at all?"

"No."

"All very puzzling, but no matter. We'll uncover Jomini's identity in one way or another. The first step is to get Hank back here, and the sooner the better."

"I think I've come up with a way to do that," she said.

"Let's hear it."

"We can send him a personal invitation through his very own email. That will tell him we've hacked into his account. He'll know we have possession of all his incriminating correspondences as well as the video. Best of all, he won't have a clue who we are."

"Perfect." He held her chair as she sat down and then took a seat beside her.

"There's just one thing though," she said as she

turned and faced him. "We haven't discussed what we'll do once he arrives. For instance, where do you think we should meet him during our initial contact?"

Wolf lifted a shoulder as he drew in a breath. "I'm afraid my love, you aren't invited to this party."

A look of indignation flashed in her eyes. "No, Wolf, you will not keep me out of this! And while we're on the subject—once we're on the other side of the portal, if you think for one minute I'll stay at home while you and your crew conduct your rescue missions, then you have another 'think' coming, sir!" she huffed. "If those are your intentions, then you might just as well leave me here!"

He lifted his hand to halt her words. "Wait just a minute and hear me out. If you don't agree with what I have to say, we'll discuss it further, all right?"

She merely raised a tempestuous brow and waited for him to speak.

"Hank is not only greedy, he's cunning. Therefore, I believe that only a ghost, and in this case several frightening ghosts, have the power to maintain the intimidation factor we need to accomplish this goal. After our initial contact with Hank, he'll know that we shadow his every step, and hear every word he speaks. How will he know this? We'll appear to him randomly, once every hour, no matter where he is or what he's doing. He'll know there's no place he can go or hide that we can't find him. We'll tell him if he doesn't do everything we tell him to do, we'll be his constant companions for the rest of his miserable existence."

As he laid out the plan, her brow relaxed, and her smile grew ever broader. A delightful giggle accompanied a nod. "Excellent strategy, Captain. But your 'party' would be even more effective if one of you could speak Spanish. Perhaps I could teach you some key phrases before he arrives? After all, we don't want him to know you can't understand what he's saying to Mercado."

Her brilliant statement spawned an additional step to his plan. He leaned back in his chair while the idea played out in all directions and covered every scenario. Despite the light of day, he could keep her safe enough. The boat would shield her presence most of the way. They'd encounter a variety of trees, bushes and tall weeds during the short journey they'd cross on foot. That would keep her hidden from view if they encountered anyone along the way. Besides, should someone happen across their path, he'd simply hide her face the same way he did at the apartment complex in Barranquilla.

"Not a bad idea," he murmured more to himself than he did to her. "Not a bad idea at all. But I think we can do one better than that. At least, I hope we can."

"What are you talking about?" she asked.

"I mean, my love, you have just been invited to the pre-party plan, and while we're on the subject—I do intend—and have always intended—to include you in our missions once we're home. More importantly, I don't think I could bear to part with you for any length of time."

"Good. Now that we have that settled, what will you have me do during this 'pre-party' plan of yours?"

"Speak to the spirit of a long-dead Jesuit priest and convince him to help us," he replied.

"What Jesuit priest?"

Wolf grinned. "The one we encountered on our

way to Barranquilla, of course."

Her beautiful eyes filled with confusion. "Sorry. I don't remember seeing one."

"You didn't? He stood right there near the gate of that cemetery we passed. The man even wished us a good evening. At least, I think that's what he said before he disappeared into his church."

"And you want me to speak with him," she said.

Wolf rose from his chair and took her hand. "Yes, I do, and there's no time like the present to get it done. I mean, should he refuse to help us, we'll need that crash course in Spanish."

As he tugged her toward the door she looked down at her clothes. "Um, Wolf? If you want me to talk to a Jesuit priest, then I should probably get dressed first."

He whirled around. She wore the lovely gown from the lighthouse. A grin stole across his face. "Oh, I don't know. I think you look mighty fetching just the way you are, Miss Montijo. So much so, I know the poor man won't stand a chance when you make your request."

Laughter accompanied the slight shake of her head. "A wolf in sheep's clothing if I ever saw one." She opened the door and ushered him out. "I'll be out in just a minute."

While Wolf waited, he presented the change in plans to his crew. Aliyana emerged from the cabin minutes later, to the sounds of their uproarious laughter and excited chatter.

"What's going on?" she asked, looking around.

"We're just discussing the inevitable capture of our notorious trio. As you can see, they've come up with various strategies for optimum effectiveness."

"Yes, I can see that. Puts a shiver down the spine. Are we ready to go then?"

Wolf put a hand on her waist. "That we are."

"Ahem," said Andries as he approached them with a bowl of porridge in hand. "Aliyana should eat before she leaves the ship, *Kapitein*. You know as well as I that we can't have her fainting for lack of food before she gets there."

"Dear Andries," she said. "You're always so good to me."

The man blushed. "Naught but a pleasure, Aliyana. Naught but a pleasure."

****

The uneventful journey took them to the rusty gates in front of the cemetery and abandoned church. The moment Wolf had them opened, the ghostly priest appeared. He gazed first at Aliyana and then at him. The man seemed mystified that a 'ghost' would have a mortal at his side. Wolf looked at the priest and smiled.

"*Buenos días, Padre*," he said in greeting.

"He's here?" asked Aliyana, as her eyes darted about the area.

"Yes, he's standing right in front of me. At this moment, he's looking at me with a bit of suspicion. So, perhaps you should take charge and give him the assurance he needs right about now."

Aliyana fixed her gaze in the exact same spot as Wolf. She placed the palms of her hands together. As she raised them to her chin, she bowed respectively to the clergyman she couldn't see.

"*Hola Padre. Me llamo Aliyana Rosa Montijo, y yo nesacito tu ayuda desesperadamente,*" she said, giving him her name and asking for the help they so desperately needed.

He manifested himself to her then and bestowed a kindly smile. The mature priest, wearing nineteenth-century robes, swept a hand toward the church. "*Venga hija, podemos hablar de tus nesacidades dentro de la iglesia.*"

Aliyana gazed at Wolf as she smiled. "He's going to hear us out. Come on. He's invited us into the church."

They followed the priest up the crumbling walk and into the dilapidated structure. He led them through the broken glass on the floor and passed the weathered pews. They then went around the side to what remained of his office.

The priest seated them on a rickety wooden bench in front of a decrepit desk. As he sat down, he gave her an encouraging nod. "*Que puedo hacer para ti mi hija?*"

"He wants to know how he can help us," she said.

"Good. Why don't you fill him in?" Wolf put a hand over his heart as he dipped his head toward the priest.

"*Mi amigo y yo estamos tratando de detener el asesinato de varios hombres inocentes, y sus esposas y sus hijos.*" As she told them about Emil Mercado's plot to assassinate the DEA officials and their families, the priest leaned toward her.

A mixture of anger and anticipation flashed through his eyes. "*Cómo puedo ayudar?*" His words and his very demeanor spoke of his desire to help.

Aliyana took a deep breath and launched into a detailed explanation of their plans. She told him about Emil Mercado—how the drug lord had already

275

murdered an unknown number of people, including her brother. As she spoke, she described the physical and mental cost of his illicit drug empire on those he ensnared around the world. She told him of her own work and involvement as an agent for the DEA. Finally, she laid out their plans to capture Mercado and his cohorts, as well as the part they hoped he would play in making that happen.

The priest leaned back against his chair. His gaze traveled toward Wolf before it wandered back to her. He paused for a moment and then rose from his seat. With a single wave of his hand, he beckoned them to follow. They trailed him down the hallway and to the back entrance of the church. Once outside, he led them to the cemetery. While they walked past row upon row of graves, he talked.

Aliyana turned her gaze toward Wolf. "He said that many who are buried here have fallen victim to men such as Emil Mercado and his cohorts."

The priest pointed to a fragmented stone, and then another and another.

"He said that the blood of these innocent men, women and children will compel him to leave his sanctuary for the first time since his death and give you the help you need," Aliyana said. "He has but one request."

Since the priest directed the question to Wolf, Aliyana paused so that he could answer. Wolf bowed his head. "Name it, and it's yours."

The priest returned a grateful smile. "I'd like a moment to speak to my little flock and tell them why I must go. Many of them will panic otherwise, for you see, even now, they are still in need of a shepherd."

As Aliyana translated his words, a young man from the nineteenth century emerged from the mausoleum. He glided toward them and stopped in front of the priest. The shy ghost peeked over at Aliyana, and then with a slight bow of his head, gazed at the priest. "*Perdón por la intrusión, Padre Romualdo.*"

"*Si, Pedro?*" the padre asked.

Aliyana covered her mouth as she listened to their entire conversation. Once they arrived at an agreement, she turned toward Wolf. "Pedro overheard our earlier discussion with the father. He said he feels it's his right and his duty as a soldier to continue in the defense of his country from men of Mercado's ilk. Pedro would consider it an honor to help us achieve our goals. Then Padre Romualdo could remain with his flock, many of which so desperately need his guidance, he said. This arrangement is agreeable to the father, if it's agreeable to us."

Wolf extended a hand toward Pedro, who grasped it in the instant. "We're grateful for your help."

Before Aliyana could translate Wolf's words into Spanish, Pedro waved a hand and smiled. He held up his hand, and all but pinched his thumb and index finger together. "I speak English, little bit," he said, then thrust a thumb behind him. "My companions wish to come as well?"

An additional four spirits, from the same era as Pedro, stepped out of the mausoleum and joined the group.

Wolf flashed a grin. "Even better," he said.

Later that evening, as the boys welcomed their ghostly companions on the top deck, she and Wolf retreated to the cabin below. She sat down at the computer and stared at the screen.

"Do you have any ideas as to how we should word this email for greatest effect?" she asked.

"Let me think on it for a minute," he replied as he paced within the small quarters.

"All right. While you're doing that, I'll check his bank records and see if they can pinpoint his current location."

"That's a very good idea," he replied.

The boisterous laughter above her made her smile. But as she delved into the latest transactions posted on Hank's bank account, her smile faded. "Wolf?" she called out without bothering to turn around.

He ambled up from behind and knelt down beside her. "Did you find something?" he asked.

She pointed at the latest posts. "Hank is either already on his way here, or he's here. This transaction is for his plane ticket. The one just underneath it is for reservations at the Sonesta hotel, in Barranquilla."

"Looks like we won't need that email after all. Everything I need to say, I can say in person." He gave her a joyous kiss and then strode toward the door.

"Where are you going now?" she asked as she rose from her chair.

"I'll gather some of the crew, along with our new friends, and head for Barranquilla," he said. "We should make sure Morris receives a proper welcome, should we not? In the meantime, keep an eye on that email log. Let's see if he contacts anyone while he's here."

"But Wolf, it's the middle of the night."

He grinned as he raised his brows. "Yes, my love, I know."

Chapter Twenty-Two

Wolf asked Andries to watch over Aliyana. He warned him that she might do something stupid—like leave the ship for instance and head toward the Sonesta hotel. Never mind they would return well before she could cross even half the distance to the city. He assigned Johannes and Laurens to keep tabs on, and record, every word coming out of Mercado's mouth during their absence. They could ignore the conversations of all the lieutenants unless they received a direct order from the drug lord. If that should happen, Johannes could stay with Mercado, while Laurens followed the lieutenant.

"Is everyone ready?" he asked as he stepped toward the portside of his ship with Aliyana in tow.

"Aye, *Kapitein*," Conrad said.

"Ready, willing and able," Joris added.

"Then let's get this done," he said. As his men gathered, he turned toward Aliyana. "I don't think we'll be very long. With the plans we now have in place, I'm pretty sure Hank will cooperate with us."

"If the man is in any way normal he will," she said. "I just wished I could see the look on his face when you all go storming through the walls of his hotel room without an invitation."

Wolf flashed a grin. "Do you want us to record it for you, *lieveling*? One of the men could hold a video camera without too much trouble."

"I must admit, I'm sorely tempted by the offer. But I don't want to claim responsibility for anyone's lack of concentration when it comes to producing those gruesome faces. Just take note and give me a detailed briefing after you return. That'll satisfy me well enough."

"I can do that; in the meantime, try to get some sleep," he said as he leaned down and gave her a kiss, followed by a second.

An exaggerated clearing of the throat interrupted his farewell. So did the quiet laughter.

"At this rate, *Kapitein*, we won't arrive at our destination until daybreak," quipped Conrad. "By then the man could be gone!"

"You know, you remind me very much of another *kapitein* we were all very well acquainted with," Joris said.

"My thoughts exactly," said Johannes. "Warms the heart though, doesn't it?"

"Let's just hope this *kapitein* doesn't boot us off his ship in the same way," Pieter replied.

"Not going to happen. We have too many contracts awaiting our return, and I'll be hanged if I do them myself." Before Wolf backed away, he gave Aliyana a final kiss. "Now, let's get this done."

Within minutes, they arrived at the hotel in Barranquilla. They paused just outside the glass doors and checked out the interior. The front desk lay directly ahead with elevators on both sides of it. The lobby was sparsely populated. A solitary clerk yawned, and then stretched his arms behind his neck. The man then leaned on the counter and spun a ring of keys in tiny circles. *Perfect. No distractions.*

"Getting Hank's room number should only take us a minute." Wolf turned toward Pedro and placed a hand on top of his shoulder. "Can you whisper to the man in Spanish and suggest he look at the room number they've assigned Hank Morris?"

"My pleasure, *Capitán*," he replied.

Once Pedro completed the simple task, Wolf waved the rest of his men inside the building. "Fifth floor and room 521."

They stood outside Hank Morris's door and waited for his orders.

"Give me just a moment to see where he's at before we storm the fort," said Wolf. "If we're lucky, we'll find him in the bathroom and in a compromising position." Raucous laughter followed the comment.

Wolf stepped inside the room and found that Hank had already retired to his bed. His clothes lay in a disheveled heap on the floor and a half-emptied bottle of spirits rested on top of the nightstand next to the bed, as did his weapon. He picked up his gun and removed the round inside the chamber then emptied the magazine of all its bullets. He shoved Hank's ammunition inside his pocket and put the pistol back where he found it.

"All right," he said as he returned to the hallway. "Hank is already asleep. He's had quite a bit to drink, if the bottle next to his bed is any indication. If that's the case, we may have a problem bringing him around."

"With what we have planned, he'll sober up soon enough," Pieter replied.

"I've no doubt of that," Wolf said. "You all know what to do, so let's get in there and get it done."

Wolf led the way through the door and took his position at the head of the bed. The rest of his men formed a semi-circle around it. With the force of their combined energy, they levitated the bed five feet off the floor.

"Hank," Conrad whispered. "Wake up, Hank. You have guests."

Pieter laughed. "Come on, Hank. We're waiting."

Joris grabbed the bedding and slid the bundle all the way down Hank's body.

Pedro and his buddies conjured freezing temperatures. Hank, his eyes still shut, lifted his hand off the mattress. He searched for, and then clutched his blankets. As he drew them up high around his neck, he snuggled a little deeper into the covers. Joris waited as he drifted toward deeper sleep and then repeated the process. This time, he yanked a little harder. Hank stirred and rolled onto his back. Several minutes passed before he sat up, bleary-eyed, and puzzled over his bedding near the foot of the bed. He expelled an exasperated sigh, gathered a generous handful, and while holding on to his prize, turned to his side. But just as he shifted his body to make the turn, Wolf met his startled gaze head on. He flashed the twit a malicious grin.

Hank's eyes bulged from their sockets. He inhaled a sharp gasp, snatched his gun and rolled off the bed. He fell with a thud to the floor, not taking his eyes off Wolf. In adrenalin overdrive, he ducked and rolled to his side. The idiot squeezed the trigger without even taking careful aim.

Hank gulped numerous times when nothing happened. Several more jerks against the trigger accompanied an increase in labored breathing. Morris lunged to his feet. Then, as he tightened his grip on the pistol, he flung his weighted fist into Wolf's face. Hank's hand went right through him. His eyes bulged even wider. He drew in a deep breath and held it while throwing multiple punches, all of them futile.

Wolf, without so much as a flinch in return, maintained both eye contact and grin. Morris fell back onto his haunches and stared. His eyes were now filled with both fear and disbelief.

Joris's deep, slow, evil laughter echoed throughout the room.

Hank gasped anew and flung his head away from the unholy sound. A moan escaped his lips as his eyes fell on the hideous sight that stood just off to his left. Klaus appeared as a faceless specter dressed in the black-hooded robe of the grim reaper. Wolf's other men appeared in similar fashion. Some used skulls, and some manifested themselves with rotting flesh that dripped from their skeletons. At once, they converged upon their hapless victim.

Morris dropped his mouth, threw back his head, and bellowed at the top of his lungs. He scurried to his feet and bolted for the door, which was still locked and chained. As he twisted the handle and tugged, Pedro and his companions poked their heads through the steel door and growled like savage beasts. Blood dripped down the corners of their mouths as they pinned their gazes to his. Hank squeezed his eyes shut and backed away from the door. His shoulders slumped forward as he groaned.

"Watch it," Pieter warned. "He might pass out."

"Wouldn't surprise me any," Klaus scoffed.

Finally, his adrenalin spent, Hank turned a full circle, collapsed to the floor, and cried. Tears trickled down his cheeks. His shoulders shook as he lifted a trembling hand and covered his mouth. He moaned. "What do you want with me? What do you want?"

Wolf approached him but didn't speak. He held his silence until Hank took in a deep breath, tilted his head upward, and looked him in the eye.

"Your soul," he said.

Joris laughed again. The members of his crew crowded around his first mate and joined him in his laughter.

Hank gulped several times, and it appeared that he might puke. His eyes slammed shut. He rubbed a hand beneath his nose and sniffed.

"You deserve no less than suffering endless, fiery damnation in the underworld, is this not so?" asked Wolf, using a tone of disdain. "Admit it. Your soul belongs to us."

Morris shook his head. "No, I've done nothing to deserve this."

"Have you not?" asked Wolf.

"He lies," Cornelius jeered. "His list of heinous deeds goes on and on."

"No," Hank said yet again. "You're wrong."

"Oh, I don't think so," said Wolf. "But perhaps you're so rooted in your vile actions you need a reminder of your wasted life? So be it."

Wolf provided every sordid detail that they had uncovered, uttering each word with slow deliberation. He left nothing out.

The hands dropped from Hank's face. His wide-eyed gaze filled with shock as his jaw slackened. Yet he said nothing in return. What could he say?

Wolf finished his narrative with what he and Aliyana uncovered within his personal email and bank accounts, including the acquisition of the submarine. He then leaned in close to his face.

"To top it all off," he spat, "to this hour, you search for an innocent woman, so you or one of your cohorts can take her life. A woman you should've protected at all costs, for she's one of your own."

"Enough talk. This man knows his sins well enough. I say we take him now and move on," Joris rasped, without an ounce of pity reflected in his tone.

"No, please," Hank moaned. "I'll do anything, I swear. I swear…"

"I don't see where there's anything you can do to get yourself out of your current dilemma," Wolf said. "Your life is a mess and it's much too late to make corrections. Better for you then, if we take your soul now before you get into deeper trouble. Your drinking binge has given us the means. Didn't you know? You're half-dead already," he whispered.

"No. There has to be something, please—" Hank rose to his knees and clasped his hands together as he begged. "I don't want to die."

Joris snorted, shook his head and looked away. "Isn't that what they all say? He is not worth our time."

"I concur. Does anyone see any other option for this man?" asked Wolf as he gazed into the eyes of each companion.

Pedro stepped forward and held up a hand. "This gringo brings shame to my country. He helps the likes of Mercado and his loathsome drug cartel, which even now, we work tirelessly to eliminate from our soil. He complicates everything we do. The prospect of having one less piece of vermin brings me a measure of joy."

"Then we are all agreed?" asked Wolf with lifted brow.

"No, wait! Please. There must be something…" Hank held up his hands as if that action alone would ward them off. "I…I…can help you."

"Help us? Do what?" asked Wolf in a scathing tone.

"I don't know—anything. Anything you want! Name it and it's yours…please."

Pedro gazed at Hank with contempt. "Shall we test him?" He changed his form to one of black swirling mist, save his head, and then slowly circled their victim over and over again. Each time he paused inches away from Hank's face, he stared deep into his eyes. "*Uno momento, Capitán.* I might be able to use this man's particular talents after all."

"If that's your wish," said Wolf. "He's within your domain at present. It matters not to me if we take him now or we collect him later."

A glimmer of hope sprang into Hank's eyes. He focused on Pedro. "Yes! Anything. What do you want me to do?"

Pedro halted and morphed into his true spiritual form. "You'll arrange a meeting in which both Jomini and Emil Mercado are present. In this way, we can take possession of them both without delay and without the cost of additional innocent lives. In exchange for this service, we give you the opportunity to redeem yourself."

Hank shook his head. "Impossible. Neither of those men will agree to such a meeting."

Pedro studied Hank for a moment and then gazed at his companions. He jerked his head toward Morris. "Take him. I have no further use for this scum."

Terrifying grins appeared on the faces of those who chose skeletal forms. They slowly advanced then, with bony arms outstretched.

Then, just as Klaus grabbed hold of Hank's wrist with elongated fingers, Morris screamed. "No, wait! I have an idea. Please, you must give me the chance to explain."

"You can speak," said Wolf. "But know this: your time is almost out." He nodded at Klaus, who promptly released him from his grasp.

"I…I think I can arrange to have both men sh-show up at the same place at the s-same time, but only if uh—only if they believe they're coming to meet someone else. Yes, that will work. And um—"

Wolf didn't say a word as Hank wiped at his face over and over again. The man's eyes darted all around the room as his chest heaved despite the shallow breaths he took.

"Cartagena! Yes—I'm quite certain I can convince each of these men to visit the city." Hank's gaze flitted between each of the phantoms, before they settled on Wolf. "I…I can make them believe they are…that I'll introduce them to one of the uh…one of the um…well-known drug lords from Asia. One of you can act the part, or find someone, right? I'll tell Jomini as well as Mercado that he's here vacationing with his family and that…that he wishes to discuss the possibility of a…of a partnership with them and that…and that…"

"I don't really care what you tell either of the men," Wolf cut in as Hank's scenario faltered, and the mere sound of his voice grated on his nerves. "Just as long as they are both in attendance at the same time and in the same place, you buy yourself a reprieve. At least you will until you do something else that cancels the mercy we give but once."

"All right." Hank swallowed. "Give me two days to work out the details and arrange the meeting. Upon your return, I'll give you all of the—"

"Oh, no. No, no." Wolf shook his head. "We're not leaving you, Hank. We'll ever remain at your side and shadow every step you take. We'll be your constant companions until we've collected either the souls of Jomini and Emil Mercado, or yours. Furthermore, your attendance at this collection is required. Only in this way will you have fulfilled your end of the bargain. If you fail to meet any of the agreed upon terms, you'll forfeit not only your life, but your eternal soul. And by the way, you have just twenty-four hours to finalize your plans and arrange this meeting. You have an additional seventy-two hours to make it happen."

Hank bolted up and raced to the bathroom.

"*Kapitein*? Why don't we ask him for the identity and position Jomini holds within the DEA?" Joris asked. "Surely Aliyana could use this information now."

"I thought of that," Wolf replied. "But, we've convinced Hank we're all-knowing phantoms from hell. If we should reveal our ignorance on this matter, he might feel inclined to deliver someone else in Jomini's place."

Joris nodded as he turned his gaze toward Morris. "I didn't think of that. You're right, of course."

"I hope he'll say the name on his own, or you'll

discover it when he contacts the man," Wolf replied.

"You know, I don't see any reason for all of us to stay here now," Conrad said. "As long as we keep a constant presence, Hank will toe the line."

"Aliyana will worry over your absence if you're gone overly long," Klaus reminded him. "Why don't you head back to the ship and let her know Hank has chosen to cooperate. Let the rest of us handle things on this end. We can figure out a schedule for shifts if we need them."

Wolf nodded. "Sounds good. I should speak with Aliyana about the plausibility of the Cartagena location. We must find someone she can trust who has the authority to take these men into custody as well."

"If it's all the same to you, *Capitán*," Pedro cut in, "I, along with my companions, would like to remain with Morris until all three men are apprehended and handed over to the authorities."

"I'd feel better if you did." Wolf glanced at Hank who still had his face over the commode and a hand against his gut as he vomited. "All right, I'll let you all take it from here then. Anyone coming with me now?"

When no one volunteered, he chuckled. "As you please, just don't get too carried away with your, uh, fun, hmm?"

"One or two of us will be along soon enough, *Kapitein*," Joris said. "You needn't worry. We'll keep you informed and updated as the need arises."

"That's good enough for me." With a nod, he vanished from their view and returned to the *Wieven*. As he approached his ship, he spied Aliyana leaning against the rail. *Didn't she get any sleep at all?* She clasped and unclasped her fingers as she searched the terrain on the starboard side of his ship. Her worry was evident by the grim set of her lips. He didn't think they had tarried long enough to cause concern. Nonetheless, he boarded his vessel, and approached her from behind. The minute he wrapped his arms around her waist she whirled around. Before she could speak, he kissed her quite breathless.

"Wolf!" she whispered the moment he released her. "I was so worried about you. I thought perhaps something had gone wrong."

"You shouldn't have worried. The light of dawn has barely touched the sky."

"Yep, over an hour ago it sure did," she countered. She gazed all about the deck. "Where is everyone else?"

"They stayed behind for a while. I think now that Hank has agreed to our terms, they'll make sure he doesn't falter—in one way or another."

"So, I take it you left him quaking in his boots then?"

He flashed a grin. "In a manner of speaking. I suppose you could say we accomplished our goal."

Chapter Twenty-Three

At the end of Wolf's tale, Aliyana pondered the details of his story. A small part of her felt pity for Hank and all he endured at the hands of her captain and his crew. The rest of her quashed it.

"So, you really had him believing that you and your pack were part of the devil's dominion, huh?" she asked.

"Yep, I think we did. This is the only reason we didn't ask for Jomini's real name. I'm pretty sure he assumed we already knew that information."

"You're probably right about that, and really, it doesn't make any difference. We'll discover who he is soon enough," she said with a firm nod of her head.

"Will Cartagena pose a problem? Because if it will, I'll have Hank change the location."

"No, I don't think we should do that," she murmured as her mind raced through all her options. "Hank believes you're gathering their souls for a journey to hell, right?"

"Yes, he does."

"Then we can't have him think location is a factor, and he does have a point. Cartagena is a beautiful resort city visited by people from all over the world. Therefore, it's the perfect place to carry off this ploy without a whole lot of suspicion."

"Do you have any ideas as to how we'll proceed

once we have them rounded up?" he asked.

"Well, we can't risk using the local authorities. There's a chance Mercado has a man working on the inside who would tip him off before we can nab him. I can't use any of the DEA agents right now, either, so…" She nibbled at a nail as she considered their quandary. Suddenly, then, the solution presented itself. She met his gaze and nodded. "The U.S. Department of Justice, Criminal Division. They have an office in Bogota. I can contact the marshals, present my evidence, and have them meet us in Cartagena at the chosen time and place."

"You can trust this agency?" he asked.

"Yes, I think I can. I don't know why I didn't think of them before."

"Because you had us. Hence, the need for an outside entity didn't exist."

She smiled. "You've proven that more than once. But this time, we'll need someone outside the DEA who has the authority to take our trio into custody. The U.S. Marshals fits that bill."

"Will we have to travel to Bogota to get their help?"

"Probably, but land travel is no good. To meet all the time constraints, we'd have to commandeer Mercado's other plane, piece of junk that it is. If we did that then we could fly in and out—"

"I'd rather not do that Aliyana," Wolf cut in. "You'd have to land in an airport. In so doing, we run the risk of undoing everything we've worked for this far. Not to mention, if you stole his other plane, Mercado would know you're here."

"Then our only other choice is to get the marshals

to come to us."

"How would we go about doing that?" he asked.

"Presentation of evidence." Aliyana considered the dilemma. She ran the risk of discovery if she used her satellite phone. Contacting the U.S. Marshals through the internet remained a viable option, but how quickly would they see or even respond to her message? Wolf gave Hank just one day to set his plan in motion and an additional three to make it happen. That didn't give them any time to waste. She needed to talk to them and the sooner the better.

"Aliyana? What are you thinking?"

"I'm just going over the list of alternatives," she replied and then a workable idea struck. "I need another cell phone. One that Jomini can't or won't trace."

"Mercado's compound is the closest place to get one. I could get in and out of there in a matter of minutes."

"Begging pardon, *Kapitein*," said Andries as he approached with her breakfast. "I could get the phone for you. After all, I've got nothing better to do at the moment."

Wolf nodded. "Thanks, we would appreciate that."

Aliyana accepted the tray with a smile of thanks. "Just don't bring me one that belongs to Mercado or any of his lieutenants, for that matter. See if you can find one that belongs to one of the women, and I need you to make sure it has a full charge. I'll probably need to use it a couple of times before we finish this part of our plans."

"Not a problem," Andries replied. "I'll only be gone a few minutes."

Once Andries disappeared, Wolf said, "If you can

convince the marshals to attend our little get together, where will you have them meet us?"

"Good question. We really only have two choices: back at the cave or the shack in Barranquilla. However, if we have them meet us at the cave, we run the risk of having one of Mercado's men take note of the unusual activity. I mean, the marshals would have to use some kind of vehicle in order to get them close enough to find us. The guards might hear or spot them coming in. So, I think our best shot is in Barranquilla."

"The boat is right here, so we can keep you concealed while we cross the river. We can also time our departure so that we arrive in Barranquilla well after sunset," Wolf replied.

"I'll see if I can get them to meet us about nine thirty then. That'll give us time to set up inside the cellar." She settled her gaze on the steps that led to the captain's cabin. "However, before we do any of that, I need a phone number. So, come on, let's go find one."

As she powered up the computer, she looked over at Wolf. "I just had another thought."

He sat down. "I'm listening."

"In order for us to tie everything together, I'll have to tell them about our plans to stop the assassination by disabling the submarine." She typed in her search request for the marshal's office and then clicked the link to the website.

"That stands to reason," he replied as the desired page popped into view.

"So, they'll want to want to meet you and perhaps ask questions." Before he could speak, she held up a hand to stop his words. "Let me finish. We can take a couple men from your wolf pack along with us. I'll have you all stay in the shadows while I explain that you're undercover, and don't want your faces exposed. Trust me, this is something they understand. They'll keep a respectable distance because of that. The thing is—they might have questions about the sub only you can answer."

"You're probably right. I can get Joris and Cornelius from the hotel in a matter of seconds in the moment they're needed."

A rap at the door announced Andries's return. He entered with a pink phone in hand.

"Did you have any problems?" she asked.

"Nope, not a single one," he said. "The young lady I appropriated the phone from was wasting this beautiful morning by snoring away in her darkened bedroom. She didn't have a clue I was there."

"Thanks, Andries, you're a sweetheart." She dialed the phone number as Andries slipped out of the room.

"U.S. Marshals, Greg Donner, speaking," said the gruff voice at the other end.

Aliyana's mouth dropped. "Greg?"

A lengthy pause followed. "Yes—may I ask who's calling please?"

She shook her head as she glanced skyward and smiled her thanks to the heavens above for this unexpected gift. "Marshal Greg Donner, this is Aliyana Montijo."

"Aliyana?"

She detected a bit of hesitancy to his tone, as if unsure she identified herself truthfully. "In the flesh. Well, at least I am on this side of the phone and right now? That skyscraper in Miami seems a lifetime away. How is that bum shoulder after all these years?" she asked.

"Aliyana, my darlin' girl. It *is* you! I recall hearing a nasty rumor awhile back. Something about a plane crash and no evidence of survival?"

"You know you can't believe everything you hear," she countered. "Not in our business, anyway."

"Well, you're living proof of that," he said. "But wait a minute. You must've called this office for a reason. Are you here in Colombia? Are you all right? Do you need some help?"

She laughed over the rapid succession of questions. "Yes, I'm in Colombia, I'm all right, and I do need your help."

"Anything, sweetheart. Just name it," he said.

"I can't discuss any of this on the phone. So, if you're willing, I'll meet with you, along with a few of my friends, in Barranquilla. There's a deserted shack on the outskirts of town, complete with cellar. If I give you the exact GPS location, can you meet me there about nine thirty this evening?"

"You bet I can. Give me the location, and we'll be there."

****

They arrived in front of the shanty at nine fifteen. Wolf made a thorough check of the building before Aliyana descended the steps. She grabbed her nylon bag and while Wolf held her glow-stick and backpack, she dug around inside for her small propane lantern. Once she had the thing lit, she carried it over to and rested it on top of the large wooden crate against the wall. Wolf placed the laptop beside it.

"Now, I think if you stand against the wall just opposite the light, neither Greg nor his companions will see your faces with any distinction," she said. "That'll add credibility to what I'll tell them."

Wolf tested her theory by leaning against the wall. As she peered into the darkness she could just see his silhouette, the shadows of his beard, but nothing more. "That will do fine."

"All right, it'll only take a few minutes to get to the hotel and return. In the meantime, I would feel better about this whole thing if you waited up in the tree," he said.

She nodded as she acquired a satellite signal. "I'd already planned on doing that. That way I can watch for them. Let me get this set up, and I'll head outside."

Wolf returned to the site with two minutes to spare. He and his men waited until she spied Greg Donner coming toward the shanty. He had two marshals at his heels. She hurried down from the tree branch and brushed the debris off her pants.

"That's him," she whispered. "Go ahead and get yourselves in position and I'll bring them inside."

"Know that I can hear you, so scream or call out if you need me," Wolf said before he disappeared into the darkness.

"Don't worry, I will."

Greg's voice broke the silence. "Aliyana?" he whispered.

Smiling, she stepped from the shadows, and beckoned him to follow her down the steps. Once inside, she turned around and faced him. He stood so close they almost collided. The hug that followed all but squeezed the life from her body. Wolf shook his head, shifted his stance, and folded his arms against his chest.

She gave Wolf a helpless little shrug as she stepped back and gazed at her dear friend. "It's so good to see you, Greg. It's been a long time."

"You too darlin', and it's been far too long. How have you been?" he asked.

She took a moment to look him over. Even though the marshal now approached his fiftieth year, his physical condition rivaled that of any man half his age. He stood about six feet tall, had just a touch of gray in his otherwise dark brown hair and his hazel eyes twinkled with delight. The last time they worked together, he had dubbed her the daughter he never had, but wished he did. High praise indeed, coming from a man with such a distinguished reputation.

"All things considered, I'm doing very well. And standing right behind you is the reason I can say that. Without the invaluable assistance of these fine men, I wouldn't be here right now."

Greg and his companions turned their gazes toward Wolf and the boys.

"They're deeply entrenched in their current assignment and are working undercover at the moment. They mean no disrespect, but please understand their desire to remain in the shadows. For now, I'll introduce them to you only as the wolf pack."

Greg studied what he could see of their forms and gave them a conciliatory nod. "Gentlemen. You have my gratitude for taking care of my little girl."

"Our pleasure," said Wolf.

Greg gazed at Aliyana. "Now tell us what this is all about."

"Come on, I'll show you what I've gathered." She led the men to her computer. "Let me begin by telling you that during my most recent mission, I worked undercover inside the compound of Emil Rios Mercado. My mission was to gain intelligence on the inner workings of his drug cartel and gather enough evidence to put him away for life."

"Did you succeed?" asked Greg.

"Yes, I did," she replied. "But on my last day, after I slipped inside his office to download the information I needed, I found something quite unexpected."

"Which was?" Greg prodded.

"A plot to assassinate the DEA administrators and their families on American soil. This action is scheduled to take place very soon."

"Have you given your commander this information?"

"No. Unfortunately, I can't. Right now, I don't know who I can trust within the organization." Aliyana launched into a detailed explanation of everything they had uncovered to date.

She showed them every shred of accompanying proof. Greg and his men asked detailed questions along the way and by so doing, Wolf, Joris and Cornelius finally gleaned the specifics surrounding her escape from the compound. The revelation produced broad grins on the faces of Joris and Cornelius, which they promptly hid as best they could. Wolf scowled. She wished she could see inside his mind and know his thoughts. He didn't look the least bit amused.

She ended the narrative by laying out their plans to incapacitate the sub through the wolf pack. In so doing they could capture Hank, Jomini and Mercado with the help of the marshals. They were all on board with the mission.

"You've neglected to show these men Mercado's private logs," Wolf said.

Aliyana closed her eyes, tilted her chin upward, and sighed. That was the last thing she wanted Greg to know. She needed to kill herself a Wolf and she'd do it when the meeting ended.

"What logs?" asked Greg as he glanced first toward Wolf and then back at her.

"The one that offers two million dollars for her demise," Wolf said. "Go ahead, Aliyana, show him."

Yep. I am definitely going to kill him.

"Aliyana?" Greg pressed.

The marshal taking meticulous notes stepped a little closer. She turned around and pounded out the URL address on the keyboard and smacked the enter key with a little extra oomph. Emil's password followed in much the same manner. As the men gazed at the screen, she turned toward the captain. He topped his irritating smirk off with a wink. But just then, several expletives from Greg's mouth interrupted her irritation.

Wolf swept a hand toward the computer. "I thought it important that you read the logs for yourself. This way, while we're taking care of business in Cartagena, we'll all take extra care in watching over Aliyana."

"You needn't worry about Aliyana, trust me," Greg replied. "Now then, do we know exactly when this phase of the operation is going down?"

Before Aliyana could open her mouth, Joris moved a half-step forward. "Yes sir, we do. Mercado and Jomini, unbeknownst to each other, have agreed to meet our fictional Asian drug lord this coming Saturday, at one o'clock in the afternoon. A drug lord we must provide, by the way.

"They'll meet at Club Naútico marina thirty minutes apart. They'll look for a yacht named Florencia once they arrive. Our phantom drug lord promised he'd send the occupants of his yacht to the city for a day of shopping. Thus, he guaranteed uninterrupted solitude between the principles. However, you and your men will be hidden inside that yacht," he said.

"Excellent," Greg replied. "We'll have our team in place well ahead of schedule. We already have a warrant for Mercado, so that won't pose a problem."

For the next two hours, the men planned their strategy for apprehending Hank Morris, Jomini, and Emil Mercado down to the smallest detail.

At last, Greg turned toward Wolf. "What about the sub?" he asked. "How do you and your men plan to disable her?"

"The sub has compartments we can conceal ourselves in until we're well on our way. When the moment's right, we'll use our technology and override the controls. Once we have control, we'll set a course toward Puerto Rico. About an hour outside our intended destination, we'll render the sub powerless."

Broad grins appeared on the faces of the marshals. Greg nodded his approval. "If you'd like, I can contact the coast guard in the morning and let them know they can expect you anytime within the next two weeks. When you're ready, just pick up the radio. Tell them the Wolf pack is about to deliver their package and give them the location. They'll understand and take care of the rest."

"Sounds good, I'd appreciate that sir," Wolf replied.

At the end of their planning session, Greg gazed at Aliyana as he took hold of her hands. "You have my personal cell phone number. If any of you need anything at all, between now and Saturday, just give me a call—anytime of the day or night. If I don't hear from you, we'll meet the pack at the dock around noon. In the meantime, we'll pick you up at the designated location at 0600 hours, and follow the plans as outlined."

A short while later, she and Wolf boarded the boat and headed for the *Wieven*. Joris and Cornelius returned to the hotel.

Wolf broke the silence first. "Donner seems like a nice enough man."

She nodded. "Yes, he is."

"He seemed pleased to see you." Wolf had a slight edge to his tone.

Aliyana smiled. "Did I forget to mention that he likes to think of me as the daughter he never had? Apparently, he likes my spunk—a thing which is absent in most females of his acquaintance, he said."

"Yes, well, that spunk has a tendency to alarm me at times." His gaze drilled into hers as he shook his head. "You took on an armed guard with nothing but a knife zipped up inside your backpack?"

She waved a hand of dismissal. "There's no need to look at me like that. I wouldn't have done it unless I had complete confidence in my ability to carry out the maneuver."

He muttered something in return she couldn't quite hear, but she didn't miss the tone. *Better just to keep quiet, and give him the opportunity to calm down, right?*

The passage of time, the serenity of the night, and the gentle lapping of the waves underneath the boat calmed his inner beast. She wouldn't awaken it by bringing up Mercado. Instead, she dropped her hand over the side of the boat and played with the water.

"You seem a little more relaxed since we've had our meeting," Wolf said as he worked the oars.

"Everything is coming together, and I just feel like this huge weight has been lifted from my shoulders." She gazed into his eyes and smiled. "Thank you, Wolf. I couldn't have done any of this without you."

"There's no need to thank me, *lieveling*. I volunteered for the assignment, remember? As it turns out, this journey of ours gave me far more than what I gave in return. In just under two weeks, we'll head to open sea where we'll seek a storm and a portal. Once I find both, I'll take my beautiful wife-to-be home, where I promise I'll love and cherish her for every single day of forever."

Her tummy did about a half-dozen flip-flops over the way he looked at her just now. The heat rose in her cheeks. Not that she cared. "You don't know how wonderful that sounds. As you might have already guessed, it's been quite a while since I've had a place I could really call home."

"Well, you have one now," he said.

"Tell me about it." She turned around and leaned her back against the side of the boat.

"Well, the front exterior of our home faces the sea," he began.

"Now why doesn't that surprise me," she teased. "And I suppose you anchor your ship just a short way off in the distance."

"Of course." A devilish grin accompanied a wink. "You never know when we might need a quick getaway."

The comment, most likely spoken in truth, made her laugh. "What about the interior of your home?"

"The interior of *our* home, you mean?"

"Yes, our home," she clarified.

"The place is filled with all kinds of furnishings from centuries past that you, my love, are allowed to rearrange to your heart's content. We have things stored in the basement should you choose to use those pieces instead. If nothing we own suits your fancy, we can go shopping for something that does."

She wondered if anything she now imagined even came close to what she'd see in the very near future. "I can hardly wait to see it."

"Not too much longer now and you will," he replied. "That, my love, is a promise you can count on."

A curious wave of apprehension shot through her body. A thing born, perhaps, from years of insecurity and fear. She sought at once to banish it and held on instead to the promise.

Chapter Twenty-Four

Cornelius propped an elbow on top of the port side railing and gazed down river. "Here they come again," he said.

Aliyana couldn't hear the boats yet, but they would come into view in a minute or two. They had arrived in groups of three all throughout the night. No one on board uttered a single word as they loaded Mercado's drugs into the sub. Not a soul at the compound said anything concerning the imminent arrangements either. The night's activity had simply proved their plans to move the drugs.

She didn't have a clue as to the appointed hour they would leave or in which direction they would sail. Those unknown details drove her to distraction.

"How many do you see this time?" she asked as she approached the railing and peered into the darkness.

"Same three as before," Wolf said.

"That's twelve loads so far, then." Aliyana chewed on a fingernail as she considered this quandary. They had a little over twenty-four hours before Greg would arrive and whisk them away to Cartagena. But, what if the sub left before they returned? Dare they take the chance that it might? Her heart hammered in slow, even strokes against her chest as she thought of the best way to bring the problem to Wolf's attention. There wasn't one. "I think we might have a dilemma."

"What kind of a dilemma?" he asked.

"Well, in light of what we've seen tonight, we must face the very real possibility that this sub will leave before we take care of our mission in Cartagena."

Wolf shrugged as if it wasn't a concern. "So what if it did?"

"So, it might be best if you stay with the ship and handle things here, while I go to Cartagena with Greg." She held her breath and waited for his reaction.

"Absolutely not." Wolf shook his head as he firmed his jaw. "You're not going there alone."

"I'm not going to be alone. Have you forgotten? I'll have several well-trained U.S. marshals and five Colombian ghosts with me at all times."

"Okay, then let me say you're not going without me. None of them will protect you like I will," he countered. "Besides, I think we'll have time to spare."

"What if we don't?"

"Then we'll just catch up to the sub once we've finished the job in Cartagena," he said.

"You know that won't work, Wolf." She shook her head as she placed a hand on her hip. "First of all, you have no idea the direction that sub will go. Therefore, we won't be able to find it once it leaves. Second, once the architect of the assassination plot is unmasked, I'll have to give a final, detailed report to the DEA. That will take even more valuable time away from the ship. I just don't see how we can possibly—"

"Then tell me something," he cut in. "If such is the case, how will you find us at the conclusion of your task, if I leave you in the hands of the marshals and a handful of inexperienced ghosts?"

"Well, um," she stammered as she sought a quick

solution. "We could set up a rendezvous point and when we've both completed our assignments, we'll meet up at the designated place."

"In following that same line of thinking, you and I, as a team, could do the same thing. We can simply have my men sail my ship to this meeting place and pick us up after they take care of the sub and its occupants."

Aliyana sighed and glanced toward the deck. "You must be on board the craft alongside your men, Wolf. You've already told me that it'll take all of you to incapacitate the thing."

He hesitated for only a moment. "Yes, I did say that. But it's possible my men can accomplish it without me," he argued.

"It's also possible they can't. Will you really let the success of this mission hinge on possibilities? We must make sure those men never reach Virginia. If they do, everything we've done this far will count for nothing."

Wolf said nothing in return. Nonetheless, she could see his inner struggle as he dropped his head, closed his eyes, and blew out a ragged sigh. At once she pressed her advantage.

"I promise you, I'll be all right and lest it has slipped your mind, I do have a few skills of my own, Captain. After all, as I have reminded you often enough, I've made it through in one piece this far."

Wolf shook his head. "Aliyana—"

"No, Wolf," she said. "There's nothing more important than keeping that sub from reaching Virginia, and you know it. You also know we must get it close enough to U.S. territory to give the coast guard the authority to take over. Sinking the thing in Colombian waters won't complete the mission."

"This isn't a decision we must make right now," Wolf replied. "Let's just wait and see what tomorrow brings. Keep in mind that the sub can carry a very large cargo. I should think it might take a couple of nights to load the thing to full capacity."

"*If* they load it to full capacity with drugs. We don't know how many men will sail inside it. Bodies take up valuable space, as well you know."

Before she could argue further, Joris emerged from the sub. He waved a recorder in the air while he crossed the area between the ships.

"I take it someone finally spoke?" asked Wolf.

Joris nodded as he handed Aliyana the device. "Yes, indeed. I just recorded a short conversation between the captain and one of Mercado's lackeys. I thought you should listen to it now, in case they said something of value."

Aliyana pushed the playback button. Wolf gazed at her intently as she listened to the exchange. Her facial expression must have translated the subject matter for him. He dropped his gaze and sighed as she turned off the device.

"According to this conversation, they'll leave a couple of hours before Greg is scheduled to arrive," she said. "They also said—"

"Do you know where they'll drop off their contraband?"

"No, they didn't talk about that. I only know that according to plan, they'll make one other brief stop. They didn't say why or for what. But if I had to guess, I'd say they'll load additional drugs from another area along the river."

He remained silent for several uncomfortable

minutes. What could she say that would put him at ease? She didn't like the idea of a separation any more than he did.

"Wolf—"

He held up a hand to stop her comment. "Don't say it, Aliyana. Please, not right now."

She lowered her gaze as she nodded. "All right. I'll wait for you inside the cabin."

****

Wolf didn't say a word as she headed to his cabin. He couldn't. Everything she said smacked of truth, but that didn't mean he had to like it. And it certainly didn't mean he could quash the fear that had suddenly seized him. A fear that something might go wrong, that something would happen to prevent her from sailing away with him.

Every vision he created of Aliyana at his side and within his realm, crashed into his mind. Their marriage, the joyful expressions he conjured as she explored the unique beauty of his world, the intimate moments in the home they would share, the long walks, and the grand adventures that awaited them. He couldn't endure the pain if something happened to take those hopes and dreams away from him.

Wolf strode aft of the ship and focused on the rhythmic, rippling water until the faint light of dawn reflected her colors. Joris and Cornelius had the good sense to stay away from him as he struggled to come to terms with the inevitable separation. At last, he drew in a deep breath of the damp earth that surrounded his ship, slowly released it, and made his way to the cabin.

He found Aliyana seated, with an elbow on the table and a curved hand bracing her chin. The oceanic map on the computer screen had her full attention. He approached the back of the chair and combed his fingers through the length of her hair, several times over. "What are you looking at so studiously?"

"Possible places for us to meet once we've finished our assignments." She pointed to a small group of islands just to the right of the screen. "These islands are off Puerto Rico. I think they would suit our purposes best since the ship will ultimately head in that direction. Specifically, the atoll called Desecheo, right here. It's a small, uninhabited island that's now closed to the public. I know I can get permission to wait for you there should I finish ahead of you."

"I know that island well, and it's a good choice I think," he said as he knelt beside her. "Let's meet right here on the northwestern boundary. There's a bit of a clearing as I recall. If you arrive first, we'll be able to spot you easily. We can row the boat over and pick you up in no time at all. If we arrive first, we'll simply moor the ship as close as we can get her to shore and wait."

She nodded. "That sounds good to me."

"I have only one question. How do you purpose to get there from Cartagena?" he asked.

"I'll let Greg figure that part out for me," she said as she finally turned and gazed into his eyes. "He has the authority to arrange things like that."

"Speaking of Greg, he should know about this change in plans. I'd like to be the one to tell him, if you don't mind."

"I don't mind," she replied. "Do you want to call him now or wait until the sun is a little higher in the sky?"

"Now is as good a time as any, and he'll need all

the time he can get to adjust his plans."

She took the stolen phone, found the marshal's number entered earlier, and handed the device off even as it rang.

"Greg Donner here," said the voice at the other end.

"Donner? This is the captain of the wolf pack, speaking."

"Hey, buddy. Everything still going according to plan?" he asked.

"Unfortunately, we have an unexpected change," he replied. "I hate to bail on you at the last moment, but we've just received intelligence that the sub is leaving in less than twenty-four hours. Therefore, my men and I can't lend a hand in Cartagena as planned."

"No problem," said Greg. "We can take care of things ourselves well enough. I have plenty of good men here that can take up the slack. We're still on schedule to pick up Aliyana as per plans though, correct?"

"Yes, she'll be awaiting your arrival in the designated place and at the specified time. And Donner—although unnecessary I'm sure—I need to remind you that Aliyana has a heavy bounty on her head. I need to know you'll take good care of her in our absence."

"She's very precious to me as well, sir. We'll keep her safe and sound. Count on it."

"There's one more thing. Once you've finished your objective in Cartagena, Aliyana will need safe passage to Desecheo Island with enough supplies to last a couple of days in the off chance she arrives ahead of us. Can you take care of that?"

Debbie Peterson

"Yes, I can. You needn't worry about a thing on this end. All you need to do is make sure that submarine, Mercado's lieutenants, and those drugs never reach Virginia."

"They won't."

Despite all the marshal's assurances, Wolf worried all throughout the remainder of the day, though he didn't let Aliyana see it. Instead, he occupied their time with an abundance of laughter, lighthearted conversation, and the making of plans for their future together.

Hours after she had sought her bed for some much-needed sleep, Joris approached him.

"*Kapitein*, do you think I should gather the men and bring them back to the ship now? We have but a few hours before the sub is scheduled to sail."

Wolf blew out a sigh and nodded. "Yes, I suppose it's time. Bring Pedro and his companions up to speed before you leave. Let them know we cannot be there to help them in apprehending our targets. Ask him to please take special care in watching over Aliyana during the forthcoming operation."

"Don't worry, Wolf." Joris gently squeezed Wolf's shoulder. "I'll make sure he understands the importance of that duty."

"I'd appreciate that," he said.

"All right then. I'll be back shortly with men in tow."

Seconds after Joris left the ship, he turned toward the unmistakable patter of Aliyana's footsteps. She wore a white, oversized, button-up, short-sleeved blouse meant to conceal her weapon and a pair of white slacks. A charming blush stole across her cheeks as his gaze meandered over her form.

She lifted the sunglasses she clasped in her hand. "Do you think I'll blend in with the rest of the natives at the marina?"

He drew her into his embrace and shook his head. "I'm afraid, *lieveling*, you'll always stand out in a crowd, no matter what you wear."

A small smile turned a corner of her mouth just before he covered it with a searing kiss. He followed it up with another and then another. Wolf found he couldn't get enough of her sweet kisses. Not when he must leave her so soon. When at last he let her breathe, she stepped back and traced her lips with her fingers.

"If you keep that up, I won't be able to concentrate on my job," she said.

"You mustn't do that. I just want to make sure you don't lose sight of our ultimate goal."

"Don't worry. I won't. I couldn't."

He swallowed his fear, for it served no purpose at the moment. "I love you, Aliyana, more than I ever thought it possible to love anyone. You're my whole life. Please remember that, and stay safe while we're apart."

A hint of moisture gathered inside her eyes as he made the declaration. "In return, keep in mind how very much I love you. Please, don't take foolish chances on board that sub. Get that vessel to American waters, incapacitate the thing, and get out."

Wolf chuckled, turned his gaze heavenward, and tsked. "Of all the things that cause you worry—" he sighed and shook his head. "You needn't concern yourself over us, Aliyana. We have the easy end of this quest."

"And a thousand things could go wrong in the attempt, especially when you get cocky."

"I'm never cocky," he said. When she lifted a brow, he added, "Almost never—and certainly not when we're in the middle of a mission. We always give each of our assignments our full and undivided attention."

"I certainly hope so, because in just a few days we'll be on board this ship, heading into the triangle looking for a portal to take us home."

He cupped her face with his hands and drew close to her lips. "Nothing will stop that from happening. That, *lieveling*, is a promise," he whispered, just before he kissed her.

Their time together ended a short while later as the crew of the *Witte Wieven* returned, ready for duty, and not a moment too soon. Boats bearing Mercado's lieutenants and a small number of other personnel drifted into view. The hatch of the sub lifted as the boats drew alongside the craft. One by one, the men entered into the vessel.

Aliyana turned toward him as the activity finally slowed down. "Shouldn't you board now as well?"

"No, we won't board until we're heading out to sea and only then to determine our destination. That task will only require a single member of the crew. Once he discovers our destination, he'll return and report. Then, when the time comes to chart our course toward Puerto Rico, we'll all board the *Barracuda*."

"How will you reach her if she's diving deep?" she asked.

"We'll swim down, of course." A quiet chuckle accompanied the light caress against her cheek. "Don't look so concerned, my love. We've accomplished it before and without harm. Besides, with our line attached to the sub, we can control her depth and rate of speed from the *Wieven*."

She nodded and nibbled at her lower lip. "I know we've already gone over this, but please, Wolf, don't take any unnecessary risks."

"I won't if you give me the same assurance," he countered.

"You have my word."

In less than half an hour, the sub set sail as the *Barracuda* towed the *Wieven* slowly behind her. Wolf trailed them both as he rowed the ship's boat toward her point of rendezvous with Greg Donner. They crossed the river in silence, each, he supposed, lost in their own thoughts. Finally, as she gazed down at her GPS, Aliyana swept a hand toward the riverbank.

"Anywhere in here," she whispered.

Wolf merely nodded and turned the craft toward the west bank. Once they exited, he tied off the boat. He took hold of her hand as well as her backpack and together, they headed for the interior of the jungle.

Just before they entered the boundaries presented by the tall grass and variety of trees, she stopped and turned to face him. "Will you be able to catch up with your men if you walk with me to the clearing?"

He nodded. "As long as I don't dally overly long."

"You don't have to provide an escort, Wolf. Greg should be along soon, and I'll be all right during the few minutes I'm by myself. The glade isn't that far away."

"I know." He swung her around to face him. "But leaving you here is a little more difficult than what it might seem, so indulge the whim, all right?"

"Okay. Just don't miss your ride."

"I won't." He cocked his head to the right. "Come on. The faster we get this done, the quicker we can be together."

If all goes well...

Chapter Twenty-Five

The clearing loomed before them much sooner than she anticipated or desired. The lump in her throat grew larger as they stopped underneath the boughs of a nearby plumeria tree. All the while, she hoped she wouldn't make a silly spectacle of herself by crying like a baby before he left her.

He scanned the horizon before he captured her gaze. "The helicopter is approaching," he said. "I can hear it."

She could only nod in response.

For a moment, he looked heavenward. As he gathered her close to his chest, he kissed the top of her head. He then gazed deeply into her eyes. "I love you, Aliyana."

"And I love you," she whispered as traitorous tears threatened to tumble down her cheeks. She gulped as she placed the GPS in his hand. "I'll see you soon."

"Don't keep me waiting."

The kiss he gave before he disappeared was unlike any he had ever given her before. Within that kiss was the staggering depth of his love, and it was a mighty and powerful gift indeed. She responded as best she could. Once he ended the kiss, he disappeared.

The thunderous sounds of the helicopter helped her gain control over her emotions. She wiped at the corners of her eyes, sniffed, and walked toward the outer rim of the clearing.

The chopper hovered high above the trees for several minutes. Branches and bushes swayed violently from the force of the blades. Aliyana spied Greg now. He, and a couple of the other marshals, made a visual sweep of the area. They had their weapons poised and ready. At last, he signaled the all clear to the pilot. Seconds later, the copter landed.

Donner and his men leaped to the ground with their assault rifles raised shoulder height. The moment she stepped into the glade, he waved her forward and helped her board. Yet he never once took his gaze off of their surroundings. But really, she expected no less after Wolf's stern lecture.

Minutes later, the helicopter took off. The rotorcraft turned around and headed toward Barranquilla. There, they'd trade their current mode of transportation for the airplane which would then take them to Cartagena.

If all went according to their well-laid plans, in just a few hours' time, the marshals would have Emil Mercado, Hank Morris, and Jomini in custody. They would uncover the mole's identity and determine if anyone else was involved in the assassination plot. She'd then give her evidence and final report to the DEA. After she finalized that report, she'd hand in her resignation—effective immediately—and then she'd go to Desecheo Island where she would await Wolf's arrival.

If all went well...

Greg leaned in close and gave her knee a gentle pat. "You look a little pensive this morning. Is everything all right?" he shouted above the engine roar and whirling blades.

Aliyana flashed a smile as she tucked her backpack underneath the seat, between her feet. "Yes, of course. Everything is just fine. Why do you ask?"

He swiped a hand back and forth against his mouth as he gazed at her with a bit of doubt. "Worried about your boyfriend?"

She breathed out a quiet laugh and shook her head. "My boyfriend?"

"Oh, come on, Montijo." He snorted. "You don't really think you hid that fact from me, did you?"

She shrugged as she touched the tip of her tongue to the top of her lip. "Well, at the very least, I gave it my best shot."

"Didn't work. I know you too well." He lifted a brow. "Tell me something, sweetheart, is the fierce captain of the wolf pack worthy of your affections?"

"Every bit of it and then some. I only hope I'm worthy of his."

Greg blew out a derisive breath and waved her comment aside. "Don't be ridiculous. There isn't a man on this earth who wouldn't beg on bended knee to have you at his side. You can tell him I said so. Furthermore, you can also tell him if he doesn't treat you like the exceptional woman you are, he'll have to tangle with me."

Aliyana laughed as she fought off the urge to tell him that after this mission ended, he'd probably never see either of them again.

"In the meantime, give your captain a little credit," he said. "I think with the extraordinary set of skills he has, your man can handle his job well enough."

Aliyana laid her hands in her lap and nodded. "Yes,

he can. He's very good at what he does."

"Then don't worry." Greg winked. He leaned back in his seat, and for the duration of the flight, he maintained his silence.

From the airport in Barranquilla, they boarded the plane for Cartagena. Upon arrival they were met by a warm, gentle breeze and a sky dotted with white, puffy clouds. Both helped bolster her spirits. Greg led her toward two black, late model Cadillac Escalades, parked off in the distance.

"We'll split up the team," Greg informed her as he escorted her toward the second car. "I already have several men in position at and near our base of operations. I'll send a couple of these men in their direction now. The rest of us will follow in about fifteen minutes."

Aliyana nodded. "Sounds good."

He pulled a map from out of his pocket and spread it out on top of the car's hood. He pointed to the top, right-hand corner. "This is the most logical route for our targets to follow on their way in. However, it's not impossible for them to enter the marina here or even from here. We're keeping all roads under surveillance. In the meantime, we'll move into position and await their arrival."

"You already have our decoy family and staff on board the yacht?" she asked.

"Absolutely. We've had them there since early Thursday morning. From all reports, they've enjoyed acting the part of the spoiled, rich tourists," Greg said. "We have enough bodies on board so that no one will notice our exchange of places as they vacate the craft."

Aliyana glanced down at her watch. The appointed

hour swiftly approached. Had the principal players already arrived in Cartagena as well? She looked up from the map. "Keep in mind that Mercado will have appointed surveillance teams of his own. He'll watch for the smallest sign of a trap and act accordingly if they suspect our presence."

"We've already located his surveillance teams and they're under our observation as we speak." Donner folded his map, shoved it back inside his pocket, and opened the car door. "They arrived yesterday morning, and I'm told they all seem a little bored with their duties. I've assigned members of my task force to take them out of the game and place them under arrest the minute Mercado boards the *Florencia*. We'll discuss the details on our way to Club Naútico."

Forty-five minutes later, their luxury vehicle entered the marina. Greg turned toward her then and gave her a nod. "Are you ready to go?"

She exhaled a deep breath, donned the oversized sunglasses, and grabbed her backpack. "Yes, I am."

"All right then, let's get to it. We've a trio of men to take into custody."

Laughing, they exited the car. He slipped an arm around her waist and pulled her close. After he planted a kiss on her lips, he led her toward the pier, keeping a leisurely pace.

At the far end of the dock, she spied the *Florencia* and the spiritual form of Pedro awaiting her arrival. He swept a hand toward her and bowed. She acknowledged his presence with a slight incline of her head and a smile. In continuance of the plan, she and Greg boarded the boat next to the *Florencia*. Once they stepped on deck, the captain cranked over the engines, as if they were about to set sail. Ten minutes later, amidst a continual hubbub of activity and noise outside, the agent players left the target ship for their scheduled "shopping trip." During the commotion, Aliyana and Greg stealthily boarded the *Florencia,* while the decoy ship they boarded minutes earlier backed out of the berth.

"How many agents have remained on board?" she whispered as Pedro sidled up next to her. She didn't see any of his companions, at least not yet.

"Six," Greg replied as he placed his earpiece into position and handed one to her. "Four of them are hidden from sight. Nonetheless, they can still guard the entrance and passageways in the event one of our targets decides to get creative or we receive some uninvited guests. I have one man positioned just across from the library. That's where the meeting with Marshal Randall Lee, our Asian "drug lord," will take place. Once our targets are inside the room, we'll move in according to plan. Come on, I'll show you the layout."

Greg led the way down the steps and into the lavishly decorated salon. Empty and partially empty glasses sat on top of the bar. The seat cushions lay scattered about and leftover food sat abandoned on the plates. All of which gave credence to their ruse. They moved down the corridor and toward the library. One of the marshals stepped out from an adjoining room and into the hallway to give an updated report. While they spoke, she inched her way toward Pedro.

"Has either Hank or Mercado arrived?" she whispered behind the hand that rubbed her nose.

The ghost shook his head. "Not yet, but they're on

their way. At this time, my companions ride inside the vehicle to guarantee Hank's continued cooperation. We'll remain at his side until your men have him in custody."

A bit of humor washed over her as she envisioned a terrified Hank, still surrounded by ruthless ghosts who looked for the slightest excuse to seize his soul. Would that she could witness it.

"Aliyana," said Donner as he turned toward her, "I'll have you step in here with Marshal Burnham. I'll wait in the cabin across the hall. After Mercado walks through the library door, and Morris vacates the area, we'll move in simultaneously. At that point we'll take him down. Any questions?"

"Will you take him off the boat before Hank returns with Jomini?" she asked.

"No, I won't draw anyone's attention to what's taking place here until after we've secured Jomini and Morris as well. You know as well as I that when someone is in handcuffs, it draws a curious crowd. We'll keep Mercado subdued down in the crew's quarters until we're ready to escort all our targets off this vessel."

Pedro leaned close to her face. "There's no need for worry, *señorita*. I'll have one of my companions keep the drug lord quiet and in place. He won't become a problem."

They secreted themselves away in their designated positions and waited. Minutes ticked off the clock. Aliyana didn't hear anything but the gentle waves slapping up against the yacht. Then, just as she again glanced at her watch, Pedro cocked his head toward the pier.

"They're coming," he said.

Aliyana nodded and withdrew her pistol. Marshal Burnham followed suit. The sound of footsteps accompanied the gentle rocking of the boat as their targets boarded. The footsteps hesitated for just a brief moment before they resumed their path. She lifted her eyes upward and tracked the steps down the deck and over to the stairway. A minute, maybe two, passed before she heard the sound of muffled voices. Another minute passed. She could now understand every word of their conversation.

Hank gave Mercado last minute instructions. She could detect the trepidation in his tone even if Emil didn't. Hank just informed his companion that the Asian drug lord demanded the utmost respect and privacy. He then finished this warning by saying he would knock at the door, and when "Gan Teo" invited them to enter, he would make a brief introduction and leave them to their business. However, he added, he'd wait just outside the door to escort him off the ship. Mercado merely grunted in response.

A knock at the door sounded. A male voice with a heavy Asian accent bid them enter in Spanish. One set of footsteps proceeded inward. Hank made a quick introduction and the door closed. Her heart hammered inside her chest as Morris tiptoed down the hall and off the boat. She held her breath and waited for Burnham to receive a signal from Greg. Seconds later, the marshal nodded. With skilled precision, they converged into the hall and burst through the library door.

Mercado whipped around. His eyes bulged as he stared first at her and then down the barrel of her gun.

She lifted a contemptuous brow. "*Hola*, Emil,

cómo estas?"

Mercado clenched his teeth and hissed. His gaze darted between the pair of armed marshals that flanked her, but he said nothing in response. He slowly raised his hands skyward and placed them behind his head. Marshal Lee advanced from behind, and taking one arm at a time, cuffed Emil's hands behind his back. Randall kicked Mercado's legs apart with his foot and patted him down. The marshal extracted a small pistol tucked inside Mercado's belt, and a knife hidden inside his boot. Burnham escorted him to a cabin down below where another marshal would stand guard over him.

"Mercado's men have all been rounded up quietly and without incident," announced Greg once Burnham returned. "Now we just have to apprehend Morris and this Jomini character."

Aliyana let go of a breath. "They should be along soon enough."

"All right, let's get back into position everyone, and wait for their approach."

Seconds turned to minutes, first five and then ten. More than once her mind slipped away from the here and now and wandered toward Wolf. Each time she shook away her worry. She corralled her concentration, reining it back to the here and now. Pedro, still at her side, lifted his chin and gave her a signaling nod. Once again, she withdrew her pistol as she awaited the sound of footsteps. Hank and Jomini ascended the steps and strode down the length of the hall in total silence. A knock on the library door accompanied a sharp intake of breath. "Gan Teo" commanded the men to enter. The door creaked, inching toward closure. Before it latched, Burnham gave her a firm nod and together, they burst into the hallway. Greg, a half step ahead of them, grabbed Hank's arm. He twisted it behind the man's back, whirled him around, and forced him inside the library.

Jomini gasped even before he spun around to assess the threat. His gaze darted about the room and then landed on Greg Donner. Aliyana briefly wondered at the shocked expression twisting the mole's features into a mask of disbelief and horror. Jomini whipped back his coat and yanked at the gun resting inside his holster. He aimed his weapon at Greg. She leaped forward to intercept. Marshal Lee jumped from behind, swung his arm around Jomini's neck, and pulled the man backward. Jomini coiled his body in her direction as the gun fired.

In the ensuing melee, Aliyana lost her balance, but didn't know how or why. She was falling both sideways and backward, despite all attempts to halt the descent. Voices echoed inside her head as she hit the floor, but she couldn't make out a single thing they said. The swirling blackness that engulfed her mind pulled her away from the feeble effort.

****

"Aliyana...," the voice whispered close to her ear. A large hand gently rubbed the top of hers. "Can you hear me, sweetheart? Aliyana...open your eyes."

She met Greg Donner's concern with confusion. The agonizing pain in her head barred her from any kind of response. She didn't want to open her eyes. The marshal swore under his breath and then asked for the doctor's ETA. Someone said, "About five minutes or so."

He heaved a sigh. "Why can't the man hurry?

She's been unconscious too long, if you ask me."

A doctor? Why did he need a doctor? Who was unconscious? She struggled against the heaviness and pain in search of a memory that would make sense of this current situation. Finally, she remembered. A panicked Jomini yanked his weapon from its hiding place, aimed it at Greg, and fired. She could still hear the sound of the blast and smell the powder residue that hung in the air. *Did Jomini shoot Greg?* At once she forced her eyes open. She had to know—

"Aliyana." The marshal gazed at her with concern. "Talk to me, sweetheart. Tell me how you feel."

"I'm…I'm okay…" She placed a hand to her brow as the memory of the exchange sharpened. "What happened? Are-are you all right, Greg? He didn't hurt you, did he?"

Greg shook his head and snorted. "Of all the ridiculous— No, he didn't even get close to me. The one we need to worry about right now is you."

"Me?" Other than a pounding headache, she couldn't complain. She tried to raise her head and shoulders off the ground, without success.

"Whoa, now," he said, pressing her back. "You have a nasty gash on your head and it's bleeding quite heavily. I'm putting pressure against the wound to staunch the flow. So just hold still and wait until medical help arrives."

She lifted a hand toward the center of her pain. "How did I injure myself?"

"I'm not quite sure how that happened, to be perfectly honest with you. Warren Holtz drew his weapon, but as he fired, Randall threw him off his aim. You went down at that precise moment and for a minute there, we all thought you were hit. The angels must've watched your back because, miraculously, that bullet missed you. However, you struck your head on the sharp edge of that table over there and got a nasty gash. I'm pretty sure you'll need some stitches."

"Wait—wait a minute." That memory seemed hazy. If the bullet didn't hit her, why did she fall? Then she remembered a forceful, downward yank that knocked her off balance. She turned her head slightly to her right. Pedro met her questioning gaze with an almost imperceptible shrug of his shoulders and a modest grin. *Oh, of course.* For the time being, she thanked her 'angel' for saving her life with a grateful smile. He acknowledged that with a wink.

She cleared her throat. "Then my angels have my heartfelt gratitude, truly they do. Now, I think you've just identified Jomini as Warren Holtz. Who is he, and how does he know you?"

Disgust and revulsion passed over Greg's face and it took a moment for him to simmer down. "Just as you suspected, the man does indeed work for the DEA, or at least he did an hour ago. He worked intelligence. No surprise there, right?"

"No, we thought perhaps he might've worked somewhere in that division," she breathed out.

"Yes, well, in answer to your question, several years ago we worked together on a couple of tough cases, but none of that matters right now. You needn't concern yourself about him any further. I've already alerted the DEA. They're sending an officer in the morning to sort everything out. I'll brief the man and then pass off all of the evidence you gave me, unless you wish to do it yourself. From there, I'll make sure you get to Desecheo."

"Thank you." The familiar feeling of nausea took hold. She closed her eyes, hoping to ward off the need to throw up. The pressure of Greg's fingers made the side of her head throb. If it didn't hurt so badly, she might've laughed. For it seemed she injured her head very near the same location as before. *What would Klaus think of that?*

Sometime later, she awoke. Aliyana forced her eyes open and took in her surroundings. Calm, ocean waves gently rocked the yacht. They could easily lull her back to sleep if she wasn't careful. The bed in which she lay sat inside the same cabin she occupied while waiting for the arrival of their targets. Or at least it seemed so. She didn't see, or feel, any sign of her ghostly companions. Somehow, she knew they were gone. That didn't surprise her. Nonetheless, they had her overwhelming appreciation for the part they played. The mission couldn't have been completed without them.

Her head still hurt. She placed gentle fingers on top the center of her pain. Several stitches met her investigation of the wound. Just then, Greg entered in through the door, with Eduardo Romero trailing a single step behind him.

Aliyana smiled as their eyes met. "Eduardo! Hello—long time, no see."

"Getting into trouble again, Montijo?" her commander teased.

She shrugged. "Well, you know me."

His chuckle accompanied a wink. "Yes, I know you."

"How are you feeling this morning?" asked Greg.

"Morning?" She knit her brows as he leaned down and kissed her on the forehead.

The marshal sat down on the edge of her bed then and took her hand. "Morning it is and for the second time around. You needn't look so concerned about the length of your stay. After all, I think it worked out for the best."

"Why do you say that?" she asked, fighting to still her rising panic. *Wolf, did he know?*

"Because none of the gawkers caught sight of your face. Everyone has dispersed. The bad guys from this neck of the woods are in custody. All of them believe—as will the public—that Agent Aliyana Rosa Montijo is dead. We made sure the media got plenty of pictures of the linen-filled body bag, exiting the craft."

Her gaze darted a couple of times between Greg and Eduardo while she sought to absorb this unexpected information.

"We thought it for the best. If the principal players and the general public believe you died in the line of duty, no one will be looking to collect on that two-million-dollar bounty," said Greg.

"That's right," Eduardo chimed in. "We can change the look of your face if you like and give you a brand-new identity. That way you can keep working as a field agent for the DEA without always having to look over your shoulder."

A sense of relief filled Aliyana over the news and she nodded. "Perfect, except I'm handing in my resignation, effective immediately," she said.

"No!" said Eduardo, even as Greg chuckled.

"Not to worry, Romero. Her resignation has nothing to do with current events. I daresay she made these plans quite a while ago."

She swallowed. "Speaking of those plans, have you received any reports from the coast guard?" she asked.

Donner glanced down at his watch. "As of two hours and sixteen minutes ago, they still hadn't been in contact with any member of the wolf pack. Don't worry though; it's still early. Keep in mind, the sub still had one more stop to make before they sailed for open sea."

"Wolf pack?" asked Eduardo. "What are you guys talking about?"

Aliyana spent the remainder of the morning answering all of Eduardo's questions. She gave him possession of all her evidence, including everything she collected on both Hank Morris and Warren Holtz.

"Impressive, Montijo," said Eduardo at the conclusion of her tale. "Are you sure you really want to resign? We could use you."

She cast her gaze downward and smiled. "Thank you for the compliment, but I'm very sure."

Several hours later, despite the disapproval of the doctor, she and Greg boarded a plane that would ultimately take her to Puerto Rico. From there he and a couple of his marshal buddies would personally escort her to Desecheo Island and her future with the captain of the *Witte Wieven*. All Wolf needed to do was complete his phase of the mission and come get her.

Chapter Twenty-Six

"They're not leaving very much room for the men to walk about," Joris remarked. "You know that'll lead to additional panic later on."

Wolf observed as the boat crew dropped the last of the drugs and crated cargo into the vessel. "Yes, it will."

The sub had turned east toward Venezuela. Shortly thereafter, they had sailed into the Caribbean Sea, navigating at a depth of thirty meters. All the while, the *Witte Wieven* cruised just above and a little behind them. Several tedious hours later, the *Barracuda* surfaced in a scheduled rendezvous with a couple of cigar boats that belonged to Mercado. Those men set about their task with the exactness and speed born of grueling repetition.

Not that it mattered now. For soon, if they hadn't already, Pedro and his ghostly companions would infiltrate Mercado's domain. They'd light the strategically placed fuses Johannes, Pieter and Cornelius had set earlier and destroy the whole of the drug lord's empire. A simple enough task, Pedro had assured them. He and his companions would take care of the duty the moment Hank, Jomini, and Mercado were taken into custody. Wolf could count on it.

He gazed toward the west, and for the millionth time settled his thoughts on Aliyana. If all had proceeded according to Donner's plan, the marshals would now have each of their targets in custody and know the identity of Jomini. Then, when the DEA officials arrived, Aliyana would give her report, her evidence, and her resignation. But things didn't always go according to plan. If only he could somehow contact her, hear her voice and know for certain—

"She's all right, Wolf," Joris said, breaking into his troubled thoughts.

He blew out a heavy breath and nodded but said nothing in response. Instead, he focused on the activity surrounding the sub. Those manning the cigar boats now exited the *Barracuda* in a somewhat orderly fashion, all things considered. Cornelius rose up from the hatch moments before the sub's crew closed and secured it. He then went back to the *Wieven*.

"Have they assigned a new heading?" asked Wolf as his quartermaster approached them.

Cornelius nodded. "Yes, they have. The captain—bless his sweet, pointed, little head—has just entered it into the ship's computer for me."

"Good. Let's go see where they're headed." Wolf turned, strode down the deck, descended the steps, and entered his cabin with both men following close behind. He retrieved the GPS device Aliyana gave him at the clearing and then entered the numbers just as Cornelius recited them. Seconds later, the map zeroed in on Santo Domingo.

"Excellent choice for them to have made. I couldn't have asked for better," Wolf said. "The Dominican Republic is not far from Puerto Rico. If luck remains our ally, the captain and crew won't notice the slight change in heading once we override the setting."

Joris shrugged. "Even if they did, it won't be an issue. They can't change our settings once we put them in place."

"No doubt they'll try though," Cornelius added.

Wolf's thoughts raced ahead. "I wonder if they'll drop their cargo in Santo Domingo or if they merely mean to refuel."

"I don't suppose it matters; we can't let them get that far west regardless of their intentions," said Joris.

"Not if we want this over and done with in a timely manner, anyway," Wolf replied. "Let's give them a couple of hours sailing time and then we'll board the sub and change the heading to about ten miles due south of Santa Isabel. Once there, we can contact the coast guard and disable the vessel. We'll then turn our sails toward Desecheo."

"I'll need the precise location," said Joris.

"I know. Hold on a minute." Wolf entered the information into the GPS device. Once the coordinates popped into view, he turned the screen toward Joris.

He studied the numbers for a moment and then nodded. "Got it. I'll await orders to make the change, *Kapitein*."

The sub sailed at what he considered a snail's pace, probably due to the weight the vessel carried. The long voyage sorely tested his patience. Finally, far later than he desired, he sent Joris to change their heading. Joris accomplished the small task, he said, with no one the wiser. Wolf then endured another round of endless waiting, with all the fortitude of a gnat, while they cruised toward their destination. The length of the journey set his teeth on edge.

"We're getting close to position now, *Kapitein*,"

Cornelius said as he held the GPS aloft.

"About time," Wolf muttered under his breath. "Johannes, make ready to hoist the sub to within fifteen meters of the surface for the first phase of this mission."

"Aye, *Kapitein*," Johannes called back as he manned the winch.

"Drop anchor and lower the sails," Wolf commanded.

The men hastened to their assigned tasks. Once complete, he issued the order to board the *Barracuda*. Each man, in precise order, took hold of the line and followed it down to the sub. They entered through the hatch and dispersed. He and Joris strode toward the control console, while the rest of his crew maneuvered through the crowded hallway toward the engine room.

As they entered the conning tower, they spied the captain of the *Barracuda* with his brows drawn tightly together. With sweat dripping down his face, he feverishly worked the controls.

Joris gave Wolf a nudge. "Wonder how long it'll take the twit to realize there's nothing wrong with the mechanics of his vessel?"

"He won't reach that conclusion; he hasn't the time. Just as soon as I contact the coast guard, we'll rob the sub's power."

"You'll not wait for the coast guard to arrive first, then?"

Wolf shook his head. "Nope, I no longer think that'll be necessary."

Joris snickered. "Prepare for mass pandemonium."

"Yes, well, that's precisely why we'll vacate the vessel sooner than intended."

"That and the fact there's a certain DEA agent you

hope awaits our arrival on an island about eighty-five nautical miles from our present location?"

Wolf stepped around the worried captain. He requisitioned the portable radio lying on the shelf and turned toward his first mate with stolen booty in hand. "We can't very well leave the damsel stranded, now can we?"

As he switched to the channel Donner assigned him, Joris laughed.

"All right," Wolf said. "This should only take me a few minutes. In the meantime, see you if can locate some kind of a line or rope to exchange with ours, and find something that floats. The larger and heavier, the better. A bold color would be nice too. The coast guard will need something they can easily find."

Joris returned a casual salute. "Aye, *Kapitein.*"

Wolf hurried back to the *Wieven* with radio in hand. His gaze drifted in the direction of Desecheo as he raised the radio to his mouth. "Coast guard, coast guard, coast guard, this is the captain of the wolf pack. Package intact and ready for delivery, 17.8049 degrees north 66.3876 degrees west, over."

"Roger, captain, we've expected your arrival and are ready to receive the package. Please standby, over."

"Captain of the wolf pack, standing by, over." He paced the length of his ship twice before the coast guard spoke again.

"Captain of the wolf pack, this is the coast guard. We have an FRC, repeat, we have a Fast Response Cutter headed in your direction, ETA 30 minutes. More vessels to follow, over."

"Roger, coast guard. Be advised, *Barracuda* dead in the water in twenty. Look for floating device on approach, captain of the wolf pack, over and out."

Wolf tossed the radio on the table inside his cabin before he made his way to the sub. Conrad and Laurens met him in the narrow corridor.

"We have located rope enough and some to spare. Laurens found some kind of inflatable boat as well. Once we quit the sub, we can attach the rope to both sub and raft easily enough. Oh, and by the way? Those crates carry armaments. Mercado has enough explosives inside this sub to blow up an entire city block, and you should see the arsenal they carry as well," said Conrad.

"All destined for Virginia, no doubt," Wolf replied.

Laurens nodded. "And ready for war."

Wolf shook his head in disgust. "I'll give the coast guard that information once we've finished our task down here. While I'm taking care of that, I'll let the two of you switch the lines and attach the raft."

"Aye, *Kapitein*," said Conrad.

"All right, give us a couple of seconds to get inside the conning tower and we'll get this done."

Wolf nodded at Joris and together, they entered the control room. Then, in concert, the crew of the *Witte Wieven* robbed the submarine of her power. A panic ensued as the lights failed first. Minute by passing minute, the remaining electronics followed. Shortly thereafter, the engine rumbled to a halt. Voices yelled out to one another in the dark. The men stumbled and shoved past each other in alarm.

"I wonder where everyone thinks they're going?" asked Joris.

"I haven't a clue," Wolf replied. "But it's quite clear they haven't conducted a single emergency drill."

"No surprise there," murmured Klaus. "But don't they know? They should try to conserve their oxygen, not waste it."

"Yes, well, let's get out from underfoot, shall we?"

Mere seconds later they were all on board the *Wieven*. Wolf went to his cabin and retrieved the discarded radio. He gave the coast guard detailed information as to what they could expect to find inside the sub and instructed them to proceed with caution. More than likely, the crew and passengers of the *Barracuda* would embrace their rescue. They wouldn't attempt to engage a perceived enemy in a firefight, especially not in a sub. Nonetheless, one should be prepared for all situations.

Conrad approached him as he stepped back on deck. He pointed to the large, inflated boat bobbing along the waves. "I think our friends can see that easily enough."

Wolf nodded. "Yes, that'll do."

"Weigh anchor, *Kapitein*?" Joris called out from his position at the helm.

"Not quite yet, Joris. I think we'll wait for the coast guard's arrival in case they need assistance. After all this, I don't want the mission to go awry now."

By the time the coast guard arrived, the weight of the sub tugged the raft downward and water trickled inside the craft. The cutter circled the floating raft several times over before the captain of that vessel cut her engines. Three members of the cutter's crew approached the port side of their boat and gazed at the raft while they talked.

"They seem a bit perplexed," said Joris.

Laurens nodded. "Perhaps they've never rescued a

sub before."

"They could be waiting for those other vessels to arrive," Cornelius said.

"Possible," Laurens replied. "And it's also possible they're adjusting their strategy now that they know about the armaments."

"I think I'll head over there and see what they're talking about," Wolf said. "Perhaps I could offer a mental suggestion or two if they find themselves stumped. If all seems well in hand, we'll go ahead and turn our sails toward Desecheo."

Joris dropped his foot from off the bottom railing. "I'm coming with you."

Laurens and Cornelius echoed the declaration. They arrived on board just as four men in diving gear splashed backward into the ocean. Wolf made his way up to the deck and passed into the bridge. He could see the captain of the cutter engaged in conversation on his radio.

"Affirmative. The sonar readings indicate vessel length at seventeen meters as per wolf pack report. We're retrieving the attached line and securing the vessel, over."

"Roger, salvage crane en route, ETA ninety minutes, over and out."

The captain of the cutter replaced the radio and turned to exit the bridge.

"Wait a minute, Captain, you have a call on the satellite phone," said a member of the crew.

The captain blew out a heavy breath as he shook his head. "Who is it, Ensign?"

"A United States Marshal by the name of Greg Donner, sir."

Wolf exchanged a glance with Joris. The captain of the cutter grabbed the phone, lifted it to his ear, and stepped out onto the deck. Wolf followed close behind.

"Marshal Donner? Captain Peyton, here."

"Do we have an update on the wolf pack?" asked Greg.

"Yes, sir, we do. They've completed their assignment with admirable exactitude and have passed the package to us. All is proceeding according to plan."

"Very good. I don't suppose they gave you the opportunity to speak with them in person?"

"No, I'm afraid they didn't. Our only communication was over the radio. By the time we arrived they had already vacated the area."

"I'm not surprised to hear it. Nevertheless, they're very good at what they do."

"That they are, sir. They've accomplished their part of the mission and we're prepared to take it from here. I don't perceive any problems."

A lengthy pause followed the remark.

Captain Peyton knit his brows. "Donner? Is everything all right on your end?"

Greg cleared his throat. "We have the principals in custody. Unfortunately, we have sustained a casualty while meeting this objective. Agent Aliyana Montijo lost her life in the line of duty. You should record this event in your report and we'll note it in ours."

The bottom of Wolf's gut gave way; the breath left him as he closed his eyes against the pain.

"I'm so sorry, Greg. I know it's not easy losing one of our own—"

Wolf didn't wait around for the remainder of their conversation. He clenched his teeth as he whirled around, strode aft of the ship, and dove into the ocean. Joris and Cornelius both called out to him repeatedly, but he didn't respond. He couldn't. Not right now. Right now, he wanted solitude. So he swam. He swam until at long last he saw a large rock protruding from the waves close to the beach and it reminded him so much of the one Aliyana hit when she first crashed—

His throat burned, and he struggled to swallow past the lump as every memory they shared engulfed him like mountainous waves crashing down on a sandy shore. He climbed on top of the rock and cast his gaze heavenward. The sun would set soon. Out in the far distance was the silhouette of the *Wieven* and the mere sight of it intensified his pain.

The sight intensified his anguish because Aliyana would never board his ship again. She wouldn't sail at his side or with her sense of joyful curiosity; she could never enter the portal that would take her home. He'd never again hear her laughter or be at the receiving end of her delightful temper. There'd never be another opportunity to tell her just how much he loved her— how much he would always love her. For even death couldn't destroy that. A deep, rumbling wail, born of agony and sorrow passed through his lips as he dropped to his knees, bowed his head, and lifted a hand to cover his eyes. The tears he'd restrained now broke free of their tethers. And for the duration of the entire night, hour after tedious hour, he mourned her loss.

Dark, cloudy skies that stretched forth from horizon to horizon accompanied the rising of the sun. Appropriate for his current mood. With a mix of reluctance and resignation, he rose to his feet and gazed out over the ocean. The *Wieven*, with the wind at her sails, swiftly approached his position. In a matter of minutes, Joris would row the boat over to fetch him. Centuries of almost constant companionship told him that his crew would remain respectively quiet and simply await his orders. He still didn't know what orders to give.

He wrestled all night with the need to contact Greg and lay claim to Aliyana's body. After all, she didn't have any close living relatives. Instead of some unmarked, forgotten grave, he could take her home for burial. He could build a magnificent mausoleum out in the center of his opulent garden. Aliyana might like that environment. Still, in order to accomplish that, he'd have to find a way to sidestep a personal meeting with the marshal. He didn't know Donner well, but he couldn't imagine the man handing over Aliyana's remains without a face-to-face meeting. He'd want to shake his hand or give him a pat on the back and that would never do. Perhaps he could find out where they intended to take her and just go in and get her—

"Wolf!" Joris stood up in the craft and waved.

As if he needed such an action to attract his attention.

One final time, Wolf turned his gaze in the direction of Desecheo Island and released a ragged sigh. Then with a heavy heart, he returned to the *Wieven*.

As expected, no one uttered a word as he boarded. Most everyone avoided his gaze altogether. Only Joris, it seemed, was brave enough to break the silence.

He cleared his throat as he stopped a few paces in front of him. "I'm not sure if it was by accident or design, but the men inside the *Barracuda* have all met their demise. What remains of their venture is now at the bottom of the sea. I thought you might want to know that."

The unexpected statement startled him. "Are you telling me the sub exploded?" he asked.

"Yes, it did—seconds after the arrival of the salvage ship with the crane. We don't know if the men chose to end their lives or if someone did something stupid."

"I'm guessing the latter," said Klaus. "In all the time I spent in their presence, they never once impressed me with their intelligence."

"You have that right," Laurens muttered.

Wolf didn't feel any pity for the men who perished on board the sub. Those who sought Aliyana's death didn't deserve any.

"*Kapitein?*" Joris cocked his head to the right and with a bit of concern, peered into his eyes. It seemed he awaited a response to something said earlier.

"I'm sorry, did you say something?" he asked.

His first mate shook his head, heaved a sigh, and placed a gentle hand on top of his shoulder. "We also mourn her loss, Wolf. We loved her too, you know. Each in our own way."

He swallowed past the knot in his throat and nodded. "I know."

A lengthy silence followed as each of them appeared lost in their own thoughts.

"So where to from here, *Kapitein?*" Cornelius finally asked.

Time to make a choice. Should he give his men a say in the matter? Wolf glanced down at his boots before he lifted his gaze. He looked at each member of his crew in turn, and then nodded.

"I've a decision to make, and I believe you should all have a say in the matter," he said. "We can sail toward the Atlantic now and look for a portal, or we can get a hold of Greg. Perhaps we can somehow find a way to take Aliyana home for burial before we leave."

"I don't see where this even needs discussion," said Joris. "You promised Aliyana you'd bring her home, did you not?"

The memory of that vow stormed his mind and he dipped his head. "Yes, I did."

Joris waved a hand in dismissal. "Then it's settled. Give Greg a call, and let's go get our lady."

All of his men agreed. Wolf strode toward his cabin, flung open the door, and made his way to the desk. He grabbed hold of the phone and stared down in horror at the darkened screen. Despair overwhelmed his resolve. Somewhere between the Magdalena River and Puerto Rico, the final battery died. And without the connecting cable, he had no way to recharge it. Even if they set a course for Colombia right now, by the time they made shore, traveled to Bogota and located the marshal's office, it'd be far too late. They would already have buried her. Aliyana Rosa Montijo, the only woman he had ever loved—the only woman he would *ever* love—was beyond his grasp.

With his heart full of sorrow, he quit the cabin and made his way to the helm. His men said not a word as he stood behind the wheel. He turned slightly to his left and heaved the useless phone into the ocean.

"Weigh anchor." Wolf could hear the raw pain in his own voice as he issued the command. "Put on all sails."

After the crew carried out his orders, he turned his rudder east. With any amount of luck, they'd find a storm well before they could see the Bermuda Islands with the aid of their telescopes. It was time to go home.

Chapter Twenty-Seven

"Marshal Donner? Captain Peyton, here."

Aliyana held her breath as Greg gave her a thumbs up. She had endured a lengthy layover during the flight from Bogota to Panama. The flight from Panama to San Juan, tried what little patience she had left. But at long last, she sat here inside the U.S. marshal's office in Hato Rey, Puerto Rico. Once Greg completed his reports, the marshals would take her to a small airport in Mayagüez, where a helicopter waited to fly her to Desecheo. Dare she hope that Wolf already awaited her arrival?

"Do we have an update on the wolf pack?" asked Greg.

"Yes, sir, we do. They've completed their assignment with admirable exactitude and have passed the package to us. All is proceeding according to plan."

She slowly released the breath she'd been holding. Though not on Desecheo yet, Wolf had at least completed his task and from all indications, completed it successfully. That meant that at this very moment, he sailed toward the island. Her anticipation swelled.

"Very good. I don't suppose they gave you the opportunity to speak with them in person?"

"No, I'm afraid they didn't. Our only communication was over the radio. By the time we arrived they had already vacated the area."

A smile flitted across her face.

"I'm not surprised to hear it. Nevertheless, they're very good at what they do."

"That they are, sir. They've accomplished their part of the mission and we're prepared to take it from here. I don't perceive any problems."

Greg locked his gaze onto hers. A conspiratorial wink accompanied a deliberate pause.

"Donner? Is everything all right on your end?"

Greg cleared his throat as he assumed a somber expression no one else would see, and it made her laugh. "We have the principals in custody. Unfortunately, we have sustained a casualty while meeting this objective. Agent Aliyana Montijo lost her life in the line of duty. You should record this event in your report, and we'll note it in ours."

"I'm so sorry, Greg. I know it's not easy losing one of our own—"

"No, it isn't and most especially, this one. Agent Montijo was an exceptional woman. Nonetheless, I'm sure the media is going to exploit her demise for several days to come. That's why it's important you have an accurate account in your reports. In addition, you might want to prepare a statement for the press."

Aliyana rose from her chair and headed toward the window while Greg spoke with Peyton. She battled fatigue alongside a bit of dizziness and nausea. But there would be time enough to rest once she boarded the *Wieven* and sailed for home. Home. She closed her eyes for a moment and again envisioned what *home* might look like. Wolf told her their home faced the ocean, but she didn't really know how far away the shore sat from the house. Did sandy shores surround their property, or would she see trees, bushes and flowers? If so, what brilliant colors and delightful scents would delight her senses?

"Aliyana?"

She whirled around. Greg stood not two feet away from her. "Hmm?"

"Sweetheart, you look dead on your feet. There's a very comfortable couch in Demitri's office. Why don't you make use of it? I'll be here for another couple of hours at least, sorting through all the paperwork."

If she had to wait another two hours, she might just as well get some sleep. "All right, if you insist."

"I insist. You're still far from recovered." He put an arm around her shoulder as he led her into the office. "Don't worry. I'll come and get you when it's time to leave."

In what seemed more like minutes than hours, Greg woke her from a deep, restful sleep. She sat up, tossed her blanket off to the side, and rose from her berth.

"Are you feeling any better?" he asked.

She nodded as she smothered a yawn. "Yes, much better. Thank you."

"Good, you probably have a captain anxiously awaiting your arrival. So, now that we have everything taken care of here, let's not keep him waiting any longer, hmm?"

"I'm all for that—just let me get my backpack and we can go."

He put a hand at her waist and led her through the open door. "Unnecessary, it's already in the car. Oh, and uh, by the way? The coast guard just informed us of an unfortunate accident at sea."

Her brow shot upward. "An accident? What kind of

an accident."

"The sub exploded before the salvage ship could bring her to the surface. They believe the men inside the sub might have inadvertently set off some of the explosives she carried. All hands perished."

"Oh—" She rubbed her lips together and nodded. "I see."

"They will, of course, recover the debris and do a full analysis as to the actual cause, but that will probably take several months. In the meantime, we can take satisfaction in knowing the DEA officials and their families are safe."

"Yes, we can do that. You have no idea how relieved I am that this is finally over."

"I'm happy to hear you say it. Then nothing should hamper your future with your captain." He held the office entrance door open and followed her through it. His arm draped around her shoulders as they headed toward the car. Along the way, he gave her a sideways glance, opened his mouth, and then clamped it shut.

"Go ahead and ask it," she said. "You know you want to."

"All right. I know he works undercover for some unnamed agency, but I'm a little tired of referring to your captain as 'your captain.' Can you at least give me his first name?"

Aliyana gave him a broad smile and dipped her head. "Wolfaert. But you can call him Wolf if you like."

"Ah! That explains that, then."

She merely laughed in response.

All the way to Desecheo, she tried to keep her focus on the conversation between Greg, Demitri, and their companions as they discussed the demise of the *Barracuda*. She failed miserably. Wolf commanded the greater portion of her thoughts. Yet a small part of her wondered about the disaster that destroyed Mercado's submarine and all her occupants. Did they blow the vessel on purpose? Did they find death preferable to life in prison? Or did something happen on board that caused the explosion? Thankfully, Wolf and his crew were gone well before the event occurred.

"We're here," said Greg, bringing her out of her silent musing.

Aliyana turned her gaze toward the ocean and searched in every possible direction for the *Wieven*. She didn't see it. She bit down on her lower lip as worry set in. Greg gave her a gentle pat as they approached the tiny island.

"Don't look so concerned. Wolf will be along shortly, I'm sure. He and his crew had to sail some distance. They were out and away from Santa Isabel and from what I hear, they're sailing against a pretty fierce wind. That can slow things down a bit."

She nodded as the lowered chopper hovered just above the ground. The men exited first, carrying her equipment and supplies. She trailed close behind.

"Thanks for everything, Greg," she said once he dropped his burden and turned around to face her. "We couldn't have brought this mission to a successful conclusion without your help."

He leaned down and kissed her cheek. "My pleasure, sweetheart. Would you like us to hang out until your big bad Wolf arrives?"

She laughed and shook her head. "No, that won't be necessary. He'll be along soon and until then, I'll be just fine. I promise."

"All right, until next time we meet—" He gave her a hug and then he and his companions headed for the chopper. Just before he boarded, he turned around one final time. "Send me an invitation to the wedding, do you hear?"

She gave him a smile, nodded, and then waved as the helicopter lifted off and turned toward Puerto Rico. It grew ever smaller and then finally disappeared from view altogether. With nothing to do but wait, she turned her attention to the pile of supplies the marshals had strewn hither and yon.

The small tent made her laugh. So did the medical kit and sleeping bag. What made them think she would need any of that stuff? They also left mounds of food and a couple of cases of water. She shrugged. Perhaps Andries might be able to put the food to good use during their voyage home. After all, she didn't have any idea how long it would take them to find a proper storm. Once she organized the mess and made it easier to load, she took a walk and checked out her surroundings.

Every few minutes she turned toward the ocean. Yet the *Wieven* remained elusive. An hour passed, and then two. Worry set in. Surely, Wolf should've been here by now. She resisted the urge to call Greg on her satellite phone. He'd probably tell her not to panic and give them some more time. She continued her solitary vigil.

About a half an hour before sunset, the unease she had carried for the past several hours turned into a sudden feeling of dread. Panic overtook all rational thought and settled into her soul. Something terrible had happened. She raced toward her supplies and grabbed her backpack. Her fingers shook as she unzipped the bag and yanked out her phone. She called Greg's number several times over before it dawned on her that he had already boarded a plane headed for Colombia. She wouldn't be able to contact him until the morning.

Despite all attempts to banish it, the dread grew stronger with each passing hour. A growing notion that Wolf and his crew never left the sub took firm hold. The conscientious men of the *Wieven* could very well have remained behind to ensure that all went according to plan. The thought of such an occurrence made her sick to her stomach. What if they could die as she had always feared? What if they died in that sub along with Mercado's men? She couldn't sleep, and she couldn't eat. All throughout the long hours of the night, she restlessly paced along the shore, waiting, hoping, and praying.

By the time the gloomy morning arrived, what little hope she'd carried throughout the long night dissipated. Somewhere in her heart, she finally accepted that her beloved captain wouldn't be coming for her. Not now. Not ever again. Excruciating pain accompanied that knowledge. Her heart shattered into an infinite number of pieces. Even though she had endured such pain many times before, it had never assaulted her with the intensity it did right now. She didn't know if she could survive it. Indeed, she didn't know if she *wanted* to survive it.

As if all those in heaven understood her anguish and added their grief to her own, a bolt of lightning flashed across the sky. An interminable rumble of thunder followed. Rain splashed down on her cheeks, lightly at first. But as time passed, the drops increased in both size and pace. She paid them no heed. The raging storm simply attended her sobs and mingled its tears with her own.

Exhaustion finally drove her to sit on a rock near the shore, worn smooth by the continuous pounding of ocean waves. She cast her gaze out over the endless horizon. The storm had abated and most of the clouds had disappeared. The sun would soon set for the second time since she arrived on Desecheo. Tears trickled down her cheeks as she sorted through her short list of options. One of those options called more loudly than the others did. The louder it called the more she desired it. Yes, that's what she would do.

Tomorrow she would call Demitri. She'd ask him to send someone to pick her up and then she'd make her way to Alaska. Perhaps there she could find her Wolf amidst the dancing lights of the aurora borealis. If she looked very carefully and truly believed, he might call for her there…

She lifted her face toward the sky and closed her eyes against the pain. "Oh, Wolf," she moaned with all the agony of her soul. "You promised you wouldn't leave me. You promised…" She dropped her head and sobbed. "Please," she whispered brokenly, "Please, don't leave me…"

****

Wolf stood at the helm, his gaze fixed, but not seeing. The fierce wind they'd battled during the storm finally abated. Yet the sound of it still haunted him. More than once, he fancied he heard the sound of Aliyana's voice in the billowing breeze. Each time, the experience renewed his pain. He shook his head in despair, took in a deep breath of the salty air, and slowly released it.

"Oh, Wolf! You promised you wouldn't leave me... You promised..."

Those words echoed first inside his mind, and then resounded throughout his entire being. He heard them loud and clear. This time, he could feel her anguish and it matched his own.

"Please. Please don't leave me..." A heart-wrenching sob followed the mournful words.

Call him crazy, but those pitiful words sounded as if they drifted into his mind from the west. His heart pounded against his chest as he mulled over a possible reason for the strange phenomena. He tossed it aside as absurd. For surely he wanted so much to believe that she hadn't perished in Cartagena—

Wolf paused and for a moment, he reconsidered the impossible notion. After all, he'd seen impossible before, in the guise of a lovely witch named Lissa. Suddenly, he had to know. He had to know for sure.

At once, he whirled the wheel all the way to the right, turning headlong into a favorable wind. One way or the other, he would find out if Aliyana was alive. Startled gazes shot toward him as they abruptly changed direction.

"Wolf! What do you think you're doing?" Joris hollered as he strode toward him.

He firmed his jaw and said, "I'm going after Aliyana."

His men hooted and cheered over the declaration, but they didn't understand. They believed he set his course for Colombia in order to retrieve her body. Not even close—for he'd turned his rudder west, in the most direct path to Desecheo.

Hours later, he saw the island looming toward them. Unable to wait a moment longer, he took hold of his telescope and aimed it toward the clearing. He strained to see the terrain ahead but amid the light of the moon and stars, he could only see silhouettes and shadows. *No matter.* He tossed the instrument aside.

"Conrad, lower the boat. Joris, take over the helm. Drop anchor once you get as close to the island as you can," he called out. He abandoned his position and strode down the deck.

"Aye, *Kapitein*," said Joris.

He could hear the uncertainty in his tone. He wouldn't address it. Not right now.

No one else said a word as he vacated the ship and boarded the boat. He rowed toward the island with all the speed he could muster. Once he made shore, he dragged his craft onto the sandy beach and dropped it. He ran toward the clearing. His heart doubled its pace even as his footsteps slowed and then halted. He turned first to his right and made a careful sweep of the area. Yet only vegetation met his gaze. He turned to his left.

Wolf saw her then. He wanted to raise his voice high to the heavens and shout for joy. Yet he restrained the need as he approached her. She looked so tiny curled on top of her sleeping bag, nestled away in the bushes. Her hands pillowed her face as she breathed deep and evenly. Under the light of the celestial orbs, her cheeks were still damp with tears. He swore under his breath, knowing his delay caused her sorrow. A deep sigh escaped as he knelt down beside her. For just a moment, he drank in her beauty.

A gentleman would let her sleep. But then again, he never claimed such a title and right now, he ached to have her in his arms. He brushed the tangled hair away from her face.

"Aliyana," he whispered. She barely stirred. He traced the length of her jaw with light, feathery strokes. "Aliyana—"

In response to his voice, she took in a breath and held it.

"*Lieveling*, you need to wake up now. I'm so sorry for the delay, but right now, we've a portal to find."

Her eyes moved underneath her lids. A slight grin curved a single corner of his mouth. He leaned down then, and placed a soft, gentle kiss on top of her lips.

Her beautiful sea-green eyes fluttered open and for just a moment, they gazed at each other. Then, as if understanding crashed into her consciousness, she bolted upright, and gasped.

"Wolf!"

If he hadn't leaned away at the precise moment, she would've fallen straight through him. Instead, he just managed to wrap his arms around her and hold her tight.

"You're really here," she said in a half-whisper, half-sob. She lifted a trembling hand and rested it lightly against the side of his face. The other, she placed at his chest.

He answered her astute observation with a kiss that grew both in passion and in intensity. The whistles, cheers, and joyous laughter coming off the *Wieven* cooled his ardor for the time being. He drew her to her feet alongside him and gazed into her eyes. With a smile on his face, he cocked his head toward the

Wieven.

"Are you ready to go home, my love?"

Tears filled her eyes. She bit down on her trembling lips and nodded. "Yes, I'm ready to go home."

"Then let's get out of here."

****

In less time than it took Andries to prepare something for her to eat, the *Wieven* turned her sails away from Desecheo. Aliyana stood at the helm, with Wolf's arms encompassing her body. She couldn't bear to leave his side, nor would he allow her to leave his. The experience of each, thinking the other dead, made this physical contact quite necessary.

During the countless hours of their voyage, they talked about what had transpired at the conclusion of their separate missions. Wolf spoke of his utter devastation when he heard Greg announce her death. The raw pain within both his gaze and voice touched her deep inside her soul. Aliyana wept as she confessed that she too had thought him dead, and how that assumption had broken her heart. Wolf kissed away her tears as he held her close. Klaus tsked and fussed over her latest injury. Andries insisted on bringing her enough food to feed an army. Everyone else simply hovered. She didn't mind.

"I think we finally have us a storm brewing again, *Kapitein*," shouted Cornelius from the bow.

A broad smile appeared on Wolf's face as he lifted his gaze to the sky, as did she. The wind increased in strength as the thick storm clouds turned purple and the darkest shades of gray. They swirled and churned as they sped across the sky.

"All hands ready!" Wolf shouted the command even as he held her more firmly against his body.

Innumerable bolts of lightning crackled ominously as they shot out of the heavens in a downward spiral. She held her breath in anticipation. Soon, balls of light lit up the ocean and bounded all around them. All the while they emitted their eerie wails.

"Do you see anything yet?" called Joris.

"No, not yet," Cornelius replied.

Aliyana twisted her head from side to side, searching all the while for the formation of a vortex.

"There's one forming, portside," hollered Laurens.

"Not that one," returned Pieter. "Wrong formation."

"Turnabout, *Kapitein*," yelled Conrad. "Hurry! We have one behind us."

Wolf whirled the wheel all the way to his left. The ship pitched precariously from side to side as the *Wieven* sailed directly toward the billowing tunnel. Aliyana anchored her feet just before the bowsprit entered the portal. The exhilarating head-to-toe vibration and the hum of the ship increased her excitement. The jagged, colorful lights soon crept over the sides, onto the deck, and then slithered up the masts. She fastened her gaze on the yardarms as those lights spewed forth their amazing colors.

"Hang on tight," Wolf whispered into her ear as the vibrating current encompassed everything and everyone on board the ship.

Flashes of light intertwined with flashes of darkness during the journey through the portal. Finally, cloudless skies, in a shade of brilliant blue she had never even imagined, loomed just ahead. She peeked up at Wolf, met his jubilant gaze, and returned his smile in kind. He wrapped a single arm around her waist and cuddled her close against his chest. Then, second by precious second, his warmth crept into her body. Scant moments later, his physical form increased in solidity.

She noted the contraction of his muscles and the beat of his heart as he drew her closer still. He nuzzled his cheek against hers and this time, she felt the stubble. She gasped and whirled around to face him. He broadened his grin and winked.

Without taking his gaze away from hers, he called out, "Helm, Joris."

Wolf took hold of her hand and twined his fingers around hers. Now she could return the gentle pressure and the ability gave her an amazing amount of pleasure. She lifted her face toward the sky and laughed. Wondrous delight filled her entire being as she absorbed every aspect of her surroundings. She strived to take in everything at once and failed miserably at the task.

Wolf's ship didn't in any way look like the seventeenth-century pirate ship that had carried her here. All kinds of interesting looking instruments now surrounded the exquisitely crafted helm. The *Wieven* itself looked far more modern in ways she just couldn't describe or even understand. Yet.

Once Joris arrived, Wolf gave up the helm. He led her down the steps, across the deck and over to the railing at the bow. She gazed toward the panoramic vision before her. A variety of colorful seabirds chattered high above, and they were just as beautiful to behold as were the mischievous, rainbow-colored dolphins that played alongside the *Wieven*.

In the hours that followed, they sailed in a continuous southeasterly direction. All the while, Wolf and his crew filled her head with information concerning everything she'd feel and see in the days ahead. Her anticipation rose to even greater heights. Then, just before a glorious sunset in colors she didn't have words for, Wolf directed her gaze to a flourishing island on the starboard side of the ship.

Her jaw dropped as she drew in a sharp breath. For there, ahead in the distance, on a narrow peninsula, stood four magnificent spires rising straight up out of the ocean. They mirrored the ones in her dream, as did the antediluvian temple they encompassed. Wolf then pointed toward the other end of the magnificent island. She beheld a palatial structure, every bit as ancient as the temple, and its splendor filled her with amazement.

His lips played over hers for a single moment. "At last you've come home, *lieveling*. At long last you've come home."

Chapter Twenty-Eight

"Where have your thoughts taken you, my love?" asked Wolf as he gathered her into his arms.

Aliyana gazed at the absolute beauty and mystique of the ancient temple's interior. This structure had stood the test of time for over eight centuries, as had their home. Her gaze wandered over the brilliant stone walls, the likes of which she had never seen before or even imagined. In response to the sunlight that filtered through the tall cathedral windows, those walls shimmered like diamonds in every color imaginable. High arched ceilings and intricate marble flooring in shades of cream, chocolate and gold completed the picture. The splendor of it left her speechless. Richly scented candles still lit the aisle way leading toward the alabaster altar where she and Wolf had repeated their vows in a simple, but beautiful, ceremony earlier that afternoon.

Several hours before the wedding, he'd collected her at the door of his bedroom where she had passed her first night. She had slept in a massive, four-poster bed, made of mahogany wood. The bed complimented the rich shades of burgundy and blue Wolf had used to dress out the definitely masculine room. Settled atop bureaus and tables rested the most interesting objects she had ever seen. She couldn't identify a single one of them. Had he collected them in the various *kátholoses* he had visited?

Wolf led her down the oak, Tudor-style stairway, through the grand hall, and outside to the resplendent garden. The beauty of it was something to behold. She still had trouble believing that Wolf actually owned this beautiful piece of heaven on earth. Well—that *they* owned this beautiful piece of heaven on earth. They strolled down an ancient stone pathway that led to a sparkling pool surrounded by spectacular flowers in glorious, vivid colors.

He took hold of her hands then and gazed into her eyes. His were full of so much love and tender emotion that it brought her feelings to the surface as well.

"I didn't do this properly before, and I'd like to rectify that right now, if I may. So, bear with me—"

She opened her mouth, but he put a gentle finger to her lips and shook his head.

"For several centuries I've wandered between realms, without any real sense of purpose. I filled my time with countless adventures and exploits. Yet none of them ever truly satisfied me. None of them, that is, until I met you, and together, we embarked upon the greatest adventure of my life. Something stirred inside my heart the moment I lifted you from Mercado's plane and held you in my arms. As I gazed down upon your beautiful face, I didn't realize how much I'd come to love you. But I did know I couldn't let you pass out of my life without discovering the reason you affected me the way you did. And so, despite your initial reluctance to accept our help, we began a most wondrous journey. One that I'll thank the heavens for, every day, for the rest of my life."

"Oh, Wolf, you—"

"Shh." He paused.

He swallowed several times as he fought for control of his emotions. A single tear traveled down her cheek in response to that emotion—a tear that he gently wiped away.

"As you know, thinking you dead almost destroyed me. I knew my love for you traveled deep; I just didn't know how deep until Greg Donner reported your death while I stood on board the cutter. The pain I suffered at that moment shattered my soul. I never, ever want to feel like that again. I need you at my side, each and every day, for the rest of my life and even beyond that."

As he held onto her hands, he dropped to a knee. "To make that far more than a simple desire, I'm asking you again to marry me. Will you, Aliyana Rosa Montijo, be my wife?"

Tears streamed freely down her cheeks now. A ragged breath slipped past her lips as she tugged him to his feet, yet all the while she held his gaze. She wiped a hand across her trembling lips, shook her head ever so slightly, and sniffed.

"I wished simple words could tell you just how much I love you, Wolfaert Dircksen Van Ness. I'm afraid there's nothing in any language that can describe it though. You know the anguish I suffered when I, too, believed you were lost to me forever. I can't ever lose you again—not even for a single moment. I don't have the strength to endure it." She nodded. "Nothing on this earth, regardless of dimension, will give me more pleasure than being your wife."

Wolf slipped a hand inside his pocket and withdrew a ring made of small, dazzling stones that simply didn't exist in the world of her birth. He took her hand and placed it on her finger. The exquisite ring fit perfectly. He tilted her chin upward, leaned down, and kissed her many times over.

Wolf led her to a lavishly carved stone bench, all but hidden in the lush foliage that surrounded it. As they sat down together, he took hold of her hand. He gazed into her eyes. "Would a simple wedding please you?" he finally asked. "Or would you prefer something elaborate and grand?"

"Simple, please," she murmured as she wiped away the last of her tears.

From the charming grin on his face, she must've given him the answer he desired. "That's good. Would you be opposed to marrying me then, in say, an hour or so?"

She brushed her fingers through his hair. "I would *love* to marry you in an hour or so."

"I'm pleased you said that," he replied. "Because the minister will be here shortly as will just a small number of our guests. By now, you'll find a variety of dresses in our bedroom. I hope one of them suits you."

"Really?"

He chuckled. "Really."

"Do you have a favorite from among them?"

"I must confess I haven't seen them. Ellie made the purchases once I told her what I had planned. She said I didn't have any sense about such things, and the old girl is probably right. Personally, I'd just as soon you show up at the altar wearing that enchanting gown we acquired from the lighthouse. In case you're unaware, it's, ah, a personal favorite of mine."

She drew her brows together. "It is? Why?"

"Oh, I don't know. For one, you look quite

delectable in the thing. Two, it never fails to remind me of that adorable temper tantrum you had, when first you wore it."

Her mouth dropped. "My 'temper tantrums' aren't meant to give you amusement, Wolf."

"That notwithstanding, I wouldn't object in the least if you wore the thing to our wedding."

She burst out laughing. "That would cause quite a stir, I'm sure, and in all probability, the minister would be quite scandalized."

"Perhaps you're right at that. All right, I'll concede. You can wear it just for me later. And speaking of later on, where would you like to go for our honeymoon? There are so many places that will fill you with absolute wonder and delight. Mountains, canyons, lakes, each of them with amazing ruins—"

"I'll let you choose one of them. However, I have a single request before we take off on such a journey."

"Name it, and it's yours."

"Let's begin our honeymoon right here. You've yet to give me an extensive tour of our beautiful home, or this island. I'd like to stay here long enough to feel settled in, if you don't mind."

He shook his head and leaned close to her lips. "I don't mind at all."

The man held her captive for so long then that she was almost late to her own wedding. Not that she had minded the delay.

Wolf cleared his throat in an exaggerated manner, bringing her back to the present. He lifted a brow as he awaited an answer. Where had her thoughts taken her? Her lips curved slightly at the corners as she shrugged.

"Over the events of this most incredible day. I

thought I'd take a moment before we leave this beautiful edifice and make sure every single moment is safely tucked away inside my heart, alongside the rest of my treasures," she said.

He leaned down and grazed his lips against hers. "But the day is not yet over, Mrs. Dircksen."

"I know. But do you really think you can top what has already taken place, Captain?"

A roguish gleam entered his eyes. "Ah! The wife issues the husband a challenge. Very well. The husband accepts."

Without further delay, Wolf placed a hand about her waist and turned her toward the doors. He led her out of the temple and down the steps, disregarding any kind of leisurely pace. Yet, just as they arrived midway, he stopped their journey and turned to face her. He gathered her into his arms and for a moment, he simply looked at her. She could see the strength of his love, his elation, and just a bit of humor within his gaze.

"If I remember correctly, you said we were standing just so, in that dream you had aboard the *Wieven*? Am I right?" he asked.

She bit down on her lip in a futile attempt to hide her smile. "Yes, I believe so."

"And as I recall, in that dream I gave you a kiss on these very steps, did I not?"

The incredible sense of joy she experienced throughout the day upped itself a notch. All the while, swarming butterflies deep inside her belly stoked the smoldering embers there until they reached a raging flame. She could quite literally feel the heat of those flames rising, as obviously, so could he. "Mm-hmm."

****

At least for this moment, Wolf fought the rising passion she so easily roused within him. He wouldn't fight it much longer. "I'm trying to recall. Let's see now—"

Just then, somewhere in the back of his mind, a very sweet and familiar voice entered his thoughts. One he hadn't heard in quite some time

"You must forgive the intrusion, my dear friend. Since I have so anxiously awaited this day, I just couldn't let it pass without telling you how very happy we are that you have finally found each other," said Lissa Capoen Van Locken. "Perhaps one day we'll meet again. In the meantime, give your new bride our love."

The voice receded as quickly as it arrived. In a more convenient time, he would ponder the meaning of the message, but not now. Right now, someone far more important demanded his attention.

He cleared his throat, leaned down, and gave his beautiful wife a sweet, simple kiss, just as he had when she first told him about her dream. A quiet breath of laughter followed the gentle peck.

He grinned at her lecherously. "Was it something like that? Or—was the kiss more like this?"

This time, he put a little more duration and effort into his kiss. In response, Aliyana's smile grew a bit broader. She tilted her head to the side but said nothing in return. He caressed the length of her back in slow even strokes and the very action caused a delightful shiver to pass through her body. Wolf tightened his hold.

His lips played tantalizingly against hers. "Maybe," he whispered, "it was more like this." Every memory they shared, every emotion she had ever inspired, found its way into the kiss. With that kiss he expressed how very much he loved her, how much he would always, always love her.

Her arms tightened around his neck. The exquisite kiss she gave in return spoke of the incredible depth of her love for him, and he gloried in the gift of it. He loosened his hold only to gather her closer still. The next kiss left both of them very short of breath.

Wolf blew out a ragged breath as he controlled his rising passion. Well, at least he'd control it long enough to see her home, anyway.

"Now, beloved wife," he said as that alluring look in her eyes sealed her fate. "About that lighthouse gown..."

A word from the author…

Making an impossible love quite possible after all…

I am an author of paranormal and fantasy romance, including *Court of the Hawk*, *Love Letters from Heaven*, *Bound by Oath and Honor*, *Spirit of the Revolution*, *Spirit of the Rebellion*, and *Spirit of the Knight*. I have (and have always had) a soft spot for fairy tales, the joy of falling in love, making an impossible love possible, and happily ever after endings. I love music, art, beautiful sunrises, sunsets, and thunderstorms.

When I'm not busy conjuring my latest novel, I spend time with the members of my very large and nutty family here in the lovely, arid deserts of southern Nevada. I also pursue my interests in family history, mythology, and history.

Please visit me at www.debbie-peterson.com

www.ingramcontent.com/pod-product-compliance
Lightning Source LLC
Chambersburg PA
CBHW051128030726
47504CB00004B/756